Distance & Dragons

Distance & Dragons

DOMINIC N. ASHEN

4 Horsemen
Publications, Inc.

Table of Contents

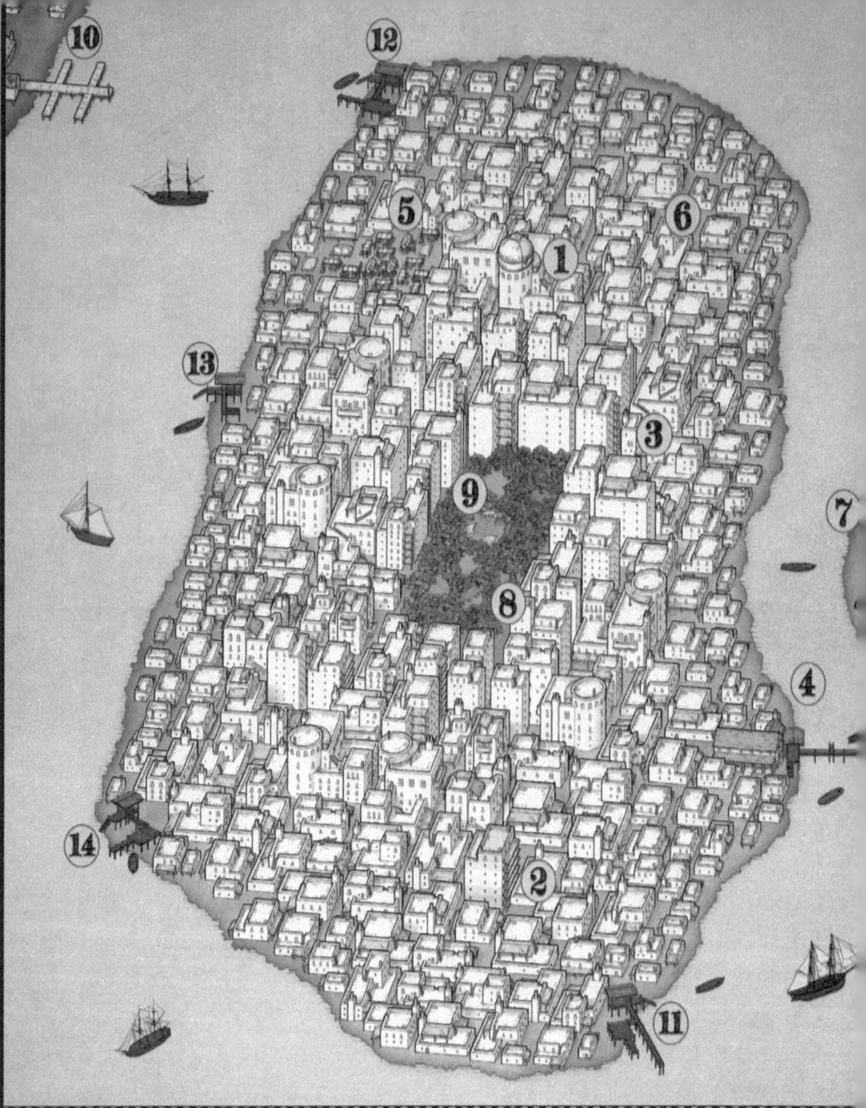

Map Key

1 City Hall
2 Moonbright Inn
3 The Black Rooster
4 Shipyard
5 Magic Market
6 Safe House 12
7 Testament Island
8 Paramount Park
9 Undead Camp
10 Lorana
11 Dock to Venzor
12 Dock to Lorana
13 Dock to Urkinom
14 Dock to Vertel

Kiweni
Fish & Gentle Waves
Map Key
1 Timid Oak Tavern
2 The Salty Salmon
3 Royal Ship
4 Bathhouse
5 Refugee Camp
6 Maname Guard HQ
7 Prince Max's Camp
8 Hurskett Family
9 Training Ground
10 Kiweni Forest

Dedication:

In memory of David Keith. Wherever you are, I hope it has a nice, big library.

Chapter 1

Khazak

"**I**s that a dragon?"

"No, I think it's a thunderbird!"

"What are either of you talking about?" the third gnome in the trio to my left comments. "It's just a weird cloud. Look, it's already gone."

I return my gaze to the heavens where, like the first gnome, I *swear* I just saw a dragon. And I wasn't alone; the only reason I even left the inn was because of the others rushing outside, and I can see dozens of people along the street who did the same. But the longer I look up and see nothing but the clouds, the more I start to question myself. *Perhaps it was just a trick of the light…*

As everyone begins to return to their mornings, I take a sip of coffee from the mug still in my hand and immediately cringe at the bitter taste—I forgot the sugar. With a sigh, I return to the Moonbright Inn to remedy the situation, electing to pick up a second mug to bring up to the room for David when he wakes up.

It is rare that I am the first one awake, but seeing as he managed to have a nightmare-free evening, I am going to let him sleep in as much as possible. I'm not sure what caused my own nightmare, still remembering the images of tendrils and black wolves. The wolves were new, but it was not even two weeks ago that I had an almost identical nightmare featuring the tendrils. At least in this dream, I was able to successfully protect David. Perhaps that will be the last of it.

After climbing four flights of stairs, I quietly and carefully open the door to our room. Setting David's coffee on the nightstand, I watch as his chest softly rises and falls with his breath, my eyes roaming over the soft curve of his hip. Taking a seat at the small table provided to our room, I pull a pen, paper, and some ink from my bag. We have a busy day ahead, and now would be a good time to write home to my family and update them on what has happened.

Orda, Ruda, and Jarda,

It's been three weeks since my last letter, and over a month since I first left V'rok'sh Tah'lj, and it has been stressful to say the least. The trouble started when we noticed we were being followed by a pair of men who we learned were members of the infamous Blackbriar Guild. We managed to turn the tables on them and thought we had the situation handled, but it wasn't long before their allies caught up and captured us. We escaped with a little bit of outside help and made our way to the newly established township of Richardton, only to be captured *again*.

Nathaniel, a previous member of our party, had business with the self-appointed "prince" of Richardton, Richard Calvinson III, or at least with his father, from whom he had stolen a valuable and rare cockatrice egg. However, the prize Calvinson ended up wanting in the end was David— and he threw the rest of us in a dungeon in an effort to keep him. He planned to have us fight a group of lions, and when that failed, a *werewolf*, which is what ultimately led to his downfall. We managed to work with the other prisoners and use the confusion of those beasts getting loose to our advantage and overthrow him.

Do not worry: everyone made it out safely. We managed to restore a semblance of order to the town before leaving, heading for our current location, Manamequohi. We're here searching for Naruk Redwish, and I cannot wait to make him pay for all the pain and destruction he wrought, especially for what he did to David—

"Mmmm." A sleepy moan pulls my attention from my letter to the bed.

I watch as David flounders on the bed before lying flat on his back and stretching out all of his limbs. After they flop back down to the bed, he sits up with a yawn, rubbing his eyes as they adjust to the light. Then, with a scratch to the back of his head, he finally turns to me.

"Morning," he says with a dopey smile.

"Good morning, pup." *Spirits, he is adorable.*

I stand and take two quick strides toward the bed, sliding myself beneath the sheets next to him. I quickly wrap my arms around him, pulling us together as he greets me with sleepy open-mouthed kisses. As I nuzzle against his neck, his hands roam down my back.

"Aww, you're all clothed." He pouts, sticking his hands under my shirt so he can reach my skin.

"I went downstairs for coffee." I kiss away his frown and nod toward the still-steaming mug on the bedside table. "I brought you some."

"Yessssss!" His mood changes swiftly, his left arm reaching out feebly toward the cup. "You're the best."

"You say that now," I roll over him, allowing him to grasp his prize, "but will you feel the same way after you've had the chastity cage on for another week?"

"I barely even notice it's there," he fibs, letting out a small moan of pleasure after his first sip.

David and I have a unique relationship, or at least it would appear that way to anyone outside of Tah'lj. I am not referring to the fact that we are both men, though I have learned firsthand that not everyone in the world is as accepting as my home. Our relationship is one of love, respect, and understanding, but it is also one of command and obedience, of dominance and submission.

In my language, we have specialized terms for each of our roles. David is the *avakesh*, which refers to the submissive partner, who is owned by myself, the dominant partner called the *kavan*. Just as it sounds, that means David is subservient to me—both in and out of the bedroom. He is the "pup" to my "Sir," and we would not have it any other way.

I know how that may sound, but it is not as though the entirety of our relationship is based around me ordering David around. In fact, I would challenge anyone to spend time with us and see for themselves that we are no different than a more "traditional" relationship. We have our own rules, which my pup is *usually* willing to follow, and when he isn't, there are plenty of ways for me to correct him in private—such as the chastity cage he is wearing right now. By the same coin, it is my responsibility to look after and protect him—which can be rather difficult given how willing he is to throw himself in harm's way. But that selflessness is also one of the reasons I love him.

"It's still early, and I doubt any of the others are out of bed yet," I tell David as I run a hand down his chest. "The city's administrative office should open soon, so after breakfast we can head there and ask about Redwish."

"Do you think they'll be able to tell us if he's in the city?" David asks, sipping more coffee.

"I honestly have no idea," I admit with a sigh. "I am not sure what records they keep nor for how long, but it is at least worth a try. I wish I were still Ranger Captain of V'rok'sh Tah'lj. I might be able to do more."

"Well, Ranger Hazatin *did* kind of officially tell us to come here in his place," David points out. "Or you could just, you know, lie. I doubt word from the secret orc city travels very fast."

The "Ranger Hazatin" David is referring to is a former coworker and subordinate of mine, one who we have run into twice since leaving the city. Before I resigned from my position as captain, my last act as leader of the V'rok'sh Tah'lj rangers was to send out Hazatin in pursuit of an escaping Redwish. Obviously he did not have much luck, and last we spoke, he was still in Richardton, helping the locals sort out some of the mess caused by Calvinson. Since we managed to not just catch up to but pass him, I have retaken the responsibility of tracking down this criminal so that he can be brought home to pay for his crimes.

Naruk Redwish is... Well, I am not sure how much I actually know about the man. I am not even positive that "Naruk Redwish" is his real name. He immigrated to V'rok'sh Tah'lj about two years ago, where he worked as a legal advocate for individuals arrested who lacked counsel. Our positions were not connected, and I had no say in his hiring, so I do not know about his credentials and whether or not they were falsified. By all appearances, for those two years, he seemed dedicated to his position—until the day David and his friends arrived.

I'd love to tell you that our first meeting was through some sort of cute happenstance, but the truth is the first time

I met David, he attacked me, and I arrested him. Technically, he was not the *first* one to attack—that honor belongs to Nathaniel, who remained behind in Richardton—but he was one of the last we subdued. After knocking him out myself, I carried his unconscious body back to the city and placed him in a cell alongside his friends, with Redwish assigned as their advocate.

You might see where this story is going. Through a series of misunderstandings and half-truths that Redwish intentionally left vague, David challenged me to what he's referred to as a "trial by combat." He lost and, as he was expecting a fight to death, was surprised to learn that instead he would become my property.

Things were tense that first week, with neither of us quite understanding the other, despite our obvious attraction. After some mishaps and poor decision making on both our parts, we finally managed to see eye to eye. Then, after even *more* communication and misunderstandings (including some involving his twin brother which were resolved only days ago), I can finally say that the two of us are truly on even footing. Or at least, even in the way we like it.

Redwish's treachery led to some difficult moments between us, but nothing could compare to only months later when we discovered he was working in concert with a group of my own rangers seeking to gain control of my home, naming themselves the Cult of Zeus, likely before setting their sights on larger targets. We came upon them one night in a ruined Olympian temple on the outskirts of our territory, and in the process of rescuing our friend Nylan from certain death, David was killed when Redwish drove a sword directly through his heart.

I have never experienced as deep a despair as when I watched the life and blood drain from David's body… only for him to awaken not a minute later with barely a scratch on him. He wasn't just healed; he was also supernaturally strong and fast and seemed not to be himself. David saved multiple lives that day, and one of the reasons we are here in Maname is to figure out how he was revived and what it means.

After some more cuddling and coffee, I extract myself from the bed again and finish my letters home. Now caffeinated, David takes it upon himself to check on our friends, and once enough of them are awake, gathers everyone for breakfast downstairs. Today's offering is shellfish harvested from the island's own shores, served over buttered and spiced cornmeal with scrambled eggs on the side. An excellent start to the day.

"Did everyone sleep alright last night?" Adam asks the rest of the group, sitting together at one of the dining room's many long tables.

"Yeah, pretty good," Liss answers first. "Though I'm not used to being this high up."

Adam and Liss are both human like David with Adam being one of David's oldest friends. Liss (full name Elisabeth) met the two of them at the Northlake Academy of Knighthood, located in the Lutherian city of the same name. The three of them had each individually determined they no longer wished to be a part of it, due in large part by what sounds like extremely poor and untrustworthy leadership. Things were bad enough that all three abandoned their posts under the cover of night together, without a word to anyone, not even their families, before they left the small island-country entirely.

Adam is a tall muscular man with blond hair and blue eyes. An excellent fighter, he is our group's unofficial leader, easily taking the lead when a situation calls for it. He is a good man with a kind and fair heart, so we get along well— and he has also been known to join me and David in bed on occasion.

That last part may sound surprising, but our relationship is more open than most—something that the unique type of relationship we share lends itself to, though we still have plenty of restrictions. While at first I think perhaps David may have harbored a small crush on the man, once he "got it out of his system" (David's words), their normal level of camaraderie and friendly rivalry quickly took over… sometimes even *during* sex. Not that I am complaining.

I believe Elisabeth grew up in the same city, but I do not think the three of them met until the academy. As tall and strong as David and Adam, she has short red hair she typically keeps covered; when I first met her, it had been dyed brown. Her personality is dry and more serious than her two friends—a trait I greatly appreciate at times. She is an excellent warrior, and I have noted her tracking skills improving while on the road together.

"The beds are great," David agrees. "I slept like a rock."

"They were very comfortable," I concur. *For more than just sleeping.*

"We slept well, too," Corrine answers from my other side.

"No complaints here!" Tsula declares, the final member of the group.

Corrine is a human also from Lutheria, though not the same region as the others. I do not actually know very much about her past, only that she was raised by a church, which I suspect might mean she is an orphan. She is kind and very soft-spoken with light blonde hair she normally keeps tied in twin-tails on either side of her head. She's also a divine spellcaster, using her abilities to act as the team's healer. Her reason for joining the others was to act as a "missionary" for her church, though the more I spend time with her, the more I wonder if there is something she isn't telling us about.

Tsula is the newest person to join us on our journey, having met us only a few weeks ago in Pákannon. She is technically closest to me in age, even beating me by ten years at forty, but as a full-blooded elf, her emotional maturity is much closer to the early-twenties of the others. The cousin of my good friend Nylan—the same Nylan David died trying to protect—she asked to come with us after an unexpected adventure seemed to whet her appetite for more. She keeps her long black hair in a single long braid that runs down her left shoulder, often playing with it when nervous, which as this is her first time away from home is fairly often.

"So, what's the plan for today?" Liss asks before lifting another spoonful of breakfast to her mouth.

"We're gonna head to the city's admin office, right?" Adam looks over to confirm. "To see if they have any record of Redwish entering."

"Correct." I nod. "I am not sure how successful we'll be, but we can at least try. Though I am not sure we *all* need to go."

"So, the rest of us could say, wander around the city?" Liss intimates her intentions for the day.

"I don't see why not," I tell her with a shrug. "The only other thing on the agenda is returning to Mr. Adcaryn to see if we can learn more about David's abilities, which you technically wouldn't need to be present for either."

"We could always look around and then meet you all back there afterward?" Corrine offers. "As long as we know where we're going."

"I think that sounds fun," Tsula says with a nod. "I can remember how to get to Uncle Atsadi's, so that shouldn't be a problem."

"Woo, girls' trip," Liss says with mock excitement. "That alright with you guys?"

"I see no issues," I respond with a short nod.

"Sounds fine to me." Adam nods as well.

We finish eating not long after that and say our good-byes, splitting into two groups. While the ladies decide to see what awaits them on the west side of the island, David and Adam join me on a path toward the center where the city's administrative offices reside. As someone with a fear of heights, walking past the rows and rows of tall buildings towering over us is a dizzying affair. Some of them have as many as a dozen floors—I cannot even fathom working in a place like that.

Finding the building is not difficult, both because of its size and the large signs proclaiming its name in both Pukwudgese and Common in bright gold lettering. Large flags line the entrance, each bearing the city's symbol: the Testament of Unity, a giant statue of a gnome that sits off the island's coast, the torch in its hand burning the same bright green as the statue's hair and providing the city with its magical protective dome. That very dome is the reason we are here.

When we enter the building, the kind human woman at the front desk is happy to guide us to our destination: the Immigration Office, which is located on the eleventh floor. While several of the city's taller buildings have magic-powered lifts to take you from floor to floor, this is not one of them, which means climbing up eleven flights of stairs, or as David puts it, "its own section of hell." When we finally reach it, between the exhaustion and nearly hyperventilating because of the height, I am out of breath, but the name of the office above the door is still a welcome sight.

"Hello, how may I help you?" a gnome woman sitting behind the desk welcomes us as we enter.

Behind her sit rows and rows of shelves, each stuffed to the brim with papers, like a sea of information. I can see other employees behind her, quickly moving from shelf to shelf as they organize and reorganize the seemingly endless sea of files. It's as fascinating as it is intimidating; how do they even know what they are looking for?

"Good morning," I greet as we approach the desk. "We are here seeking some information."

"What sort of information?" She looks at us skeptically.

"It is regarding someone who we believe may have entered the city in the past few weeks," I start to explain. "We were hoping you might be able to tell us if they were still here or not."

"I'm sorry, but that's not the sort of information we give out." She begins to eye us all with suspicion. "If you're trying to find someone, perhaps you would be better off hiring a private detective."

"I understand it is an odd request, ma'am." I lean in, dropping the volume of my voice as I decide to take a risk and reach into my bag, pulling out my old ranger badge. "I'm a ranger from the Shad'rok Logging Camp. The man we are seeking is a criminal."

"A criminal? Oh dear." The "Shad'rok Logging Camp" is the name we use for V'rok'sh Tah'lj with outsiders, allowing us to still trade with other cities while maintaining our secrecy. The badge, while old, still looks entirely official, and though she eyes it closely, she is unable to read the words written in Atasi on the front. "I… I'm still not sure we can—"

"I know this is weird," David suddenly joins the conversation on my right. "But please, this man is dangerous. We've been tracking him for almost a month now."

"I… I understand, but…" She seems to gather herself together mid-sentence, adjusting her glasses. "We deal with hundreds of individuals every day. The dome's primary purpose is to help us track the magical items being imported and exported from the island. We don't have time to use it to track down individuals for everyone that sees us. Not to mention that even if this man is a criminal, if he requested sanctuary upon entering the city—"

"He wouldn't have," I quickly assure her. "In fact, I doubt he even gave you any of his real information at all."

"Please, ma'am," Adam finally joins in. "I know you're busy and we're asking too much of you, but he's hurt a lot of people, and we only want to stop him before he hurts more."

"We just want to know if he is still in the city," I try to make the scope of our request seem as small as possible. "That is all."

"Alright," she agrees after some internal deliberation. "But just this once. How long ago do you think he entered Maname?"

"Thank you so much," I tell her with a small bow. "It could have been as early as two weeks, maybe three." I'm being generous due to all of our own delays and not knowing how exactly Redwish has been traveling.

"Tyreene, Bolun, please bring me the immigration records for the last three weeks," the woman calls out as she turns in her seat. "And what was his name?"

"Naruk Redwish," I tell her. "Though I have a feeling he used a false name when he entered."

"We can still try. Spell it out for me, please." She passes over a blank sheet of paper and pen. "We can also try using his other features. I know he is a man, but what about his age, species, and hair and eye color?"

"He is an orc, somewhere between twenty-five and thirty-one, with dark red hair and dark green eyes." I hand her back the sheet with the spelled-out name as two of the other workers, a male gnome and a female human, each carrying several tall stacks of paper to the front desk, dropping them with a thud.

"Alright, first we'll try the name." The woman holds her hand over the first stack of papers, her hand and eyes glowing a light pinkish color as she casts a spell, using her magic to search through the stack. She repeats this on five other stacks, shaking her head when she is finally finished. "There's no record of anyone with that name entering Manamequohi in the past three weeks. I'll try with his description now."

She goes through the same motions as before, using a slightly different spell to research the stack. This time, after she finishes with the second stacks, she makes what looks like a tally mark on the sheet with Redwish's name before moving onto the third. She repeats this six more times before she's through with the final stack, handing the sheet back to me when she is finished.

"In the past three weeks, there have been seven individuals fitting that description who have entered the city," she explains. "Two of them have already left, but the others appear to still be on the island. But I'm afraid that is all the information I can give you."

"Thank you, ma'am. That is exactly what we needed." I accept the sheet, folding it and sticking it in my pocket. "We greatly appreciate your cooperation."

"Yes, well… Have a good day." She bids us an awkward farewell, obviously flustered by the encounter.

"So was that good or bad?" David asks as we begin the trek back downstairs.

"Do we still think he's in the city?" Adam asks next.

"I'm choosing to believe it's a good thing, and that he is," I answer them both as I steel myself for the many flights of stairs. "Depending on where he is trying to go next, it's entirely possible he's been stuck here waiting for the right ship to come in or for a trader to be passing through."

"How do we find him though?" David asks next. "It's a big city."

"It is," I agree. "And I think the only thing there is for us to do is legwork."

"You want us to search for him?" Liss asks somewhat incredulously. "The whole city?"

"Just the areas around the docks," I clarify. "I don't expect us to set up a full patrol, but if we search those areas for him, it might lead to something."

"Alright," Liss agrees with some skepticism. "We can at least try and get out to each one at least once a day and ask around if anyone's seen him."

"Precisely." I nod, happy that I don't need to convince her further. "We can decide who should look where after lunch."

"So, has there been any luck with … that?" She juts her chin behind me, toward the spot on the roof where David is speaking with Atsadi and his friend Shira.

"Not yet," I tell her. "But they are working on it."

It is late in the morning, several hours after our morning trip to the administration office. After leaving, we returned to Atsadi's apartment, where we were surprised to find a few of the man's friends waiting for us. Two of them we already knew, Onas and Wari Bearfoot, two gnome brothers who are skilled enchanters and are responsible for creating my magical satchel. The third person was new, a human doctor and healer named Shira Tuvat. Atsadi invited all of them himself, thinking their skills might be useful in uncovering the mystery of David.

Deciding that there would be more room to work up here, Atsadi led us all up and out onto the roof of his apartment building. Or at least most of us… I have barely taken a step outside of the door leading up here, not able to bring myself to move closer to *any* of the roof's edges. I am honestly surprised I've held it together as much as I have.

Once we were up here, Shira took the lead, asking David all sorts of questions and using magic to scan different parts of his body. She had him run through some basic exercises, seemingly to test things like his base speed and strength. About two hours later, Liss, Corrine, and Tsula returned from their excursion, eager for a chance to sit and rest, and no doubt looking forward to lunch—which we will be having as soon as we finish things up here.

"So anger and/or trauma seem to be the triggers for these abilities." I listen as Dr. Tuvat explains our current working theory, given the last two times we witnessed David's sudden increase in strength and speed. "And since we can't recreate any of those events…" She looks to her left at Atsadi.

"No, Shira, we are not going to intentionally traumatize David, even in the name of research," the man says with a sigh.

"I know," Dr. Tuvat continues after a sigh of her own. "We're going to focus on your emotions and see if we can't provoke a response that way."

"Okay…" David agrees, though I suspect he's not completely following, which is fine because I am. "So what do you want me to do?"

"Get angry," the doctor tells him plainly. "I want you to try and bend this." She hands him a thick metal rod, at least half a meter in length.

"Uh, sure." David accepts the item, testing its weight before grasping it in both hands. "Just … be angry?"

"Exactly," Dr. Tuvat says with a nod, after moving back to stand with Atsadi, leaving David at a "safe" testing distance. "And I mean I really want you to feel it. Let the anger flow through you."

"Okay." David shakes out his limbs before closing his eyes and holding the rod up with both hands.

Everyone on the roof watches in silence as a look of concentration crosses David's face. With a grunt, he attempts to bend the bar, his hands struggling as they grip it tightly, but it doesn't seem to give. David stops and takes a breath, waiting another moment before he tries again, but still, nothing happens. Even opening his eyes so he can glare at the object while he tries for a third time doesn't help.

"It's not working," he says sullenly, turning back to the two researchers.

"Maybe it's that you're not angry enough?" Atsadi offers.

"Or maybe the trauma is a necessary component," Tuvat wonders, chewing on a thumbnail as she thinks.

"Try thinking about what was going on the last two times it happened," Adam suggests from his spot on the roof on the opposite side of David. "Run through the events in your head and see if you can get back into how you were feeling then."

"Alright, trying again." David takes a breath and raises the bar in his hands again.

Unfortunately, this round goes much like the last, with the rod not bending a millimeter. Even focusing on the events of the past doesn't seem to help David, the frustration on his face growing by the second. With a growl, he drops it to the ground with a *clang*.

"This feels stupid," he complains. "Maybe I'm not supposed to—"

"I have an idea." Knowing my pup's personality does not typically lend itself to patience, I take a breath and step out onto the roof. "Pick up the bar and close your eyes again."

"Okay." David does as I ask, returning to his previous position. "Now what?"

"Now you are going to imagine yourself in a *new* scenario," I inform him, taking a mostly steady step in his direction.

"What?" He peeks one eye open at me. "Seriously? You want me to play pretend?"

"Yes, seriously." I make sure my tone leaves no room for argument. "And for this to work, you are *really* going to have to try. Understand?"

"I understand," he replies with a sigh, closing his eye again.

"Alright. Now imagine we're back out on the road," I start to set the scene. "The six of us, traveling together by foot."

"Where are we going?" David asks.

"We're returning to Pákannon," I answer the unexpected question. "We just left Rakatune that morning."

"This feels silly," David complains again.

"*David*," I warn, "you and I both know you have done much, much sillier. Now focus on my words."

"Yes, Sir," he acquiesces, resealing his lips.

"It's late, and we have decided to set up camp for the night," I return to setting the scene. "You and I have just gotten into our bedroll when we suddenly hear the sounds of fighting as someone attacks our camp."

The small growl I hear from David tells me he's finally letting himself get into the scenario.

"It's the Blackbriars again. They've gone back on their word and are planning to capture us to bring back to their base," I continue, watching as David's hands clench into fists. "We fight valiantly but are even more outnumbered now than we were before. One by one each of us goes down—except for you. In all of the confusion, you manage to escape into the forest while the rest of us are loaded into a carriage."

I can see the anger crossing David's face as he pictures Kez and her crew ambushing us in the night once more. I am not sure how much truth there is to what I'm saying, as I do not really expect to hear from Kez ever again, but you never know what the future may hold. Either way, my words seem to be working on David.

"You follow them, fully intent on rescuing us. Tracking the carts as you stalk through the forest, you can overhear Kez making jokes about how she betrayed us." This next part is a bit of a gambit. "She says she can't believe how *stupid* you were to trust her."

I watch as David's nostrils flare when I use the very common and much-hated insult from his childhood. It means the anger he is feeling right now is real. Time to go in for the kill.

"When they finally stop to make camp themselves, it's all you can do to hold yourself back from rushing in and taking them all on." I take another few steps toward David, my voice getting lower as I close the distance between us. "But you bide your time and wait for them to sleep. You sneak your way into camp, ready to release us from our carriage, but there is a problem: Instead of wooden doors, you find solid steel bars."

"You can see all of us on the other side, bound, gagged, and struggling," I continue. "Those bars are the only things standing between us, David. You just have to bend them: so *bend them*."

After he hears me say "bend" for the second time, David does just that. His face screws up in exertion as he grips the bar, trying to bend it with all his might. I am just about ready to declare my attempt a failure when to everyone's shock—and with a roar from David—the bar bends.

All of us stare in stunned silence at the now L-shaped rod in David's hand, even David himself. And once it appears that the normal side-effect of him becoming a feral warrior has not taken root, David holds the rod aloft like a trophy as a cheer goes up around the roof. *It worked!*

"It worked!" David agrees, jumping up in excitement before quickly kissing me on the lips.

"Wow," Wari says, his voice barely above a whisper.

"That was amazing!" Dr. Tuvat quickly steps into David's personal space, already writing in her notes. "Can you describe to us exactly what it felt like?"

"Uh, really angry, I guess?" David answers unhelpfully.

"Was there a particular moment where you could feel your strength kicking in?" Tuvat asks next. "Did a certain thought or memory trigger it?"

"I'm not sure," David admits. "I was just trying to imagine what Khazak was telling me, and it just kinda … happened."

"What I'm more interested in is if you felt anything else," Atsadi tells us as he comes to stand with Tuvat. "You told me that when this happened before, you also seemed to undergo some sort of personality change and had access to knowledge that you shouldn't have. You said you even spoke a language you've never heard before, but once the moment had passed, you had no memory of it. Did you feel or remember anything this time?"

"I don't think so." David shakes his head. "I only felt it for a second."

"Do you think you could do it again?" Tuvat looks at the rod expectantly.

"I can try." He looks at me with a smile.

"I'd like to try *without* Khazak's help this time," Atsadi requests. "Now that we know it's possible, we should limit external influences so we know our findings will be accurate."

"Alright," David agrees with some reluctance. "Let's go again."

"You can do it, pup," I praise as I step back, hoping this is a good sign of things to come.

Chapter 2

David

"**Hmm, he only managed it a little that time.**"

"I'm still counting it. That makes four."

I glance over at the two older humans, not really appreciating Dr. Tuvat's use of "only." We've been at this for half an hour—no, *I've* been at this for half an hour, standing up here in the hot summer sun struggling to keep bending this damn piece of metal while they watch. And it isn't easy! In fact, it's been getting harder and harder each time, and I don't know why.

After Khazak helped me, I managed to bend the bar a second time by running myself through his scene in my head again, but after that, it was less effective. It took me almost ten minutes to bend it a third time and even longer for the fourth. It's weird. With a clearer head, I can actually *feel* when it happens, like a switch being flipped, but whenever I try and reach for it, I lose it. It's unbelievably frustrating.

I take a few breaths and shake out my limbs before I close my eyes to try again. The way everyone is staring at me is making me feel like a trained monkey. But I try to wipe all that from my head and imagine Khazak and the others in trouble again.

I've been trying to switch it up at least a little in my head, swapping out the villains or other details. This time it's Richard Calvinson, the creep who tried to kidnap and brainwash me, who's captured everyone. No, wait, *I'm* the one he's captured. I can see him on the other side of the cage he's thrown me in, his smug, punchable face mocking me, daring me to come at him. And I will, as soon as I *bend. This. Bar.*

"That's five!" Mr. Atsadi declares with a cheer.

"A big one too," Dr. Tuvat seems to accept. "We might need to get another rod for the next one. There's no way the tensile strength on that is still any good."

"Another one?" I ask with a whine.

"Perhaps we should let him rest for a moment?" Khazak suggests, coming to my rescue.

"Lunch is ready!" Just in time, Corrine comes up the stairs behind Khazak with a tall plate of sandwiches in her hands.

Tsula is right behind her carrying a bowl of fruit, mostly apples. They offered to get lunch ready for us after getting back with Liss about an hour ago. Khazak normally does the bulk of the cooking for our group--and he is *really* good at it—but that doesn't mean the rest of us don't pitch in when we can. Khazak wanted to stick with me up here on the roof, which I know isn't easy given his fear of heights.

"Alright, I suppose now would be a good time to take a break," Atsadi agrees with Khazak's suggestion, probably because he's a little hungry himself.

"Hmm, maybe we should start thinking about the ways we can test some of his other abilities," Dr. Tuvat wonders as she takes a sandwich for herself.

"Speed and agility should be easy enough," Atsadi says, the two of them taking a seat at a small card table that's been left up here. "But speaking Ancient Olympian? That will be tougher."

I decide I'll let *them* worry about that as I take some food of my own, thanking Cory and Tsula and taking a seat against the outside of the stairwell with Khazak. We only ate a few hours ago, but I'm *starving*. Bending metal with your bare hands can really take it out of you. After I finish my first sandwich, I go back for a second, and then a third, not to mention the two and a half apples I devour. Only about halfway through one, when I'm finally feeling full, do I realize that Atsadi and Tuvat are both staring at me.

"Have you always been so ... *ravenous*?" Atsadi asks, looking at the half-eaten fruit in my hand.

"Uh…" I'm not really sure how to answer.

"Yes."

"Yes."

Apparently Khazak and Adam are.

"Though it has gotten more extreme since the incident," Khazak adds. "Particularly after doing something strenuous."

"Hmmm…" Atsadi suddenly looks lost in thought. "It would make sense that his abilities would require an excessive amount of stored energy."

"So maybe it's a fuel issue…" Tuvat starts to scratch her chin, lost in thought. "If it works like other strength-enhancing magic, maybe we can figure out how *much* energy is being used."

"It might even be possible to find a way to harness an external energy source…" Atsadi jumps up, taking Tuvat by the arm. "Come on. We can use my office."

I watch as the two "scientists" scurry off to figure out … whatever they were talking about. I've never really thought much about my eating habits, except I guess for the way I lost and then regained all that weight and muscle in the months since leaving home—which some may have recently pointed out could very well be connected to everything. So I guess what they're saying makes sense, but it's not something I can control, I don't think.

"If I hadn't seen it for myself, I'm not sure I would have believed it," Onas tells me.

"Same with this sword," Wari, the second of the Bearfoot Brothers, adds. "The enchantments on this thing are top-notch. Where'd you say you found it?"

I first met Onas and Wari yesterday when Khazak brought me to their shop so I could buy one of their magic bags. It turns out they're also friends with Nylan's dad Atsadi, and as skilled enchanters, he asked them to come take a look at my weapon, the Harpe, a sword supposedly capable of cutting through anything. They've been off to the side all morning, watching me work while they inspect the weapon, even casting some sort of scanning magic on it.

"Buried in a long-forgotten temple almost 700 kilometers to the south," Khazak answers for me. "Though it is supposedly Olympian in origin."

"I've never seen this type of metal before." Wari holds the hilt near his eye so he can stare down the blade. "I'm not even sure how you'd sharpen the blade."

"If the enchantments on it are as solid as they seem, I don't think you'd ever need to," Onas points out. "But if the sword is as old as you say… There are legends of truly skilled enchanters, whose spells can last hundreds or even thousands of years, but this may very well be one of the oldest."

"How would you even be able to figure something like that out?" I ask, not sure it's possible.

"There are spells you can use to date magical energy, and a decent sorcerer might be able to get at least a basic idea," Wari answers, already thinking. "Actually, would you let us take this back to the shop? We've got some tools there that might help, and I'd really love to take a closer look at this thing."

"Uhhh…" I pause and turn to Khazak. "What do you think?"

"It is your weapon, so it is ultimately your decision," Khazak starts. "You cannot exactly use it in the city, so I do not see the harm in allowing them to hold onto it for a short while."

"Alright." I nod in agreement. "You can take it for the day. I'll swing by the shop tomorrow to pick it up."

"That should be plenty of time," Onas declares before grabbing his brother by the shirt. "Let's go. We're burning daylight."

Khazak and I watch as the two men leave, hauling a (relatively) oversized sword with them. With everyone finished eating, I take a moment to relax, which we really haven't had the chance to do much of since rushing here from Richardton. Or even before that, really.

But I guess I do have to get back to work eventually, Atsadi and Dr. Tuvat rejoining us on the roof after they finished with whatever it was they were trying to figure out. They brought me a fresh steel rod, and while I get back to work trying to bend it, Khazak talks to the others, apparently figuring out a plan for Adam, Corrine, Liss, and Tsula to patrol around the docks in search of Redwish. After a few goodbyes, they're all off.

It's several hours later when everyone finally makes it back, and in the time they were gone, I have only managed to tap into my strength *twice*—and I'm barely counting the second time. I don't know what's wrong with me, but it has the two researchers questioning the "energy" situation.

"How did the search go?" Khazak asks Adam as the others rejoin us on the roof.

"Not great." Adam shakes his head. "No sign of him."

"We even tried asking if anyone had seen an orc with red hair," Liss adds. "Still nothing."

Hearing that combined with the hours of my own failure gets to be too much for me, and I toss the metal rod to the ground with a frustrated growl. The noise gets everyone's attention, all of them turning to stare at me. Thankfully Khazak comes to my rescue again before I have a chance to make more of a scene.

"It has been a long day," he announces, meeting my eyes with sympathy. "Now seems like a good place to stop. After some rest, we can come back tomorrow and try again."

Tuvat seems reluctant to let us go, but plans are made to return after lunch tomorrow. It's late as we all make our way downstairs and out of the building, late enough that they're serving dinner by the time we get back to the inn. I can pretty much always eat, but Khazak tells the others to go on without us and has me wait in the lobby while he runs up to our room to grab his bag. Apparently, we've got plans tonight.

"Where are we going?" I ask as we leave the inn. "Are you sure I don't need to change?"

"It is a secret," Khazak informs me. "And you will… when we get there."

My Sir leads me through the streets toward our unknown destination. It's only my second day in the city, so I have no idea where we're going. Khazak seems confident, even though I think it's been like, ten years since he was last here himself, so whatever this place is, it must be good.

"Here we are," Khazak announces about twenty minutes later.

"Are you sure?" I look up at the building, confused as it appears to be a bookstore.

"Of course." He looks at me like I said something funny. "Come on. I cannot *wait* to show you around."

Walking inside confirms that yes, it is in fact a bookstore. A kind old lady sits behind the counter, her head full of curly bright white hair. She greets us with a smile, and Khazak steps forward, bending over to ask her something quietly. The store behind her is nothing but shelf after shelf of books, and I see maybe two other customers browsing them. This is where he wanted to bring me? I know he likes reading, but sheesh.

"This place seems … nice." I do my best to seem grateful for whatever this is as we start to walk through the shelves.

"Really? You like it?" he asks me in return, and it takes me a second to get that he's being sarcastic. "Not quite there yet, pup." He winks.

"We're not?" I follow him farther into the shop, not sure where else he could be taking me.

Toward the back of the store is an entrance to a small side room. Before we can enter it, two dwarves come stumbling out, both men and both seeming more than a little drunk. As they pass us, I swear they both give me and Khazak a once-over with their eyes, and I think they like what they see. They're not unattractive, but who gets drunk in a bookstore?

The room we enter doesn't look any different than the rest of the store, just smaller. There's another customer in here, turning his head as we enter. Khazak gives him a small nod and walks straight to the far wall of the room. I stand with him in front of a bookshelf, his eyes perusing the titles until they land on the one he's looking for. He reaches for it, but he only pulls it out about halfway. There's a *click*, and the entire bookcase swings inward.

"*What?!*" I ask in shock as an entirely different room is revealed.

"*Now* we have arrived." Khazak guides me through the new entryway, closing the hidden door behind us.

The room we've entered is not very large with unpainted brick walls. Ahead of us, a gnome sits behind a counter that takes up most of the corner, and there are doorways to the left and right of us. I can hear what sounds like the low thump of music coming from the left, as well as what I think are … moans?

"Good evening, gentlemen, and welcome to the Leather Rooster," the woman at the counter greets us. She looks to be around our age, her green hair cut short and styled almost like a mohawk, though it's her clothes that really stand out: almost dangerously-thin straps of leather wrap around each of her breasts, barely covering her nipples. "Have either of you visited our establishment before?"

"I have, though it has been many years," Khazak tells her as we approach.

"Well lucky for you, things haven't changed around here in a long time," she tells him with a smile. "With the exception of our prices. It's two silver a piece to enter, and for another three, we have private rooms available to rent."

"Just the locker, please," Khazak says as he hands over the payment.

"Thank you," she replies before reaching under her counter, sliding a key across the desk, and pointing to the room on our right. "You'll find your locker in there, and once you are ready you can proceed into the club."

Khazak takes the key with another thanks and leads me to what is apparently a small changing room. He quickly finds our locker among the hundreds of square wooden doors along the walls. I still have absolutely no clue what is going on, but when Khazak sets his bag down a bench and pulls out our leather harnesses, I start to get a hint.

"Strip," he orders without giving it a second thought.

"Right now." I look around at the empty room. "Everything?"

"Everything," he replies with a grin.

I have to psych myself up, but I manage to remove my clothes, imagining that I'm back in one of the changing rooms at school. While I'm stripping, Khazak lays out the outfit he's selected for me on the bench: the leather harness he had made for me a few months ago and a dark blue jock that does absolutely nothing to hide that I am locked in a chastity cage. I'm not exactly surprised after seeing the outfits other people were wearing.

After pulling on the jock, I pick up the harness, ready to pull it over my head. But just as I do, a flash of gold catches my eye—the scar on my chest. The one I received after Redwish drove a sword through my chest. I haven't worn the harness since the festival back in Tah'lj, and even though one of the straps cross over the scar, it doesn't do much to hide it. I'm frozen, staring down at my own chest, feeling self-conscious while at the same time trying not to relive the memory of its creation.

"I happen to like your scar." Khazak's voice snaps me out of my trance. "Not the way it was created, but it is something that brought us closer together. And I think it looks distinguished. But if you are feeling unsure, we do not have to—"

"No. It's okay. I want to," I reply with a smile, his words all the encouragement I need.

After helping me with my harness, I openly stare as I watch Khazak getting changed, pulling on his trademark brown leather vest over a harness of his own, ending with a white jockstrap and some black leather shorts. He looks hot. *We* look hot, made even hotter when Khazak finishes our outfits by clipping the leash onto my collar.

With a growl of approval, Khazak pulls me by the leash into him, kissing me firmly on the mouth. When I feel his tongue pushing at my lips, we end up having a small make out session right there, interrupted only when we hear someone else walking in. It's an elf wearing little more than a leather thong with *huge* metal rings pierced through each of his nipples, but before I can think too much about how he's seeing what *I'm* wearing, Khazak is pulling me by the leash out of there. We cross the entry room, the woman behind the counter nodding appreciatively at our outfits as Khazak leads me into the *next* room.

"Where are we?" I stare around in wonder as we enter what truly seems like a magical place.

It almost looks like a tavern—there's even a fully stocked bar centered on the back wall and some tables and booths off to the side—but the rest of the place… Everything is black, even the walls, which are either painted or have a sheet hung on them. It's dark, but not so dark that I can't see thanks to the red and blue lightstones set into the ceiling, along with the occasional candle on a table or counter.

People dressed like me and Khazak fill the floor, some wearing things I've never seen before, some completely naked, and a few with a leash and collar like me. It helps with the anxiety I'm feeling, but only a little. While one side of the room has more average looking seating and furniture, the other is filled with all kinds of benches, frames, and crosses, often with someone tied to them. There are people of all types being tied up, spanked, paddled, or even just fucking.

"This is the Leather Rooster," Khazak tells me as he walks us to the bar. "I learned of it the first time I visited the city, and it was an amazing experience. I've been dying to come back ever since, but I wanted to find someone to bring with me first. So you can imagine how excited I was once I knew we were coming."

"So it's a … secret club? For people like us?" I ask as Khazak orders us both some beer.

"It is a place for people like us to meet each other and socialize," he explains while we wait for our drinks. "It has been an open secret in the city for some time. When it first opened, it *was* an actual secret, but as its membership grew, it opened up more to the public."

"Open secret?" I scoff as Khazak pays for our drinks and grabs our mugs. "The entrance is in a bookstore, hidden behind a bookshelf."

"The bookstore is owned by the same people who started the club—we passed one of them when we first walked inside," Khazak explains as he leads us to a booth. "They've kept the hidden entrance in the bookstore for the history and atmosphere. I would say it has paid off."

Khazak slides into his seat but stops me before I can follow him. Instead, he points at the floor next to the booth—where a plush red pillow has been placed. A quick glance around reveals other submissives kneeling on these pillows at the feet of their own owners, and so before I can think too much about it, I follow their example. I hear a hum of approval from Khazak above me as his hand strokes my hair—and a mug of beer is passed over.

Khazak continues to pet me as I take in our surroundings. I know it's rude to stare, but I feel like in a place like this it's a little more acceptable since people are dressed to get attention. I mean, some of them are literally putting on shows. I watch them, transfixed, caught between wanting to see more and feeling nervous that Khazak might pull me up there himself.

There's an elf man bent over a sawhorse, his pants pulled down around his ankles with each of his ass cheeks being paddled by two different women. There's a dark-skinned halfling woman tied to a bench on her back as another woman drips hot candle wax onto her breasts, making her gasp and writhe. And in one corner, a red-skinned orc has his wrists tied to a bar, bent over while an elf—oh my gods, did he just stick his *entire* fist up the guy's ass?!

"Enjoying the shows?" Khazak asks as I choke on my beer.

"I didn't even know places like this *could* exist," I tell him, wiping my mouth on my arm. "It's like the *Uzi'gor* festival in Tah'lj."

"It is very similar," Khazak agrees. "This is less open, but it also exists year-round."

As we continue to watch the club's other patrons and sip our drinks, I start to relax, leaning against the side of Khazak's leg. At least as relaxed as I can get while being extremely horny in a chastity cage. I'm so enraptured by all of the kinky sex things going on that I don't notice someone approaching us.

"Good evening." I turn to see two men approach our booth. "Me and my boy couldn't help but notice you from across the club. Would you mind if we joined you?"

He is a tall elf with pale skin and short, light brown hair, wearing a tight black shirt with long sleeves that seems to hug him in all the right places. His black pants are equally tight, and he's wearing black leather gloves on each hand. The "boy" he's referring to is anything but, a stocky and muscular dwarf with tan skin that is covered neck to ankle in body hair. He's wearing a harness like me, though he is at least allowed shorts instead of just underwear. He grins when he catches me staring, making me blush.

"Go right ahead." Khazak gestures to the opposite side of the booth. "I am Khazak, and this is my pup, David."

"Thank you. My name is Cillian, and this is my submissive, Novus," the man greets as he slides into the seat, his boy dropping to a pillow of his own. "Are you two enjoying your evening?"

"It has been very pleasant so far," Khazak answers. "Just relaxing and enjoying the evening."

"This place is perfect for that." Cillian salutes Khazak with his own drink before taking a sip. "I'm not sure I recall seeing you two here before. Are you new?"

"I have been here previously, but it has been a very, very long time," Khazak answers before moving a hand to my hair. "This is David's first time."

"First times can be fun." Novus says his first words to me with a grin, in a deep, gravelly voice that makes me shiver.

"They certainly can be," Cillian agrees in an equally sexy tone. "Are you staying in the city long or just passing through?"

"We have some business that will keep us here for at least a few days," Khazak replies. "As you likely guessed, we both tend to find interesting ways to spend our free time."

"Then I hope you don't think me too forward for asking, but would you and your pup be interested in joining me and my boy in our private room?" Cillian leans forward, eyeing both of us lewdly.

"Hmmm." I hear Khazak considering the offer before his hand tugs at my hair to look up at him. "What do you think, pup? Would that be something you would enjoy?"

It only takes me a second to look over at Novus, who I am apparently pretty into, before I nod. Then I remember my words. "Yes, Sir."

"Please lead the way, Cillian," Khazak responds to his fellow dom.

"Wonderful." Cillian wastes no time in standing. "Follow me."

Novus jumps to his feet, quickly catching up to his owner, and I stand as Khazak slides himself out of the booth and takes my leash in hand. We follow the two men past the "floor shows" and into a hallway with at least a dozen doors. Given the muffled sounds of smacks and moans I can hear behind them, these must be the private rooms.

Ahead of us, Cillian opens a door and beckons us inside. The room contains a small bed against one wall and a couch on the other. There's also a small table next to the bed with a tidy stack of folded towels on top of it but not much else. Cillian moves to sit on the couch, leaving space next to him for Khazak.

"Here, boy." Cillian snaps and points between his legs.

Novus scurries over and immediately begins mouthing at Cillian' groin. Not to be outdone, I do the same after Khazak takes his seat and spreads his legs. As I nuzzle my face against his clothed crotch, I catch Novus undoing Cillian' pants from the corner of my eye and releasing a massive cock.

"Thank you for joining us," Cillian says, as though Novus isn't already sucking him off.

"Thank you for having us," Khazak replies, releasing his own dick so I can do the same.

"So, you say it's been some time since you were last here?" Cillian asks.

"Over ten years," Khazak answers. "Though I have been wanting to return for some time."

"That is quite a long time. Where do you hail from?" There's a gagging noise as Novus chokes himself on Cillian. "Do they have anything like this there?"

"I'm from a small village far to the south, and David is from Lutheria," Khazak answers for me as I take him into my mouth. "And no, not exactly, though we do have a small community of like-minded individuals."

"Places like this wouldn't exist without those communities," Cillian tells him, lust bleeding into his voice. "Novus and I both hail from Maname. We actually met here at the Leather Rooster six years ago."

"You make for a very attractive couple," Khazak compliments, his hand on my head moving me up and down his shaft.

"As do the two of you," Cillian replies. "I noticed when you walked into the club. The golden scar on your pup's chest, in particular. It's very *unique*."

I freeze at Novus's mention of my scar, mid-blowjob. Unique isn't exactly an insult, but it's still more attention on it than I wanted. Before I can spiral in my thoughts any longer, Khazak starts to pet his hand slowly through my hair, and I relax.

"That it is," Khazak says as I resume my blowjob. "Though perhaps not something to discuss at the current moment."

"Of course, I apologize." I can't see his face, so I'll have to assume he's being genuine. "It was actually Novus who requested that we talk to you."

"Really now?" The two carry on their conversation like we're not here. "Why us?"

"My boy is something of a switch," Cillian starts to explain. "And I recently promised him a reward: a play session with a sub of his own to dominate."

"That's very generous of you." Khazak pulls me all the way down his dick and holds me there, making me gag.

"Not as generous as you're thinking because it won't be me. I have no interest in being submissive, nor a bottom," Cillian continues as he fucks Novus's mouth on his prick. "But when you and your boy caught our eye, it got me thinking. How would you feel about these two putting on a little show for us?"

"I think that sounds like it could be a very pleasant way to spend the evening." Khazak's cock pulses in my mouth at the thought. "Does your boy have much experience domming?"

"Some. We've been known to share the occasional sub together," Cillian replies. "He knows what he is and isn't allowed to do. In addition to your own rules, of course."

"Would you like to play with Novus, pup?" Khazak pulls me off his cock so I have to actually answer.

"Y-Yes, Sir," I stammer, blushing as I look over and see the sexy man already grinning back.

"Alright, then why don't you move to the bed?" Khazak helps me to my feet, giving me a quick peck of a kiss and turning to my new playmate. "Novus: no choking, no pain, and no marking him up beyond reddening his rear."

"Understood, master," Novus says with a bow. "Thank you for allowing me to play with your pup."

"He's very well trained," Khazak comments as Novus leads me toward the bed.

"I'm a very strict trainer," Cillian replies with a laugh.

"That must be nice. My pup has a tendency to get into trouble," Khazak jokingly (I hope) complains. "Though he thrives under a strong hand."

Standing at the foot of the bed, I blush at my owner's words while Novus beams at his. I wonder if I look the same when Khazak praises me. Still wearing a smile, Novus reaches one hand up to the back of my head, pulling me down for a sloppy kiss. As a dwarf, his height is somewhere between four and five feet tall, shorter than anyone else I've been with so far. But I can adapt.

"Put him on his knees, boy," Cillian instructs from the couch.

The hand on my neck guides me downward until I'm kneeling, but with our height difference that's still not quite enough. In order to get eye level with his crotch, I've got to sit back on my heels, but it's worth it when I see the size of the mound he's rubbing. As he unbuttons his shorts, a *huge* slab of meat falls out, far bigger than I would have guessed.

"I think you know what to do with that, pup," Khazak tells me.

"Yes, Sir," I answer, already licking my lips.

I lower my mouth over the head of his cock, grinning internally at the moan I hear from Novus above me. I swirl my tongue around the head, already tasting his precum before taking in more of his shaft. Even as low as I am, his cock still has to be pointed up at an angle, and I wonder for a moment about how him fucking me might work. My own dick seems to like the thought, untouched in its cage and fighting its metal bonds.

He's content to let me work at my own pace for a bit, but soon enough, his hand is tangled in my hair, and he starts moving me the way he wants. He's not *quite* fucking my face, so I'm not gagging, but Novus clearly knows what he wants me to do, and I don't fight him. He seems worked up, not wasting time in taking charge. Does Cillian let him do this often?

"Sirs, I think I'm ready to move us onto the bed," Novus informs our men. "If that is alright with you."

"Any objections?" Cillian asks Khazak.

"None from me, although…" I hear some rustling and then something scraping against the wooden floor as two small objects bump into my leg. "You may need those."

Novus pulls himself from my mouth before I start drooling all over myself, though my lips and jaw are still plenty sore. Looking down, I see a vial of oil and my cleansing charm—everything I'll need to get ready for what comes next. Novus helps me to my feet as I hold the charm against my belly, and after another kiss, he turns me around and pushes me over the bed before kneeling down behind me.

"Unnnhhh…" I moan as the dwarf spreads my ass and buries his tongue in my hole.

His scruffy beard feels rough against my skin, sending little jolts of electricity down my body and making me shiver. As Novus's tongue slips in and out of my hole, I already know I'm leaking precum in my jock pouch. By the time he finally finishes with a *spank*, there's probably a whole puddle on the floor.

"He seems eager," Khazak comments.

"I make him work hard for rewards like this," Cillian tells him. "Not that I don't enjoy the show."

"Move up on the bed, pup," Novus gives me his first direct order with another *smack* on the ass.

"Yes, sir," I answer automatically, shuffling forward.

"Seems like your pup is more well-trained than you thought," Cillian praises me to Khazak.

"He's a natural sub," Khazak responds, "and even more of a natural bottom."

The mattress shifts as Novus climbs onto the bed behind me, his hands immediately moving to my ass. After giving it a few squeezes, I feel something cool dripping down my crack. His fingers chase the slick liquid to my hole, rubbing circles around it before daring to press a finger inside. With all the fucking me and Khazak have been catching up on, there's hardly any real stretch, at least not until two more fingers join it and are sliding in and out with ease.

The next thing I know, my ass is empty as a slick cock is smacked against my hole, making me tense up. Novus grinds himself against me as he waits, and once I'm relaxed, he reaches down to take aim at his prize. As he presses inside me, I focus on not tensing up again. I know Khazak is big, but Novus's proportions are throwing me off, and I don't think it'll be clear exactly how much dick I'm dealing with until he's all the way inside.

The answer is "a lot." When he's finally bottomed out and his hairy thighs and belly are scratching against my ass, I feel thoroughly filled up. He's not as thick as Khazak, but he's almost as long, which is plenty long enough. I let my chest fall to the bed as he starts to fuck me, the down-ward curve causing him to press into my prostate on each in-stroke.

I don't last long in that position. Once he's set himself a good pace, a strong hand pulls on the strap of my harness, forcing me up onto my hands. Now that he has something to grip me by, his thrusts get stronger, our skin meeting with a loud slap each time. I'm so caught up in trying to adjust that I don't even realize the loud moans I hear are coming from my own mouth.

"You weren't kidding," I hear Cillian say offhand. "He certainly seems to be enjoying himself."

"You have not even seen the half of it," Khazak informs him, wearing what I'm sure is a cocky grin.

I know exactly what Kazakh is getting at, too. There's a pressure in my lower half, right around my groin that has been steadily building since Novus started fucking me. My toes curl every time I feel the thick column of his cock press back inside, and with only two more thrusts, the anal orgasm finally washes over me, my hole pushing feebly against the welcome intruder. I groan loudly, loud enough that I'm sure anyone in the rooms around us can hear, and I'd give any-thing to bury my face in a pillow to hide my shame.

Novus's reaction is to fuck even harder, finally releasing my harness so that his hands can grip my hips tightly. He's spearing me on the full length of his prick on every stroke, which is exactly what to do if he wants me to make me cum again—which I very quickly do. Now free to fall to the bed, I bite into the mattress to muffle my next moan as best I can.

"Master, I'm—" Novus starts, sounding out of breath. "I'm getting close."

"Cum whenever you're ready, boy," Cillian gives his permission.

"Thank you, sir!" Novus replies happily, completely changing his tactics and rapidly humping into me.

I brace myself against the sudden anal onslaught until, with a growl, Novus cums. I feel him practically climb on top of me, grinding against my ass to ensure his seed is planted as deep as possible. His body jerks each time he fills me with another shot of warm stickiness, only becoming still when he's finally finished. He straightens his body as his knees once again reach the bed, not quite ready to pull out and stretching his back as we both catch our breath.

"Boy." ***snap*** Cillian is ready, though.

At the snap of a finger, Novus pulls out and moves off the bed, leaving me an open gaping mess. I distinctly hear a gagging sound, but before I can see any of the action, I'm flipped over as the bed shifts again, coming face to face with Khazak. There's a pause, a moment where his hand cradles the side of my face and he looks into my eyes, searching for any sign of trouble or distress. And when he finds none, he kisses me.

That's the stuff. I smile as his tusks bump against my cheeks, always content to have my orc's mouth on me. As he plunders my lips, his hands take me by the back of my thighs, bending me at the waist as he hooks them under his arms. Breaking our liplock for just a second to spit in his hand so he can slick himself up (*god that's hot*), the head of his cock prods at my still-open hole as he licks his tongue into my mouth.

His dick finds little resistance as he sheaths himself inside of me, taking a moment to enjoy the wet heat of my ass. He must have been working himself up on the couch while he watched Novus stretching me open, because he doesn't wait long to start thrusting. He takes advantage of the mattress, using his body weight to bounce himself up and down at a rapid pace. Elsewhere in the room, I just barely make out the sounds of someone moaning, followed by more gagging.

"Fuck, thank you both for that," Cillian says to us, out of breath. "What do you say, boy?"

"Thank you again, sir, for allowing me to play with your pup." Novus's voice sounds a little hoarse; Cillian really must have gone to town on his throat.

"You're welcome." Khazak slows down, breaking our kiss and kneeling upright to answer. "Thank you for the fun evening."

"I believe we are going to turn in for the evening. I trust I can safely leave the room to the two of you?" Cillian asks as he tucks himself back into his pants. "No wanton destruction of the furniture after we're gone?"

"You have my word," Khazak answers, looking at me with a hungry grin.

"Then enjoy the rest of your night." A door opens. "I neglected to say earlier, but I'm actually one of the owners, so my boy and I are here often. Hope to see you again soon."

As the door closes, Khazak returns to what's important—fucking my brains out. He presses my legs back toward my chest while he stays upright, his eyes aimed down, locked on his cock sliding in and out of my no doubt sloppy hole. When he's had enough, he drops down with a growl, his face hovering just above mine.

"I hope you enjoyed that, puppy," he says with a growl. "I enjoyed watching."

"You always like watching me get fucked," I reply, cockier than I should. "Think you can't do the job yourself?"

"*Someone* doesn't want to get out of that cage any time soon," he warns me, never once stopping his thrusts. "More fun for me."

That's what you think. With my taunts fueling his fire and Khazak filling me to the brim, I can already feel another orgasm starting to work its way out of me. His thick green rod slams its way in and out of me, the heavy sack of his balls slapping against my ass on every thrust. When I cum for a third time, I wrap my arms around his neck just to keep myself grounded.

It won't be long until number four is here. Thankfully though, I don't think Khazak is going to last very long either, and almost like clockwork, we cum one after the other, my hole spasming weakly around him as he breeds me. I swear his cock gets even bigger when he shoots, almost like he's trying to lock all of it in there.

Khazak shudders when he's finished, his body sagging over mine, our chests both pounding. He allows my legs to slip from his arms, and I wince as I stretch them back into a normal position. All the movement causes Khazak's half-hard cock to slip from my hole, a mess of cum and lube surely following onto the sheets.

"That was a welcome return," Khazak says as he rolls us on our sides, pulling me in for a cuddle as we come down from our sexual high.

"Not bad for a first timer, either," I add. "And we made friends with one of the owners."

Things aren't always that intense, but I think we both needed more than a little stress relief after everything we've been through lately. I'm not even upset about still being caged. Honestly, all I want to do right now is sleep.

"Ah ah, no falling asleep yet." Before I can nod off, Khazak is moving, climbing off the bed to retrieve a towel. "We've still got to get back to the inn."

"Can't we just sleep here?" I whine.

"I'm afraid they don't do overnight stays, pup," he informs me with a huff of laughter.

He wipes us both down as best he can, but we will definitely need to shower once we get back to the inn. After making sure I'm feeling alright—I've learned subdrop is no joke—Khazak helps me to stand, leading me by the waist rather than leash. I'm a little too exhausted to worry much about everyone paying us attention as we walk back through the club, but I don't think any of it was bad.

Back in the changing room, Khazak helps pull off my harness before pressing a waterskin into my hand and making me drink from it. After he gets me back into my clothes, he takes care of his own, and by the time we're walking back through the secret bookcase, I'm starting to feel a little more like myself again. The clothes help.

"That was fun," I tell Khazak as we walk together hand in hand back to the inn. "Thank you for taking me there."

"I'm glad you enjoyed yourself," Khazak replies with a smile. "If you'd like, we can come back in a day or two."

"I would. Maybe we can even put on a show," I tease, knowing there's a decent chance we'll do exactly that.

The air outside is cool and refreshing. I'm gonna sleep great tonight; I just know it. I squeeze Khazak's hand, swinging it as we walk like a pair of children in school. I just feel happy.

So of course, that's when everything goes to hell. From off in the distance, we hear the booms of an explosion and screaming.

That didn't take long.

Chapter 3

David

"What was that?" The ground shakes again as Khazak and I look for the source.

"I am not sure… Wait." Khazak points over my shoulder, where a column of smoke can be seen rising in the distance. "Let's go."

The two of us take off in the direction of the smoke. It's late, so there aren't a lot of people out right now, but as we get closer to the chaos, we start to see some people running our way looking terrified. I can make out the red glow of fire up ahead, turning a corner to see flames already starting to engulf some of the buildings.

"What could have done this?" Khazak looks up with worry as more people flee the destruction.

"I don't kn—" I see movement from the corner of my eye, turning in time to see something disappear behind a building, just as the ground shakes again. "What was that?"

"David," Khazak calls to me.

"No seriously, did you see that?" I take a step toward whatever it was. "It was long and kinda pointy on the end."

"*David*," Khazak repeats.

"In the light of the fire, it almost looked like it was covered in scales," I finish, just as the ground starts to shake again. "Kind of like a lizard tai—"

"DAVID!" I finally turn to a now-yelling Khazak, who is facing the opposite direction and looking up at a… at a…

"*Dragon*," I say barely above a whisper as the creature's large, scale-covered head hovers above us.

At least I think it's a dragon. I've never seen one aside from paintings and drawings—almost no one has. It's huge, easily reaching four or five stories tall, covered in dark scales with two large horns atop its head. As it rears its head back and opens its mouth, I see a row of large and no doubt deadly teeth—and an orange glow coming from behind them.

"MOVE!" Khazak shouts, grabbing me by the arm and rushing us both into an alleyway.

Not a second later, a fiery inferno blazes down the city streets. Only feet away, the heat nearly singes my face, like standing to close to a blacksmith's forge. If Khazak had been even a second slower, we'd both have been burnt to a crisp.

"I… I…" I stare in shock at the charred stone that lines the exit to the alley. "A dragon? An *actual* fucking dragon? How!?"

"We need to move." Khazak is already in business mode, heading the opposite way down the alley. "We have to get away from that thing."

"What? We can't just run away," I start to argue as I follow him. "There's people—"

"We're not running away," he answers confidently. "We're going to help, but we need to get to the others. And our equipment."

"Shit, my sword!" I exclaim. "The Bearfoots still have it."

"Keep your voice down," Khazak warns me, looking apprehensively to the sky. "You will just have to make do with the one you still possess. We may be able to find a replacement."

"Maybe." I silently curse at myself, my best weapon out of reach.

The trek back to the inn is tense, but we manage to get there without the creature noticing. By now people are starting to wake up to the sounds of destruction, coming out of their homes confused and concerned. I hear the word "dragon" shouted more than once, and I'm sure it won't take long for the news to spread. I jump when a siren starts to blare all around us, like a city-wide alarm spell.

The entire inn is in a state of panic when we get inside. Khazak and I run upstairs, splitting up to wake our friends. I do my best to tell a groggy Adam and Liss quickly about what's going on, but I wait until everyone is dressed and in the lobby for Khazak to fully explain the situation, which sounds crazy.

"A dragon?" Liss doesn't sound convinced. "That's impossible."

"I understand that it sounds far-fetched, but we saw it with our own eyes," Khazak assures them.

"More than that, it breathed fucking fire at us!" I add, remembering the heat. "It almost singed my hair off."

"If that's really what's going on, then they're going to try and evacuate the city," Adam says, crossing his arms over his chest as he thinks.

"People could be hurt," Corrine adds with concern.

"If we head toward the fires, we can help people get to safety, maybe at one of the city's ports," Adam concludes with a nod.

"My thoughts exactly," Khazak agrees.

"I can get on board with that." Liss finishes tightening her boot laces and stands from her chair. "Let's go."

"Follow us. Not that you'll miss the smoke," I say as we all stand, and I lead everyone out, pausing when I realize someone isn't following. "Tsula? Are you coming?"

"I... I..." she stammers, still in her seat, nervously twirling her braid.

"It's okay if you're scared," I tell her, realizing she probably isn't used to running *toward* danger like this. "If you want to say here, you—"

"No, I... I want to help." She takes a deep breath, grips her staff tightly, and stands. "I can do this."

"You have the rest of us to back you up," Liss assures her. "And I doubt we'll be the only ones out there."

Liss is exactly right. Once we're outside, we see members of the city guards posted along the streets, using the glowing wands in their hands to guide people away from the destruction and toward the ports. A few of them shout at us as we run in the opposite direction, though none actually try to stop us. Their hands are already full.

We slow down once we get near the area where me and Khazak were first attacked, not wanting to run face first into our fire-breathing friend. It's oddly quiet, other than the people already working to put out the fires and rescue those still trapped inside buildings. We start to pitch in when we feel a distant rumbling, realizing the dragon must have moved deeper into the city—until we feel a second, much closer rumble.

"I-Is there more than one?" Tsula asks nervously.

"I do not know," Khazak answers, already looking in that direction. "But we may need to find out."

"I'll catch up," Corrine tells us, already using her magic to heal the burns of some of the fire's victims. "I can't just leave these—"

"We understand," Adam assures her. "Stay safe and find us when you can, okay?"

"Okay." Cory nods with a smile. "You stay safe too."

I don't love not having our healer with us, but she's right: those people need her more than us right now. We head toward these new sounds of destruction, which only seem to be moving farther and farther away. But it doesn't take long until more people are running past us in the opposite direction, some screaming in terror.

"Over there!" I point ahead with a shout, already running toward someone in trouble.

I spot a man being backed into a wall by two assailants, one of them menacingly swinging a rope lasso above their head. It's only when I get closer that I see that these assailants are much bonier than I'm used to dealing with. *Skeletons. They're all fucking skeletons!*

I skid to a halt as one of them turns their skull toward me, its red glowing eyes staring right at me. Even I want to scream when it hisses at me menacingly, striking out with my sword in a panic—and lodging it firmly in its skull. I try to shake it loose but only succeed in losing my grip as the undead creature screeches in anger.

I'm actually scared, at least until Khazak rushes in, slams it into the wall, and it crumples into a pile of bones. Before the second skeleton can finish turning around, he gives a solid kick to its ribcage, forcing it to do the same. He quickly kneels and drives the hilt of his sword into the skull, shattering it and freeing my sword while Liss rushes in to do the same to the other.

"An *army* of skeletons…" Khazak shakes his head as he helps the man who was nearly captured to his feet. "Are you alright?"

"Thank you so much," the man thanks us in a panic. "Those… Those things… They're capturing people!"

"We'll do our best to help them," Adam tells the man before guiding him in the direction we came from. "You'll find help that way. The people there will be able to help you get to safety."

"Remember, they have no flesh or blood. Crushing or bludgeoning will be more effective than a blade," Khazak tells me while handing me my sword.

"Have you fought them before?" I ask as I return it to its sheath.

"No, but I ran drills with the rangers," he answers.

"And pretty much everything 'dies' when you destroy its skull," Liss reasons.

"First dragons, now the undead?" Khazak starts walking. "Not the most ideal time to be without our cleric. We need to hurry. You heard that man; others are in trouble."

It doesn't take long before we come across more people and even more skeletons. Like, a small army of them, marching down the road toward us as everyone else runs away. Some of them carry rope, other chains, but all of them are doing the same thing, grabbing and attacking anyone they can before binding them tightly.

"Try and free anyone you can," Khazak orders, already rushing forward despite the danger. "We can at least try and stop their advance."

We work to rescue as many as we can, focusing our efforts on the skeletons with bindings that seem to be doing most of the capturing. We manage to free a few more people, but we're outnumbered almost four to one, and they quickly overwhelm us. We're split up, and I'm backed against a wall with Tsula at my side, no exit in sight.

"I don't suppose you have spell that'll make these guys back down, do you?" I ask the relatively inexperienced wizard.

"I... I..." She holds her staff in front of her, her hands shaking.

She tries to steady herself, closing her eyes. Her hands begin to glow as she tries casting a spell, but it's too late. The skeletons are on us. Bony hands grab onto my wrists with more strength than I would have expected as a rope is thrown and tightened around my shoulders. I thrash against our attackers, Tsula screaming as they do the same to her. Feeling a sudden burst of strength (*Did I just…?*), I manage to shake them off, grabbing Tsula as I rocket through the crowd and pull us both into an alley. I pull off the rope as we run, not stopping until the sounds of bones clicking against the ground have faded.

"We have to go back," I tell Tsula as she leans against the wall, out of breath. "We can't leave the others."

"How… How are we supposed to stop them?" She stands up, twisting her hands around her staff in worry. "I-I couldn't even rescue myself."

"Don't think like that," I tell her. "You're still new to this and did what you could."

"And what do we do now?" She bites her lip.

"You need to go and find Corrine," I answer. "She'll be able to help us."

"W-What are you going to do?" she asks with worry after she realizes I'm not coming with her.

"I'm going to follow them," I say, already turning back. "See where they're taking the others and figure out why, and maybe try and find an opening to free them."

"A-Are you sure?" She's still scared, and I don't blame her. "What if you get caught?"

"Then you and Cory will just have to rescue me too," I tell her, offering her a quick hug. "Find her and then us. Hurry."

"I will!" With a nod, she continues down the alleyway while I turn around and run back the way we came.

It's not hard to track a giant army of skeletons. The bones they leave behind after combat are like a trail of breadcrumbs. I catch up to them pretty quickly, though I make sure to keep my distance, sneaking quietly around corners as they continue their march. I can make out a disarmed and surrounded Khazak and Adam in the crowd but can't do anything to help.

They herd the people they capture toward the center of their group, forcing them to march as the "soldiers" in front grab anyone else. It doesn't seem like they're taking any specific route, but eventually I notice that they've stopped trying to find people and turn toward the center of the island. What are they planning to do with hostages—and how is it connected to the dragon?

I follow them as they move toward a tall building, some sort of office, I think. I can't read the signs, and even more skeletons are posted outside like guards. As the group with my friends approaches, these skeletons quickly start to separate the capturees, roughly checking their bindings and confiscating their belongings before pushing them inside the building one by one.

As I hang back watching all of this unfold, a *second* group of skeletons with their own hostages approaches from the west and does the exact same thing. *What the fuck is going on here?* I have to find a way inside if I'm going to get anyone out of there.

Which is easier said than done. I circle around the building at a safe distance, but I can't find an entrance that isn't guarded. Somewhere else in the city I hear the sound of glass breaking, and it gives me an idea that has served me well more than once: going up.

The building people are being thrown into is tall, and so are all the others around it. So after sneaking through the alleyways to get a little closer, I start to search for a way inside one of the places next door, lucking out when I find an unlocked door to the east. Maybe some kind of apartments? Inside, the lack of sound tells me it's either long abandoned or has already been searched by the skeleton squad.

I run up eight or nine flights of stairs until I reach the door to the roof, moving to the edge that faces my target and leaning over to try and gauge the distance. It's pretty far, and these buildings are about the same height, but I'm not working empty handed; I've still got the rope they tried to tie me up with. And lucky me, the building across the way has something this one doesn't: stone gargoyles.

I tie one end of the rope into a loop, and though it takes me a few tries, I eventually manage to throw it across the gap and over one of the gargoyles. I give it a few *really* good tugs to test the weight before I step up onto the edge, both my hands firmly grasping the rope. *Seems sturdy enough… Khazak is going to kill me when he finds out about this.* After taking a breath and saying a silent prayer to any gods up there willing to listen, I jump.

The rope pulls taut as it takes my full weight—and thankfully holds steady as I swing across the gap! While that part of the plan works perfectly, I seem to have misjudged the distance because from where I grabbed the rope, I'm about to swing directly into a window. A closed window. I brace myself as my body shatters the glass, rolling onto a wooden floor with a hard *thud*.

Okay, yeah, that was pretty stupid, but you're inside! And *you somehow managed to avoid getting cut by any of that glass. Shit, did the skeletons hear the glass breaking? Can skeletons even hear? I mean, they don't have ears, but they don't really have eyes either, and it sure seemed like they were looking at—THERE'S NO TIME FOR THIS!*

I shake the silly thoughts from my head as I stand, carefully brushing off any remaining bits of glass. I'm just going to assume the skeletons might have heard me and play it safe. The floor I'm on seems like it's for storage, boxes stacked into rows against the wall. I find the stairs and quietly sneak my way down, stopping at any sign of noise or movement, which is a lot with these creaky wooden floors.

It's not until I reach the second floor that I find any skeletons, four of them all congregated around the final flight of stairs down to the first. I briefly entertain the idea of taking them all on, but a dozen more could be right at the bottom of the stairs waiting to join in. I'm going to have to find another way down.

I sneak my way to the opposite end of the floor and find a lot of offices, none of them useful, but when I reach the back corner, something catches my eye: a lift. Or at least something resembling one: an open doorway covered with a grate, a rope and pulley just inside. That must be how they move those crates from the upper floors around the building.

I open the grate and stick my head into the shaft, pleased to see it drop down another floor. A strange purple light shines in, but I can't make out what it is from up here. I climb inside, hanging on to the two thick ropes that pull the dumbwaiter up and down to lower myself to the ground floor as quietly as I can. Pleased to not see any of the undead in the immediate area, I open the grate and carefully climb out.

I'm surrounded by desks but not in an organized way. They've been pushed here haphazardly from the center of the room, where there appears to be a glowing black cage—the source of the seemingly purple light. And inside of that cage are Khazak and everyone else they've captured. The entrance and the stairs are both on the opposite side of the cage, which is also where all of the skeletons are.

No one's noticed me yet, so I sneak toward the cage, staying low to the ground. I spot Khazak pretty close, but as I get closer, I see another of the captives accidentally touch the cage's side, pulling their arm back in pain when they receive a nasty magic shock. That's gonna make it tougher to get Khazak's attention.

I get an idea, grabbing a piece of paper from the top of a desk and crumpling it into a small ball. I line myself with Khazak and a gap between the cage's "bars," taking careful aim as I toss the paper ball through the gap and into Khazak's shoulder. The impact gets his attention, his eyes flitting from the ball, to the direction it came, to me. Tugging on Adam's sleeve, they try to get as close to the cage's edge as possible while trying to make sure no one else notices.

"David?" Khazak says barely above a whisper.

"Just hold on," I try to reassure him. "I'm here to rescue you."

"What?" Adam keeps looking from me to the skeletons, worried they might notice.

"You need to leave before they capture you too." Khazak sounds annoyed.

"I am *not* gonna leave you here," I tell him. "I'm getting you guys out of there."

"*How?*" Adam looks at the cage separating us.

"Give me a minute and I'll figure it out!" *Maybe a few minutes.*

"No, you need to get help." Khazak shakes his head. "Whatever they're planning, this is just a holding area for now, but I don't know how long that will last."

"I can't just leave you—"

"David, *please*," Khazak implores, reaching through the gap to take my hands. "You need to get out of here, maybe even out of the city."

"I'm not leaving the city!" I hiss-whisper. "I don't run away from a fight."

"I'm not asking you to run away, David. I'm asking you to send for help." Khazak looks anxiously at his captors. "Get messages to the people in Richardton, Pákannon, even home—anywhere. Just tell them what is happening here so they can send reinforcements. You can't help us if you get captured yourself or *worse*."

"Fine." I hate when he's logical. "But I don't like this, and I'm still coming back for you."

"I know you will," he says, squeezing. "And when you do, you can do whatever insane plan you come up with."

"I'm holding you to that." *Gods, I wish I could kiss him right now.*

With a lot of reluctance, I let go of Khazak's hand and sneak back to the lift shaft, climbing back up to the second floor. You'd think getting out would be easier than getting in, but I didn't really have an exit plan in mind when I swung across the building, and swinging back the other way isn't an option.

My best chance is probably gonna be to find a window and drop from the second floor. I find one, but then I have wait for a gap in the patrol walking around the building. I'm spotted as soon as I hit the ground by skellies on either side and take off as fast I can down the alley, not stopping until I'm several blocks away from the makeshift prison.

Looking around, I can see the glow of multiple fires in the distance all around the island. Actually, I think I'm near the shopping district—which means the Bearfoot Brothers' shop. Might as well get my sword while I'm here, right? Then I can figure out how to get out of here and get help.

Sneaking through the marketplace is no less stressful than the rest of the city, moving from alley to alley. Compared with how bustling it was yesterday, right now it's a ghost town. The streets are empty other than a few evacuees, scurrying away with bags strapped to their backs. Everyone else is either already gone, hiding, or somehow still asleep.

I find the brothers' shop in the magic district, right where I remember it. The door is locked, but it's also made of wood, and I make the quick decision to break it open. After making sure the coast is clear, I step out into the street before charging at the door shoulder-first. The door gives way easily, but I didn't stop to consider that a pair of enchanters might have other types of security in their store—like the loud alarm that's now blaring in my ears.

"WHO'S THERE!?" Onas pops up from behind the shop's counter, blue energy crackling in the hand he has aimed at me.

"David! It's David!" I throw my hands up, hoping he can hear me over the alarm.

"What? David?" The pukwudgie raises his other hand, dismissing the alarm with a gesture. "What are you doing here?"

"What was that? Are those boney bastards he—Aahh!" Wari comes charging downstairs and promptly trips, tumbling to the bottom with a thud.

"Are you okay?" Onas asks after scurrying over and helping him to his feet.

"I'm fine," he answers gruffly, adjusting his tunic. "What's going on?"

"It's just me," I announce again, stepping forward with my hands still up. "Sorry about the door… I came to get my sword, didn't think anyone would be here. I'll replace it, I swear."

"We can worry about the door later, kid," Onas tells me, motioning for me to put down my hands. "The city's gone to shit."

"I noticed." I relax a little. "That's why I'm here for the sword."

"It's all yours." Wari steps behind the counter, returning with the Harpe. "But even with this thing, you're not gonna stand a chance against those dragons."

"Dragons? As in, more than one?" I look between them, worried.

"Saw at least two." Wari confirms, holding up his fingers. "We were over at the western dock, trying to help people evacuate to the mainland."

"It was a mess, everyone screaming and fighting to get on board," Onas continues explaining. "We managed to get a lot out, but the rest were all forced back when that damn thing started boiling the bay!"

"Then a damn army of the undead cuts us off from the other end, sending everyone into a panic trying to escape." Wari shakes his head. "It was chaos."

"We barely made it out." Onas sighs. "Came here to get some supplies before going back out… Where are the rest of *your* friends?"

"Captured," I admit, dejectedly. "Most of them, at least."

"Shit." Wari looks at his brother then back at me. "You know where they are?"

"In a tall building to the west." I half-shrug. "But the place is crawling with skeletons at the moment, so you can't really miss it. They're keeping people in a cage inside. I already tried breaking them out once, but just getting into the building was hard."

"Okay." Onas walks around, chewing on a thumb as he speaks. "If we can find enough people, we could probably raid—"

"Actually…" I cut him off, in disbelief at what I'm about to say. "I need to get off the island first, so I can send for help. *Then* I'm allowed to come back and 'do whatever insane plan I come up with.'"

"That's probably a smart idea," Wari admits, deflated at his plan being nixed. "No telling who actually made it out and what they're gonna do."

"There's a spell-o-gram office in Lorana, where the northern ferry usually docks," Onas tells me. "You could try and send something from there."

"How do I get there though?" I ask them both. "If one of the city's ports were attacked, the others probably were too. Even if I snuck in, they'd see me as soon as I got on one of the boats."

"Well, lucky you." Onas grins. "You happen to know two guys with a boat of their very own."

"This is it?"

"Why? What's wrong with it?"

After a half-hour trek through the city, the brothers and I make it to somewhere on the island's northwest coast where they keep a boat tied to a small and mostly unused dock. It wasn't easy getting here. Not only did we have to avoid a couple of skeleton patrols, but we actually passed a few skirmishes between them and the city guard. I think I even saw some fighting. It was hard not to join in and help—but I've got a job to do.

"Nothing." I try to cover my accidental insult. "I just thought it'd be bigger. And that we wouldn't have to row it ourselves."

"Row it *yourself*," Wari corrects. "Besides, an engine would be too loud or flashy."

"You're not coming with me?" I look between the brothers.

"Afraid not." Onas shakes his head. "This is our home. We're not leaving it to whoever or whatever is behind this."

"Alright." I understand how they feel, and I know I'm not running away exactly, but I still wish I could stay. "Two of my friends, Corrine and Tsula, they're still out there. Corrine was helping with some of the fires on the east side of the island, and Tsula left to find her after everyone else was captured. Find them. They might be able to help you."

"We will," Onas says with a nod. "And then we'll try and rescue the rest of your friends."

"I'll get back as soon as I can." If I work fast, I could be back on the island before dawn. "I'll find you."

"Hold on." Wari touches the hull of the rowboat as he casts a spell, a cloud of fog slowly forming around it. "That should give you at least some cover on the water."

"Thanks." I reach for the gnome's hand and shake it. "Stay safe."

"You, too." Onas shakes my hand as well. "Now get in the damn boat before——"

The sounds of bones marching, which we've all quickly become familiar with, start to echo from the street.

"Shit." Wari pushes me toward the boat. "You gotta get moving."

"Don't worry. We'll hold 'em off," Onas tells me as he unties the boat from the dock and kicks me out to the bay with his feet. "Try to stay quiet until you're far enough from shore."

"Wait!" But it's no use. Both brothers are already walking away, their hands glowing with magic.

I want to stay and fight, but that would make everything we just did pointless. So with a quiet grumble, I stick the oars in the water and start to row. Pulling away from the dock, the sounds of fighting echo across the water. As I get even farther away, I can see the glow of fire across the island through the magical fog—and the shadow of a dragon as it flies over the city and out into the bay.

I follow it with my eyes, terrified it might see me, but it passes by harmlessly and lands on Testament Island. It starts to climb the statue, making me hold my breath when I expect it to topple, but confusingly, there's no further destruction. Happy that I'm still unnoticed, I keep rowing.

I turn to look behind me, trying to find lights on the coast that will point me toward Lorana. Just up ahead, a glowing green line sits on the surface of the water—the border of the security dome that covers the city. As my boat passes through it, I'm bathed in the dome's green glow, which normally isn't visible from the inside.

A loud *crack* suddenly rings through the air, right before the light of the dome flickers, and then fades entirely. A second later, it's back, but instead of green, the color is a dark, almost sinister-looking red. No one ever mentioned anything about it changing colors.

I start to row the boat back, curious about the sudden change, but the hull bounces off with a *thunk*, the dome glowing at the point of impact. *The fuck?* Leaning over the edge, I bang my fist against the magic wall and receive the same result. *Fuck! Am I locked out? How am I supposed to get back inside?!*

I panic for a minute, smacking my oar against the dome in a futile attempt to break through. Of course it doesn't work, but it does give me an idea. I pull the Harpe from its scabbard on my back. This thing is supposed to be able to cut through anything, right? So what about a magical wall?

Carefully standing up, I grasp the hilt with both hands, raising the blade above my head. I bring it down in a smooth, quick motion and watch as the blade easily pierces through the dome—right before it explodes in a loud, bright flash of light. I'm immediately blown back into the water, everything going dark and cold as I drift into the deep.

Chapter 4

Khazak

"I still can't find Liss, and they haven't brought in anyone new for a while."

"Perhaps she managed to escape like David and Tsula?"

It's the best I can offer Adam in our current predicament. After getting overrun by an army of the undead, the two of us were thrown into a makeshift prison with other civilians. Our other companions seemingly managed to evade capture, and David even broke into the building in a misguided attempt at freeing us.

Misguided because he had no actual way to free us. Aside from being massively outnumbered, the "cell" we are being kept in seems to be formed by some kind of magic—and given the undead army, likely necromantic in origin. As it is in an entirely different division of magic, my meager nature-based magical ability is of no use.

I convinced David to escape and get help, even telling him to leave the island. Given how quickly the situation turned, I am not sure there is any safe harbor left in Maname. I hope he escaped and take the fact that he has not been thrown in the cell with us as a good sign. But that still leaves me trapped here with Adam and dozens of others.

"I hope so." Adam looks around at our fellow captives. "I'm not sure I like our odds here."

"Agreed," I concur, taking in our fellow captives. "Everyone else captured appears to be a civilian."

"Not that I don't trust David to get help," Adam starts, "but we may need to start thinking of a backup plan."

"Agreed again," I reply. "This is obviously only a temporary holding place for us, so our best chance at staging an escape will be when they start to move us to the next location. But we will have no idea what may be waiting for us outside."

"Maybe we could ask some of our more able-bodied friends here if they're willing to fight with us?" Adam looks around the room, unsure.

"Good idea. I will do the same." This may be our only chance.

We slowly mill about our fellow captives, gauging which of them might be able to help in our escape. Many of the skeletons confiscated our weapons for their own use, the rest of our equipment thrown into a pile outside as we were being led in, too out of reach to be of any use. None of the skeletons guarding us seem to actually be paying attention to us, but I have heard that necromancers are capable of hearing or seeing through the bodies of their minions, so I do not trust being around them.

Over the next few minutes, we find a few individuals willing to fight with us, including some members of the Maname city guard. However, we still lack a concrete plan for actually escaping and are forced to bide our time and wait for an opening. They'll have to open the cage eventually to get us out of there, and when they do...

Red light suddenly beams in through all of the windows, casting a crimson glow on everything inside. While it immediately gets the attention of all of the captives, the skeletons seem entirely unbothered. And when it does not go away, the collective anxieties of the group shoot through the roof.

"What the hell was that?" Adam stares at the red glow.

"I have no idea." I've never seen anything like it before. "But I doubt it is anything good."

Not long after the world goes red, something happens outside that does manage to get our jailers' attention. I can't quite make it out through the windows, but I can hear the sounds of a fight or struggle just outside. Almost all of the skeletons collectively turn toward the exit and march their way outside to take care of whatever may be happening.

Before I can so much as turn to Adam, more noises of destruction are heard, this time *inside* the building, above us. A large set of bones clatters down the stairs in the north-western corner of the room, followed by the four individuals who sent them tumbling: Corrine, Onas Bearfoot, and another human and gnome, both wearing the uniform of the Manamequohi City Guard. The guards quickly dispatch the skeletons that remain inside on the first floor with their maces while Onas and Corrine use magic.

"Cory!" Adam calls out cheerfully as the four come to the edge of the cage. "You're alright."

"It is very good to see you," I tell her myself.

"Good to see you both too," she says between the flowing purple bars. "Give me a second. I'll get you out of here."

"We need to hurry," Onas tells her, looking behind to the outside. "Not sure how long our distraction is gonna last."

"Working on it," Corrine responds while concentrating.

She holds her hands up to the edge of the cage, her fingertips already glowing as she prepares her spell. As she murmurs her incantation, she takes the golden dove hanging from her neck into her hand, which also begins to glow. The light from her hands glows brighter until it flashes bright and fades, the cage dissipating into nothing.

"There," she finishes, out of breath.

"Alright, everyone," one of the guards announces to the group, "follow us out and we'll—"

A high-pitched scream cuts him off. *Tsula!* Adam and I rush outside with our rescuers to a terrible scene. In front of us, Tsula and Wari Bearfoot, along with three other Maname guards, are being restrained by more than a dozen undead warriors. A dark red sky hangs above us as countless more undead begin to approach from seemingly all angles.

"Follow my lead," the human guard says to her partner, "if we go for the three on the left, we can free the others and maybe open a path for the civilians."

"I've got it," Corrine requests as she steps forward.

As the skeletons converge on us, her hands begin to glow once more. While one grabs at the focus hanging from her neck, the other grips her staff tightly. Both begin to glow a bright light-blue until Corrine slams the base of her staff against the ground. An explosion of light emanates from the point of impact, spreading around us in a dome that causes every skeleton around us to literally fall apart.

"That… That should…" Corrine's knees buckle.

"Cory!" Adam rushes forward to catch her before she can collapse to the ground, unconscious.

"Is she alright?" Tsula asks as she carefully steps around the bone-covered ground.

"I think so. Just took a lot out of her," Adam responds after checking her pulse. "Are *you* alright?"

"Yes." The timid girl nods a little shakily. "I think so."

"How were you able to find us?" I look around for signs of Elisabeth or even my pup.

"You can thank David for that," Onas says from behind me.

"You saw David?" I turn to face the shorter man. "Where is he?"

"Outside of the city, hopefully." He nods toward his brother Wari. "We put him on a boat ourselves."

"He told us where we could find you," Wari continues. "Not long after he left is when the sky went all … red and evil looking."

"Is that not normal?" Adam asks, looking up.

"No," I reply. "And I have absolutely no idea what could be causing it."

"They've hijacked the dome somehow," the human guard from inside says. "Officer Yuta here. My best guess would be that they've turned it into some kind of barrier."

"Is that possible?" My knowledge of the magic powering the dome is lacking.

"It would be pretty easy for someone who knew what they were doing," Onas explains.

"The difficult part would be getting to the room housing the spells," Wari says next. "And given the dragon we saw landing on Testament Island right before everything went red, I'd say that's probably what happened."

"You're sure David made it off the island?" I ask with concern.

"Pretty sure," Wari admits with a grimace. "We didn't see him make it to shore, but we pushed the boat from the docks ourselves."

While I don't like hearing that the ambiguity, I have to have faith that David is alright. I hate to admit it, but I am a little surprised he actually listened to me and left for help. I'll have to remember to reward him well once we are reunited, which will hopefully be sooner rather than later.

Most of the other guards are working to keep the freed citizens calm, and also together—a few have already run off, intent on returning to their homes or finding their friends or family. Those of us who remain begin to scour the felled skeletons and equipment pile for our personal belongings. I feel much better with my weapon back in my hand.

"We need to move before whoever they were holding us here for shows up to collect," another of the guards tells us.

"Do you have a safe place we can go?" Tsula asks him.

"We were in the process of setting one up at one of our stations," Yuta explains, "but we were overrun before we could finish. A few of us were captured, and we followed as they were brought here, which is where we met the rest of you."

"When we all realized we were after the same thing, we came up with our plan to rescue everyone." Onas gestures to his brother and our friends.

"We could try holing up in another station," a second guard suggests, "but it feels like that might be an obvious target."

"Yeah, we need some place more covert," Yuta agrees. "Then we can get our bearings and try contacting someone in the city's command structure and figure out what the plan is to fight back."

"I … may know of a place," I hesitantly offer, "but it is very unconventional."

"Unconventional sounds perfect," the first guard says with a nod of her head. "Anything is better than standing out here at the moment."

Let's hope you still feel that way after you see the slings hanging from the ceiling. "Then everyone, follow me."

The distance from here to the Leather Rooster is not too far, but still farther than I would like given our current conditions. We are able to stick to smaller roads and back alleys for the most part, hiding as we wait for any undead patrols to pass us. Things work out well, at least until we come upon some of the dragon's destruction, crumbling buildings blocking our path forward.

"Shit," Wari says as we try to look over the rubble. "We're either going to have to take a huge detour around, or we risk it and take one of the main roads for a bit."

"The detour could end up being more dangerous," Adam suggests. "No telling what could be down there or even how far it would take us."

"I think I agree." I nod. "I'd rather risk that for a few minutes then add spirits-know how long to our journey."

Decision made, our group inches our way toward the nearest main road. Of course, *this* particular road (16th Street) runs right alongside Paramount Park, which sits at the center of the island. We'll need to make it at least two blocks down before we can duck back onto our more concealed path to the Rooster.

Yuta sends two of her fellow guards to make the first run, checking that it is safe for us to move and then verifying that we have a way out further down the road. While one of them runs back to inform us of the situation, the other remains at our "exit" point, ready to receive civilians as we start to send them.

"Hey, are you seeing that?" Wari asks his brother after nudging him with his elbow.

"Seeing what?" Onas follows Wari's finger, which is pointing at the park. "Dammit, is that a fire?"

"Wonderful," Yuta deadpans. "A fire breaking out in Paramount Park is *exactly* what the city needs right now."

"Hold on." Onas reaches into his bag, pulling out an odd-looking pair of binoculars. "Hmm."

"What is it?" Wari asks as a guard escorts another civilian to the exit point.

"Well, it *is* a fire but a controlled one," Onas answers, gazing through the lenses. "A campfire—someone's setting up tents in the park. Which, you know, isn't really ideal right now."

"That does seem odd." Camping during a disaster like this? "Can you see anything else?"

"Not from this distance." Onas shakes his head. "All I can really make out is the light of the fire."

"Camping in the park at a time like this?" Yuta crosses her arms as she thinks. "Could be civilians trying to take shelter. But they would be sitting ducks out there."

"Maybe some of us should try and gather them, bring them back with us?" I suggest, sharing Yuta's worry, memories of protecting V'rok'sh Tah'lj's population as a ranger running through my head.

"I'd go myself, but I'm the highest-ranking guard in the group." And being the leader, she should not be running headfirst into danger. "Any volunteers?"

"I can go," Onas offers first, raising his hand.

"I'll go as well." And I am next, my protective instincts leaping at the opportunity.

"Uh, Khazak, what about the shelter?" Adam asks, still holding an unconscious Corrine.

"If you can tell us how to get there, we can guide the others and meet you there afterward." Yuta seems to have taken charge. "I don't want to leave anyone out here if we can help it."

"Alright, but you may need to trust me. On 67th Street, between 22nd and 24th, there is a small, nondescript bookstore," I start to disclose the location to Adam and the others. "There isn't even a name on the sign. Go inside, all the way to the back, and into a small attached room. In that room, on the northern wall, four shelves from the right and three shelves down, will be a red book, a biography of King Hyrieus of Olympia. If you pull—"

"The Leather Rooster," Wari cuts me off with a sly grin. "Pretty smart. I shoulda pegged you as someone to frequent that place, but—"

"Not to be rude, but could we maybe start moving?" It's Wari's turn to be cut off, this time by Yuta.

"Of course," Wari says apologetically and then turns to me. "You and Onas go check out the park. I'll make sure this group gets to the Rooster safely."

"Thank you." I appreciate being able to delegate the task to someone who knows where they are going.

"See you later, brother." Onas quickly forces a hug on Wari.

Our group splits, Onas and I moving into the park. Though the park seems empty, we still have to move carefully from cover to cover, ducking behind some trees to avoid detection by a nearby patrol. Everything is made all the more tense by the eerie red glow that bathes the entire city.

I let Onas lead the way, as he was the one who noticed this strange campsite in the first place. We're nearing the center of the park when I think I see a small fire in the distance. There's some sort of structure around it, and what appears to be people milling about. But as I start to plan a route toward it, Onas pulls us both into a bush.

"Are we not getting closer?" I ask. I am not sure how he expects us to see much of anything from here.

"Don't need to." From the pack on his back, Onas produces the set of binoculars that he holds up to his eyes. "Let's see what we're dealing with."

Aiming toward the makeshift camp, he begins to adjust some knobs on the top and side of the item. Knowing the pukwudgie and his brother are skilled enchanters, I have to assume the object is magic, and I'm very curious to learn how. After a few more adjustments, he seems to be set.

"There we go," he comments. "Shit, I don't think it was that big before. And it looks like they're building something."

"Who is 'they' and what are they building?" I ask at his side.

"Skeletons, and it looks like a cage or something," he answers. "Wait, I think I see a person. A *live* person. An orc."

"What?" *There is no way that it could be him...* "Are they being held captive?" We may need to regroup with the others before plotting any rescues.

"No, I don't think so." He hands the binoculars to me. "Look."

Peering through the eyepiece reveals that they do more than just magnify things across distances; they also make the image brighter and sharper. It takes me a moment to adjust, but once I do, I quickly peer around the campsite. Just as Onas said, there are at least a dozen skeletons milling about, and it does look like they're building some sort of metal cage. But what really gets my attention is the orc there with them: Naruk Redwish.

"I know that man," I tell Onas, still in disbelief. "That's who we've been trying to find."

"No shit?" Onas sounds as surprised as I am. He pulls a second eyepiece from his pack, this one only fitting over a single eye.

"You're right. It doesn't look like he's being held captive." He actually looks to be gesticulating rather wildly. "I think he might be yelling?"

"Really? Hold on." Onas tugs me down before clicking another button on the binoculars. "There."

I'm not sure what's changed as everything still looks the same, but as I aim the binoculars once more, I realize they are now emitting sound. The soft roar of the campfire, the shuffling of boney feet on the ground—whatever I am currently looking at. And so I turn them on a huffing and puffing Redwish.

"—demand you take me to your master *immediately*!" He stomps his foot on the ground. "Stop ignoring me!"

"He doesn't sound happy," Onas says dryly.

"No, but they aren't attacking him either," I note. "And it would seem he is familiar with their 'master' as well."

"So that's the guy you've all been chasing?" Onas asks about Redwish. "Small world."

"Not small enough," I grumble. "As much of a shock as it is, I'm not surprised someone like him would be connected to—"

Before I can say more, the red dome above us suddenly flickers out of existence, revealing the dark night sky above. But only a moment later and it's back, leaving both Onas and I puzzled as to why. At least until we see the dragon landing near Redwish and the campsite.

The creature is more than three times the size of my house, its black scales looking more obsidian under the red light of the dome. Some sort of a necklace or collar has been chained around its neck, a large jewel at its center, and it carries what look like saddlebags on its flanks. The dragon extends its left arm and wing along with it—and I can just make out a hooded and robed figure using it to slide down to the ground.

"There you are!" Redwish practically shouts at this dragon rider. "What is all this?! Explain yourself!"

"Good to see you too, Red," a man speaks in an accent that sounds vaguely like one from Albion but just a little off. "No 'Hello?' 'How are you doing?' 'Congratulations on bringing dragons back from the dead!' Rude." He laughs at himself, which goes on a little too long…

"That's a different dragon than the two I saw earlier," Onas mutters quietly. "And I think that guy in the robe is our necromancer."

"And the source of the city's dragon problems," I add, still shocked that someone could tame a beast like that.

"You were *supposed* to pick me up by boat!" Redwish continues angrily. "Not do … whatever this mess is!"

"What's the saying about killing two birds with a dragon?" The hooded figure pokes Redwish in the chest before laughing again.

"Are you alright?" Redwish is as uncomfortable with the man's demeanor as I am.

"I have *never* been better, Red!" He pulls his arms above his head, stretching out his back. "You may need a ride, but I have other business here to conduct."

"He won't be happy about this," Redwish warns.

"How do you know he hasn't already approved this entire operation?" the figure responds coolly before laughing again. *Who is this 'he'?* "Because *maybe* I've finally found exactly what he's been searching for."

"I'm sure," Redwish grouses, clearly not believing him. "Can you please finish whatever this is so we can go?"

"What are you talking about?" The man pulls a dagger from his waist. "I only just got here, and there's still *so* much to do."

He walks away from Redwish, toward his dragon, specifically the saddlebag. Once he's close enough, he drives the knife into the material, dragging it as he walks from one end to the other. He tears a huge rip across the bag, making all of its contents spill out: bones. Hundreds if not thousands of bones pour from the bag onto the ground. I think I even see some weaponry mixed in.

Satisfied with the mess he's made, the man wades through the lake of death he just spilled out into the park. He raises his hands above him, both glowing with the same sickly purple light the bars of my earlier prison were made out of. The mass of remains in front of him takes on the same glow until each individual bone seems to move on its own, rolling and sliding together to form small piles, rearranging themselves until they have formed an entire skeleton. There are hundreds of them, seemingly of every species, including some that must be animals or monsters.

"How... How powerful is this guy?" Onas asks in shock.

"I have heard of necromancers who can summon dozens of undead minions," I stare in disbelief. "But *hundreds*? If not thousands, considering what is already roaming around the city."

"We… We need to get out of here," Onas says shakily. "Like, now."

"I agree." We won't stand a chance if they discover us here.

The two of us quickly backtrack our way out of Paramount Park, eager to put as much distance between us and the necromancer's army as possible. The sun should just be getting ready to rise, though thanks to the new red dome in the sky, it's impossible to see. Much of the city seems oddly quiet as we trek our way toward the Leather Rooster. Anyone left in the city is likely hiding for their safety, though I almost envy anyone able to sleep straight through the chaos of the night. There is no telling what the day will bring.

We pass the occasional skirmish between the undead and the city's defenders, though given our priority of rejoining our friends and family, we only stop to assist when it is needed. We pick up a handful of stragglers this way, specifically two small families we manage to pry from the invaders' bony clutches. We become extra cautious once we approach the bookstore, not wanting to risk someone following us inside.

The door is unlocked and the interior of the shop empty, though I am still cautious as I lead our small group through to the back room. The bookcase swings open just as it should when I pull the book, revealing the hidden entrance to the club. All seems quiet until Onas and I first step inside.

"Who goes there?!" Wari hops up onto the front desk, both of his fingers glowing and pointed at us. "Oh thank gods, it's you."

"Glad you made it here safely." Onas hugs his brother after he hops to the ground.

"Same to you." He looks toward me, then the others. "And you brought friends."

"Half of the city has gone to hell, and the other half is only just waking up," I inform him after closing the door once everyone is inside. "How are things here?"

"There were already a few people hiding here when we came, the owners and a few of the regulars," Wari explains as he leads us farther inside. "They've had no problem with us being here, but I'm not sure how much space we really have left."

"Khazak!" Adam calls to me as we enter the main room. "You're safe."

"Thankfully," I reply. "How is Corrine?"

"She's okay, just sleeping in one of the, uh, private rooms." Adam has the tact to dance around the club's purpose and why I knew of its location. "What happened out there?"

"Redwish," I respond.

"Wait, *he's* behind this?" Adam's eyes furrow in anger.

"Not exactly, but he's on a first-name basis with the necromancer who is," I start to explain. "We only heard a small portion of their conversation, but it seemed like Redwish was not expecting the attack, only a ride out of here."

"It sounded like they were both working for the same person," Onas adds. "Oh, and this guy is also responsible for bring the dragons back from the dead."

"He can bring actual, whole dragons back to life?" Wari asks in disbelief. "How powerful is he?"

"Powerful enough to summon hundreds of the undead to attack and trap half the city in a single night," I point out. "What about here?"

"There's not enough beds or supplies," Adam starts, "but we're taking stock of what we do have and figuring out how to get more."

"The guards we came with were already talking about plans to take back some parts of the city," Wari continues.

"That's good." I nod, attempting to get my bearings. "We should start looking into fortifying and concealing our position as much as we can."

We split up, each with a different task ahead of us with plans to regroup once we've finished taking stock of our supplies and a headcount. I'd like to think we won't be here too long, but we should start planning in the event of an extended stay regardless. Hopefully, David will return with help soon, and we can put a stop to whatever nonsense Redwish and his friend have planned now.

"Khazak!" a familiar voice calls to me as I walk around the building to assess the layout.

"Cillian," I reply, surprised to see the elf when I turn around, his boy at his side, "it's good to see you are both safe."

"Likewise." He nods. "We weren't surprised to find people already hiding here. It was one of the first places we thought to come that might be safe."

"Where's David?" Novus asks, looking around for my pup.

"Not here, I'm afraid," I say with a small sigh. "He made it off the island to get help… I hope."

"I'm sure he made it," Cillian tries to assure me. "We almost did too, but then our boat had to turn back when a dragon tried setting the bay on fire."

"We tried to get home, but there were too many skeletons," Novus explains. "Which is when we had the idea to come and hide here."

"I can see that you and your friends are all ready to turn this place into a veritable stronghold," Cillian continues. "So please, tell me and my boy how we can help."

"Anything at all, sir," Novus says.

"At this point, I think we are still trying to assess what our current situation is," I tell the two men. "But I know for sure that we are going to need more supplies. Aside from the bar, there is not much in the way of food or drink in this place."

"There's a grocer about two blocks north of here," Novus offers. "I work there. I've got keys to the whole building, including the stockroom."

"That's my brilliant boy," Cillian praises as he pulls Novus in for a kiss.

"That sounds like just what we need," I reply, somewhat relieved that one of our issues might be solved. "Give me a few minutes. I'll speak with some of the others, and we can gather a group to head out there together."

"Sounds good, Khazak," Cillian says, still making eyes at Novus.

I smile at the two men as they embrace, ignoring the pang of sadness I feel in my heart as I turn and walk away. I am just so worried about David. I have to believe that he's okay and that we will see each other again soon because anything less is not an option.

Chapter 5

David

It's dark outside, and I'm running. Running toward some-
*thing for once, something that… Okay, I don't really know what
it is. It's some kind of warmth, a light that I can physically see
ahead of me.*

*I'm weaving through trees, climbing over hills, running through
fields, all chasing after this golden orb that only seems to move farther
and farther away. No matter how hard or fast I run, I can't catch up.
I keep reaching for it as it fades over the horizon, threatening to leave
me here in the dark. Then I hear it.*

"…avid…"
"…David…"
"DAVID!"

"Nngh…"

"Ma, I think he's waking up!"

I slowly open my eyes, my vision blurry as I stare up at
a vaguely beige colored ceiling. A ceiling that's flowing in
the wind because it's made of fabric. Sitting up as the rest

of my body starts to wake up, I find myself in the back of a covered wagon.

Around me are four concerned faces, an older woman, two teens, and a young girl. They all seem to be halflings, and judging from their tan skin and brown and black hair, I'm guessing they're from around wherever... *Wait, where am I?*

"H-Hello?" I tentatively start, watching their concern morph into relief.

"Oh thank goodness, wasn't sure what we might get when you finally woke up," the older woman says first.

"You're awake!" the teen girl happily declares. "We were so worried."

"I-I'm sorry, but," I start, my head still feeling foggy, "what's going on?"

"What's that last thing you remember, hun?" the woman asks next. "Because we found you washed up on the shore near Lorana about three days ago."

At hearing her words, memories of the last few days begin flooding back. Arriving in Maname, working with Atsadi and Dr. Tuvat, the Leather Rooster, and then... dragons. The whole city was under attack. Khazak was captured, and I... I was supposed to get help.

"Where are we?" I ask in a panic. "What... What happened?" Then I have another realization. "Why am I naked?"

"I'm sorry about that," the woman apologizes, "but your clothes were soaked, and we don't have anything in your size."

"You were wearing pretty interesting britches," the teen girl comments with a blush.

"And some funny looking 'jewelry' too," the teen boy finally speaks.

"Jules, Cam!" the older woman admonishes what I'm assuming are her children.

Oh god, the cage. I glance under the covers to confirm that, yep, I am still very much locked into the chastity cage. Not that it really could have gone anywhere, I guess. But to know that other people have seen it? I bury my face in my hands.

"We're just glad you're awake," the woman attempts to reel in the conversation. "I'm Marna, and these are my children Julie, Cameron, Yina, and Jact Jr." She points at each of the children in turn.

"It's nice to meet you," I greet as best I can. "I'm David. Thanks for rescuing me the way you did."

"Well, we weren't just gonna leave you half-drowned on the beach," she replies. "My husband Jact is up front driving."

"Did anything else happen to wash up with me?" I ask, worried about more than just my lack of clothing.

"There was a bag hanging from your shoulder and a sword on your back." Yina, the younger girl eagerly points to a corner of the wagon where I can see my spacious satchel sitting on top of my now dry clothes. Right next to it are two scabbards, only one carrying a sword.

"That's great." I reach my hand out, hoping one of them will pass them to me. "I don't suppose there was anything else on the beach? Like, a second sword?"

"Nope," Julie says as she hands me my things. "Just this one."

"Great," I mutter to myself. *Good job, David. You're such a fuck-up that your ancient magical weapon is probably sitting at the bottom of the ocean.*

"Hey, Ma?" The youngest kid, Jact Jr., is peeking out the back of the wagon. "I think that wolf is still following us."

"There's no way a wolf has been following us for three days." Cameron rolls his eyes.

"Wolf?" The word gets my attention as I awkwardly try to pull on my pants under the sheet still covering me. "What color is it?"

"Black," the kid responds. "I saw it first right after we left Lorana."

Sona? Now at least partially clothed, I climb over to the edge of the wagon and peek outside myself. There's a forest on either side of us, the sky above mostly clear. Just down the road behind us, I can make out something black and furry darting in and out of the brush as it follows us.

"I'm sorry, but do you think we could stop for a minute?" I turn and ask Marna.

"Well, it is almost lunch time…" I can tell she thinks the request is a little odd, but she moves toward the front of the wagon to talk to her husband at the reins. "Hun? That boy woke up, and it's about time for lunch."

I hear a man make an affirmative noise as the wagon slows to a stop, and I hop out of the back to the ground. I whistle twice, high-pitched and in quick succession, a signal I've been using with Sona the past few weeks. Almost on cue, she hops out onto the road, and I crouch down as she rushes over to me, her tail wagging behind her.

"It's so good to see you," I say as I pet her fur. She steps back and licks a long swipe across my face. "Ugh. Missed you too, fuzzface."

She makes some grumbling noises in her throat as she presses her snout into my chest.

"Have you been following me this whole time?" I ask Sona as I hear the family exiting the wagon behind me.

"Dang, I guess it was following us," Cameron comments as he climbs down the small ladder hanging from the back of the wagon.

"Wow mister, is he your pet?" Yina asks next as her family starts to set up camp.

"She," I correct. "And… Kind of. More like a friend."

Sona makes more grumbling noises, not that I expect her to understand and respond. But it does make me feel better that she's here. And for her to have followed me the way she did, she has to at least know *something* is wrong.

"Well isn't this a sweet reunion," Marna comments as she steps forward, her sons already spreading a blanket on the grass to my left. "After three days, you must be starving."

"I hope you don't mind, but all we really have is bread and fruit," Julie says, pulling an apple from her basket. "I know it's not much."

"We didn't exactly have time to restock in Lorana before things went to hell," the man who must be Jact Sr. says before he's smacked on the arm by his wife. "I mean heck."

"This is more than enough, honestly." I happily accept the food, shoving the bread into my mouth. My stomach started growling as soon as they reminded me I was hungry. "Fank you fo much."

"The name is Jact Hurskett, and I think you've already met the rest of my family." He offers me a handshake.

"I'm David." I take the man's hand after swallowing. "David Cerano. And I really can't thank you all enough."

"In times like these, helping each other out is all we've got," he replies, leading us off the road and toward the blanket.

"What happened after you found me?" I look around at our unfamiliar surroundings. "And where are we, exactly?"

"We were in the process of fleeing Lorana ourselves." As Jact takes a seat on my left, Jact Jr. and Yina both cautiously approach Sona on my right. "I take it you saw the dragons?"

"Yeah," I confirm. "I only barely made it out of the city… I was supposed to get help." *Three days ago…*

"I think you had the same idea as just about everyone else." Jact continues speaking, watching while Sona allows his two youngest children to gently pet her. "About half of Lorana left when they saw the dragons, and the other half took off after the dome turned red."

"It's some kind of barrier," I explain, my final memories still a little fuzzy. "I only just made it out before it went up."

"That's what we've heard from some of the others who've passed us on the road," Jact confirms. "I'm guessing Venzor and the other towns around Maname went the same as Lorana with everyone fleeing to nearby towns for safety. We're only about a day or two out from Kiweni."

"And how far is that from Maname?" I ask, knowing the answer probably won't make me feel any better.

"About 250 kilometers." My mind reels at that number. "We've been pushing our horse, Vic, pretty hard to try to make it there faster."

"Do they have a spell-o-gram office?" I ask one question, and then realize I need to ask another. "And, sorry, but can I ride with you all the rest of the way there? I can pay you."

"They should," Jact answers my first question. "And nonsense. We're happy for you to tag along. Though I'm sure we can find some things around the wagon that you can help with."

"I'm happy to earn my keep," I offer with a smile. "What is it that you do?"

"We're traders," Jact starts to explain as he and everyone else sit down and start to eat. "You know, buying things in one place and selling them in another."

"What do you usually deal in?" I saw some boxes with food in the wagon but not much else.

"Rugs, art, sometimes even furniture," Marna lists. "All sorts of unique crafts you might not find anywhere else."

"Cameron and Julie have been trying to get me to branch out." Jact looks over at his two oldest. "Into things like games and toys."

"Hey, we sold every one of those dolls in Lorana," Cameron points out before biting into an apple.

"We did," Jact concedes. "I'm just still surprised about it."

"Do you have a normal route?" I don't know much about being a trader.

"Not exactly," Jact continues. "There are seven or eight neighboring towns we make regular stops in, but Maname's marketplace is the biggest so we always tend to come back to the area."

"We actually just sold the last of our stock the day before we found you!" Julie informs me cheerfully.

"And then a bunch of dragons attacked before we could restock the next day," Cameron says flatly at her side.

"Oh no." I bet a ton of people have lost their livelihoods after the attack.

"We'll be alright," Marna assures me and her children. "We've got plenty of savings and supplies."

"We don't normally go as far north as Kiweni, but we've been there before," Jact points out. "After we buy some new stock there, things will get back to normal."

I can appreciate the confident words but can't help but feel like there's some underlying worry over how their routine has been upended. After they finish with their food, Yina and Jact Jr. return their attention to Sona. She seems eager for it, the young wolf happily chasing the two young-sters around the wagon with a wagging tail. Even Cameron and Julie seem a bit taken with her, stroking their hands through her fur when she comes close.

It's a happy little scene, but one that we quickly sober up from when we notice a horse-drawn cart coming up the road toward us. Its driver and passenger look tired in disheveled clothing, and the back is filled with bags, chests, and even furniture—another person fleeing the chaos and a reminder of our own situation.

"We should probably get moving," Jact says with a sigh as the cart pulls away.

There isn't really anything to reload onto the wagon, not having really made "camp." Jact is once more taking the reins while the rest of us climb into the back. I check to make sure that Sona is following alongside us, then take a seat near the head so I can talk to Jact and Marna some more.

"This is a nice wagon," I compliment. It's much bigger than I would have expected for a family of halflings, but they're probably used to carrying a lot more than just a human and need the space for whatever they're trying to sell.

"Thank you," Jact replies from the wagon's front seat. "When you spend most of your time on the road, it's the closest thing you have to home. It's been in my family for a long time—though I'm not sure it still has any of the original parts left. The Hursketts have been maintaining and upgrading it for generations."

"Jact comes from a family of traders," Marna tells me. "He's been doing it since he was a child, and he actually took over for *his* father."

"It was during one of my first trips to Maname after my father retired that I met Marna." I can hear the smile in his voice. "Took me nearly a dozen more visits to finally woo her."

"Try two dozen," she teases. "We've been together ever since."

"This wagon has been through a lot," Jact says wistfully. "Heck, Cameron was born in this wagon!"

"*DAD!*" Cameron shouts at the revealed information.

"Have the children always been on the road with you, too?" They would have to be if they're always traveling, right?

"Since they were babies," Marna confirms. "We teach them all their school lessons ourselves."

"While showing them all there is to know about the trading business at the same time," Jact adds.

Night falls before long, and I assist the Hursketts in setting up a proper camp. I'm impressed again when Jact slides a long, wide board of wood from the back end of the wagon, folding and latching it in place to provide a shelter large enough for him and his family to sleep under. Unfortunately, there's not really enough room for a full-sized human, nor do they have any sleeping rolls in my size, but they do allow me to sleep in the back of the wagon in my previous "bed."

I sleep just fine, with thankfully no nightmares. We pack up after a quick breakfast of bread and some fruit and are on or way. The rest of our travel that day goes just fine, at least until just after lunch. We stop when we come across a lake not far off the road and take the opportunity to refill our water stores.

"JJ, don't wander too close to the shore," Marna warns her youngest.

Everyone is taking the opportunity to stretch their limbs before we get back on the road. Even Sona stretches out on the grass, enjoying the warm sun. My own waterskins are filled, and I hop back into the back of the cart to wait for the others. Then someone screams.

I grab my sword and leap out of the back of the wagon, ready for a fight. I spot the source of the scream—Marna— and the reason for it: a monster staring down Jact Jr. It looks and sounds almost cat-like, and it hisses threateningly at the young halfling. But it's covered in scales instead of fur and clearly lives in the water. Sharp fins run along its spine, almost like a dragon's, and it moves its dangerous-looking tail like a whip in the air behind it.

I'm not sure the kid even realizes he's in danger, and the rest of the family seems frozen, except for Jact Sr. and Cameron carefully trying to inch closer. I cut a wide arc around them, wading into the water farther down the shore. Sona is growling at my side without even calling for her.

I make sure to splash around enough that the creature notices me once I'm in the water. I want to get it to focus on me *without* the small child between us. When the creature turns to me and takes a step forward, I stand my ground, even puffing up my chest to try and make myself look bigger. Sona has the same idea, her fur bristling as her growls get louder.

I let it take a few more steps toward me before I start to walk backward, trying to lead it farther away from JJ. Jact Sr. picks up on my plan, and as soon as he sees an opening, rushes forward to grab his son and flee back to the wagon. But the gurgle of surprise the little one makes once he's snatched pulls the creature's attention away from me.

"HEY!" I shout, making a quick stride forward and make sure to kick up a lot of water when I do.

That manages to kick things off, the creature growling menacingly before it begins to charge. I don't even have a chance to defend myself before Sona leaps into action, jumping at it with bark. Her jaws land somewhere around its neck or shoulder, and the two of them immediately begin to struggle in the shallow water. As quickly as it started, the two animals separate, Sona once again at my side, hackles raised.

The fish-cat raises its tail, the end of which I can now see is as sharp as the fins on its back. It swiftly brings it down, forcing me and Sona to dodge away from each other as it cracks like a whip in the water between us. As I see it start to raise it high again, I barely manage to bring my sword up in time to catch it.

The tail wraps around my sword, causing the creature to yowl in pain as the blade slices into its flesh. Sensing an opportunity, Sona leaps into action and bites down hard on the stretched-out tail, earning us another yowl. It tries to pull back as quickly as it attacked, but it's a struggle, especially shaking Sona from its tail. Looking between us and the Hursketts, who have all moved far inland from the shore, it gives us another warning hiss before turning and leaping into the water, a trickle of red following its tail as it sinks under the surface. *Phew.*

"Oh David, thank you so much," Marna tells me, full of gratitude as she hugs me tight. "You saved my baby."

"I'd say you've more than paid us back for your rescue and ride," Jact tells me, relief clear on his face.

"It was nothing," I say, partially out of habit at this point. "What *was* that thing?"

"A *mishipeshu*—a water panther," Jact explains. "Dangerous things, but they usually keep to themselves. We probably got a little too close to its nest and it was just trying to defend itself."

"That was so cool…" I hear Cameron say to his sister, looking at my still bloody sword.

"Are you two hurt?" Marna asks, fussing over me and then Sona.

"Sona's got a few scratches, but I think we're okay," I tell her as I check through the wolf's fur. "Just wet, mostly."

I clean and sheath my sword, and with the excitement over, we get back on the road. We reach Kiweni in the early evening, just as Jact said we would. The first thing I notice is how much cooler the air is. Despite summer having started weeks ago, we're far enough north and close enough to the ocean that it doesn't matter. The second thing I notice as we approach the town proper is the large encampment that seems to have been set up just outside its borders.

"Other refugees from Maname, probably," Jact informs me when I stick my head out to look.

"What do you think they're all gonna do?" Not to mention what Jact is going to do himself.

"Hard to say," Jact responds with a grimace. "Some folks might have somewhere else they can head to for safety, but most of these people probably just lost the only home they've ever known. And I imagine some of them are going to want to take it back."

Here's hoping.

Not wanting to have to fight for space, Jact takes the long way around the camp to scope out a suitable spot for the Hursketts to make camp of their own. Sona happily trots up as we hop out, sitting patiently as I help the family once more. Once we have a small fire going and Marna starts to talk about dinner, I figure it's time to make my exit.

"Jact, Marna, I want to thank you and your family again for rescuing me and getting me somewhere safe," I say to the group. "Sorry to leave, but I need to get to the spell-o-gram office in town before it gets too late."

"Of course," Marna tells me with a nod. "We're just happy you're alright and that we were able to help someone. And I can't thank you enough for rescuing little JJ."

"If you see us on the road or in town, don't be a stranger." Jact shakes my hand again. "Take care of yourself."

"You too." I smile.

"Aww…" Jact Jr. frowns.

"Goodbye, mister." Yina looks just as sad. "Goodbye, puppy." *Ah, it's not me they're sad about; it's Sona.*

After the children say their goodbyes to Sona, I head through the camp and into the village. I see people of all ages and species, and this close, it's easy to see how unhappy, scared, and even angry some of them are. Most of them barely have more than the clothes on their backs.

The town itself isn't much better, seemingly crowded with more people fleeing from Maname. I don't like what that means for my odds of getting a room at an inn later, but I'll deal with that when I need to. For now I'm just happy that the collar Khazak bought for Sona is doing the trick with most people not sparing her more than a glance when they see her walking at my side.

I'd never even heard of Kiweni before, but it seems like a nice place. Most of the buildings look similar to what I'd expect this far north, with walls made of thick logs that almost make them cabin-like. Some of the older buildings look a little more like cone-shaped tents, large, seemingly permanent ones wrapped in thick hides. I wonder what it's like up here in the winter.

"Excuse me!" I call out to a woman standing outside what looks like a general store. "Can you tell me how to get to—"

"What are you saying?" She pulls her head back in confusion.

"I'm just trying to ask where the spell-o-gram office is," I finish, annoyed.

"I don't speak… Common, I think?" She continues to look at me like I'm missing my head.

Then I realize her lips aren't moving in concert with her voice. Dammit. My hand goes up to my ear, touching the metal translator I picked up in Maname from Onas and Wari. Of course she can't understand me. With a sigh and an awkward smile. I do my best to silently apologize and move along.

It takes a bit of searching and asking around—a few people seem to blow me off, and I have to check beforehand that they can even speak Common—but eventually, I find the spell-o-gram office attached to the post office.

"Alright, wait here, girl," I tell Sona, holding up a single hand as a signal and hoping she understands what it means. "*Stay.*"

She huffs but takes a seat on the ground outside of the post office, watching me but not moving as I open the door. It doesn't seem too busy, but there are three people in line ahead of me for the spell-o-grammer. All three of them seem to be from Maname, and I can overhear two of them sending messages to their families letting them know they are safe.

"Next," the spell-o-grammer announces when it is my turn. "How can I help you?"

"I need to send a message to Pákannon," I tell the woman, who I'd guess is somewhere around the age of forty.

"Alright, that shouldn't be any problem." She smiles, dipping her pen in her ink while pulling a blank sheet of paper toward her. "Who in Pákannon does the message need to reach?"

"The mayor. Mayor Aust—Mayor Elajor," I finish when I can't remember the man's first name.

"You want to contact the city's mayor?" the 'grammer seems surprised by that, and I realize how I must sound. "People don't usually go through us for officials like that."

"I do. He knows me. If you say it's from David Cerano, he'll read it. Or… Maybe we can send it to the head of the city guard?" I offer instead. "Marshall Velxina. I… I'm not sure who it might be better to—"

"We can still send your message to the mayor's office," she assures me. "I am just not sure how soon it will actually get into his hands. Would you like to send a second message to this Marshall? Perhaps the same one?"

"Yes." I sigh in relief, thankful for her help. "That would be perfect."

"Excellent, now: what should the message say?" she asks me next.

"That… That Manamequohi is under attack, and my friends are trapped there and in trouble," I start. "That we need help."

"Okay." She writes my words on the paper in front of her. "What else?"

"I… I…" *I'm drawing a blank.* "I don't know."

She gives me an odd look, but seriously, I don't know what else to say. I have no actual plan for getting back into the city to free Khazak and the others. Do I ask them to send an army? Does Pákannon even *have* an army?

"Perhaps you could let them know more about where you are and your current condition?" she offers.

"Right." I nod and sigh. "Please say that I'm here in Kiweni, and that I'm alright, but I'm trying to find a way back. Oh! And can you ask—one of them needs to get in touch with Khazak's family in his hometown. That's K-H-A-Z-A-K. They'll know what that means." *I hope.*

"Alright." She appends the note to the end of the letter. "Anything else?"

"Not that I can think of." I shake my head. "Is there a way for me to find out if and when they send back a response?"

"We record all messages as we receive them," she starts to explain. "If you already have a temporary residence set up in town, we can have it delivered the same day; otherwise, you can check back in with the office yourself for anything under your name."

"I don't have a room yet, so I'll be back later," I say earnestly, trying to disguise the frustration I feel with myself. "Thank you."

"Alright." The woman places her pen back in its pot. "Connecting to the office in Pákannon."

Still in her, she lifts her arms at her side until they are both outstretched, palms up. Swirls of yellow colored energy begin to gather above her hands as her hair and the fabric of her clothing ruffle as if there was a breeze in here. When these swirls finally solidify into glowing, golden orbs, she opens her eyes to reveal that they are glowing with the same energy.

"Connection established," she says, allowing her hands to fall, the magical orbs moving to float above her shoulders.

Her head tilts down as she looks over the written message. Right now, the spell-o-grammer in Pákannon should be receiving a visual image of my letter, literally seeing through the eyes of the woman in front of me. From what Mikey's told me, the two spellcasters are able to hear each other's thoughts and also silently communicate the message and other information at the same time. Magic is awesome sometimes.

"Your message has been sent," she tells me when she's finished, the glow of her eyes and the orbs fading away. "I asked that they get them into the hands of who you requested as soon as possible."

"Thank you," I tell her. "I'll check back in tomorrow morning for a reply."

"Have a good evening, sir," she says as I turn and leave.

I feel foolish and frustrated as I walk back outside, dropping to the ground next to Sona. Maybe sensing my mood, she leans into me, and I throw my arm over her and pull her close. I don't know what I expected to happen there, probably because I didn't really think about it beforehand at all. Was I just going to raise an army and take back the city on my own?

You need to think *David—something the old you never used to do before rushing into danger. We're supposed to be past that. Now we think through our plans, just like Khazak would. So what would he do in this situation?*

Raising an army is probably out of the question, if only because I'm not sure exactly how you go about doing that. So maybe not an army, but I did walk through a giant camp of disaffected and angry people who are probably also wanting to take back their home. Maybe if I get enough of them together, I could—

"Excuse me." I'm pulled out of my pity party by a woman that seems to have exited the post office behind me.

"Yes?" I stand, taking in this new stranger, a gnome wearing some sort of uniform—one that I think I remember seeing in Manamequohi.

"Let me start with an apology because I swear I wasn't trying to eavesdrop," she starts, standing in front of me in Sona. "But I couldn't help but overhear that you might have some friends trapped in Maname and were looking to help them?"

"That would be accurate," I tell her with some apprehension. "Is there something I can help you with?"

"My name is Twyla," she starts with an understanding look. "I'm a member of the Maname Guard." That might explain the uniform.

"I'm David." I take and shake her hand. "What's this about my friends?"

"There are a lot of people that call Maname and its surrounding villages as home," Twyla tells me. "And most of us aren't happy that we've had to flee."

"Does that mean you have a plan to get those dragons out the city?" I ask, still not entirely trusting this stranger.

"We're working on it," she tells me. "And there are a whole lot of other people who want the same thing."

"How many is 'a whole lot'?" I narrow my eyes.

"You saw that massive camp set up just outside of the city, right?" I nod my head yes. "Then come with me, and I'll introduce you to my fellow guards. We have a lot of work to do."

I watch the woman walking away with a spring in her step before deciding to follow her. Whatever plan she's working on is better than the complete lack of one I'm dealing with at the moment. Maybe she really can help me get back to Khazak and the others. One way or another, I'm getting back to my Sir.

Chapter 6

David

"So I take it you just made it into town?"

"Yeah, barely even an hour ago."

Seeing as I have nothing left to lose, I follow Twyla back to camp with Sona at my side. She seems nice, and while I don't love that she was apparently listening to my attempts at finding help in the post office, if she hadn't, I might still be sitting on the ground feeling sorry for myself. This is the least useless I've felt since getting here.

I wish I could say the same for the rest of these people. As we reach the camp's outskirts, I'm once again met with the faces of scared and upset refugees. Their clothes are disheveled, their tents crowded together, and I even hear a baby crying. It's just awful.

"It's rough," Twyla says after seeing my reaction. "All of these people barely had a moment's notice before they had to pack up everything they could and leave. Half of them aren't even from Maname; they're from Lorana or were just passing through."

"Do you know how many people actually made it off the island?" I must have been the last one.

"Barely a third, but we expect more arrivals over the next few days," Twyla tells me with a sigh. "The Kiweni officials have been incredibly accommodating, but there's only so much room and so many supplies to go around."

"How long have you been here?" There have to be over a hundred people here.

"Since yesterday morning," she tells me as we move toward the camp's center. "I came with one of the first evacuation groups."

"You got all of this set up in a day?" I'm exhausted just thinking about it. "How?"

"We had a little longer than that," she starts to explain. "As soon as the evacuation order reached Lorana, we sent our two fastest riders north to Kiweni. They started preparing for when the rest of us would follow."

Twyla leads me into a large circular tent, a flag bearing the Maname skyline hanging next to its already opened entrance flap. The area around it is more open than a lot of the camp, but I'm guessing that's because they have a lot of people who need to be able to move through here quickly. Further out between the camp and the forest is a large open field where some guards have paired up and are sparring.

The inside of the tent is a little stuffy, but it's also crowded. A circular wooden table sits at the center of tent with about half a dozen people dressed in the same armor as Twyla standing around it. They're having some kind of discussion, and from the frustrated tones, I'm not sure it's going well.

"I don't care. We *have* to get a message—"

"Syris," Twyla interrupts an older, very muscular human, "I found another new recruit in town."

"Yeah?" The man eyes me from head to toe. "What's the name, kid?"

"David." I reach out my hand to the man. "David Cerano."

"Lieutenant Syris Longfellow." He shakes it. "Normally I head up our operations in Lorana, but currently, I'm heading up everything else it would seem."

"Sir, should we—" one of the guard starts.

"Take a break," he cuts him off with a sigh. "Maybe we'll think of an idea if we cool off."

"Everything alright?" I ask nervously.

"It's fine." He waves me off, steps around the table, and approaches Sona. "Who's this? I love her coloring."

"This is Sona," I answer, reaching down to scratch behind her ears as she starts to sniff the new people.

"David here wants to help us take back the city," Twyla continues for me.

"That's great because we're going to need all the help we can get," Syris says as he shakes my hand.

"How many people have joined up with you so far?" I ask as we all gather around the table.

"We've got about sixty or so able-bodied people," Twyla tells me. "Unfortunately, only about twenty of them actually know how to fight, and training the other forty has been no easy task. Please tell me you know how to use that sword on your back."

"I've been told I'm pretty decent with it," I tell her. "I was in the city with my friends. We were trying to help with the evacuation when everything went down."

"Does that mean your friends can fight too?" she asks me next.

"Uh, yes, but they're actually all still in the city. Some of them were even captured." My heart sinks when I think about Khazak in that cage. "And that was three days ago."

"Sorry to hear that," she responds, trying not to sound grim. "Try not to worry. We're hard at work on a rescue plan."

"Yeah?" That sounds promising. "What have you got so far? Is there anything I can do to help?"

"We're still in the planning stages," Twyla admits, "but we'll have something concrete soon. I'm certainly trying to train everyone like we're ready."

"Right now, we're trying to figure out how to get messages in and out of the city," Syris tells me plainly. "That and coordinating with our other evacuated forces."

"How are you gonna do that?" I can't see how a courier could get through that dome. "Will magic work?"

"No, whatever they've done to the dome is repelling magic the same as it is anything physical," Syris says with a shake of his head. "Everything we've tried to throw at it just bounces off."

"*But,* from what our scouts have told us, the dome seems to flicker off and on occasion," Twyla follows up. "We think we might be able to slip something in when that happens."

"They've only seen it happen a handful of times, and it never lasts more than a few seconds," Syris continues to explain. "But if we have a druid or another shapeshifter waiting just outside it, they might be able to quickly cross over before it came back up."

"How many people are still in Lorana?" I didn't exactly see the town when I was passing through it. "Are they safe?"

"Half a dozen," Syris says. "Enough to keep an eye on things but not draw any attention."

"We left scouts in all four ports around Maname when we were evacuating," Twyla tells me. "We've been using carrier falcons to communicate with them and our other split-up forces."

"I never expected to actually *use* them, but the Manamequohi City Guard has had an evacuation plan on the books for decades," Syris sounds surprised but proud. "At least someone had the foresight to think that with a city that big and crowded, it was important to have a plan for where to send everyone in case of an emergency."

"I know we didn't even get half of the people off the island, but considering how badly we were taken by surprise, I think we've done the best we can. Each port has a different location to evacuate to, a town or settlement a day or two out," he continues. "We obviously came here, Urkinom and Vertel would have gone west to Borrham, and Venzor to a trading post southwest."

"A trading post?" I can only think of one place that fits his description.

"Yeah, it's not the biggest place, but enough traders pass through to support a small camp." Syris nods his head confidently. "I think it might even have a new name these days."

"If it's the one I'm thinking of, it's not small anymore." Which is a good thing, hopefully. "I passed through with my friends on our way to Maname. It's going by 'Richardton' these days."

"Richardton?" Twyla wrinkles her nose. "What kind of name is that?"

"An arrogant one." I get angry just thinking about that dickhead. "But let's just say that through a series of weird events and a story too complicated to get into right now, the guy that was in charge is no longer in charge."

"Really now?" My information seems to worry Syris. "I hope that won't mean any problems for the evacuees."

"It shouldn't, I don't think. I trust the people we left running things." *Here's hoping Kignun hasn't had any problems with those guards… Wait a minute.* "And actually, they've got a lot of able-bodied men who should already know how to fight with very little else to do at the moment."

"That's … intriguing." He's less worried now. "And you know the people currently in charge?"

"I do." I nod. Here's hoping there haven't been any issues since leaving.

"He *also* knows the mayor of Pákannon," Twyla volunteers for me.

"I think I can see why Twyla brought you right to me."
Syris looks at her and me both appreciatively. "You seem
well connected."

"Yeah, she found me right after I sent a 'gram off." I nod
and smile. "I'm sure they'll be willing to help."

"They might be a little far out to get to us in time, but
that's still something." Syris starts to think. "And Richardton
sounds promising too."

"I can totally get in touch with them too." Finally, something to do! "They don't have a spell-o-gram office, but I
could go write them a letter right now."

"Actually, if it's alright with you, I'll have someone write
something up for you to look over. That way we can work
things out directly," he tamps down my excitement. "We'll
tell them you directed us to them, of course, and have you
sign it so they know we're not making things up."

"I guess that makes more sense." I deflate. "Is there anything else I could maybe help with?"

"Right now, we're just trying to coordinate everything
to put together a response." Syris offers me a small smile.
"But we'll have something solid for you to do very soon,
I promise."

"Ah, okay." I try (and fail) to not show my disappointment.

"I'm going to be running some training drills in the
morning," Twyla tells me. "You should come by. Not that I
don't trust you, but I'd like to see what you can do. Maybe
you could even help me train everyone."

"Sounds good," I lie. It's an obvious consolation, and I'm
clearly being dismissed. "I'll see you in the morning, then.
I should probably try and figure out where I'm crashing
tonight anyway."

"We'll see you tomorrow, David," Syris tells me
with a wave.

"Come by tomorrow so you can sign the letter," Twyla
requests with a smile.

"Will do." I wave at the two and turn on my heel, walking out of what I'm gonna call the "war tent."

It's hard not to feel frustrated as I make my way out of the camp. I'm sure they're doing the best they can, but can't they do it any faster? The longer I'm here, the longer Khazak and the others are trapped in the city. In that cage.

Sure, maybe they don't have a way to actually get back into the city yet, and I get that having to organize a response to something like this when your forces are split up takes some time… *And I am just some random guy they've never met before today…* I groan, wiping my hand down my face.

Sensing my mood, Sona whines at my side, and I crouch down to pet her. Seriously, what was I expecting? That they were just going to welcome me in and put me in charge of leading the defense? And who could blame them? They don't even know if I can fight yet.

Which means I'll just have to come back tomorrow to prove myself. Maybe I can even get the ol' super strength working again, but I'm not gonna hold my breath. Right now though, I need to find a place to sleep for the night.

I don't have any of my camping equipment—I only grabbed my armor and spacious satchel when we were gearing up in Maname—so my options are pretty limited. I know it's a longshot, but I can't help myself and decide to try for a room at the inn anyway. Can't hurt to ask.

Kiweni is big enough to have two inns, and the first I check with is the smaller one. I can't read the sign, but I overhear someone outside call it *The Timid Sparrow Tavern.* Just walking in, I can see how overcrowded the place is, every seat in the common area already taken. Thankfully though, there isn't a line at the front desk.

"Hello," I greet the young woman working behind it. "I was wondering if you had any rooms—"

"We're all booked up," she answers before I can even finish. "No clue when something will be available, either."

"Right." My shoulders sink, even though I knew that would probably be the case. "Well then, can you at least point me to the other inn in town?"

"Heh, good one." It takes a second for her to realize that I'm serious. "You know they're going to be just as full as we are here, right?"

"Probably," I admit with a shrug. "But I'm still gonna check anyway. The worst they can tell me is no." *And it's not like I have anything better to do right now.*

I thank her after getting my directions, returning outside to a patiently waiting Sona. The second inn is located farther in the city, practically across the street from its port. I can smell the salt in the air as we pass by and notice a large and very well-kept ship tied to the docks. It's not flying any colors, but on its bow is a figurehead carved into the shape of a wolf. It looks expensive. I wonder who it belongs to.

"Alright girl, wait out here," I tell Sona as we approach *The Salty Salmon*. "I'll probably be right back out again."

This place is just as crowded as the last. There are even people trying to set up camp in some of the common areas, curling up on couches or booths in the dining room. It's looking rough all around.

There are six people ahead of me at the front desk, most looking to be around my age. They're all dressed similarly, shirts ranging from black to gray and their pants the same shade of brown. None of it resembles what I've seen the locals wearing, so I assume they're together. They're also all weirdly tall and muscular, even the dwarf in their group. A traveling group of adventurers or maybe mercenaries?

"What do you mean you don't have any rooms left?" One of them, a human with tan skin and short black hair asks the halfling behind the desk, sounding irked.

"I meant exactly what I said, sir," the clerk responds, unimpressed. "We have no available rooms."

"Not even one?" He changes tactics and pouts.

"Not even one." He shakes his head.

"Are you sure that you're not just doing this to drive up business?" he challenges, full of suspicion. "Claiming you're sold out to make this place seem more appealing to potential customers?"

"Max…" the blond man at his side says worryingly.

"How would that even work?" one of the women in his group wonders.

"*Sir*, I'm not sure if you noticed, but Kiweni is currently sheltering hundreds of refugees from Manamequohi." The halfling is getting annoyed now. "We have not had a single room available for the past two days."

"Well when will some open up?" *This guy really isn't gonna give up, is he?*

"I don't know, sir." The halfling sighs. "All of our guests are currently booked for multiple days, and we have a waiting list for those still seeking one. I can add you to it, if you'd like."

"Please. And how much would it cost us to get bumped to the top of that list?" the cocky dickhead propositions. "Hell, how much to get us in a room right now anyway? I'll pay you double your normal rate. Triple!"

"*Max!*" the blond practically hisses before turning to the man behind the desk. "I'm sorry. We understand. Thank you anyway."

"But I—"

"Stop," he pleads to Max with his eyes. "Didn't you hear him about these people being refugees? They need this more than we do."

"Alright, Sunshine," Max relents, turning back to the man at the desk. "I apologize for my behavior. Thank you for your time."

"We can always just sleep on the boat again," the blond man suggests as all six turn, walking around me on their way to the exit.

"*Ugh*, no," Max complains when they reach the doors. "The constant rocking makes me seasick."

"We do have everything we need to set up a camp..." one of the women in the group suggests before the doors close behind them.

Who the hell was that guy? Just openly trying to bribe someone like that, throwing his money around in public. That takes some balls, but it doesn't make the guy seem like any less of an asshole. If I ever get rich, I hope I don't start acting like that. I bet that was his boat I saw at the docks.

"Hi," I greet as I approach the desk for my turn. "I don't suppose you were just lying when you told that guy you had no rooms because he was being a huge dick, were you?"

"Oh, no, I'm sorry." He frowns. "We really don't have any rooms at all."

"I figured." I sigh but still give him a smile. It's not his fault. "Thanks anyway."

"I think if you check with some of the people in the camp right outside the city, they might be able to help you," he offers instead.

"I'll do that." I mean, it is my only option at this point. "Have a good night."

I step back outside, looking for Sona to call back to my side, but she's already occupied. The six people who were in front of me inside are now out here, all standing around the wolf. In fact, that Max guy is crouched down next to her and is petting her fur. She certainly doesn't look agitated or angry, more curious than anything as she sniffs at him and his friends.

"Can I help you?" I ask as I approach the group.

"Oh, sorry, is she yours?" Max looks up at me with a grin.

"Yeah." Saying that is going to be easier than explaining that she belongs to my boyfriend every time someone asks, so I'm just going with it.

"She has a beautiful coat," he says next, still petting her.

"Thanks." I mean, it's not like we brush her or anything. "Sorry, but we've gotta get going."

"Oh, of course." He stands, flashing an apologetic smile. *Where was that charm inside?* "Have a good night."

"You, too." I try not to give any of them a weird look at what I think is odd behavior.

I let out a short whistle, getting Sona's attention and calling her back to myself. *Was he just sniffing the air?* Once she's at my side, I give a quick wave to the group. Whoever or whatever they were, they were weird.

We make our way back through the town to the camp outside the city. I know the innkeeper told me to talk to Syris's group, but I have a better idea. I head for the spot I last left the Hursketts in and am pleased to see them sitting around their own campfire eating from bowls.

"David!" Marna greets as she sees me approach. "Good to see ya again."

"Hope you were able to contact your friends," Jact says next.

"I managed to get a message out," I reply with a nod. "But there's no place for me to sleep in town, and I don't have any of my camping gear. I don't suppose I could sleep here with your family for another night?"

"Of course, sweetheart," Marna assures. "We can get you set back up in the back of the wagon."

"Thank you," I say with some relief. "I can look in town tomorrow for a bedroll and get out of your hair."

"Stay with us as long as you'd like," Jact tells me. "I'm not sure we're leaving the city right away anyhow."

"I really appreciate it." Having a place to sleep is one thing off my to-do list. "And if there's anything I can do to help around camp, just let me know."

"Will do," Jact replies with a stern nod.

"Go ahead and sit down," Julie says, hopping to her feet. "I'll get you some dinner. Hope you're okay with rabbit!"

The kind teenage girl quickly brings me a bowl of stew, even placing a second one on the ground for Sona, and we both eagerly dig in. It's not bad, and whoever made it clearly knows how to cook, but all that makes me think about is Khazak and *his* cooking. I wish he were here, making dinner over the fire right now.

Those feelings follow me all the way to bed. I tell Sona goodnight, watching her curl up by the fire before climbing into the back of the wagon. I lay on the small makeshift bed Marna set back up for me, staring at the cloth-covered ceiling of the wagon, missing my orc, my owner, my *kavan*. I think this might be the longest we've ever spent apart since meeting. I guess most couples probably don't spend literally all of their time together the way we have, but there have been some pretty extenuating circumstances. Also, I don't care: I miss him.

I miss everyone, honestly. Other than the time when Calvinson had me separated from the others (when I wasn't exactly in my right mind), I haven't been alone in almost four months—since I left Northlake with Adam and Liss. Even in V'rok'sh Tah'lj when they were all in jail, I still had Khazak, and other than in Richardton, we haven't spent a single night apart in all that time. I'm glad to have Sona, but fuck, I wish I could talk to anyone right now. Adam, Cory, I'd even take Nate. I almost wish Mikey hadn't left when… *Oh shit, Mikey!!!*

I shoot up, quickly scrambling for my satchel and reaching inside for the enchanted vellum journal I just bought a few days ago. They come in pairs, and what I write in one appears in the other. My twin brother Mike has the other copy, which I gave to him specifically so that we could keep in touch, and I can't believe I already forgot about it. I plop the book in my lap, opening to the first page to find my brother has already been writing to me. A lot.

So I know we're supposed to be in trouble, but the way all of the other students keep coming up and congratulating us is making it hard to remember.

Ugh, Piper and I have a meeting in an hour with Headmaster Barmasai and the disciplinary board. Wish us luck!

Well, we got chewed out by pretty much everyone. We've both been assigned extra kitchen and laundry duties for the next month. Of course, immediately afterward they started asking us for details about the teleportation. They want to start doing more test runs right away.

Okay, seeing as you're the one who bought these, it's kinda lame that I'm the only one using mine!

Hey, are you okay? Some people here have been hearing some weird things about Maname.

Okay, seriously D, where are you?

Brooooooooooo.

I'm going to bed. If you don't respond by the time I wake up, I'm porting back to Maname to find you myself!

That's the last entry written, not that I have any way of knowing *when* it was written—but I think it should be morning over there now, so hopefully I'm not too late. With that barrier up, I'm not even sure teleporting would work. If magic messages aren't getting in or out, who knows what would happen if a whole-ass person tried to cross? I quickly reach back into my bag for a pen.

Hey! I'm okay. I'm here, I respond. Do NOT teleport to Maname. It's not safe.

I sit there, anxiously waiting for a response for a few minutes, before I see pen strokes on the page forming letters, and I sigh in relief.

DUDE! Where the fuck have you been? Mike replies. I've been freaking out over here.

Funny you should ask. I'm in some town to the north of Maname called Kiweni. He might already know where that is.

Gonna have to look that up.

Guess not.

So you and the others managed to make it out? Does that mean dragons are really attacking the city?

No, I'm the only one who made it out. The others are still trapped. I feel guilty writing that. But the dragons are real. Wouldn't have believed it if I hadn't almost been burnt to a crisp by one myself.

Holy shit. Are they okay?

I don't know, I admit. I tried to leave the city right after the attack so I could get help, but literally the second I got on the other side of it, they put up some kind of barrier. Nothing is getting in or out, not even magic.

How is that even possible?

How should I know, mister magical genius? But there's a giant fucking red dome around the city that no one can get through. I even jammed my magic sword into it, and it blew up in my face. I leave out the part where I lost said sword. And the dragons aren't the only problem. There's also a literal army of the undead.

What?!

Skeletons. I saw dozens of them. I still remember the creepy glowing eyes. Probably way more than that, though. They were rounding people up and throwing them into these magic cages.

Dozens? Only a necromancer could do something like that.

Duh.

I know. They grabbed Adam and Khazak, and that was three days ago. I hesitate, a lot, before writing more. I know you hate him, but... I'm scared, Mikey. Really scared. What if something happens to him? What if it's already happened?

There's a delay before my brother's next response, but he doesn't leave me hanging.

You can't think like that, D. You have to believe that he's okay right now because I do. As much as I don't like the guy, he's capable. He can take care of himself and the people around him. He's okay, I'm positive.

I really want to reply snarkily that it's impossible for him to know that for sure, but I'm too touched by the fact that he said it at all, even if it was just to make me feel better. See? They'll get along one day.

Just like Mikey said, I have to believe he's okay. He's probably worried about me just as much as I am him. I have to believe that I'll see him again soon.

Chapter 7

Khazak

"David? David!? Where are you?"

"Khazak!? I'm over here!"

I am in my bedroom, back home in V'rok'sh Tah'lj. Only things are different, like the room is somehow bigger. When I step into the hallway, it is much longer than it should be, going on for miles in both directions with dozens of different doors.

"Khazak!" David cries out from behind one of them.

"David?" I throw open the door I thought his voice came from, but it just leads me back to my bedroom.

"Khazak, help!" he tries again, this time from farther down the hall.

I run in his direction, but the hall seems to stretch on forever. I start to throw open random doors in an attempt to find him and get out of here, but they all lead me to a different room of the house—none of which have David or any other exit.

"Khazak!" I finally manage to find a door to the living room, where I see David clinging to the frame of the front door.

The windows and doorway behind him are pitch black, and inky tendrils are coiled tightly around his limbs. I can see the strain in his arms as he struggles to keep a grip on the doorframe, fighting whatever it is that is trying to pull him back. I rush to help him, but I'm too late.

I wake with a start, covered in a sheen of sweat. *Another damn
nightmare.* Though they have been a fairly regular occur-
rence the past few weeks, it seemed as though they were
getting better. But of course with David missing, all of that
worry and guilt has managed to bubble right back up to
the surface.

I stand, stretching my limbs before reaching down to
pack my bedroll. There are only eight beds in the club, and
we've given them to those hiding with us who need them
the most: the injured and elderly. Corrine has even turned
one of the rooms into a makeshift healer's office. The rest
of us have made do with the floor.

It's been three full days since we escaped from our prison
and discovered Redwish alongside the necromancer in the
park. And a stressful three days it has been. We wasted no
time in doing our best to fortify The Leather Rooster, setting up alarms and barricades in the bookstore that acts
as the club's front. We have to be extremely careful when
coming and going or else risk someone we don't want following us back.

We lucked out in our choice of shelter as the walls, floor,
and ceiling of this building have all been lined with lead.
This prevents any magic from getting through—meaning
we are hidden from any potential detection spells. Cillian
informed us that this was necessary to protect the privacy of
the club's patrons, and though I do not agree with infidelity,
I can only be thankful for the precaution.

Thanks to Novus, we have been able to gather supplies from his place of employment, but those won't last

forever. Especially not if we keep taking more people into our shelter, which we've done on our last three outings—it's not as though we are going to leave someone in need out there on their own. One of the first things we did was retrieve Atsadi, who had just so happened to be "entertaining" Dr. Tuvat the evening of the attack. But we are running out of space and need to figure out what we are doing next and soon.

I make sure to carefully step over those who are still asleep as I exit our shared room. Out in the main area, I can see some of the others are already awake, mainly the Maname guards. I wave at the Bearfoot Brothers, currently wrapping up their shift on watch duty in the entryway, as I make my way to the bathroom.

I take care of all my usual morning business, ending with a splash of cold water to the face. Then I head to the bar, which we have turned into a pantry and kitchen during our occupation. I smile when the aroma of freshly brewed coffee hits my nose. We managed to snag a box of it during our first supply run, though we are already running low.

"Morning," Adam greets on my left, reaching for a mug of his own. "How'd you sleep?"

"Not well," I reply, adding sugar to mine. "I had a bad dream about David."

"Aww, I'm sorry." He frowns.

"It is alright," I tell him. "It wasn't the first, though at least in the past David would actually be here for me to see for myself that he was alright."

"I'm sure David's fine," Adam tries to assure me. "He can take care of himself."

"In some ways." *In others…*

"Good morning, you two." Yuta, the woman in charge of the guard contingent we are working with, joins us as she pours her own coffee. "Looks like everyone else is getting up too."

Indeed, more and more people are entering the club's main room, several still rubbing the sleep from their eyes. To our left, a line has formed leading into the club's bathroom, which also happens to contain the facility's few showers. Like many others in the city, they draw water directly from the bay around the island and use magic to heat and filter it. Though it has only been a few days, there have already been enough arguments over hot water usage that everyone is limited to fifteen minutes each.

"Good morning everyone," Atsadi greets us chipperly.

"Good morning, sir," Adam responds while I offer a silent bow of the head.

"I hate to be a bother, but it would seem our shower issues extend beyond time management," he starts with a slight grimace. "We are running low on soap and shampoo."

"I suppose it is time for another supply run then," I reply, already mentally preparing a list.

"Some of the other guards have been putting together a list of their own. Let me grab it and I'll head out with you." Yuta has been adamant that at least one of the Maname guards is a part of each outing in the hopes of running into any of their compatriots. "Just a small group. We don't need to attract more attention than necessary."

"Sounds good," Adam agrees. "I'll ask Wari or Onas if one of them wants to come with."

Aside from Corrine, Tsula, and to a much lesser extent myself, the two gnome brothers are the only trained spell-casters in our group. There are not many capable fighters at all, leaving the rest of us to pick up the slack. I am exhausted, and this cup of coffee may be all that stands between us and a horde of the undead today.

"I'll retrieve the key from Novus," I volunteer.

"Perfect." Yuta nods and quickly downs the rest of her still-steaming cup. "Okay, finish waking up and taking care of what you need to, then get in your gear and meet back here in half an hour."

"See you then," Adam says with a wave, already going to talk to the brothers.

After I finish my coffee, I turn and scan the room, spotting Novus and Cillian both in line for the showers. The two have proven invaluable, taking the initiative to take down or hide many of the more questionable and explicit objects within the club. And with Novus, we've gained access to an entire grocery store, one we have been sure to lock behind us so we can continue returning.

"Good morning, gentlemen," I greet as I approach.

"Morning, Khazak," Cillian replies. "Everything alright?"

"For the most part." I nod. "We are going to make another supply run in about an hour, and I was hoping I could borrow your key again, Novus."

"Of course, be right back." The dwarf scurries off.

"How are you holding up?" Cillian asks me next. "Without your pup."

"It has been ... stressful," I answer honestly. "I cannot help but worry about him."

"I understand. I'm sure I'd feel the same if something forced me apart from Novus." He leans in and lowers his voice. "Now, if you are in need of any 'stress relief,' I would be happy to volunteer my boy's services to you for the evening."

"That is a very generous and tempting offer, but I will have to decline." Even taking into account our separation, I do not think David would appreciate me fucking someone else while he's been gone—I'd certainly feel that way about him.

"Understood. But if you change your mind, the offer stands," Cillian finishes with a knowing look, just as Novus returns.

"Here you go, sir," he tells me, a small chain poking out of his fist.

"Thank you." I catch the key he drops into my hand. "If there is anything in particular you would like us to look for at the store, I can do my best to find it for you."

"I wouldn't say no to a bottle or two of wine," Cillian requests.

"Red, please!" Novus adds on.

"I will do my best," I tell the two men.

With that finished, I need to change into something more appropriate to venture outside than the simple shirt and pants I slept in: my armor. I make my way to the back rooms where my equipment is when I see Tsula and Corrine entering the room. Corrine is clearly exhausted, all of her time taken up lately with her healing duties. Each time we have returned from a venture outside, we have inevitably brought back more civilians with us—many of them injured.

Tsula has taken it upon herself to act as her nurse, assisting where she can. Which, given the circumstances, is a lot. Even the healthy among us have become anxious hypochondriacs, forcing both of them to spend many of their waking hours just trying to keep people calm.

"Are you alright?" They look like they've barely woken up.

"Yes, I'm fine," Corrine assures me. "All of the healing spells just take a lot of my energy."

"I'll be okay. I'll just need a nap a little later," Tsula jests.

"I just want to make sure you both know how invaluable you are," I tell the two women. "We will be leaving for another supply run shortly. If there is anything I can get either of you, you need only say the word."

"Thanks, Khazak," Corrine replies with a smile. "I can't think of anything I need right now, but there was something…" She turns to Tsula, the two sharing a look.

"Oh, right!" Tsula shakes off her confusion, though now she's blushing. "A few of the women here are in need of, um..." She leans in and says the next part in a whisper. "Feminine hygiene products."

"*Ah*, of course. Not a problem at all." I have two sisters, so it would hardly be the first time. My twin Ayla was so terrible at planning and preparing that when we were teenagers, I had to run home more than once on her behalf. "Is there a particular type I should look for?"

"The women I spoke to specifically requested menstrual cups," Corrine answers, lacking all of Tsula's embarrassment, "but there are a few girls on the younger side, so you may want to pick up some basic pads as well, just in case."

"Will do." I make a mental note of the items to grab.

"Thank you." Tsula gives me a little bow of her head, her face unnecessarily red as a beet.

After that, I return to my room and gather my belongings, changing into my armor and pulling the sword scabbard over my shoulder. Ideally, we will not have to do any fighting, but it is better to be safe than sorry. Once I'm ready, I wait for the others in the club's lobby, eager to get started.

Unfortunately, we discovered during our first attempt at a supply run that the skeletons have been able to see through the strongest invisibility spells we could muster—a feat that had us once more worried about our villain's power level. But there are other ways to use magic to keep us camouflaged and silent.

"Alright, first things first." Wari, the brother accompanying us, turns to me after pulling out pieces of what I've learned are the molted skin of a lizard, and presses it against a bare part of my arm. "*Eskomasina*."

His hands glow a soft green as the spell is cast, which travels into my arm and through my body. It feels strange, like all my hair suddenly standing on end, but it's not painful. When he pulls his hand back, the lizard skin is gone, and my body, or at least its color, begins to change to match that of the floor beneath me and the wall behind me.

While I cannot explain all the specifics, a typical invisibility spell works by manipulating the light around the chosen target or area to make them vanish in the eyes of anyone looking at them… *Unless* of course you are an even more powerful spellcaster, capable of crafting a spell to see through it, as our necromancer seems to be.

But *this* spell isn't something a counterspell can see through. This spell actually changes the physical properties of our bodies—clothing included—to match the color and appearance of our immediate area. We may not be completely out of sight, but this is not a bad alternative. When moving, the camouflage is less effective, but when we are still, we are nearly imperceptible.

After repeating the spell on Yuta and Adam, he releases the switch that swings the bookcase out, and we all step into the backroom of the bookstore, closing the bookcase behind us. The store is much messier than my first visit, forcing us to step over the fallen shelves and spilled books. This is all by design. Making it look as though the place has already been ransacked should signal to other looters that there is nothing of value and nobody left here. As a secondary purpose, they can act as a barrier should we ever be forced to defend ourselves.

Outside, the city is the same as it has been for two days— eerily silent and empty, aside from the periodic patrols of skeletons roaming the streets. The dome that once acted as a form of security for the city now bathes everything in a disturbing blood-red glow. We learned that first day that it had become a solid barrier, preventing any further escape. Only a fraction of the people living here were able to evacuate, and those who are still here are hiding in their own homes, terrified to come out lest they be captured.

It's only about five blocks from the Rooster to the grocery, and we stick to smaller streets and alleys, not wanting to risk alerting anyone of our presence. I pull Novus's key from my pocket as we approach the back door, unlocking it and granting us access to the store's stockroom and from there the rest of the store. It is large, no doubt servicing many of the surrounding neighborhoods and taking up almost half of the city block. We split into two groups, me with Adam and Onas with Yuta, dividing up each side of the store between us.

We first stop near the produce. While none of the fruit is fresh (seeing as no one has been here to restock it), it isn't rotten either—yet. As the Leather Rooster does not have any sort of oven or stove, we are forced to stock up on things that require no cooking. My personal diet has consisted of a lot of jerky and other dried meats, as too many fruits and grains give me an upset stomach.

"There's still a lot of bread over here that should still be good," Adam calls to me from a short distance, standing in front of the store's small bakery. "There's even some cake."

"Bring it," I tell him as I approach, my bag already open. "It may brighten someone's day."

Thanks to my magical satchel, we can transport large amounts of items without having to worry about the weight of carrying it all or it expiring. Onas and his brother claim to have originally designed them several hundred years ago, which I have no way of confirming or denying—gnomes have a lifespan that rivals the elves—and with one of his own, he can stock up as much as I do.

Finished in the bakery, we walk around the store for a short while until I find the section carrying things like bandages and medicinal remedies and begin searching. I find a row of individually wrapped menstrual cups next to several stacks of pads that are bound together with twine. Adam does not say anything as I pull them all into our bags, though given how he looks away, I assume he's embarrassed. Silly.

"Okay, the only other specific thing that was requested was some wine," I tell Adam while closing my bag and throwing it over my shoulder. "Only a few bottles were requested, but…"

"Seeing as how depressed everyone seems, it might do us some good to stock up?" Adam finishes for me. "I'm with you there. The liquor in that place won't last much longer."

The two of us make our way to the back corner of the store where wine and other alcohol is kept. We pass Yuta and Onas, the two searching through the store's small butcher shop for anything already dried and preserved. We already cleared out as much of the fresh meat as we could that first day. Right next to it is a large ice box filled with different types of cheese, of which we have also already stocked up on.

"You know a lot about wine?" Adam asks me as we start to look over the bottles.

"Not much." No one in my family was ever much of a drinker, but one of my fathers did run his own restaurant, where I worked as a server for a couple of years. "You chill white wine, while red is left at room temperature. Supposedly, the older the vintage the better, but that is far from a guarantee."

"Sounds right to me," Adam attempts to confirm. "I'll grab the oldest looking bottles I can find. I've only had wine a few times. Usually, I just drink whatever beer the tavern is serving."

"I am much the same," I concur. "I enjoy a good ale myself, but I've never been a big drin—"

The sudden heavy *bang* that seems to originate outside of the grocery's front door makes us jump. We wait for a moment, hoping it was somehow nothing, when there's another, and then another, all in rapid succession. Someone is here, and they're trying to break in. Adam and I both rush to our companions.

"What the hell is that?" Onas asks, staring at the entrance in the distance.

"Not exactly sure," Yuta starts, "but I'm willing to bet whoever's out there is lacking a pulse."

"If we hurry, we might still be able to sneak out the back—" As I plan, a loud *crash* signifies that the store's front doors have been forced open. "Shit."

Taking cover behind the butcher's counter, we watch as the undead begin to pour inside. More than a dozen skeletons scan their unnerving gazes across the inside of the store, forcing us to duck down behind the counter before any of them can notice us. Our magical camouflage is still active, but also much less useful at close range. The more complicated the backdrop, the harder the spell has to work to replicate it, so shelves filled with items of all sorts of different shapes, colors, and sizes are not ideal. *This is not good.*

"Did they follow us?" Adam asks in a whisper.

"No, they would have used the back door," Onas answers. "They know we're here, but not how we got in, I think."

"We may be able to sneak back out the same way then," I say, quickly coming up with a plan. "Stay close, quiet, and low to the ground."

We leave our shelter behind the counter in a single file line, crouching as low as we can without having to crawl. The door to the back isn't far, but I can hear the skeletons shuffling closer and closer. I peer carefully around the shelf we hide behind before darting across to the next when I see we are in the clear.

One by one, the others follow until we are once more safely behind cover. We only need to repeat this tactic once more before we reach the still-open stockroom door. After we're out of the building, we can—

crash

"…Sorry," Adam whispers with a grimace as we all turn to see the broken jar he must have accidentally knocked off its shelf.

I know logically they had to have heard that, but I am still hopeful enough to peer my head around the next shelf on the off chance they didn't. Instead, I see a trio of skeletons all marching in our direction. One of them points a bony finger in my direction, opening their jaw to release an unsettling *hiss*.

"We've been found," I tell the others, already reaching for my sword.

"Guess we're fighting our way out," Yuta follows my lead.

"Really sorry, everyone," Adam apologizes again.

"Worry about that later," Wari tells him, cracking his fingers.

"Fan out. Do not let them box us in," I tell the others, just as the wave of enemies reaches us.

My sword clashes with that of the first skeleton, overpowering it and sending it flying to the side. I quickly follow that up by slamming the hilt of my weapon against the side of its skull, smashing it against the wall and causing the rest of its body to crumble. While I turn to my left to block an axe swung by the second skeleton, Onas rushes past to take down the third on my right.

"*Isiwepane!*" Onas shouts, pelting our enemies with jars and other items that go flying from the shelf behind him.

On my right I hear Yuta and Adam clashing with their own. I look over the rows of shelves to the entrance and count more than a dozen already inside, more still entering through the front door. With so many opponents, running may be our only option.

Seeing an opportunity, I ram my shoulder into the wooden shelf at my side. It topples over, hitting the next shelf and knocking it over, hitting the *next* shelf and cascading on from there—trapping about five of our attackers who happen to be standing between them, but there are still plenty more.

"So I'm not saying I'm worried," Adam starts, preparing as the next wave approaches, "but do we have a plan here?"

"If we can make it to the back room, we can try to block the door and leave the way we came in," I share my idea aloud.

"We'll have to make sure none of them are able to follow us," Yuta notes as she parries a skeleton's sword with her own. "There could be even more outside. We may have to lead them the wrong way and then double back when we lose them."

"Alright, Yuta and Wari will go first, then Adam—" I start trying to coordinate things when I'm interrupted.

"They must be in here!" a voice shouts.

It came from outside, not terribly loud but audible enough that we all heard it. It does nothing to stop the undead already encroaching on us, aside from a few near the door who turn and step back outside. There's a small explosion and then a shower of bones is blown inside, followed by three individuals in Maname Guard garb, a gnome and two humans. *Spirits, is that—*

"Liss!" Adam joyfully cries out while dodging a swinging mace.

"Adam? Khazak?" she calls back once she sees us on the other end of the shop.

"It is so good to see you!" I yell while kicking in a bony rib cage.

"Where have you been? I've been looking for you everywhere!" She swings her sword upward, decapitating the skeletal dwarf in front of her. "And why do you look so weird?"

"Camo spell," Wari answers proudly. "I can show you how—"

"Not to interrupt the touching reunion," the gnome who came in with Liss starts, knocking a skeleton's legs to the side then jumping onto its skull when it tumbles to the ground, "but maybe you should do the thing first?"

"Crap, sorry ma'am," Liss replies with realization.

After knocking the now headless skeleton to the side, she sprints forward, stepping onto one of the toppled shelves and leaping into the air. From inside her pocket, she pulls a glowing crystal, which she throws to the ground near the center of the store. The crystal smashes against the hard wooden floor, releasing a bright flash of light that spreads outward to cover almost the entire room.

"Who is *that*?" Yuta asks as Liss lands on her feet a second later, in awe.

"Elisabeth." I smile as skeletons around us crumble.

Whatever trick Liss pulled, it works on everything except for a few in the shop's corners. Both groups quickly work to dispatch the remaining enemies until all is silent, both in and outside of the store. Once we are sure the coast is clear, we enter the back room, barricading the door so it is safe to talk.

"What was that flash?" Adam asks about the bright light.

"A reponiam charge," the gnome with Liss explains. "Carrying a spell that disrupts the undead."

"Lieutenant Gwar." Yuta quickly salutes the woman. "I am *so* happy to see you."

"The feeling is mutual, Yuta." She returns the salute, before looking over the rest of us. "Where is the rest of your squad?"

"Back at our current safehouse, ma'am," Yuta explains. "We were just out gathering some supplies."

"Those two are actually some of the friends I was telling you about," Liss says to Gwar and her other companion. "Adam and Khazak. And that guy's name is…"

"Onas," the pukwudgie finishes with a grunt.

"I'm Lieutenant Anika Gwar of the Manamequohi City Guard, this is my deputy Raso, and you already know our newest recruit, Liss," the lieutenant introduces her team.

"It is nice to meet you," I say, grateful for their sudden appearance. "You may have just saved our hides back there."

"I'm glad you found us when you did." Yuta sounds relieved. "My squad attempted to hole up in our station as everything went down, but we were overrun. These fellows actually helped us find and set up the makeshift safehouse we're in now."

"Good work. I've been trying to get an idea of what our remaining defenses look like." Gwar looks around our small group again. "You bring us to six, at least that I know of."

"Are you the one in charge, ma'am?" Yuta asks with concern.

"Lieutenant Pules and Lieutenant Greenhilt have been helping me run things." Gwar shakes her head. "There's been no sign yet of Captain Revik, but I'm hoping he's out there doing the same thing we are and just haven't run into us yet."

"What about the city council?" Yuta asks next.

"No sign of them either." Gwar doesn't quite frown. "But that is not entirely unexpected. Nothing gets in and out of our safehouses unless we want it to. Have you all found anyone else?"

"You're the first of the Maname Guard we've run into." I wish that I had a better answer for her. "Regarding *our* safehouse, we can bring you back with us now if you'd like."

"That would be great." That at least seems to brighten her spirits. "How many others are with you?"

"A little over thirty by our last count, but there's only about a dozen of us capable of fighting," Yuta tells Gwar as we exit the store. Despite the chaos inside, I still lock the door behind us. "Half of that is my squad, and the other half are civilians like these three."

"Every little bit helps," Raso says as we step farther down the alley. "Between our five safehouses, we've rescued over a hundred civilians, and the number keeps growing."

"How are you able to keep everyone hidden?" Onas asks, and I find myself just as curious.

"They're large safehouses," Raso explains. "We have about twenty of them tucked away around the city."

"Their existence is a secret to all except high-ranking city officials," Gwar adds. "Or at least they were. We'll probably have to move them once all of this calms down."

"So what happened to you?" Adam questions Elisabeth. "We lost track of you after that skeleton attack. We've been worried you were still locked up somewhere."

"It was so creepy." Liss gives a small shudder. "They managed to grab me and slap a pair of cuffs on my wrists, but before they could get me marching, I smashed the one holding me against a wall and broke away from the group."

"David and Tsula managed to get away as well," I tell her next. "Corrine and Tsula are currently at the safehouse."

"What about David?" Liss notes his absence.

"Hopefully, he is off the island." I try not to let my worry show. "I sent him to get help, but I have no idea—"

"David's fine," she says confidently. "He's so stubborn that he came back from the dead. A combo dragon/skeleton attack is nothing for him."

"I appreciate the vote of confidence." It does help, a little.

"I found a place to hide until it was safe, and then I wandered around until I found Lieutenant Gwar and her group," she continues. "They were able to get the cuffs off of me and I've been helping them ever since. That and looking for the rest of you."

"Liss has been invaluable on our scouting missions," Lieutenant Gwar says proudly. "She was the first to notice the patterns among the captives."

"How do you mean?" I ask, not sure what patterns she is referring to.

"Well for one, they only seem to be capturing people that are able bodied," Liss explains. "Mostly between the ages of twenty and fifty with no injuries or disabilities."

"We've seen them walk right past children and the elderly without so much as a second glance," Raso adds.

"Now that you mention it, more than half the people we've rescued have been kids and their grandparents," Onas says, deep in thought.

"There's more," Liss continues. "We've also seen some of these groups *feeding* their captives, giving them water, even taking them to the bathroom."

"What?" *They're taking care of them?* "That makes no sense."

"Right?" Liss responds. "If anything, you'd think a necromancer would want them dead so he could add them to his army."

"Which means he has some other kind of plan for them," Onas says ominously.

"Unfortunately, that's also what we've concluded," Gwar says with a sigh.

"We've been trying to find and liberate any holding pens," Liss continues to explain. "We're not sure why, but once or twice a day, they move one of these groups into Paramount Park, and they don't come back."

"We've been there," I reveal. "Not that I know what he is up to, but that seems to be where the necromancer established his base."

"You've seen him?" My words have Gwar stopping in her tracks. "What can you tell me?"

"He is a human, or at least appeared to be," I recall the man who slid down the dragon's wing. "His accent was one I was unfamiliar with; he certainly wasn't from around here. Maybe around thirty years old? Though that is a little harder to tell with someone like him."

"Anything else?" Gwar is eager for something to fight back with.

"Only that he seems to be extremely powerful," I say with disappointment. "I saw him raise more than a hundred of the undead in a single casting, and in addition to the armies of skeletons, from the way he spoke, it seemed like the dragons are his doing as well."

"The *dragons* are undead?" Raso asks, shocked. "They don't look like it."

"I've heard of necromancers who can restore the bodies of their undead minions," Gwar says gravely. "But it's one of the more difficult things for them to do. I can't fathom how he could have pulled it off at that scale."

"That's not even everything we learned that night," Adam says next. "Khazak saw the necromancer talking to Redwish."

"What? Really?" Liss's reaction is instant, her eyes opening wide in surprise.

"It would seem he and the necromancer behind this are somehow connected," I confirm.

"Figures that after spending the day trying to find him, he'd show up later that night and cause us even more problems." Liss scoffs in disbelief.

"Who is this Redwish character?" Gwar looks between the three of us.

"Naruk Redwish , the man we have been chasing up the coast for weeks, all the way here to Maname." *Just saying his name makes my blood boil.* "He's responsible for many deaths, including that of my p— partner," I nearly slip and call David by his pet name.

"I am so sorry to hear that," Gwar offers solemnly.

"It's okay. He got better," Liss comments offhand, causing Yuta and Gwar to share a strange look.

"Well, I've never heard of him," Gwar tells me as we resume our trek. "But when we get to your base, I'd like to know all about him. If they're working together, I want to figure out why."

"Happy to, ma'am," I respond with a nod.

"Wait, does that mean that whatever those two are up to here is connected to everything that's been going on with David?" Liss asks next, her mind clearly racing.

"We have no idea," I answer honestly, "but at this point, it would be stranger if they weren't."

"We're almost there," Yuta announces as we reach the end of an alley.

After checking that the coast is clear, Yuta is the first to exit, running toward and opening the door to the bookstore. We each follow, one by one, sprinting across the road before ducking inside. Locking the door behind us, things seem to be exactly as we left them.

"A bookstore? Really?" Liss turns her gaze on the toppled shelves, unimpressed. "This is where you've been hiding?"

"Oh boy, this is gonna be fun," Adam starts, a grin on his face.

She gives him a strange look but allows herself to be led by the shoulder into the back room. I chuckle as the rest of us follow, eager to see our friend's reaction to both the false bookcase and the secret club behind it. I just wish David were here to see it with me.

Chapter 8

Khazak

"This place is ... interesting."

"That's one way of putting it."

Liss, Adam, and I stand together at the Leather Rooster's bar, looking around over our makeshift safehouse. Liss was surprised by the door hidden behind the bookcase, and then again when she looked around and realized what sort of establishment it is. Raso was equally surprised, though Lieutenant Gwar's lack of reaction was a tell that she was already aware of its existence.

The other members of Yuta's squad are as excited as she is to see the lieutenant and waste no time in updating her on the situation, stumbling over each other as they try to fill in any gaps. Gwar seems happy with our current arrangement and assigns Yuta to continue overseeing it, something that (judging by Yuta's reaction) she feels honored to do.

While we show the newcomers our supplies and add the spoils from our outing to the "pantry," Onas and Wari explain how we are managing our defenses. Now that we've made contact, we'll be able to share any needed provisions with the others and they can do the same for us, hopefully making up for anything the other is lacking. We will also be able to coordinate things like patrols and ensure the civilians under our protection remain safe.

"I'm guessing this was your doing?" Liss directs her question at me, gesturing to the room.

"I might have suggested it," I admit. "It has suited our purposes well enough so far."

"I can see that." She nods in agreement. "Honestly, I'm impressed. Very resourceful."

"Liss!" Corrine calls out, crossing the room as swift as a rabbit. "I'm so happy to see you."

"It's so good to know you're okay," Tsula adds, both of them looking slightly less exhausted than they did this morning.

"It's good to see you both too," Elisabeth says as she hugs them both. "What have you been doing for the past couple of days?"

"Mostly just trying to survive," Adam answers. "It hasn't been the easiest."

"That and helping Yuta reconnect with the rest of the Maname Guard," I add next. "She has really been the one in charge."

"We've just figured that since it's their city, they should do any big decision making," Adam clarifies.

"And we have really appreciated it," Yuta says, joining us with Captain Gwar and Raso. "Lieutenant, these two and their friends have been invaluable to our survival here."

"I saw for myself firsthand." Gwar looks over us appreciatively. "Elisabeth has been doing the same with us. The city thanks you for your help."

"Only doing what's right," Adam says for us all.

"Ma'am, I'm sorry, but we really need to be getting back," Raso interrupts with some reluctance.

"Right," Gwar agrees before turning to us. "Yuta's already coming with us so we can get her up to speed on things, but if you wouldn't mind, I'd like some of you to accompany us as well."

"Are you certain?" I am interested but was not expecting it.

"You showed me yours; it's only fair I show you mine," she jokes. "We can clue you in on our current operations."

"I would be happy to," I answer.

"I'm in, too," Adam says with a raised hand.

"I've had enough 'outings' for one day," Onas grumbles as he walks off.

"I'm gonna stay here, just in case I'm needed," Corrine tells us as she finds a seat in the common area. "Be safe, everyone."

"I may be able to send another spellcaster or two here to help with the healing duties," Gwar says to those of us still gathered.

"We would greatly appreciate that." *Anything* would help. "Corrine is our only trained healer, and I have been worried about what we would do if the worst were to happen."

"Having them here won't matter much if you're suddenly forced to defend yourselves," Gwar agrees as she watches the woman walk away.

"We appreciate the assistance, Lieutenant." Yuta joins us, still beaming from her recent praise. "We are ready to go when you are."

"Let me just give a few final words to the others," Gwar says, returning to the remaining guards.

"Khazak," Tsula calls for my attention, "I'm going to stay here with Corrine, but did you happen to get the…?"

"Oh yes, of course." I quickly reach into my bag to retrieve the requested items. "I tried to get enough for anyone else that may need them, but just say the word if we start to run low."

"Thank you," she replies, taking the boxes of pads from me. "I have a feeling this isn't something that ends up on many supply lists." *Not the ones written by men, at least.*

After Lieutenant Gwar finishes what looks like a pep talk, our group gathers up once more. Yuta leads the way out of the Rooster with Gwar taking over once we're outside. It is like walking through a ghost town, the quiet, eerie streets. It is painful to think of those people fearfully hiding in their homes, too afraid to draw attention to themselves or else risk getting captured and rationing what little food they may have. *Spirits, I hope this siege does not last—*

"Did anyone else hear that?" I ask after hearing a crash in the distance.

"No, what?" Raso and the other humans would not likely have caught it.

"I heard it," Gwar confirms and points east, down a street to our right. "Sounded like glass breaking, somewhere over there, maybe a block away."

"Maybe it was—" Before Liss can finish, there is another crash—and then a scream loud enough that *everyone* turns their head.

"What was *that?*" Adam looks around, concerned.

"Someone in trouble! Come on." Gwar is the first to start running.

We look for the source of the noise as we run down the road and are led to a small general store. The question of the first noise is answered by the broken window we see next to an open door, and the second is answered when we step inside: children. Three of them: a human, a gnome, and an elf trapped under a toppled shelf.

"Aaahh!" the gnome screams when he notices us enter.

"Scatter!" the human yells before she and the gnome run deeper into the store.

"Don't just leave me here!" the elf calls to her friends, half-angry and half-scared, before turning back to us.

"It's alright." Gwar speaks calmly, crouching down to her. "We heard your scream and came to help."

"Can we start by getting that shelf off of you?" Raso jokes as he steps forward.

"O-okay." The girl nods hesitantly, and Liss and Adam squat down on either side to lift up the shelf, allowing her to crawl out from under it.

"Are you hurt?" I ask her next, getting down on one knee.

"M-my arm kind of hurts," she answers tentatively, showing him the injured limb.

"Well, I don't think it's broken," I tell her with a smile after giving it a quick examination and then cast the only healing spell I know. "But that should keep it from getting sore."

"Th-thank you." She worries her lip as she takes in the four of us.

"What is someone like you doing here?" Gwar asks her gently, no longer crouching as she actually seems to be shorter than the girl. "And what about your friends?"

"We are not going to hurt you," I call to the back of the shop, cupping my hands around my mouth. I have not heard any doors or windows being opened, so they must still be inside.

"Are you okay, Kira?" a small, worried voice replies.

"Yeah," Kira confirms. "It's safe. You can come out."

The two other children peek out from behind a counter before slowly making their way back to us. They look to be of similar ages, between eight and ten, though given the different species, I may be completely incorrect. Neither gets too close, looking to Kira for guidance.

"Are you children alright?" I ask them both as gently as I can.

Both nod silently.

"What were you doing here?" Adam questions.

"Looking for food," the human girl explains. "Remo said—"

"Ssshhh!" the young gnome at her side silences her with a glare.

"Why are you here alone?" Raso looks between the three of them. "Where are your parents?"

"I haven't seen my mommy since we saw the dragons…" Kira is the only one to say anything after silence fills the air. "We were going to the port when we got separated in the crowds of people running away."

"And you've been taking care of yourselves since," I conclude. They must have all been separated from their families in the attack.

"Where have you been sleeping?" Gwar asks the three. "Is there anyone else with you?"

"Well, we've been over—"

"Ssshh!" the gnome shushes her again.

"I know we're strangers, but I promise, we're the good guys. See my badge?" Yuta tries to assure her. "Because of those dragons, the city isn't safe right now. But we can help make sure you guys have food, a warm place to sleep, and maybe even help find your parents."

The three children share a look, having a silent conversation to decide exactly how much they are going to tell us.

"We've been hiding in an old apartment building on 23rd street," the human reveals.

"Muna!" the young gnome admonishes. "We're not supposed to tell people that!"

"I don't care anymore, Natch!" Muna replies, sounding near tears. "I'm hungry, and I'm tired of having to steal, and I just want to go home!"

I share a look with my fellow adults as it would appear that our plans for the day are in flux. Despite the importance of what we originally set out to do, we cannot in good conscience leave these children to fend for themselves. Now we just need to find the rest of them.

"Could you take us to your other friends?" I ask Muna, who seems more agreeable than Natch. "We want to help them, too."

"Okay." Muna nods with Natch looking on apprehensively.

Together, the children lead us a few blocks down from the general store to a tall apartment building. The entrance is wide open with no door, and it is clear once we step inside that the building was abandoned long before the city came under siege. There is refuse on the floor, a layer of dust covering everything, and several of the individual apartment doors are off their hinges or missing.

The children bring us upstairs, all the way to the top floor of the building. Things look no less abandoned up here, though some noises can be heard coming from farther down the hallway. We're led in the sound's direction, entering an apartment at the end of the hall.

"Good, you're back. How did——" a voice starts and then stops once we turn in the entryway and step inside the apartment's living room. "You brought grownups with you?!"

The voice belongs to a young boy—an orc, no older than twelve by my estimate. And he looks none too pleased to see us, glaring at us with his arms folded over his chest. Behind him are about half a dozen other children, staring up at us through fearful eyes.

"I tried to tell them not to…" Natch tells the boy worriedly before moving to join the other children. "It's Muna's fault."

"Nu uh!" Muna defends with a whine. "Kira is the one who started talking to them!"

"Only 'cuz you both left me stuck under that shelf after it fell on me!" Kira says with a stomp of her foot. "And I don't care anymore, Remo! You promised you'd take me to the shipyard days ago to try and find my mommy and daddy, and you still haven't!"

"How long have you all been here?" Gwar asks the group, and just from glancing around the apartment, it would seem a while.

"None of your business," Remo replies stubbornly.

"Only about a week?" a young halfling girl tells us.

"What are you doing?!" Remo angrily confronts the girl. It would appear there is some division in the ranks. "You know the rules!" She looks to be too young to even understand much of what is going on.

"What have you been doing here?" Raso asks as he walks around and peers into some of the empty rooms, taking in more of our surroundings.

"Taking care of ourselves," Remo answers with a cocky smirk.

"And what's this about people in the shipyard?" Adam steps forward to ask next.

"Some citizens took shelter there and have since made it into their own little base of operations to fight back from," Gwar explains as she looks over the children. "We've been trying to convince them to leave it to us and move into one of our safehouses, but they are a pretty stubborn group."

"Yeah, they've been fighting against the skellingtons!" one of the other children excitedly tells us.

"Kira thinks some of our parents might be there too!" another cheerfully declares.

Rather than yell, Remo only scoffs and looks away at their obvious enthusiasm. Elsewhere in the apartment though, I can hear someone crying. Seeking it out, I step into a small bedroom to find a young human boy with a dark complexion and curly mop of black hair in one corner, softly sobbing with his knees pulled to his chest.

"What's wrong, little one?" I ask as I crouch down.

"<Leave me alone. I am tired of being in this place and I want my mother,>" he manages between sniffles, never looking up.

"I am sure you must really miss her," I attempt to console, getting the boy to look up at me, though he only looks confused and annoyed.

"You can understand him?" Kira asks from the doorway as she and everyone else follow us into the bedroom.

"Yes, why would I not…?" I look between the two children, confused.

"Because he's speaking Galatian," Gwar informs me before stepping closer to the boy. "<When did you last see your mother?>"

The young boy looks up in shock, no doubt at someone speaking in his native tongue. At the same time, I start to worry that I may be having some sort of stroke until I brush my hand over my ear and remember what I'm wearing. I will have to let Onas know his translator works.

"<At the docks!>" he begins to rapidly speak. "<She put me on a boat without her, but it had to turn around, and when I came back, she was gone! I can't find her anywhere!>"

"<That must have been very scary.>" The young boy sniffles and nods at my pukwudgie companion. "<Do you want to come with us? We can help you look for her.>"

"Are you sure that is something you want to tell them?" I ask Gwar. I know personally from my line of work how dangerous it can be to make promises that are too big to keep.

"Unless you've got a better idea…" She half shrugs.

"What are we doing now?" Raso asks, having barely understood half the conversation.

"The kids," Liss is able to put together. "We can't just leave them here on their own. We're bringing them back to the safehouse with us while we try and find their families."

"None of us are going *anywhere* with you!" Remo suddenly declares in anger. "We're doing just fine without you."

"But Remo, they said they could help me find my mommy." Kira doesn't understand her friend's reaction. "Maybe they can find yours too!"

"*No they can't!*" Remo spits out before stomping out of the room, followed by an equally sad looking Natch and Muna.

"What's his problem?" Liss asks, though I may have already figured it out.

"He lost his parents a long time ago," I answer with a sigh. "Long before the dragons showed up. He's an orphan. I think all three of them are."

"Shit," Liss curses at her insensitivity—drawing small gasps and giggles from a number of the children. "I mean, crap."

"You should try and talk to him," Gwar suggests, the young Galatian boy holding on tightly to the hem of her shirt. "I'm a little busy right now."

I straighten up and follow after the three children, finding them in a different bedroom. Remo is crouched near a wall, softly sobbing into his crossed arms with his friends on either side, looking equally sad. The two of them look up when I enter, though Remo pointedly ignores me. Between my years of being a ranger *and* having three younger siblings, I would like to think I am good at dealing with kids.

"You have all been on your own for a while, haven't you?" I ask as I approach the three, who are obviously all very close to one another.

"A long time," Muna confirms with a sad nod.

"Remo helped take care of us when there were no grown-ups who would," Natch says next. "Taught us how to take care of ourselves."

"And he's done an amazing job." My heart breaks for these children; no one should have to live like this, least of all innocents like them. "But it is very dangerous right now to be out here on your own. You've seen all the monsters."

"I've been taking care of everyone just fine," Remo complains, finally looking up, his eyes bloodshot, wet, and angry. "You say you care, but all you're gonna do is dump us off on someone else, and they'll do the same thing, and so will the next person, over and over. No thanks."

"I know you don't know who we are," I decide to try some diplomacy, "and it sounds like you have no reason to believe us, but we really only want to keep you safe."

"Which it isn't, here," Yuta tells them next, having followed me. "We only want you to come with us until all of this craziness is over. We've got food, water, beds. Then you can go back to whatever you were doing."

"You mean it?" Remo looks over me from his crouched position with a sniffle.

"I promise." Yuta holds up a hand as if swearing.

Remo looks to both of his friends—and then to some of the other children who have also followed us in here, each with a hopeful look on their face.

"…Okay," Remo answers, standing with a sniffle. "We'll come with you."

"Yay!" Kira cries out behind me, along with several of the other kids.

"Glad that's settled." Gwar re-enters the room with the young Galatian boy still at her side. "Alright kids, grab your things, 'cause we've gotta get a move on."

Everyone immediately scatters around the apartment before returning with toys, blankets, food, or whatever other objects they have managed to hang on to. Once everyone is together, the six of us guide the nine children down the stairs and outside with Gwar, Raso, and Yuta in front and Liss, Adam, and I in the rear, shielding them between us. Spirits willing, we will not run into any issues on the journey from here to the safehouse.

"Okay, stay together, stay quiet, and move quickly," Gwar instructs carefully when we step onto the street.

"If we move quickly enough, we should be able to get there in—" I stop after turning the corner. "Oh no."

Ahead of us, a group of deadly skeletons marches in our direction, and as soon as they notice us, their red glowing eyes are locked onto our form. There are maybe ten of them, and while I would normally not worry about us having a problem with that many, we have the children with us. Keeping them safe is our highest priority.

"Children, get behind us, and when I tell you to—" I start.

"I've got it!" Liss cuts me off and runs forward.

She chucks another reponiam charge overhand toward the group of undead. Just like at the grocery store, it shatters and releases a bright light that causes the skeletons to crumble. I should ask to carry a few myself.

"Good job," Yuta compliments.

"Thanks, but that was my last one," Liss reveals. "We should get moving before another patrol comes through."

"We're not far," Gwar tells the group. "Three more blocks to the north."

A few minutes later and we are sneaking through alleys behind what look like apartments. After checking to make sure we are not being followed, we approach the back door on one of the taller buildings. Raso unlocks it, and Gwar ushers us inside.

We enter an unremarkable hallway, a long row of doors ahead of us. Walking about halfway down, Gwar pulls a small glowstone from her pocket when we reach a dark stairwell, leading us down to an equally unremarkable basement. I see nothing but stacks of crates and some old rugs, storage from the residents above.

Raso moves toward a rug spread across the floor, squatting down to lift it and reveal that it is attached to a wooden hatch, and underneath *that* is a second hatch, this one dark and metal—no doubt made of lead. He proceeds to rap his knuckles against it in a specific pattern—a code—and then sits back on his heels to wait. A moment later, there's an audible *click*, and he grabs the handle on the hatch, pulling it up to reveal an opening with light and a staircase leading down.

"That is fairly ingenious," I comment with approval on their hiding space.

"Right?" Liss responds as Raso attaches the metal hatch's handle to a hook on the back of the wooden one, allowing all three covers to be pulled down all at once. "Most people wouldn't think to check for a way farther down than a basement."

"Not as cool as our bookshelf, though," Adam comments on my left.

"What bookshelf?" one of the children asks as we start down the stairs.

"Nothing. It's not as cool as he makes it sound," Liss answers, rolling her eyes at our blond companion.

Two by two, we descend, with me at the end closing the hatch. The stairs bring us down into a small room with two guards, likely in charge of watching and unlocking the door. Both of them salute Gwar before turning their gazes to the rest of us.

"Who are they, ma'am?" the first one asks.

"Yuta!" the second announces more happily. "It's so good to see you're safe!"

"Chani!" Yuta responds equally as happily, and the two quickly embrace.

"We found the children hiding in the old Treetop Apartment building," Gwar explains, ignoring the display. "The rest are actually the friends Liss has been telling us about. They've been helping Yuta and her contingent to set up their own safehouse. Anything happen while we were out?"

"No, ma'am." The guard shakes his head as Yuta and Chani finish their reunion.

"Good." She nods at him. "Keep up the good work."

We enter a hallway and round the corner, and my eyes go wide at the large cavern of a room that opens in front of us. I hear some of the children whisper a "*wow*" as we stand on a balcony overlooking dozens of guards milling about and working, and even more civilians. The room is divided into sections, the largest of which has to be the rows and rows of bunks that take up almost the entire back half. In the corner to my left is a kitchen with a long stove, obviously designed with quantity in mind, food and other provisions stacked high against a wall as an impromptu pantry.

"Welcome to Safehouse 12," Gwar tells us.

"Welcome back, ma'am, sir." Another guard on the balcony salutes Raso and Gwar as he approaches our group. "More rescued civilians?"

"Only the children," Raso explains. "First thing we need to do is make sure they are fed, then we can start to work on reuniting them with their families."

"We have safehouses like this tucked away all over the city," Gwar tells us, leaving Raso to handle the children and leading us down a flight of stairs. "We've been working non-stop trying to protect everyone we can, but we're starting to run out of room."

She walks us through the "barracks," past a young human with curly black hair sitting on one of the bunks. To his right on his bed are a series of dark-colored crystals: reponiam. One of the crystals sits in his lap, and he begins to cast a spell on it as we approach. His hands begin to glow as does the sun-symbol hanging from his neck, and the crystal absorbs the light. When he's finished, the formerly dark crystal now glows.

"Yuta, Khazak, Adam, this is Jace," Gwar introduces us. "Jace, we found another safehouse this morning, and these two are some of the civilians helping with our resistance."

"Oh great." The young man says as he places the crystal on his left. "We need all the help we can get."

"He's responsible for that anti-undead bomb I used to rescue you," Liss explains, somewhat cockily. "Speaking of, I'm all out."

"I've been trying to help us stock up on them as much as we can, but it's a little exhausting." He does sound weary. "I've got another box and a half of these ready to go, but Lieutenant, we're running low on reponiam. We need to use whatever we've got left sparingly."

"I'll make sure word is spread to the others and see what we can do about finding more," Gwar tells him thoughtfully. "Jace is who I was considering sending back to help your healing issues."

"Where am I being sent?" he asks curiously.

"The safehouse these two are in is well hidden, but they've only got a single volunteer healer," Gwar tells him. "It's taking a toll."

"Of course, I'd be happy to help," he offers.

"That's good to hear," Gwar compliments. "Finish what you were doing and then pack a bag. I'll likely be sending you back with them tonight."

"Yes, ma'am." The young guard salutes, then gets back to his reponiam charging duties.

"Over here is what we call the 'war room.'" Gwar leads us back to the front of the safehouse, toward a table with a large map of the city spread across it.

"'War corner' might be a little more accurate," Liss jokes.

"This is where we've been working on our plan to take back the city." Gwar ignores the attempt at humor. "With your group added to the fold, we can start coordinating our operations with yours."

"That would be great, ma'am," Yuta says from behind as she rejoins us.

"We have three main goals at the moment," Gwar says, stepping onto a stool and ignoring any side conversations so she can overlook the map. "Protect and liberate the city's civilians, seek out more of our safehouses and hopefully more of our number with them, and figure out what exactly is going on at the center of town with the people the necromancer has captured."

"And how do you fare on those fronts?" I look down to see various points on the map marked with pins.

"Each of these represents one of our safehouses." She motions to the map and its markings. "The blue flags are what we currently occupy, but the red still need to be investigated. Of the seven we've found so far, only two were empty, though not anymore."

"We've been trying to fan our search outward, but it goes slower than you'd think," Liss explains. "All the skeleton patrols make it difficult. If we aren't careful, we risk them finding out these places exist."

"That combined with our rescue attempts are what take up the majority of our time," Gwar continues. "The good news is we've been prepping some of the empty safehouses to house the civilians we liberate since hopefully that number also only continues to go up."

"*Hopefully* we'll have this guy out of here before it gets too high," Liss affirms. "Which is why I keep saying I think we need to start focusing on what's going on in that park. I just *know* the way we've seen the barrier flicker is related."

"You've seen the barrier flicker?" Yuta asks, my head shooting up when I hear the information.

"Not often," Gwar clarifies. "But a few times a day, it seems to disappear for a few seconds before coming back. It doesn't seem to happen at a consistent time, so we still wouldn't be able to use it to evacuate anyone even if we tried."

"I know why the barrier is dropping," I reveal, remembering my trek to the park with Wari. "He's leaving and entering the city on the backs of one of the dragons. I saw it myself."

"You have?" Gwar is almost taken aback. "When? What did you see?"

"It was right after the initial attack," I start to recount. "We noticed something strange in the park and thought it might have been someone in trouble. I went in with another man to investigate, and we saw the necromancer creating his army with our own eyes. The dragons are carrying these massive saddlebags filled with bones."

"That's where the army came from." Gwar's nostrils flare in frustration.

"Fingers crossed that means he hasn't raided any local cemeteries yet," Liss adds dryly.

"And those dragons are their *own* issue," Gwar complains. "We've counted three of them, each a different color: red, green, and black. The red and green look similar aside from the coloring, but the black one is *huge*, at least four or five times as big as the others."

"The red one hasn't moved since it landed on Testament Island, but we've seen the green and black dragons both flying overhead," Liss adds. "It looks like he mostly uses the black one to fly around the city."

"What I don't understand is how he's able to raise so many minions at once," I continue before anyone can ask any questions. "Or how some of them seem able to cast spells themselves."

"Well, we don't know *how* they work yet." Liss turns toward a set of shelves against the wall and grabs what looks like a necklace with a red stone pendant. "But we're pretty sure it's because of these."

"What is it?" Adam picks it up to inspect its jagged shape. "It looks like an unpolished ruby or something."

"We're not sure exactly what it's made of yet," Gwar starts. "But somehow, the skeletons wearing those necklaces are able to use magic. We've only noticed a handful of spells, all necromantic in nature, so we think he's somehow sharing his powers through them."

"I've never heard of someone splitting their magic like that." The more I learn about this man, the more worried I am about what he is capable of. "How does it work?"

"No idea," Liss answers. "We have people trying to figure it out. They say it must somehow amplify his powers too."

"We might have a couple of guys who can help with that," Adam offers. "A pair of brothers, really skilled enchanters."

"We have a few, so feel free to take one back with you," Gwar tells us.

"If you take out a skeleton wearing one of those, any magic it has cast is dispelled," Liss says next. "*But* all it takes is another of them to put the necklace on to recast it, so you've gotta be fast and grab it."

"Good to know," Yuta notes. "That should make our rescue efforts a lot easier."

"I wonder if it would be possible to figure out where the bones for his army originated." I start to think of unconventional ways to gather information on this man. "That might tell us what he's doing with..." *Oh no.*

"What is it?" Adam asks after I trail off.

"What if it's not just that our enemy is leaving to get more bones for his army?" I start to realize the implications aloud. "What if the reason people are not coming back from the park is because he is taking them somewhere out of the city?"

Looks of horror slowly dawn on everyone's faces.

"If that is true..." Determination fills Gwar's face. "We can't waste any more time. How is he doing it, and why?"

"He can't be having them all ride the dragons, can he?" Liss offers.

"I'm not even sure how one person rides a dragon, let alone dozens," Adam counters. "Doesn't seem very safe. Not to mention actually making the people climb aboard in the first place."

"He had a saddle," I point out. "The seat itself was almost comically small. I doubt there was room for anyone else."

"Figuring out what exactly he's doing—and stopping it—just became priority one." Gwar's tone leaves room for no argument. "That and upping our rescue efforts. He can't take them out of the city if they never get to him."

The rest of us agree with that assessment and prepare to devote the rest of the evening to coming up with a plan. We have no time to waste and a lot of work ahead of us, but for the first time in days, I am actually feeling hopeful. I just wish David was here to share it.

Chapter 9

David

"**Awrooroo.**"

"Nngh…"

A warm wet tongue slides over my face only seconds before a cold nose pokes against my neck, waking me up with a shout. I open my eyes to be met with Sona's fur-covered face, who licks me again before making more of her wolfy grumbles. I can hear her tail *whap whapping* against the wagon's cover.

"Sorry about that," Julie's voice trails in from the outside. "I didn't even realize she had jumped up there until she started making noise."

"She sure seems happy now that you're awake though." And that's Cameron, hearing the excitement of her tail.

"Alright, alright. I'm getting up," I tell the canine after she licks me again. "Gimme a minute."

After forcing me to pet her by pressing all of her body weight against me, she hops down from the back of the wagon with a happy bark. I don't know what's gotten into her, but I guess Khazak was always more active in the mornings than I was and probably helped her burn off some energy. So far, she seems happy to hunt for her own food in the nearby forest, but if that changes, I might need to look around town for something.

I sit up in my makeshift bed, taking a moment for my eyes to adjust to the morning light. I didn't sleep great and had a few nightmares last night. Nothing too bad, but I am worried that they might start to get worse again. I was up a bit too late after talking with Mike, worrying and stressing out about Khazak and the others. I kinda just wanna stay here and lay in bed, but I think that's less about being tired and more about being depressed.

It's not the only thing I'm feeling. There's also a deep ache right around my crotch. I lift up my blanket to take a peek at my poor cock straining against its prison. Not only do I have to pee, but it has been four whole days since I last had sex. This may shock you to learn, but I am *very* horny. Not that there's anything I could do about it even if I wasn't locked up without my Sir here. It's not really painful, more uncomfortable than anything, and I'm sad to say it's something I've gotten used to feeling when wearing it in the past—which has happened a bit too often, in my opinion.

Alright, first things first, I should check and see if there are any updates from Mike. I roll over and reach for my journal, flipping to the first page and scanning down to the bottom of our last conversation. There's only one new message.

I'm headed to bed. It's been kind of wild over here. More and more people have been getting messages confirming the attack on Maname all day. The heads of the institute are supposed to be having a meeting right now about trying to help. Most of them have family living there.

Makes sense that the world's biggest magic school would have connections to a city as filled with magic users as Manamequohi. But I'm not sure what kind of help they can offer from halfway around the globe. I guess if we could somehow make sure it was safe to teleport, then maybe? Hmm.

I'm embellishing a little, but Mike should be asleep right now, so I'm not expecting a response for hours. I can check before dinner. Like I said to Mike, I'm not exactly sure how they'll help from so far away, but maybe connecting the two groups will do some good. And if it gets the Maname Resistance to take me a little more seriously, that's just a bonus. Hell, maybe some of the relatives of the people at Mike's school are here in camp!

With one thing taken care of, it's time to finish getting up and take care of the rest. I feel a little gross, so I should probably ask around about finding a place to bathe or shower. Maybe there's a public bathhouse, or one of the inns will make an exception. I'd prefer not to do it in any freezing cold rivers, but I guess if I have to, I'll make do. I pull a clean set of clothes out of my bag, change, and fold up the blankets and pillows I've been sleeping on and push them to one of the wagon's corners.

"Good morning, everyone," I greet the Hurskett family as I exit the back of their wagon, feeling groggy but at least mostly awake.

"Good morning, David!" Marna is by the fire, hunched over a large skillet. "I'm just about to finish breakfast."

"It smells great," I compliment as I stretch my arms over my head. "If you'll excuse me for a moment, I just need to go take care of some … morning stuff."

"Hurry back!" she urges as I start walking toward the forest.

Sona follows me, trotting off to find her own food when I find a tree to stop at. I know I could probably go into town, but my poor bladder isn't going to make it that far. I'll need to head there later anyway, though I'm sure that with so many people here whatever facilities are available are probably already stretched thin. I finish relieving myself, clean up at the well near the edge of the refugee camp, and head back to the Hursketts and breakfast.

"Just in time," Marna says as I rejoin them, a stack of metal plates in the crook of her arm.

She kneels next to the skillet, which is large even for someone my size. She was able to cook everything together at once, and she goes around the pan in a circle, scooping things onto a plate one by one with her wooden spatula. I see scrambled eggs, grilled tomatoes, potatoes, and beans— no meat but still tasty. She hands the finished plate to Julie or Cam to pass to someone else, and I happily take it when it is offered and dig in.

"The food tastes wonderful, Marna," I compliment the chef. "Thank you."

"Glad you like it, sweetheart," she responds. "I tried to give you a little extra, seeing as you're almost twice as tall as the rest of us."

"I appreciate it." Seriously, this is like the fourth time they've fed me, on top of everything else. "I really can't thank you enough for rescuing me, feeding me, giving me a place to sleep. I'd like to return the favor somehow, if you'll let me. I've got some gold—"

"Nonsense." Marna stops me with a raised and a shake of her head.

"She's right. There's no need for that," Jact also insists. "I'm sure you would have done the same thing for any of us. We're just glad you're alright."

They're not wrong. I wouldn't hesitate to rescue someone in trouble the way they did. But that doesn't mean I still don't want to give them some money. They've got *four* kids! I'll just need to figure out another way of doing that.

"Well, thank you again," I say, returning to my food. "If there's ever anything I can do for your family, please just say the word."

When breakfast is nearly over, Sona returns to camp, passing by me to plop down next to the fire. There are some spots of red around her muzzle, and she yawns as she begins to lazily lick at her front paws. *Someone ate well.*

"Don't you look satisfied," I comment off-hand as I watch.

She doesn't get up, only letting out a soft *woof* in response.

"Would you happen to know if there's a public bathhouse or something in town?" I ask as everyone finishes the last of their meal. "I could really use a shower."

"Yep, there's the Kiweni Public Baths," Jact answers. "It's right behind the Timid Sparrow. Not a bad place, though it's probably crowded right now."

"I should get moving then." I stand and hand my dirty dish and fork to Marna, who is collecting them. "I'm supposed to head over to their part of the camp and see about joining up with the Maname Resistance today."

"Really?" Cam, who's been silent all morning, suddenly seems very interested in the conversation.

"Yeah, I think they're checking to see who can already fight and who might need a little too much training to be useful right now," I explain, hooking a thumb over my shoulder.

"Do you think they'd let me join too?" Cam asks as I reach into the back of the wagon.

"Uhhh…" I panic, not sure what I should say.

"Absolutely not!" Marna quickly admonishes. "You're just a child."

"I am not a child!" *Well, whining like that isn't helping your case.*

"You're sixteen, which is way too young to be joining any kind of 'resistance,'" Jact joins his wife. "The only things you need to be worrying about are your school lessons and helping me and your mother with the family business."

"But I… Ugh." Cam goes silent, but I doubt that's the end of it.

"Go get cleaned up," Marna orders her son. "You and sister are helping your father in town today."

"We'll be there most of the day," Jact alerts his children so they can prepare accordingly. "We need to see if there's anything worth adding to our inventory while we're here, and then decide where to go next and plot out our course."

"Fine…" Cam stomps off to the well with Julie following much more gracefully.

Having had my fill of family drama, I grab my bag and head into town. Walking around the perimeter of the Timid Sparrow Tavern, I spot the public baths easily enough given the large amount of people crowded around the entrance. I really hope I'm not stuck here waiting forever.

It's just as packed inside, and I'm happy to learn that's because the owner is offering free use of the facilities to anyone in the camp—permitting that they don't take forever. There's a line leading to the more public shower room, but given that I really don't wanna answer any questions about the metal cage on my dick, I end up having to wait almost half an hour for one of the individual stalls to open up.

It's not the worst bathhouse I've been in. The showers at the one in Northlake don't get cleaned nearly often enough, and I wouldn't trust the bathwater. They always run out of towels, too.

I wash myself as fast as I can, forced to use my hands and the small discs of soap they provide, in a bowl just outside the showers. I'd give anything for a nice scrub down with a slightly rough sponge, especially if a pair of strong green hands were doing the scrubbing. The thought of them running over my body, grabbing my ass, slipping into my… I bite my lip as my cockhead presses futilely against the bars of my cage, willing myself to go soft again. *Now is not the time.*

All done at the bath, I return to the Hursketts' wagon for my equipment. Marna is off cleaning everything that was used to cook and eat breakfast, and I spot Jact in the back of the wagon when I reach in for my sword, looking through a book with a pen in his hand. I don't see Cam anywhere, but Julie is watching her younger siblings and waiting for her parents, and I get an idea as I pull my weapon over my shoulder. Grabbing my wallet pouch out of my bag, I take out a handful of gold coins. *This should be enough, for now.*

"Hey, Julie," I call to her, revealing my handful of coins, "if I gave this to you, could you find a way of getting it to your parents without them knowing?"

"Of course, sir," she says with a smile. "Thank you so much—they'll appreciate it even if they don't realize it."

"Perfect." *Oh boy is it weird being called "sir."* "Thank you."

Before leaving, I turn to Sona, currently still laying by the fire. "Are you coming?"

She gives me a low bark, stretching her body but not bothering to get up.

"You're the one who woke *me* up." I swear she looks annoyed at me for even asking.

I leave the Hursketts to their devices and start to focus on my own. The way breakfast was cooked with care, being called "sir" by Julie, even my poor full balls: all of it reminds me of Khazak. I miss him. I miss waking up together, eating together, sleeping together—I even miss our stupid arguments! I try to keep Mikey's words to me last night in my mind, but I'm not sure how long I can go without knowing he's okay before I go crazy.

By the time I reach the Maname Guard's training camp, the action is already underway. A crowd is gathered near the open area just outside the central tent, and when I get closer, I can see two people fighting—one of them being Twyla, the gnome in charge of training that I met yesterday. Off to one side of the circle are a line of men and women, each holding a sword—other new recruits, maybe? And right next to them is a familiar face: Cameron.

"Shouldn't you be getting ready to go into town with your dad?" I ask after making my way over to him.

"I, uh—" He jumps nervously. "I just wanted to see the tryouts. But uh, maybe I should…"

He starts to slowly slink away now that he realizes he's been caught, and I lose track of him in the crowd. I probably could have taken him back there myself, but it's not like he's *my* kid. I shake my head and redirect my attention to the fight ahead of me.

"How long has this been going?" I ask the woman on my right about the current battle.

"Only a couple of minutes," she answers. "But he's doing better than the last two guys."

Their battle is fast and intense. It looks like the human tries everything he can think of to defend himself, but Twyla is just too quick for him, circling around and throwing him off balance. While trying to prevent himself from tripping and falling, the clearly more-skilled gnome knocks the sword from the recruit's hand and throws herself at his side, ultimately landing him on his ass.

"Not bad," she tells the man as he picks himself up. "Rough around the edges, but nothing a little training won't fix. You're in."

The man rejoins our lineup with a smile as his fellow recruits congratulate him.

"David, glad you made it." Twyla notices me at the end of the line. "You even brought your own sword. Good. Are you up for going next?"

"Sure." I hope no one gets mad about me skipping the line. "Anything specific you wanna see?"

"Nope, just want to get a feel for your skill level." We both walk to the center of the ring. "You've been trained in how to use that thing, right?"

"I have." I nod. "I was a student at the Northlake Academy of Knighthood for a few years."

"Never heard of it." She's serious, but her tone is at least joke-y. "Let's see what they taught you. Remember, we're not trying to kill each other but don't hold back *too* much."

"You got it." I take a few steps back and draw my sword.

Twyla sizes me up thoughtfully, twirling her own sword at her side. I know the height difference might make this fight seem one-sided, but trust me, you never know how these things are gonna go until they're actually happening. Even though I've done it plenty of times before, fighting shorter opponents isn't as easy as you'd think.

Dwarves have their own strengths (literally—punching a dwarf feels like punching a boulder—their bodies are *dense*), but gnomes and halflings are a different kind of tricky. Other species might have them beat on size and even strength, but they've got speed and agility on their side. There are also a lot more vital areas on the lower half of the body for them to aim at than you'd think of, something much more difficult to take advantage of when your opponent is half your height. Even defending yourself requires a different set of tactics, forcing you to constantly aim your weapons and shields downward, which in turn limits any opportunities for you to make a follow-up attack.

Even knowing all that, I doubt this will be easy. Twyla comes at me first, launching forward with a horizontal slash that I easily knock to the side. I try to surprise her with an upward swing, but she avoids it by jumping back. As we start to trade blows, I realize that she's just repeating the same strategy she used on the last guy, except this time it's not quite working because I'm much faster than he was.

I'm holding my own but not exactly winning. She wants to see what I can do, which means I need to get more aggressive. I start cutting her off when she tries to slip around me, forcing her on the defense. Then, after she tries to feint by jumping back, she quickly charges right at me—and I leap over her in response, turning to face her as I land with my sword pointed at the back of her neck.

"That was amazing!" she compliments as she turns around, and I drop my sword hand. "You said you only had a few years of training?"

"Maybe a little more than that." *There was all the practice with Dad and Joseph when I was growing up.*

"Whoever it was, they did a great job," she continues. "Would you gimme a second? I wanna try something. Syris, come here!"

I look around for the man, not seeing him in the crowd, though I do notice someone else: that Max guy who was petting Sona yesterday outside of the Moonbright Inn, as well as a few of his friends, including the cute, beefy-looking blond. *What?* I'm allowed to look. What are they doing here? Most of them look like they can fight, so maybe they're here to try out too?

"What did you need?" Syris asks his fellow guard once he finds his way to us. "Oh, hi David."

"Grab a weapon." Twyla points at a weapon rack and turns back to me. "Are you up for another round? Two on one?"

"Uh, sure." *If that's what they want…* "Could I get a second sword, though?"

"How's this one?" Syris hands me a sword after grabbing an axe for himself.

"Alright everyone, back up!" Twyla shouts to the crowd, miming pushing them away with her hands. "We're gonna need more room."

I test the new weapon in my left hand, getting a feel for its weight and balance. It's nothing fancy, and it should suit me just fine for what I need, but it is a reminder that I still need to get a replacement for my own. Satisfied and with the area cleared, the three of us get into our starting positions, with them on one side of the circle and me on the other.

They split up as soon as our match begins, which is exactly what I would have expected them to do because it's exactly what I would do. I feel like I've almost gotten used to fighting multiple opponents at once lately, so having it be just the two of them almost feels *too* easy. I try to move backward, not wanting them to flank me and limit my defenses, but I don't have a ton of room.

I'm brought back to the woods outside V'roh'sh Tah'lj, to the day Khazak and I were attacked by a trio of hungry wolves. We were spending the week on patrol in the forest with the other rangers, and thanks to some slipper grass and the unlucky placement of some poisonous flowers, Khazak was out of commission. I was forced to defend the both of us with only the trunk of the tree at his back to protect us. It wasn't easy, but I did it then, and I can do it now.

Knowing that I can't hold on to my defense much longer, I step toward the center of the ring and let them both move around me, thinking they've got me trapped between them. With a sword in each hand, I'm able to deflect their blows from both sides, but it requires almost all of my focus which doesn't leave me room or time to make any counter attacks. But that's what I'm hoping they are focused on too.

After figuring out the timing of their strikes, I wait for the moment they both sync up and come at me together to leap backward. They try to avoid hitting each other instead and pull back, but they're forced to turn out of the other's way and end up overcorrecting. That puts them off-balance and leaves themselves wide open for my response.

I aim for Twyla first, hip-checking her in the shoulder and knocking her away as she tumbles to the ground. Before she can get up, I turn and charge at Syris. He's better with an axe than I expected, actually proving a decent match and meeting most of my blows. It's enough to actually start frustrating me a little bit, and as I start to concentrate, I notice a familiar feeling flowing through my body—and the next time my sword meets his axe, it hits it with enough force to knock it clear from his hands and high into the air.

"Oh shit!" Syris exclaims as the three of us—along with the rest of the crowd—watch his axe go flying. It shoots entirely over the camp and lands somewhere in the forest on the town's outskirts with a barely audible *thud*. *Hopefully no one was out there...*

"What was that?" Twyla is the first to ask. "That kind of strength, it had to be magic, right?"

"Uh, not exactly." *How do I explain this?* "It *is* magic, but I'm not a spellcaster. It's just sort of … a thing I can do."

"*How* did you do it?" is her next question. "And can you do it *again?*"

"I can try?" I offer, suddenly nervous. "I'm not really able to make it happen consistently at the moment."

"Really? Damn," Syris says next.

"Gotta say, that doesn't seem very useful." We all turn—once again, including most of the crowd—to look at who else but Max, who at least has the good sense to look sheepish at the attention he's called to himself with that unnecessary comment. The blond at his side looks like he would rather be anywhere else.

"Thanks for the info," I snark and roll my eyes. "Hadn't considered that."

"That kind of strength *would* be very useful," Twyla pulls everyone's attention back to her. "But even without it, you did great. You'll be an excellent addition to the team. Welcome to the resistance."

"Happy to be here." A small cheer goes through the crowd, but I still can't help but feel like I just screwed up. I mean, I guess I'm glad it's still something I can do, but I almost wish it hadn't happened at all because now everyone is going to expect it again. *Why can't I figure out how to get it to work?*

"So, I can already tell that the training I'll be running today is going to be way too simple for you," Twyla continues. "But I could use your help starting tomorrow. I'm going to start us on some group drills, and I'd like your help demonstrating things. Think you could come back then?"

"Yeah, totally. Sounds good." I nod, despite feeling like I'm being dismissed. "I'll see you then."

"See you." Twyla confirms before turning to the line-up of recruits. "Alright, who's next?"

No one volunteers, so she just calls one of them over as I make an exit, pushing my way through the crowd, and making sure to give that black-haired asshole a glare while I do it. I don't have anything else on my schedule today and only one thing on my mind: getting my stupid fucking super-strength to work. I never asked for it, and after everything I've had to deal with since getting it, the least it could do is *help me* and work when I actually fucking need it to.

At least the forest is quiet. I walk through the trees until I can find one with a thick, sturdy-enough looking trunk for my needs. Standing before it, I close my eyes, raise my sword, and attack. Again, and again, and again. I'm not trying to hack away or cut down the tree. I'm trying to force my strength to work.

I strike at the tree again and again, all the while thinking of my friends being captured and rescuing them. I focus on the danger they're in right now, the danger they were in in the weeks before that, anything to trigger it. But all I'm really doing is hurting a plant and sending wood chips into the air. *After everything I've done in the past two months, why can't I do* this?! In a fit of frustration, I throw the sword to the ground, pull back my fist, and punch the tr—*OWW FUCK!*

"That looks like it hurts." After hearing the surprise voice, I turn to see Max and the blond man at his side not far from me and getting closer. *Why didn't I hear them approaching?* "Is that some new type of training technique I'm unfamiliar with?"

"Is there something I can help you with?" I ask in clear annoyance, ignoring the throbbing pain in my injured hand.

"Ah, well…" He actually looks bashful for once but doesn't speak again until the blond elbows him in the side. "I wanted to apologize. I think we may have gotten off on the wrong foot."

"Uh-huh." I narrow my eyes, not disagreeing but not sure I care enough to accept.

"I'm Max, and this is my … partner, Peter." He nods his head toward the blond while holding his hand out for me to shake.

"I'm David," I reply after staring at it for a moment. I start to reach out to take it when we both see the blood on the back of my hand. "Sorry."

"Are you okay?" Peter asks, looking from my hand to the poor hacked at tree. "What were you trying to do, anyway?"

"Can I assume it was related to the feat of strength you pulled during that fight?" Max sounds intrigued. "Because it was very impressive."

"Yeah, kinda," I admit. "But like you said, it's not exactly useful if I can't do it consistently."

"I'm sorry for that, too." Max grimaces at himself. "I have a tendency to run my mouth without meaning to."

"It's fine," I relent and decide to let him off the hook. "I … actually have a bad habit of doing the same thing. I don't usually feel this prickly, but the last few days have been really, really stressful."

"I can only imagine," Max sympathizes. "I feel for everyone who's had to flee from Maname."

"So, your strength: how *does* it work?" Peter asks next. "You said it was magic?"

"Yeah, but it's not like casting a spell," I clarify. "It's… It's a really long and complicated story."

"Well, we've got plenty of time, and a first aid kit we could use to clean up that hand of yours," Max offers. "Would you like to come back to our tent and tell us about it? Maybe we can help."

I have to think about the offer for a moment. They seem nice enough (now), but I don't know these guys at all, and I'm not sure how they could possibly help me. But there's something about them that I have to admit is making me curious. Plus, my hand really does hurt, and I'm dripping blood everywhere.

"Sure," I finally decided with a nod. "Lead the way."

Chapter 10

David

"So, what are your stories?"

"Our stories?"

"Yeah, you know." I look at Max as we make our way to his tent. "Where are you from? What do you do?"

"Oh, right, that." He glances at Peter and then back at me. "You first."

"Alright…" *Does he look nervous?* "I'm originally from Lutheria, but I've been traveling around a lot in the last four or five months. Because of that, I don't really have steady work and mostly just take odd jobs whenever I can."

"I've never been, but I have read a lot about Lutheria." Max seems to have recovered. "The two of us are from Litkalaa."

"I think I've heard of it." Sounds familiar at least. "What do you guys do there?"

"Ah, well, we…" Max starts.

"Farmers," Peter quickly answers for him. "We're both farmers."

"Really? I wouldn't have guessed that." Neither of them dresses like a farmer, at least. "That must be hard work."

"It really is," Max says, already sounding exhausted. "But it's very rewarding."

"He's newer to it," Peter says it like Max needs the reminder. "But I actually grew up on a farm."

"I've only ever visited." It was on a school trip as a child. "So, what brought you here then?"

"Just … traveling." Back to simple answers. "Like you."

"Right…" *These guys aren't gonna murder me in their tent, are they?* "Well, I'm only *here* because I was in Maname when it was attacked. It's a long story, but I ended up here with the rest of the evacuees."

"Manamequohi was actually supposed to be our next stop," Max gives me a little more info. "But obviously that's not an option at the moment."

We circle around the perimeter of the camp until we reach a set of four black tents set up in a circle around a small campfire. They're big, tall enough to stand up and walk around in. Way bigger than anything I've ever slept in, and they look almost brand new.

I recognize the two people sitting around the fire from our brief interaction outside of the inn. They stand when they see us, looking from Max, to Peter, to me. Neither of them says anything though, even when we're only a few feet away.

"Ryse, Gala, this is David," Max introduces me to the two humans, a man and a woman.

"Nice to meet you." I shake the woman's hand while the man simply nods in my direction.

"Where are the others?" Max asks, looking around the camp.

"Thomas is speaking with the shipyard master, and Aria is dealing with the boat's captain and crew," she … reports? "Not sure how long we might be docked here."

"Hopefully not for too long." *So that* was *their boat.* "Gala, do you know where the first aid kit is?"

"Are you hurt?" Gala and Ryse both look at him concerned.

"No, but David is. He's with the Manamequohi resistance group and hurt himself training this morning," Max … lies and brags for me?

"I'll grab it now," Gala offers, turning to rummage through one of the tents while Ryse just continues to silently stare.

"Hi there." I give him an awkward little wave, but all I get in return is the smallest of eyebrow raises.

"Don't mind him. He's just like that." Gala returns and hands the kit to Max. "Do you need me to…?" She looks at my injured hand.

"I can do the bandaging," Peter offers, taking the kit from Max.

Max lifts the flap of a different tent, ushering me and Peter inside. If I thought the outside of the tents looked nice, the inside… There are rugs—plural—spread out on the floor, two big chests filled with clothing, a full desk and two chairs, and a huge cot. Like, you could *easily* fit two people in there.

Wait. There's only one bed, but the two of them have both been calling it "our" tent… Still standing near the entrance, I watch as Peter grabs a chair and sets it next to the bed while Max steps up behind him and puts his arm around his waist. *No, they couldn't be… Is* that *what he meant by "partners"?*

"Everything okay?" Max asks when he notices I haven't moved.

"Yeah, sorry." I shake my head, suddenly feeling more comfortable with these two. "Just … remembering something."

"Wanna come sit down?" Peter points to the chair as he sits on the bed.

"I appreciate this." I take my seat and hold out my hand as he starts to take things out of the kit. "Done this a lot?"

"Used to have to all the time back on the farm," he tells me as he pours a bottle of clear liquid onto a strip of cloth. "For myself, my momma, and my daddy. It's really easy to injure yourself without realizing it when you're workin'. Not to mention what some of the animals can do if you're not careful."

"I should really get a kit like that of my own." I suck in my breath when I feel the sting of alcohol as he cleans my wounds. "Not like I'm getting any less injured doing what I've been doing."

"You said you've been traveling, but what has you fighting so hard to get back to the city?" Max takes a seat next to Peter. "Can't say I've ever punched a tree like that."

"I have people trapped there." I take a beat to decide if I'm really gonna reveal the rest of this. "Friends and … my boyfriend."

That revelation gives them both pause, mostly Peter. He stops what he's doing, looking at me, then Max, then back to me with sympathy. I think that is a good thing.

"I'm really sorry," Peter consoles as he wraps a bandage around my now clean hand. "You must be so worried. Tell us about him."

"His name is Khazak. We've only been together for a few months." *Depending on how you look at it.* "He's… He's really great. Smart, kind, patient—which I'm learning you really need a lot of with me."

"I can tell he makes you happy," Peter says softly as he finishes bandaging me. "All done. Sorry, but I think you got some blood on your shirt."

"Really?" I look at my sleeve to see some dark red spots along the cuff. "It's fine. I'll just change when I get back to my tent."

Without thinking, I start to unbutton the top of my shirt as if I already had a clean one with me. It's not until I see Peter's eyes go wide that I even realize what I'm doing, remember my collar, and quickly try to close the opening in my shirt. Which only draws more attention to what I'm trying to hide.

"Interesting looking necklace you've got there," Max comments slyly.

"It's… It's not…" My mind is in a panic to think of an explanation. "It's just my—"

"A c-collar, right?" Peter guesses, stuttering as he puts a hand on my knee. "I-I have one too."

He unbuttons his shirt to reveal a golden necklace around his neck. It's made up of small chain links and wraps around his throat twice, a pendant in the shape of a wolf's head at the center. He then lifts the pendant to reveal the lock on the back—a collar.

"So, then you guys…" I look between them, unsure of how I should word this. "You're his. You belong to him." I point from Peter to Max.

"Correct." Max confirms with a smile. "I imagine our relationships are very different, but I *knew* there was something familiar drawing me to you."

"I thought you said that you just really liked his wolf?" Peter asks, making Max look betrayed.

"She actually belongs to Khazak," I reveal. "And we both miss him, a lot."

"So Khazak is your…?" Max allows me to fill in the blank.

"Sir. I call him Sir." I tell them both. "And I'm his pup."

"That's cute." Peter smiles. "You're his other pup."

"No, *she's* his other pup." I cross my arms, playfully defiant. "I was here first."

That makes Max laugh. "How did you end up separated?"

"It was in the chaos of the attack on Maname," I explain, my mood souring. "We were trying to help with the evacuation when he was captured by a roving band of skeletons. Yeah, I wish I had an explanation for you," I add after they both do double-takes.

"An army of the undead?" Max sounds shocked. "So it was a necromancer that attacked the city?"

"That would make sense." I hadn't given it too much thought. "I only saw the skeletons, though. Well, that and the dragons."

"*Dragons?*" Now Peter is the surprised one. "You fought a dragon?!"

"No, I ran away from a dragon," I admit with a sigh, disappointed in myself. "After leaving Khazak and my best friend in a magic cage surrounded by them." It doesn't matter to me that he was the one who told me to leave.

"I'm so sorry, David," Peter sympathizes. "That sounds awful."

"I think I understand why you were so angry at that tree," Max jokes.

"It wasn't the tree's fault." I laugh, mostly at myself. "It's not anyone else's either. I know everyone is working as hard as they can. I've just never been a patient guy. And it doesn't help that all I can think about is Khazak and my friends being captured or something worse happening to them. All I *want* to do is get back there and fight, but all I *can* do is sit around and wait. It's hard not to feel frustrated, especially when my fucking cock has been locked in this cage for almost a week now!"

"I'm sorry. Your *what?*" Max asks after finishing my rant.

"Your cock is in a cage?" Peter is just confused.

"Oh gods." I bury my face in my hands. "Could we pretend I didn't just blurt that out?"

"Oh no, I'm afraid I'm going to need to know more about this." From the evil glint in his eyes, I can tell Max is definitely a "sir."

"I'm still confused." Peter looks back and forth between us.

"I'm being punished," I explain to him. "Or I was being punished, not really sure this is what Khazak intended. Though I guess he did warn me I'd be in it for a while…"

"What exactly did you do to get in so much trouble?" Max is way too eager for more details.

"Your boyfriend is punishing you?" *That's* what Peter doesn't understand? "Why would he do that?"

"Why wouldn't he do that?" Look, even I'm willing to admit I can be kind of a brat sometimes. "He's Sir."

"Max has never punished me." He looks at his man with innocence.

"*Never?*" My turn to be shocked. "You must be *really* well behaved."

"Not once, but he's never given me any sort of reason to consider punishment," Max tells me while putting his arm around Peter. "Though I have a feeling we have very different rules for our relationship than you have with Khazak."

I mean that makes sense. I'm positive they've never even heard of V'rok'sh Tah'lj or avakeshes and kavans, but Khazak did tell me there were people "like us" all over the world. But still, no punishment? Peter's a lucky boy.

"So, Khazak punished you by … putting your cock in a cage?" Peter seems nervous to ask. "How does that work?"

"I've heard of them before, but I've never seen one in person." Max is almost vibrating out of his skin. "Would you show us?"

"*Max.*" Peter is scandalized. "You can't just ask him to show you his…"

"Uhhh… I'm not sure." I try to think if this breaks any rules with Khazak, but if they're only *looking*… "What's in it for me?"

Peter seems surprised by the question (just how innocent is he?), but Max takes it seriously. "What do you want? Money? I can't offer you sex."

"*Max!*" Peter buries his face in his hand.

"No, nothing like that." Mostly I just wanted to see what he'd say. "Let's just say that you owe me a favor one day. Don't worry. Nothing crazy."

Max silently considers my offer. "Alright, deal." He holds out his hand for me to shake.

"So, do you want me to just…" I look around the otherwise empty tent. "Drop 'em?"

"Works for me." Max sits back as if he was in a theater.

"Oh my gods…" Peter still has his face in his hands—though I see him peeking out between his fingers.

I stand and push my chair back so that I'm centered between both men on the bed. I unbutton the top of my pants and pull out my shirt—you gotta tuck everything in when you're fighting—before hooking my thumbs into both my pants and the jockstrap (no, I didn't go back to regular underwear without Khazak). *Here goes nothing.*

"Wow," Max muses after I strip myself from waist to thigh.

"Does it hurt?" Peter has finally dropped his hands and is now openly gazing.

"No, not usually." I look down at my trapped dick with a sigh. "It doesn't stop me from *trying* to get hard, and it's not exactly comfortable having my dick pressed up against the bars, especially in the mornings. But it's not too bad."

"And I assume Khazak has the only key?" Max is staring just as much as Peter.

"Yep, so I'm stuck like this until I get back to him." I pull my pants back up and tuck myself back in.

"I still don't get it." Peter shakes his head. "You … *want* him to punish you?"

"'Want' is a strong word." I re-tuck in my shirt. "It's not like he's just handing them out left and right, or even that they're that bad when he does. Usually, it's just a spanking. I know it sounds weird, but I like that he corrects me when I need it. And I … tend to need it."

"Yeah, I can see you being a handful." Max nods to himself.

"Is he always this cocky?" I ask Peter. It's not like Max can punish me.

"Uh…" Poor guy looks like a trapped deer.

"He's really never punished you, huh?" Peter shakes his head. "Not even a spank?"

"No." He shakes his head again, his cheeks turning red.

"Told you that you can't jerk off?" *That's never fun.*

"No." Even redder.

"What about like, tying you up?" I mean, that's not really a punishment, but now I'm just curious.

"N-no…" He's practically a tomato now.

"Like I said, our relationship is different from yours," Max swoops in to save his boy—as he should. "I really do understand your frustrations with the situation, though. We were actually only at the resistance camp this morning to see if we could offer any help."

"Were you guys gonna join up?" That was my original guess. "We should probably get back there then before Twyla finishes her 'tryouts.'"

"No, nothing like that," Max waves me off. "I was going to put him in touch with our—"

Peter suddenly clears his throat loudly, the two sharing a look and then going silent.

"What's going on?" I look between them.

"Nothing," Max assures. "I misspoke. We *were* actually going to—"

"I already know you're lying about who you are," I cut him off, crossing my arms. "There's no way a couple of farmers could afford a tent like this. Or the rest of camp. Or your … bodyguards?" I wager a guess.

"I don't know what you're talking about." Max gets defensive. "We told you, we work on—"

"Come on, guys." I roll my eyes. "I *literally* just showed you my dick in a cage."

The two men share a look and seem to have a silent conversation, but in the end, my argument wins them over.

"Alright," Mac starts. "But what I'm about to tell you does not leave this tent."

"Okay…" This had better be good.

"I'm not actually a farmer." *Duh.* "I'm a prince."

"A prince?" I'm not sure I believe him, and if I did, I wouldn't be impressed.

"Yes. The prince of Litkalaa." He pauses, waiting for a reaction.

"Uh huh." I cross my arms and narrow my eyes. "I've met dudes claiming to be 'princes' before, and they turned out to be pricks."

"He's not lying." Peter gives his word. "Really."

"Peter is actually my consort, and the people traveling with us are my personal guard." I'm still not convinced. So Max starts to think. "How can I prove it to you? I don't have my crown on me, but… Oh! The boat in the harbor?"

"The one with the wolf motif?" I remember it. "I figured that was yours."

"Werewolf actually," Max corrects me. "As in, the royal werewolves who rule Litkalaa. My parents and one day me."

"Werewolves?" *That's* why Litkalaa sounded so familiar! "Where exactly were you headed after you landed in Maname?"

"I'm not sure why that's—"

"Richardton?" I ask and watch their surprised reactions.

"I thought it was pronounced 'Richard*town*,' but yes," Max confirms with a suspicious look. "How did you know that?"

"I met someone when I was there. A werewolf." *Fuck, what was that guy's name?* "My friends rescued him."

"Uncle Achak?" Max asks next.

"Maybe?" That sounds kinda right. "I don't remember his name, but he was a knight, an important one I think?"

"That has to be him." Peter looks excited. "Was he okay?"

"We left him better than we found him." I'm not really sure how to describe his state without it sounding like a horror story. "He was recovering well when we left him. That was a little over a week ago."

"We're on our way to pick him up," Max finally admits. "Or were, before we got stuck here. The plan was to land just outside of Maname and travel to Richardton by horseback."

"I mean, Venzor and the other ports on the mainland are empty, but you could still probably dock there," I point out. "You don't have to be stuck here like me."

"No, that wouldn't feel right." Max shakes his head. "Litkalaa conducts a lot of trade with Maname and has considered them our allies for a long time."

"That's great!" Not having the manpower was one of Syris and Twyla's biggest concerns. "What did they say when you told them?"

"Well, I haven't talked to them yet," he admits.

"What? Why not?" That's a pretty big thing to forget to do.

"Well, you seemed upset after my comment, and Peter wanted me to apologize to you…" Max defends, looking at his "consort."

"Seriously?" I look at them both in disbelief.

"To be fair, I didn't tell him to do it right *then*," Peter defends himself.

"Look, I appreciate it, but that could help end all of this." I look toward the door. "We should get back there."

"Alright." Max stands, helping Peter up as well. "Lead the way."

When we arrive back at resistance headquarters, Twyla can be seen downfield outside of camp where she's training with all of the new recruits. And judging from their form, she has her work cut out for her. Without a door to knock on, we let ourselves into the central tent.

"Hello, Syris," I announce myself to the older man currently reading over a stack of papers.

"Oh, David," he answers after looking up, "is there something I can help you with?"

"Actually, I'm here to help you." I step aside, allowing Max to approach.

"Makseka Blackclaw, Crown Prince of Litkalaa. Pleasure to meet you." He holds out his hand for Syris to take. "I can't officially speak for my father, but I'd still like to offer our assistance in liberating Manamequohi."

"You… The prince?" Syris's eyes are wide as he looks the man up and down while shaking his hand. "Sir… Your Highness… Thank you!" He then turns to me. "And thank you for bringing him to us."

"That's not the only thing," I tell him next. "Probably less of a big deal, but I know that the heads of the Arcane Institute in Kirinyaga are also interested in helping if you can get in touch with them somehow."

"Who the hell are you, to be so well connected?" he asks with a smile, so I know it's not hostile.

"Just lucky, I guess?" I scratch the back of my head.

"Lucky for us you mean." He's pleased. "We've been working with the office in town, but they've only got two trained 'grammers in town. They've even been extending their hours for us to send late night communications, but we're talking to the guild about getting someone else out here to help."

We spend the next couple of hours making arrangements and planning. Well, most of the others do; I just stand back and watch really. It's not that I don't want to help. There's just not much for me to do. Everyone else here knows about diplomacy and military tactics and communication. I just swing a sword around.

At least it's not *just* me: Peter's been right next to me the whole time, as involved as I am. I'm not that surprised though. He's got the right build for it, but with his gentle personality, I just don't see him as much of a fighter. I guess "consorts" probably don't see much battle.

Eventually everyone else finishes what they needed (for now), with Syris heading to the town's spell-o-gram office to work out specifics with the guild. It's late in the afternoon, and I didn't even realize, but we worked straight through lunch. I still need to go into town for some shopping so I can just grab some food while I'm there.

"David, just a second." Max catches up with me as I leave the tent. "Will you come back with us to our tent?"

"Everything alright?" I ask as he and Peter start to lead me.

"Absolutely." Max nods his head. "There's just something I'd like to give you. Both to apologize for earlier and as a thank you for helping with Uncle Achak."

"Oh, thanks, but I don't need anything," I try to decline.

"Nonsense. I insist," he insists.

We get back to their small camp, where after greeting his campmates, Max brings me back into the tent he shares with Peter. He moves to one of the open chests and bends over to rummage through it. Peter just stares, clearly having no idea what Max is doing.

"Found it!" Max stands holding a small black silk bag above his head. "I thought you might find this useful."

"Thanks, Max." I accept the bag. Whatever is inside feels solid and a little heavy. "I'm sure I'll…" I open and then quickly close the bag, my cheeks burning with embarrassment after seeing my "gift."

"What is it?" Peter asks, confused after seeing my reaction.

"Nothing I need." I try to hold the bag out for Max to take back.

"From what you were telling me earlier, that seems like exactly what you could use right now." He turns to Peter. "It's a dildo."

"It's a *what*?!" Peter is more scandalized than I am. "Max, you can't just give him a… Why did you even have a…" He can't even finish his sentences.

"I mean, I had it for the two of us," Max responds without shame. "And of course I can give it to him. You saw the cage. He needs it. Besides, it's brand new."

"I… I really…" Okay, *maybe* I'm having some second thoughts. "Thanks."

"Attaboy," Max praises me with a grin. "I hope that helps until we can get you back with your sir."

"Thanks," I repeat a little dumbly. "I'm just gonna…" I point behind me and slip out of the tent.

I don't say anything to anyone as I exit their camp, just tuck the bag with the sex toy under my arm. Gods, I hope no one asks me what this is. How do I even use it? I mean, I know how to *use* it, but where would I even be able to bring it? Just the sight of the Hursketts' wagon makes me shudder.

I grab my bag, stuffing my "gift" inside, and pulling out a shirt to change before returning to Kiweni proper. As I walk around trying to find a store that might sell camping supplies, I pass the public baths and notice that it is significantly less busy at this time—which maybe gives me an idea.

I try to hide it, but I know I seem nervous when I ask to use the showers, specifically one of the private stalls. With fewer people here, there are less restrictions on time, and I'm hoping that'll be enough. I feel like everyone is staring at me and knows exactly what I'm here to do, even though that's crazy and impossible. Still doesn't stop me from looking awkward as hell as I stiffly walk to my stall, my bag slung over my shoulder.

I step inside and quickly close the curtain behind me, hanging my bag and towel on two of the metal hooks screwed into the wall. Then I turn on the shower, hoping the sound of the running water will mask the noise of what it is I'm about to do. Even behind the curtain and away from anyone's sight, I'm as anxious as I was on prom night when my then-girlfriend tried to kiss me as I reach into my bag to pull out the smaller bag Max gave me, along with a bottle of oil and my cleansing charm. *Am I really going to do this?*

It becomes apparent that I am when I find myself holding the charm to my stomach to let it work its magic. I put it back in the bag and dare to pull out the dildo, finally able to take a good look at it for the first time. Like some of the others I've seen, it's made of dark, polished wood. It's not as big as Khazak, but I wouldn't say it's small either. Probably bigger than I am when fully hard—I think, it's been so long.

I warm myself up with just a few fingers after pouring a little oil into my palm. One quickly becomes two, and then three, and I very quickly realize that I'm going to need more. A lot more. I blame Khazak for making my hole so hungry.

I lube up the dildo next, though I have to spend more time wondering what the best position to get it inside of me is going to be. I start by bracing my chest against the wall, spreading my legs, and reaching underneath me to press the toy against my hole. It's slippery, awkward, and I miss the mark more than once, but after a few false starts, I manage to hit my target and have the wooden head pressed to my entrance.

I keep adding more pressure until it pops through my ring, hissing under my breath as I feel the stretch. It's been a while (for me) so I need to take it slow, at least at first. I start to slowly push more of the toy inside, inch by inch, pausing here and there to catch my breath. I'm not sure if it's the toy or the temperature of the water, but I'm already sweating.

I know I have the toy almost all the way in when my fingers start to lose places to grip onto. Instead, I press them against the toy's base, keeping it buried inside of me while I get used to the feeling. The stretch is nice, but all it makes me think of is Khazak.

And it's Khazak I start to imagine fucking me when I pull the toy back a few inches before pushing it right back in. I imagine his thick green cock inside of me, strong hands holding me steady by my hips as he drives it in and out of my hole. My cock strains in its cage, already leaking precum onto the wet stone floor.

"*Good boy*," I can hear him whispering in my ear, his tusks scraping against the back of my neck and making me shudder.

I fuck myself faster with the toy, feeling the pressure in my groin already starting to grow. I didn't expect it to take me very long given how long it has been, so when I finally crest over the edge of my first orgasm, I bite into my own wrist to muffle the noise. And then I keep going.

No longer satisfied with that position, I try a new one, setting the toy on the floor pointing straight up and squatting above it. Without needing both my hands to hold it in place, I'm able to ride it up and down, using my free hand to pinch at my nipples or tug on my balls, once again imagining it was all my Sir doing it.

It isn't long before I cum again, looking down to see a huge glob of precum, maybe even real cum, leaking out of my cock and down the drain. This position is great, but the one thing I can't seem to match is Khazak's speed. Yet.

Next I get on my back, pulling my legs to my chest. With the toy between my legs, I push it into my hole while using my other arm to hold my leg against my chest. At this angle, I can move it a lot faster, pistoning the toy in and out of my hole at a rapid pace. I release my legs to muffle my noises when I cum for a third time, which is quickly followed by a fourth and then a fifth, and then I stop counting.

I'm not sure how long I ultimately stay in that shower for, but it has to be more than twenty minutes. If anyone knows what I was doing when I exit, they don't say anything, and I'm a little too self-fucked out to feel paranoid. I needed that, I really did, but I'm sad to report that my ass is *still* hungry. The one downside to an anal orgasm is that they don't make you any less horny—you just want more and more. And gods, do I want more.

And there's only one green man out there who can satisfy me.

Chapter 11

Khazak

"**I'm just saying, wouldn't it make more sense to send** someone younger?" The question makes everyone around the table groan. "And faster, too?"

"I've been hunting and tracking for over a decade." I feel forced to defend myself.

"And I've been sneaking in and out of that park since before you were born." I am not quite sure that is what Onas meant to say to a room full of uniformed officers, but his point stands.

"We've been over this already," Yuta repeats herself with a sigh. "Khazak and Onas have already done this before, so it just makes sense to send them."

The three of us, along with all of the other "active" members of our safehouse, are gathered together near the Leather Rooster's bar. We are discussing plans to investigate what is happening to the citizens being brought into Paramount Park, a task assigned by Lieutenant Gwar herself. And as I have already infiltrated it once before, I see no reason we cannot do it again.

Things have been looking up since our rescue two days ago. We have managed to connect with two more safehouses, bringing our total to nine. With the assistance of our new friends, we have been able to alleviate most of our supply issues and move some of our more injured and infirm residents to more secure locations where they can be better cared for. And with Jace's addition to our number, Corrine has been relieved of her duties as our only healer, letting the poor girl get some much-needed rest.

It has not been *all* good though. We still have not heard from anyone higher in the chain of command, a fact which has the lieutenant very concerned. The rate at which people are being rounded up has not slowed down, and for whatever purpose, it is starting to feel as though we are running out of time and only delaying the inevitable. *So if we could get a move on already, that would be wonderful…*

"If only those two are going, why did you gather the eight of us?" another of the guards asks.

"According to our scouts, the necromancer was last seen leaving the city on dragonback three hours ago," Liss explains. Though she is still based in Safehouse 12, she has been working closely with us since reuniting. "We're going to take advantage of that absence and hit one of 'holding pens' that isn't too far from the park."

"And it won't just be the two of them," Yuta takes back over with a nod. "The eight of us will liberate the holding pen together, and then Khazak, Onas, *and* Jace will split off for the park while we bring prisoners back here. All of us will be long gone by the time he arrives and hopefully will be there long enough for these three to get in, get what we need, and get out. Are there any other questions or objections?"

Everyone is silent, particularly the man who raised the original complaint.

"Then get ready and meet back here in fifteen," she tells the group. "Dismissed."

"Way to take charge," Liss compliments Yuta as the group splits off.

"Thanks, I think I suits me," Yuta … *flirts* back? Onas and I share a look and leave before it feels like we are intruding on something.

"Have you and your brother had a chance to examine the amulet?" I ask as we walk to the club's stockroom, which the brothers have converted into a temporary workshop.

"We did, but we're still scratching our heads over it." He pushes open the door, and I follow him in. "The stone *does* seem to be ruby—at least part of it."

"And what is the other part?" I look at him confused.

"If we knew that, we wouldn't be scratching our heads," Wari grouses without looking up from his worktable.

"You just hate not knowing things," Onas chides his brother. "The ruby is mixed with some other kind of stone, one we've never seen before."

"It's fascinating, really," Dr. Tuvat, who has taken to working with the Bearfoots, adds. "The two stones seem to have fused together."

"And watch how it reacts to magic." Onas points two fingers at the amulet his brother is inspecting. "*Wahsaya!*"

A bright light flashes in the room, stronger than any light spell I've ever seen—enough to blind someone if they weren't careful.

"Fuck!" I hear Wari yell. "What the hell!"

"Sorry." I can barely make out a grimacing Onas through my squinting eyes before he dismisses the spell. "I just wanted to show you how strong it is at amplifying magic. That spell should barely be brighter than a lightstone."

"Just warn us next time, dear." Dr. Tuvat removes her glasses to rub both her eyes.

"We need to get ready to leave," I remind the gnome of our other obligations. "I am going to get my equipment. I will meet you with the others."

Once I am prepared and in my armor, I meet the others in the club's lobby. Our group of eight consists of Yuta, Liss, Adam, Jace, Onas, myself, and two other guards. Before we can go anywhere, we all line up for Onas and Jace to cast their defensive spells. Onas starts with a camouflaging spell, with Jace stepping up once he moves on to the next person.

"*Kyapema*," he says after placing both hands on my shoulders.

Similar to Onas, Jace's hands glow as he casts his spell, transferring that glow into my body. I suppress a shudder at the strange feeling flowing through me, but I know it is necessary for what we are doing. This spell is supposed to mask our presence as living creatures, hopefully bypassing any detections spells the necromancer may have set up around his camp. If we are going behind enemy lines, we need every bit of help we can get.

After verifying that it is safe, we exit into the bookstore and then outside. Things are silent on our walk toward the center of the city, the seriousness of our mission weighing on us all. The alleys and backroads we have been using to traverse the city are starting feel cramped and claustrophobic, the entire city a prison.

"Alright, we're almost there," Yuta announces, pausing and then twirling a finger in the air. "Circle up so we can go over the plan. Liss."

"They're holed up in a local diner," she starts to explain. "Grossman's Deli."

"Aww, I love that place," one of the guards announces to my left. "They make the best apple pie."

"The quicker we clear the place out, the sooner the Grossmans can get back to making pie," Yuta replies before continuing. "There are only two entrances to the building, both thoroughly guarded."

"Normally these undead bastards consistently overlook the same thing: anything coming from above." Liss points up. It has been a good tactic so far and is even how Wari and Corrine broke me and Adam out from one of these. "Well, that won't work this time. There's no way to get to the first floor from the second without breaking a hole through the ceiling."

"However, two blocks east, there is an alleyway with quite a few second-floor balconies," Yuta takes over again. "We are going to split into two groups. While most of you are getting into position on the balconies, Officer Tone and I are going to attempt to draw some of our targets from the building and into the alley, where you will get the drop on them."

"Will that work?" Onas asks. "Are they even aware enough to only send part of their forces? What's to stop them from *all* coming to attack and overwhelming us?"

"They're smart enough not to leave their captives alone," Liss answers. "At the very least, the head skeleton can't leave because they have to maintain the force cage."

"It's a risk, but I think it's a solid plan." Yuta looks over the group. "And if it starts to look rough, we've got reponiam charges. Any questions?"

"Uh, is there a reason you picked me to … draw out the targets, ma'am?" The elf who must be Tone asks with a raised hand.

"Because you seemed so eager to remind us of your speed earlier," Liss reminds him with a tight smile. "Anything else?"

"Then let's get into position," Yuta tells us when there are no objections.

After our lures leave us, we move as a group to our target alley, splitting into groups of two and making our way upward. Some of us have an easier time climbing up than others. I have never been known for my jumping skills. But after stacking some refuse, I am able to get myself high enough to reach the bottom rung of the metal balcony and pull myself up.

"You seem to be enjoying your time with this group," I comment to Liss, whom I am paired with.

"Yeah, it's actually been pretty nice." Her face brightens at the subject. "I feel like I'm actually doing something, more than just traveling on the road or sitting in a jail cell."

"I suppose that has been the focus of your energies these past few months," I reply with a grimace.

"Not that it hasn't been a blast," she tells me, only half-sarcastic.

"No, I understand." Liss always has been the first one to volunteer when I need help around camp or with hunting. "I am glad you managed to find a way to stretch your legs, as it were."

"Thanks." She bumps my shoulder with hers. "Now, uh, what do you know about Yuta?"

"How do you mean?" I tilt my head, confused. "I have barely known her longer than you. She seems nice, and it is clear she takes her position as the head of our safehouse very seriously and acts responsibly." I am sad to admit it, but even despite the close quarters, I have not gotten to know our hosts' personal lives very well.

"Look alive," Onas announces from across the alley "I can hear 'em coming."

Sure enough, Yuta and Tone turn the corner a few moments later, looking a little anxious but otherwise unharmed. After looking up briefly to confirm our presence, they move farther into the alley and then stop to turn and face their attackers. Skeletons are not exactly the fastest runners, so there's a slight delay before the group of ten finally catches up.

Tone and Raso inch backward, almost as if they might run again—luring our targets into a better position. Once they are underneath us, Liss and I both use one hand to leap over the balcony and get the drop on them, landing with a very satisfying crunch. For good measure, I kick their skulls against the building's stone wall to shatter them.

The eight of us quickly overwhelm the few that remain, scattering their bones all across the floor of the alley. While checking to make sure they are all actually *dead*-dead (whatever that means), I take a moment to examine their weapons. Just like the others I have seen, these are all old, dull, and even rusted. But even in that poor condition, where is he finding so many?

"Good job everyone," Yuta tells us all after we finish with our "clean-up." "Liss, how much of their force was that?"

"A quarter or so by my count," she answers. "I don't think we'll have too much trouble with the rest, but we should get moving before any of their reinforcements reach us."

"I'm sure some are already on their way," Yuta says as she leads us down the alley. "Still not sure if he's directing them from a distance, or they're somehow able to share and respond to information."

We run into a second wave on our way to the deli, and though we lack the element of surprise, we still have no problems taking them on. It rarely takes more than one strike to disarm them and a second to destroy them. It is hard to believe they could ever pose a threat, but when they number in the dozens or even hundreds, it is very easy to be overwhelmed.

The rest of their forces are already outside waiting for us when we arrive, standing stock-still and silent, a statuary of eerie, frozen gazes—at least until we reach some invisible threshold and they move into an attack formation. They have almost double our number this time, but I am not worried about our chances any more than I was before. Still in the pairs we first split into, we work together to defeat our foes. Liss trips a skeleton while I finish it off with the hilt of my sword, and when I deflect the longsword of another, she rushes in for the kill strike.

"Keep moving in, everyone!" Yuta cheers us on as we fight. "We've almos—"

Suddenly, a bolt of dark magic strikes her in the side, knocking her off her feet. My eyes follow the shot's direction, landing on one of the so-called "lead skeletons" standing in the diner's entrance. One of its bony hands crackles with necrotic energy as it raises the other to fire a second bolt, giving Onas and his partner only seconds to leap out of the way. There are only a few other skeletons left, so if this one is outside, they must be getting desperate.

"*Khazak*," Liss turns to me, her face and voice filled with anger and determination. "With me."

I nod and follow our new target as it steps fully outside, already charging its next round of magic bolts. Seeing us coming, it takes aim in our direction before firing. I leap to the side, the bolt singing the hair on my arm as it barely misses me, while Liss drops into a slide, recovering and back on her feet after it passes overhead.

Liss reaches the skeleton before I do, holding her sword high as she attacks. In response, the skeleton raises its left hand and projects a shield of dark-colored energy, the blade ricocheting off. But that still leaves its right open for me, and I slam into the monster, surprised at the way it is able to hold itself together when it hits the ground. Before it can react again, I grab its necklace, pulling the rest of its body up with it and stomping it back down with a boot to the ribcage. That finally causes its body to finally crumble, and through the windows of the deli, I can see the glowing cage inside dissipate. I pocket the necklace, happy to provide each of the Bearfoot brothers with something else for their research purposes.

With that skeleton gone, it's a simple matter of finishing off any stragglers. Inside are around twenty-five people, and just like the others, they seem to all be healthy and able bodied, men and women no older than their late 40s. They are all eager for the rescue, many already trying to ask after their families.

"Good job everyone," Yuta tells us as Jace inspects the small wound on her shoulder. "We might actually stand a chance at turning things around and taking this city back."

With no time to spare, we quickly free the captives inside the building. After being wished good luck by the others, our group of three splits off and makes for Paramount Park. Once we're no longer out in the open, Onas and Jace both recast their stealth spells, just to be safe.

"Damn," I curse when we reach the park's edge a few minutes later.

"He must have added the patrols after that first night," Jace gripes, peering around the edge of the building with me.

"That's what I would have done," Onas adds unhelpfully. "Not to worry though—like I said, I've been sneaking in since I was a kid."

"How?" Jace and I are both confused at the claim.

"Follow me." Onas leads us farther into the alley and down another block—to a closed manhole.

"The sewers?" Jace asks in disgust as he realizes what Onas expects.

"The retention ponds in the park all have drains that connect to city's sewer system," he explains as he squats down and tries to take hold of the manhole cover. "And under a bridge next to one of those ponds is a maintenance tunnel—one only people outside of the city planner's office and sanitation department would know about."

"So how do you?" I narrow my eyes at the shifty gnome.

"The park is where the city holds all our events and festivals." He makes a noise of triumph when his fingers finally find purchase. "And some of those events cost money—and when you're a broke teenager, you make friends with people who work in city hall to learn how to get around things like that." With a grunt, he lifts and pulls the cover away.

"And you're sure you know the way?" Jace asks, looking at the dark ladder warily.

"Like the back of my hand." Before anyone else can volunteer, Onas starts to climb down the later.

"Here we go, I guess." Jace shakes his head, sighs, and follows after.

"Spirits help me." With a grimace and a prayer (I have been making a lot of those lately), I am the third person to feel the cold, grimy rungs of the ladder as I climb down after.

I am gagging before I even reach the bottom. The smell is horrendous, and after touching that ladder, I have no desire to pinch my nose. This is one of the foulest places I have ever stepped in.

"*Wahsaya*," Onas casts a light spell on his goggles, illuminating the sewer from his head. "This way."

It looks as disgusting as it smells, but it is a sewer I suppose. Onas leads us down a narrow walkway that runs along the river of muck to our left. I can hear rats and other vermin scattering away as we approach and hope against hope that we will be out of here soon. When I see another ladder in the distance, I breathe a sigh of relief—and gag again when I inhale.

The ladder is much shorter than the last and leads to a very small hallway. I have to crouch just to enter, and anything other than single file would be impossible. But after a very short walk and another staircase, I spot a wooden door.

"We're here!" Onas says with pride.

"This just leads right out into the park?" It seems like it would be fairly obvious to see.

"It's well hidden on the other side." Onas presses his ear to the door and then slowly opens it a crack. "I think we're good."

We exit out into Progress Park, underneath a bridge just as Onas described. Closing the door quietly behind us, I see that the other side appears to be made of the same brick as the bridge itself. I cannot even tell where the "handle" is once it is fully shut.

"Which way to the camp?" Jace asks the of us, and I defer to Onas.

"Should be that way." He points west.

We carefully move out from under the bridge and into some nearby bushes before we can be spotted. Despite the red tinge, we are still much more visible during the day and move with even more caution than we did on the night of the attack. As we move toward his camp, it becomes clear that the necromancer has made some changes to the park's landscaping.

Holes have been haphazardly dug into the park's lawn everywhere we look. They are large, large enough that it has to be the work of more than one person; I think we have discovered what he has been doing with the kidnapped citizens. And the biggest one by far is located just outside the tents that make up his camp.

It has to be at least a meter and a half in diameter and is deep enough that I can only make out some of the civilians' heads, confirming my hypothesis. Skeletons are placed all around its perimeter, no doubt acting as "motivation" to keep everyone working. Aside from the giant hole in the ground, not much has changed since our last visit except an extra tent and a number of metal cages, no doubt where they are being held when they aren't working.

"Think we're safe here?" Jace asks as we take cover in some brush.

"As safe as any other brush," Onas notes as he removes his binoculars from a bag to hand to me.

"What are they digging for?" Jace wonders in a whisper while I examine the area.

"You mean what does the necromancer have them digging for," I correct him and venture a wild guess. "Is some sort of treasure said to be buried here?"

"If there is, it's the first I'm hearing of it." Onas shakes his head, flipping down his goggles and handing his singular eyepiece to Jace.

"Why not have the skeletons digging as well?" I ask, noting that they only seem to be standing guard around the hole's edges.

"Not strong enough, probably," Jace explains, peering from the bushes with the two of us. "The magic makes them mobile, acts like muscle to move them around, but it's got its limits. With undead minions, fresher is usually better."

"That is one way of putting it," Onas mumbles, mildly disgusted.

"I don't make the rules." Jace shrugs. "Making them move is one thing, but they're still just bones. Giving them muscles would be hard for even the strongest mages."

"Even with the amulets, it must be easier to use the living," I think aloud. "Are they … themselves? Do they know what is happening?"

"Nope." Jace shakes his head. "No personality or memories of any kind. *Those* kinds of spells typically require a much fresher corpse and a lot more power."

"Think we can free any of the captives?" Onas asks next.

"Not without getting caught," I answer. "But where is—"

"—going to be back soon?" I hear a familiar voice and spot a certain red-haired bastard exiting one of the tents, clutching a glowing necklace in his hand. "I just think you may want to speed things up."

"Who is he talking to?" I look around for someone that isn't a captive or undead.

"The skeletons?" Onas guesses.

"They're not really the type for holding conversations," Jace corrects. "It's not as if they can answer."

"Just get back here." A familiar annoyance bleeds into his voice as he releases the necklace, and it stops glowing. "Why do I always work with idiots?"

"It had to be the necromancer." It is the only thing that makes sense. "The amulets must also allow for long-distance communication."

"I bet it's similar to what the spell-o-gram guild use to connect all of their offices," Jace begins to theorize. "But it would take a *lot* of power. Especially if he's getting it through the barrier! The SOG offices are all linked to local leywells or other magical power sources, and none of that is getting through."

Suddenly, the red sky above us flickers out of existence for a few moments before returning us to our crimson cage. *Someone has returned.*

"I thought we had more time." Onas notes the same thing. "We should leave before—"

A shadow passes over us, and we all hold our breaths as we look up to see the large black dragon circling above. It grows larger as it draws lower to the ground, its wings blasting power gusts of wind through the park. It's different though—the saddlebags it wore before are gone, and it now seems to be holding a set of large metal cages in its rear claws. The ground rumbles as it drops each of them before finally landing itself, lowering and spreading out its wing for its rider to slide down. *The necromancer.*

"Finally," Redwish says, looking bored as he approaches the beast and rider. "Welcome back, Corbin."

"What was so important you couldn't wait another two minutes?" He doesn't sound pleased.

"I just thought you might want to know those holdouts at the shipyard finally responded to your offer," Redwish continues. "What do you think an exploding bag of dogshit means? At least I hope it came from a dog."

"*Godsdamnit!*" The necromancer lets out a frustrated growl as he throws back his hood. "Don't they see how *generous* I'm trying to be?"

Corbin, as he is apparently known, appears to be a man in his late 30s, though with necromancers I suppose that could be deceiving. His black hair reaches his shoulders, he has no facial hair to speak of, and in addition to the amulet around his neck, he has some sort of crown atop his head. It looks to be made of some sort of silver or polished iron, thin bands that twist and wrap around the crown of his head with a large stone that matches the strange ruby used in the necklaces set into the front.

"Yes, I can't believe they would turn their nose up at your hospitality." Sarcasm drips from Redwish's voice. "How much longer am I going to be stuck here?"

"If they would have accepted my offer and helped, we probably would have already found the artifact by now!" Corbin responds, stomping around like an angry child.

"I still don't even know what it is we're looking for." *He doesn't?* "If it's so important, should really be splitting your workforce like this?"

Splitting his… That offhand comment and the cages both give me pause. What is he trying to dig up?

"I'll know it when I see it!" Even with the light of the dome, I can see the anger turning his face crimson. "Do you know they've been *stealing* from me too? I am finished playing nice with this island."

"What are you planning?" Redwish sounds more curious than nervous.

"A few things, actually. Some already in the works." He turns somewhat menacingly toward his dragon. "But obviously I can't let this stand. I need to make an example and show them what happens when you refuse me. One that will leave them absolutely *burning* with regret."

"Oh gods, you don't think he's going to…" Jace starts, already sounding worried.

"We need to leave, now, and warn them." It is not worth risking him doing anything but the worst.

"This way." Onas leads the way.

We waste no time in turning around and coming back the way we came. We do not bother using the hidden entrance to the sewers, Onas and Jace using their magic to blast through the few patrols we run into. We cannot afford to waste any time if Corbin is going to strike.

"Jace, you should return to Safehouse 12 and alert Lieutenant Gwar," I instruct as we return to traveling the city's streets and alleys. "Let her know the situation and see if she can determine how best to respond. Onas and I will continue to the shipyard to warn the people to evacuate."

"On it!" With a confident nod, Jace splits off from the two of us to do as instructed.

The two of us continue running toward the shipyard as fast as we can when we're stopped again, this time by two small birds. I don't think anything of it when one of them flies back and forth overhead a few times, but when it makes a point of zooming past our heads and then landing on the ground ahead, the strange behavior gives us pause. We are prepared to run around it until the animal starts to change shape. It grows, losing its feathers and gaining a short body clad in armor with green hair, the second bird landing on *her* shoulder.

"Told ya we'd find someone," the druid says to her companion as she shakes off the last of her transformation. "I've been looking for someone *alive* to talk to since I got in here."

"You came from outside the barrier?" Onas is as intrigued by our visitor as I am. "How?"

"Easier than you'd think." She looks up at the dome of red. "It doesn't hurt to touch, so I just parked myself on top of it and waited for it to drop when that big dragon flew in."

"You just ... fell through?" I ask, looking up at the sky. "Who are you?"

"Officer Jillian Grassfield, Venzor Station," she answers with a salute. She *is* wearing the right armor. "And I come with news from the outside world!"

"That's wonderful!" I am ecstatic that someone from the outside has made it in, but even more so that she can fly. "But first we need your help. There's an emergency."

"The shipyard," Onas continues. "The necromancer is planning to—"

A loud roar cuts him off, and a shadow passes over us on the street as the dragon flies in a wide circle around the city. Letting out another roar, it flies lower until it is hovering in the sky, right over the southeast corner of the island—where the shipyard is located. Frozen in our tracks, we watch as the dragon cries out with a terrible screeching roar before unleashing a torrent of fire at the ground.

We're too late.

Chapter 12

David

It's hot. Like, really hot. So hot it feels like the air *around me could ignite my feathers at any second.*

Below me is a city that's been set ablaze, building after building on fire, the flames and smoke climbing higher and higher. People are screaming in the streets as they flee, drawing my attention downward. But not everyone is running away from the destruction.

Someone is running toward it. Someone with green skin. Khazak? It has to be. I dive down, trying to chase the figure as it runs into a burning building, flying into the inferno without a second thought.

I wake with a start (though thankfully not a scream), sitting up inside the new tent I bought myself yesterday. Even though the sun has only just started to rise, I feel hot and muggy in my new bedroll, peeling it away from my skin like a fruit rind. That dream felt a little too real for my liking. So I tell myself that that's all it was. A bad dream. *Khazak is fine. He has to be.*

I try to push it from my mind, but the dream follows me around all morning. Even the Hursketts notice that I'm distracted during breakfast, and I try to play it off as just being preoccupied with that morning's training drills. It isn't a total lie; there's a lot of work to do.

After I'm done eating, I say my goodbyes. Sona is preoccupied, having learned it doesn't take much to get the younger Hursketts to feed her tasty treats and has grown thoroughly lazy because of it. Time to head to the training field. This will be the third day of me helping to train the new recruits. Twyla is the one running the show, using me and a few of the others to demonstrate techniques and form before we walk around correcting and assisting those who need it.

So far, it's been going pretty well. I'm hardly an expert, but I have a lot more experience than any of these newbies. Mostly I'm just happy to actually be doing *something* besides sitting on my ass waiting. Though if you ask me (and no, nobody has), it's still not going as fast as I'd like.

"Careful," I tell a man, catching him after he nearly loses his balance while practicing a sword strike.

"Thanks," he says, embarrassed.

"You're putting too much force behind your swings," I tell him. "You want them to be smooth and steady. Keep your strength even as you're extending your arm. Work *with* the weapon."

I take his sword and demonstrate a few times on one of the makeshift wooden training dummies we've been using before handing it back and watching him do the same.

"Much better," I congratulate when he seems to get the hang of it.

"Thank you for your help, sir," he tells me a little too formally, especially since I think he's at least six or seven years older than me.

Today hasn't really been much different than the last two. The techniques are getting a little more advanced, but they're still pretty far below my skill level. Most of the recruits are making pretty good progress, which hopefully means good things for whatever Syris and the others have been cooking up. I know they've been in touch with Max's people, as well as a few others, but no one has really let me in on what the plan is yet. Or if there even is a plan.

"David!" *Speak of the devil…*

"Morning, Max." I turn and see the man standing at the edge of the evacuation camp, probably having just finished talking to Syris in the central tent. Litkalaa is supposed to be sending us troops! "What's up?"

"Was curious to see how things were going out here." He looks out over the field of trainees, several of whom are still struggling.

"It's … going," I respond, trying to sound positive.

"I'm sure everyone is doing their best," he replies very diplomatically. "Peter and I were wondering if you'd be interested in joining us back at our campsite for lunch?"

"Sure, that sounds nice." I nod then look to the sky to gauge the time. "We'll probably get a break to eat in like an hour or so."

"See you then." With a wave, he departs, leaving me to return to helping training.

Once we're finished for the morning, Twyla lets everyone break for lunch. I'm a little sweaty, so instead of heading straight for the werewolves' campsite, I stop by my tent to change my shirt. I've learned over the last couple of days just how sensitive their noses are, and I'd rather not offend anyone with my B.O.

I've hung out with Max, Peter, and the others for the past few days, usually in the evenings before dinner. So far, they seem like a good group of people. I mean, don't get me wrong—the Hursketts are great, but between the parents and the teenagers, we don't exactly have a lot in common. It's been nice to be able to talk to people my own age again.

The werewolf thing was a little strange at first. I mean, back home when you hear the word "werewolf," you think of a deadly monster, but after meeting Achak in Richardton, my assumptions have changed—and knowing these guys are related to him certainly helps. It reminds me a lot of what I first thought of orcs before I got to know Khazak.

I wasn't exactly sure how much of a secret their being werewolves was at first. I figure most people are probably going to want to scream and run away from a monster before they try to talk to it. But after asking for some specifics, Max and most of the others actually seemed eager to show me how they shift—which was definitely weird to witness at first.

What *is* a secret though is Max's royal background. As far as anyone around here is concerned, he's just a visiting ambassador for the nation, not its prince. I've kept my lips sealed, not that I can see any benefit to spreading info like that around anyway. Max can seem a little … prideful at times, but I wouldn't say he's stuck up, exactly. He's way more grounded than Calvinson was, though it does seem like Peter has to remind him of what life is like for us common folk at times.

"Hello, David," Thomas, a dwarf, werewolf, and member of Max's personal guard, greets when I approach their campsite.

"Lunch is just about ready," Gala tells me, standing by the fire with Peter where two chickens are being roasted on a spit next to a large pot with steam coming from the top.

"Smells great." My stomach growls as I stare at the succulent meat and crispy looking skin.

"Surprised you can smell anything at all with a nose like that." I wasn't a big fan of Aria's jokes when I first met her, but it's grown on me. She's like an even grumpier version of Liss.

"Good to see you, David," Peter tells me with a wave as he lets Gala take over the spit-turning duties.

"Great, you made it!" Max says as he exits his tent.

"I never turn down free food." I pat my belly.

"You and me both," Thomas agrees, standing to help Gala finish off and then cut into the chicken. Those two have probably been the nicest of Max's group, aside from Peter. Aria can be abrasive, but she's fine, and Ryse…

"Mmm," he grunts a greeting before taking a seat and waiting to eat.

The chicken is just as juicy and delicious as it looks, though the turnips and potatoes they boiled could do with some extra seasoning. But these guys seem mostly like meat eaters anyhow. *Just like Khazak…*

"So David," Max starts, still chewing, "I've been curious to learn more about your … abilities."

"The rest of us, too," Peter agrees. "If it isn't magic, where does it come from exactly?"

"It's a long and complicated story." *That they probably won't believe, but here we go…* "About a month ago, someone stabbed me with a sword. A special, magic sword, inside an old Olympian temple. And I … died. But then I came back. And now I'm different."

Everyone around just stares at me in silent disbelief. And I don't blame them.

"That wasn't very long." Aria shrugs.

"You're… different?" I can tell Gala is trying *not* to sound skeptical.

"Different how?" Thomas questions next.

"It was like what Max and Peter saw the other day. I was faster, stronger." I let 'deadlier' go unsaid. "But I couldn't control it. And I don't mean like how I can't control it now—everything was 'on,' but it had my body running on pure instinct."

"Sorry, but you died and then just 'came back'?" Aria shakes her head. "That sounds made up."

"I know. I've still got a pretty nasty scar, if you wanna see." I pull up the front of my shirt to reveal the bottom half of the jagged golden mark at the center of my chest. "It goes all the way through to my back."

Not sure I've convinced anyone, but Ryse at least *looks* curious and grunts.

"Death and resurrection aside, you said you *have* controlled it before," Max points out. "What happened then? And what about the other times that you couldn't?"

"I'm pretty sure the first time was because of, you know, dying, and the second happened after my friends had all been captured and someone was threatening them." *Fucking Calvinson.* "The times I've done it on purpose, though, those are much more recent."

"What does it feel like when it happens?" Max asks me next. "What do *you* feel like?"

"When I can't control it? Anger. *Rage*," I answer after some thought. "But in reaction to something. When I have been able to control it, it's been because I was able to focus on that type of anger—but it never lasts for very long, and it's only gotten harder and harder to repeat."

"Hmm." Max thinks as he chews and swallows another bite. "That doesn't sound too dissimilar from a werewolf's shifting ability."

"It doesn't?" Not that I would know either way.

"I mean, our emotions don't trigger our transformation, exactly." As Max speaks, everyone around is listening intently, especially Peter, who looks *very* interested. "But they *can* help … or make things harder. Full moon notwithstanding."

"How does it work?" I'm open to hearing any ideas, if they can help me.

"It's a little like what you said about having something to focus on," he says next. "Normally, shifting isn't something you have to think much about; it's always kind of sitting at the back of your mind. But as soon as I need it, I can feel the urge to shift just under the surface of my skin. Then it's just a matter of focusing on *why* I need it, letting that energy flow through my body, and then the next thing I know, I'm furry and fanged. But if I'm flustered or something is distracting me? It's a lot harder."

I'm not sure I would have compared me to a werewolf, but hearing him put it that way does make me think. "There are times when I can almost feel it, just out of reach. But it's like I don't know the right muscles to flex."

"Maybe the problem is that you're focusing too much on the anger part of it," Max offers next. "What if we tried having you practice with a different goal or emotion in mind?"

"Do you think that would work?" I'm certainly open to trying. "Also, 'we'?"

"Well I figured I'd offer our help," Max says nonchalantly. "I've seen how strong you can get. Could be dangerous if you were practicing with a regular person but not a werewolf. Probably."

Aria and Thomas's heads turn at that 'probably.' I'm not completely confident that what he's talking about is going to work, but I'm not going to turn down the help it's being offered. At this point, I'm getting pretty desperate.

"Okay," I tell them with a nod. "When do you want to…?"

"We can finish eating first," Max says with a wink, digging back into his plate.

We wrap up our meal about ten minutes later, followed by another ten of waiting while our stomachs settle. Then Max leads our entire group away from camp and out into the field, not far from where the others have been training. I still have some time before we're supposed to regroup for afternoon drills, so let's see what we can make happen until then.

"Alright," Max begins, walking away from the rest of us, "we'll start with some simple hand-to-hand sparring. Don't worry. I'll go easy on you."

"You're going first?" I'm kind of surprised that he's going at all. Doesn't seem very prince-like.

"Why not? I've been itching to do more than sit around and talk for days," he answers with a grin, rolling up the sleeves of his shirt, and I know that feeling well. "Now remember, anger isn't what we're aiming for here, not specifically. If you can feel that strength coming to you, don't try to force it. Just feel how you're feeling, connect it to what you want to do, and then let it happen."

"Alright," I respond, rolling up my own sleeves and following him farther afield.

Here goes nothing. With the others on the sideline, Max and I start to circle each other like old rivals. I have no idea what I'm doing here or if any of what Max has been telling me really makes sense, but I have to try.

I let him make the first move, dodging out of the way of his fist as he aims for my chest. I can feel how strong he is from the force of the air around his arm. *This* is him taking it easy on me?!

I spend the first part of our match on the defensive, scrambling to evade his blows. I'm pretty quick on my feet, but this guy is making me look like a newborn deer still learning to walk. I have to concentrate and regain my balance before I can actually start fighting back.

Not that it ends up mattering because punching him feels like slamming my fist into a wall. I'm probably doing more damage to myself than him! I'm pretty sure the wound on my knuckles has reopened, too.

The longer we fight, the more people crowd around our circle, interested in watching the outcome. What starts as a few turns into what feels like the entire camp watching us. I even see Cam on the sidelines, as eager as I've ever seen him.

"Come on, David," Max taunts me as the fight continues. "I know you can do better than this."

"I'm trying!" I complain as I duck under his arm.

"Well try harder!" He takes another swing. "Remember why you're doing this! Who you're doing it for!"

The coaching is starting to grate on my nerves, but I try and do as he says anyway. I think about Khazak, Adam, and all of my friends back in Maname. How worried I am about their condition, how angry I am at the necromancer for causing all of this and separating us, and how happy I'll be after we're finally reunited.

The memory of me and Khazak versus those wolves in the forests around V'rok'sh Tah'lj surfaces in my mind. He was injured and the two of us cornered, but I was determined to protect him and didn't hesitate to put everything on the line—and I felt so fucking victorious after I kept us safe. Back in the real world, magic ripples through the muscles of my arm, just as it connects with Max's chest.

Our spectators gasp when he's knocked backward and tumbles to the ground. Aria and Peter are ready to rush over and help him, but Max staves them off with a raised hand as he picks himself up. He stands with a grin, feeling the spot on his chest that I just punched. Even I can't help but look from my arm to him in shock.

I did it. I did it!

"Damn." He looks at me in smiling disbelief. "You got me good! Now do it again."

"Let's go." I can do this.

We start to spar again, and this time I'm feeling a hell of a lot more confident. Max has me beat in the strength and speed departments at first, but it doesn't take me nearly as long this round to find my footing. I'm actually *excited* about my prospects this time, and I use that excitement to fuel myself even further, imagining how good it will feel to sock that necromancer right in the face, and when that burst of strength returns, I knock Max on his ass once more.

"Seems like we may have solved your problem," he tells me with a cocky grin as I offer him a hand up.

"I think you might be right," I reply as he stands. "But I'd still like to get a little more practice in to be sure. You up for it?"

"I think between the five of us, we are." Max turns toward our spectators. "Ryse, get in here."

I spend the next hour fighting with the whole group—everyone except Peter, for some reason. We stick to one-on-one matches at first, but it isn't long before I'm able to take on two of them at a time. Of course, it's not like we're *really* fighting, but it's real enough for what I need. And our crowd only seems to grow, cheering each time I "win" a match.

It's like the opposite of what happened on the roof. Now it seems like the more I use this strength, the easier it becomes, and the more I realize I can do *with* it. I'm able to jump higher than ever, leaping straight over my opponents, and if I need a burst of speed, all I need to do is find something solid to push off from. I even let myself take a few of their hits on purpose, pleased to find that their fists practically bounce off me with barely a tickle.

Super strength isn't even the only thing I'm capable of. Before I even realize it's happening, my reaction times are almost instant as I dodge and twist out of the way. I'm faster than I've ever been before, like I've unlocked some secret state of flow where my body is moving almost automatically as I dance between my opponents.

But it only works when I'm paying enough attention to get it to work. At one point, Peter sneezes, which surprises me, and everything is gone in an instant—which unfortunately means one of Gala's fists hits my shoulder, and it's finally my turn to get knocked on my ass.

"Oh gods, I'm so sorry!" she quickly apologizes after rushing over to help me up.

"Nono, 'sokay," I assure her, rubbing my shoulder. "I mean, oww, but it's good to know my limits, right?"

"I'd say that went great," Max agrees with me as everyone comes in. "In fact, I think this calls for some celebrating. You like beer?"

"As much as anyone." Although it is still pretty early in the day… "But I'm supposed to get back to help with training."

"Aww, come on." He frowns, and it's pretty effective. "I'm sure they can survive without you for one afternoon. This was a big deal!"

"I'll say." I turn to see Twyla exiting the crowd that has started to disperse now that the show has ended. "That was impressive. Seems like you figured out those abilities of yours."

"Getting there." I don't want to oversell myself. "These guys have been a big help with practicing. But we're done, so I can head back to help with—"

"Go ahead and take the rest of day off." She cuts me off with a raised hand. "If this group can get you to do that on the battlefield, then I say you focus on training with them."

"If you're sure." I feel like I'm getting demoted for some reason. "I still want to help however I can."

"And you will, by kicking that necromancer's ass." She nods her head, sizing me up. "Come by in the morning. You can help with warmups, and maybe I can come up with a few new drills just for you…"

"I'll be there." Not really sure I like the sound of those drills, but practice makes perfect I guess.

"See? Everyone wins!" Max's smile brightens in an instant. "Thomas, do we still have that keg?"

"We should," he answers, looking toward the campsite.

It's a pretty decent sized keg that Thomas has no problem carrying and setting down. I wonder if I'll be able to lift stuff like that with ease one day. Aria is right behind him with mugs and the stopcock, which Thomas uses to tap it.

"So, do you feel like you have a handle on how things work now?" Max asks as they start filling our glasses.

"I'm still gonna want to practice a lot, but yeah, I think so." I nod. "I owe you one."

"Don't worry about it. I'm happy we could help you figure it out." He grins and accepts a mug from Aria. "And we'd be happy to give you a hand with that practice too."

"Can't wait." Gotta make sure I work out all the kinks before we return to Maname.

"That was really impressive out there," Peter tells me as Thomas hands me my own mug of beer. "I've never seen someone fight two werewolves like that, that wasn't *also* a werewolf."

"Thanks, but I'm sure if they were *really* trying to hurt me, I would have had a much harder time." I accept the compliment, but let's be real. "What about you, though? Not much of a fighter?"

"Err, no, not at all." He looks embarrassed. "I've never actually been in a fight before."

"Nothing wrong with that," I assure him.

I hope I didn't make the guy feel bad. I'm just surprised because even compared to most of the others, he's a big guy. I figure working on a farm while he grew up probably contributed some, but he's also got all that werewolf strength. So why isn't he using it?

"Alright, everyone have their beer?" Max asks the six of us before raising his glass. "To David!"

It's my turn to be embarrassed when everyone follows Max's lead, even Aria. I wasn't expecting all the attention, but I couldn't have done it without their help. I'm really glad Max turned out not to be an asshole.

The seven of us spend the next few hours just drinking and hanging out around the campfire. Stories are told, jokes are made, and I completely lose track of time. Before I realize it, I've had four mugs of beer, and the sun is starting to set behind the forest.

"Alright, I should get going," I finally manage to say my goodbyes once the keg is nearly empty. "Thanks again for all the help."

"We can figure out training time tomorrow," Max offers with a wave.

"Have a good night, David," Peter tells me, cuddling up to Max's side after having several drinks himself.

"You too." I put on my best smile as I wave goodbye and turn away, ignoring the pang of jealousy and sadness in my chest. I'd give anything to cuddle up to Khaz right now.

The Hursketts all greet me when I return to our own campsite, but I'm feeling a little too tipsy to hold a conversation, so I make an excuse about being exhausted from training and climb into my tent for a "nap." I check my vellum journal to see if I have any messages from Mike, but there's nothing new to respond to. Laying there and thinking about what I want to do next, I remember that I've had *four* mugs of beer, and I really, *really*, need to pee.

It's quicker to go out into the forest than find somewhere in town, so I speedwalk myself past the treeline. I don't have to go very far to find a decent spot, letting out a soft, happy sigh as I relieve my bladder against a tree. Then, just as I'm finishing, I hear what sounds like a moan.

After zipping myself up, I quietly and carefully stalk my way through the forest in the direction of whatever that just was. I hear another moan as I get closer, taking cover behind a thick tree trunk when I finally see two figures in the distance. *Holy shit, Max and Peter?*

It is, and right now Max has Peter pushed up against a tree and is kissing him like his life depends on it. He's aggressive, his hands running up and down Peter's sides as the poor flustered boy struggles to hold on. Fuck, it's hot to watch.

They keep kissing for a few minutes until Max suddenly drops to his knees in front of Peter. The poor boy can only look down in surprise as Max undoes the front of his pants and fishes out what appears to be a decently sized cock surrounded by a large tuft of blonde fur that looks lighter than Adam's. Max gives it a few small strokes and then leans forward to take the whole thing in his mouth.

Peter's eyes roll back in his head as Max immediately begins throating his cock like an old pro, one hand on the man's head and the other holding on to the tree behind him. This goes on for a few minutes until Max finally stands and wipes his mouth, grinning as he kisses Peter again. Then he has the two of them swap spots, leaning back against the tree while it's Peter's turn to get down on his knees.

I know I should stop, not stand here watching them like some kind of creep, but I can't help myself. Even with the toy Max "gifted" me, I've still been so fucking horny. I can feel myself trying to get hard and reach down to my crotch on instinct, but as soon as my fingers brush the hard, unforgiving metal within my pants, I know my efforts will be futile.

Peter is less skilled than Max, but I've still got to give him an A for effort. He's practically gasping for breath when he's finished, but Max doesn't seem to mind when he pulls him to his feet and returns to kissing him. I watch as Max's hands roam all over Peter's body, coming to a stop on his ass before squeezing him tightly.

Max turns Peter around, placing the boy's hands against the tree before sliding his hands down the front of his body. I see him fumbling with the front of Peter's pants, sliding them down when he manages to pry open the buttons. One of Max's hands then disappears into his pocket, pulling out—oh, a cleansing charm!

He brings the charm up to Peter's stomach, using it before slipping it back into his pocket. Then Max drops to his knees behind Peter and yanks down his pants, revealing his pale cheeks to the forest and me. With a hungry look on his face, he places both his hands on Peter's ass, spreads them, and dives in.

Fuck. I shouldn't be watching this. But I've been in this cage for over a week now, and I'm just *so fucking horny*. I can't help myself, and after undoing the front of my own pants, I slip a hand down the back of them. As I watch Max hungrily eating Peter out, I brush my fingers over my own hole and imagine what it must feel like.

I bite my lip as I feel the familiar tingles of pleasure that come from rubbing my hole. Seeing Max slobbering over Peter's ass just makes me wish Khazak were doing it to me. When he finally finishes and stands, his considerably sized cock hangs in front of him—though I'm pretty sure Khazak has him beat. When I see him spit into his hand to apply to his shaft, I pull my fingers from my pants and do the same (as quietly as I can).

I tug my pants down a little farther while watching Max rub his thick, hairy prick up and down the crack of Peter's ass. Peter looks back with a whine, gyrating his hips to try and catch the cock that's been teasing him. I push a finger into my hole at the same time that Max is able to penetrate Peter, the blond's louder moan hopefully covering my own.

And so there I am, fingering myself while I watch my two new friends fuck in the middle of the forest. I can't reach anywhere near the depth that Max can, but I do my best to match his pace, fucking myself in time with him fucking Peter. I have to add a second finger before long, and even consider adding a third, not getting nearly as much of a stretch as I'd like.

Peter can only moan and whine as Max fucks him faster and faster, pressing his ass back in time with his thrusts and encouraging him for more. And Max is more than happy to oblige, growling and holding Peter by the shoulders, his hips loudly slapping against his boy's. Gods, when I see Khazak again, I'm gonna need him to fuck me just like that. And in a dozen other ways.

I keep on finger-fucking myself, half bent over and leaning against a tree while secretly watching my new friends fuck. I consider stopping multiple times, but I can feel myself getting closer and closer to an orgasm, and I just can't. At the same time, Max's movements are getting jerkier, the knuckles on his hands turning white as he grips onto Peter's hips. He gives a sudden jerk, and with a growl, bites onto the back of Peter's neck, cumming.

I cum at the same time, shoving my fingers as deep into my hole as they can go and biting into my wrist to muffle the noises that threaten to spill out of my throat. Pulling my hand free, I lean against the tree and catch my breath, and I'm sure Max and Peter are doing the same. I can feel that the front of my pants are wet and sticky from all the precum I just forced out of myself and just hope it's not obvious enough for anyone else to notice when I get back to—

"Hope you enjoyed the show, David!" I freeze when I hear Max calling over to me. *He heard?!*

I tentatively peek my head around the tree and see Max smiling in my direction, still firmly inside Peter. Peter looks over as well, clearly more than a little embarrassed as his entire body turns red. At least we have that in common.

"I— I— I'm so sorry," I sputter, mortified that I was caught. "I swear I'll nev—"

"It's fine. Once I realized it was you, I figured being in that cage for so long meant you needed to blow off a little steam." He turns back to Peter at his front. "We really gotta work on your hearing though."

"It's not like I knew to listen for someone…" Peter is still red as he pushes Max off and pulls his pants up. "But, um. It's okay, David. I, uh, hope you had fun."

"I… Yes." I nod stiffly, unsure of what else to say. "I… I'm gonna head back and … give you guys some privacy." *Which you should have given them to begin with, pervert!*

"Have a good night, David," Max tells me as I turn to leave. "Don't look at me like that, Peter. You *loved* it…"

I can't believe I just did that. I mean, I'm pretty sure I haven't broken any rules with Khazak—we've never talked about whether or not I'm allowed to watch other people have sex, and I didn't *technically* jerk off—but I still feel weird. Can't deny just how hot that was, though. Totally worth a spanking.

Chapter 13

David

gain."

"Grrrr…"

I wipe the sweat from my brow and get ready for another round. For the last three hours, I've been dodging sharp claws and deadly fangs, all while weaving left and right through the trees. I've been training with Max and his werewolf friends for two days now, honing my abilities like a fine sword, and I'm starting to feel like an old pro!

Originally, we were doing this in the field just outside of town, but when we kept drawing in crowds, we figured it would be better to move into the forest. I think we were distracting the other troops from their training. I saw poor Cam get dragged away more than once by his parents.

Out here, we're free to really let loose. Unlike Khazak and the others, I never got the chance to fight a werewolf before, but now I can say I've fought *five*. Some at the same time! The more we practice, the faster and stronger I seem to get—which forces them to up their game again and again. It started with them changing into their full werewolf forms, and then they upped it by having me take them on two at a time—and I'm starting to run circles around them.

"Rrrr!" Aria growls on my right, coming at me with her claws.

I jump back and watch as she gouges deep marks into a tree trunk instead of me. No time to make a counter attack, though, because lunging at me from behind is Thomas. I leap into the air, landing on his back with my elbow when he passes under me. I quickly roll off him, sticking out a leg to trip Aria once I hear her headed my way.

"That was a quick one," I taunt as I dust myself off.

Aria grumbles something unintelligible, both of them glaring in annoyance from their spots on the ground.

"Don't get mad. Get even," I continue, dropping into a fighting stance. I'm ready for another round.

"How about we take a break for lunch?" Max suggests instead from the sidelines.

At the mention of food, my stomach growls.

"Guess that's not a bad idea." I pat my loud belly. "Think you'll be up for more later?"

"Yeah, we should be." Max nods as the others start to shift out of their wolf forms. "It might be time to try three on one."

"I'm willing to give it a shot." I smile at the man, politely ignoring the others' nudity while they dress.

Once everyone is decent, we walk together back to their camp. It took me a minute to get used to all of them just stripping down like that before they shifted, but I get not wanting to destroy their clothes. They all seem pretty comfortable with the nudity as it is.

Sona trots happily at my side as we exit the forest. I wasn't sure what she would make of the werewolves at first, but she seems to have warmed to them pretty quickly. She's spent a lot of time with Peter, who unlike the others has sat out all of our sparring sessions. I haven't seen him shift at all, yet.

"I'll get some food started," Thomas announces as we near the campsite.

"Thank you, Thomas," Max tells him as he adds some wood to the fire.

Thomas and Aria seem to do the most of the cooking in this group, and they're pretty good at it. Not only has everything tasted great, but there's also a lot of it. If he were here, Khazak would probably make a comment about me eating almost as much as the werewolves do.

"Thanks again for all of this," I say a little later, before biting into a chicken leg. "Fo' the foo' an' th' spawwing."

"It's nothing," Max downplays, not even grimacing at me for talking with my mouth full. "Glad we can do something to help."

"I'm kind of surprised to see a prince like you eating and sleeping in a camp like this," I say after I swallow. *Calvinson wouldn't be caught dead out here.*

"This is nothing. Once a month I eat it raw." He makes a show of displaying his sharp canines. *Good point.*

"Excuse me, Pri—sir." One of the guards from camp comes jogging up our campsite, grimacing for almost using Max's title.

"Is everything alright?" He takes it all in stride.

"Syris has requested your presence in the main tent." He looks nervously at the rest of us, as if he's not sure we're allowed to hear. "It's regarding the, uh…"

"It's okay." Max tries to put him at ease. "Everyone here is in the know. Lead the way."

"Mind if I tag along?" I can't help my curiosity.

"Sure." Max is happy to include me, though I'm not sure the guard was expecting it.

We wrap up our meal early and make our way through the camp. The mood has shifted over the last few days, with people acting friendlier and more positive as their hopes for returning to their homes grow. Getting your hopes up isn't always the best thing to do, but it certainly has made things feel less depressing around here.

I see afternoon drills are just starting when get near the main tent. I've still been helping the Maname Guard with training sessions but in a reduced capacity. I want to be at the top of my game for this fight, and thankfully so does everyone else.

"Prince Makseka," Syris greets within the safety of the tent, and I manage not to roll my eyes when he, Twyla, and the other officers around the table offer the man a bow. "We've received word from Litkalaa on how many troops they will be sending and when: they ship out tomorrow."

"Finally." Max is very pleased by that announcement. "Then I guess time to start—"

Suddenly, two birds fly into the tent, startling everyone as they land on the ground near the table. Before anyone can move, one of them begins to grow and change shape—a druid, shifting out of animal form. A halfling woman—pukwudgie given her green hair—stands, stretching her arms out as the second bird flits up to her shoulder.

"Sorry for the surprise entrance, sir," she says as she salutes those gathered around the table. "I flew straight here from the city."

"Jillian!" Syris returns her salute. "Is everything alright?"

"I made it into the city!" she announces proudly.

"That's fantastic!" Syris asks, the mood of the tent growing even more hopeful. "What's the situation with the guard inside? Who's in charge?"

"Rough," she answers with a sigh. "Lieutenant Gwar is leading things at the moment. There's been no sign of Captain Dagek or any of the Maname council."

"None at all?" Syris looks dejected when she shakes her head. "That's not good. What are our ground forces looking like?"

"Gwar and a few of the other lieutenants had managed to open up and start working out of the city's safehouses," the druid continues. "They've got a decent amount of people and have been sheltering as many citizens as they can. But right as I got there…"

"What happened?" Twyla and the others go quiet at her reluctance.

"Some of the citizens had set up a small stronghold of their own at the shipyard," she sounds more somber now. "Gwar had extended an offer to shelter them, but they insisted on fighting back themselves. So the necromancer had one of the dragons burn the entire area to the ground."

"Oh gods." Twyla covers her mouth in hock.

"How many people?" Syris asks, more seriously. "Any survivors?"

"Around fifty were killed," she estimates. "Many more injured. We had only just finished the rescue operation before I left. I had a pretty small window to get back out."

"We can't allow this to go on any longer." Syris shakes his head. "We can't keep waiting."

"There's more." Though from Jillian's tone, it's something she'd rather not tell us. "He's kidnapping some of the citizens."

"*What?!*" We're all as shocked as Syris by that news.

"When I was waiting with the other scouts for an opening, the dragon he was riding was carrying two large cages," she starts to explain. "And when I was leaving, he flew out with them filled with people."

"Where is he taking them?" Twyla points to a map on the table as though Jillian should mark it. "What is he doing with them?"

"We don't know yet." Jillian shakes her head. "Some of the scouts flew off to follow him, but that was at the same time I left. And he's powerful. And riding a dragon."

"We have to stop him before he can take anyone else," Syris says with conviction. "Do we at least know which direction he was headed?"

"West," the druid answers. "We'll know more once the other scouts return."

"Then we can come up with a plan," Syris assures her and himself.

"At least we can get messages in and out of the city now," she tries to be positive. "It was easier getting in than out, but as long as you keep an eye on the dragons, it's doable."

"Not for an entire army, though," Syris muses depressingly. "We need someone on the inside to disable the dome. Twyla, where's that diagram on the dome's enchantment array?"

There's a brief pause in the conversation, so I take the opportunity to step a little closer to the table. I know it's a long shot, and I know there are bigger things to talk about, but I can't help it. I need to ask Jillan something.

"Um, hi," I call for her attention once I'm close enough. "I'm one of the new recruits."

"Nice to meet you." She looks at me with a decent amount of curiosity. "Can I help you with something?"

"Sorry, this is gonna sound weird," I start, already regretting it. "When you were in the city, did you happen to meet anyone named Khazak? An orc? Green skin, tusks…"

"I know what an orc looks like." She raises an eyebrow as she thinks. "Actually… Are you David?"

"Yeah." I nod eagerly. *Does that mean…?*

"What are the odds?" She grins as she talks. "I did meet him, and he mentioned a David he hoped had escaped the city."

"He's really okay?" I immediately need to seek confirmation. "He's not captured or hurt or—"

"He's fine," she assures me in my panic. "More than fine, practically an officer in the guard himself from what it seemed."

"What about Adam? Corrine? Liss? She also goes by Elisabeth," I start to overwhelm her.

"I, uh, didn't really have chance get *everyone's* names." She gives me a look that tells me I should calm down. "But there was no talk of anyone in immediate danger. As far as I'm aware, your friends have been pitching in a lot."

"That sounds like them." I nod, mostly to myself. "Thank you."

"No problem." She seems happy to have made me happy. "Anything you'd like me to pass along when I return?"

I pause and think of a million different things, but none of them feel good enough. Or they'd tell Jillian *way* more than she'd like to know about our relationship.

"Just that I'm okay," I finally decide, "and that I'm on my way back to him."

"Will do." She nods. "I imagine I'll be headed back there soon."

"Oh, David," Syris seems to have finally noticed me, "good to see you. How goes your 'training'?"

"Great," I tell him happily. "I'm ready to fight."

"Good to hear." Syris spreads out what looks like a map of the city. "Jillian, if you wouldn't mind?"

For the next few minutes, Jillian grabs a pen and begins to mark and annotate areas on the map. While she does this, she explains the specifics to Twyla and Syris as they watch over her shoulders. And there's a lot.

"Done." Jillian puts down her pen. "It's mostly the southeast corner of the island we have under control."

"I see that." Syris looks over the large map and shakes his head. "And with those dragons around, it won't be difficult to lose it, so we need to move fast."

"In addition to the troops we're expecting from Litkalaa to arrive in the next two days, we also have a lot of volunteers from Rakaune, Pákannon, and other coastal villages," Twyla tells the group. "Even the Lutherian colonies are offering their aid."

"Maybe they're finally ready to start playing nice with the rest of us." Syris nods confidently. "But none of that matters if we can't get our people inside."

"Getting people in is easier than getting them out," Jillan repeats. "But even then, you've got a window of ten, maybe fifteen seconds before the dome is back in place."

"Obviously an entire army is out of the question, but what are the risks?" Syris cuts to the point.

"When I was there, we found animals that were stuck, their bodies half in and half outside of the dome." Jillian explains. "Fish and a few birds. My best guess is that they were passing through when the dome dropped and were still in its range when it came back up, locking them in place. None of them survived."

"Was it the dome itself that was fatal?" Syris confirms. "Any physical injuries?"

"No." She shakes her head. "It seemed more like they had died of starvation or stress. Poor things probably panicked when it happened, not understanding what was going on." Jillian pets the bird on her shoulder who tweets sadly.

"Not the way I'd want to go." Twyla grimaces at the image. "But if someone did happen to get stuck, we would *in theory* be able to keep them alive until we could get them out?"

"In theory," Jillian confirms nervously. "But I wouldn't want to test it."

"It's clear that the necromancer has hijacked the city's dome of protection." Syris stands over the large map on the table as he speaks to the entire room. "Without bringing that down, getting any amount of people into the city will be near impossible."

"Maybe we get boats waiting around the edge, but then what? Are they going to swim all the way to the coast?" Twyla shakes her head. "Even if they could swim that far, they'd be spotted long before they made it."

"If they even make it past the barrier in time," Jillian adds.

"It has to come down all together if we going to stand a chance." Syris points to Testament Island on the map. "Someone on the inside has to reach the enchantment array. If they remove just one of the relics powering it, it'll disrupt the entire thing."

"Easier said than done," Jillian sadly disagrees, and draws a big x over an island on the map. "The necromancer has kept one of his three dragons stationed on Testament Island since the start of the siege. Probably to prevent exactly what we're trying to do."

"Someone stealthy enough could sneak onto the island and around the dragon without them even knowing." Twyla taps her fingers together, as if devising an evil plan. "We could have the rest of the troops waiting in the bay. With magic, we could cover the whole area in a blanket of fog and then get everyone to shore as soon as the barrier is down."

"The necromancer would know something was happening as soon as it was out, but he'd still have no idea which direction we're coming from or how many people we have." Syris seems to be buying into the idea.

"But without being on the inside, we don't know who is actually capable of doing any of this," Twyla notes.

"And we don't exactly have time to go back and forth." Syris is fully on board. "We'll just have to pass our plans along to Gwar and leave that part in her hands."

"Then we'll need to work out the rest of this too." Twyla points to a map of the city. "Troop placement, timing, supplies. And that's before we even make it on the island."

"The ships from Litkalaa should be here by tomorrow evening," Max reminds them.

"Someone make some coffee. It's gonna be a long night," Syris requests one of the other guards. "Alright, regardless of where we get on, we should try and push the battle toward the park to minimize damage to the rest of the city…"

I eagerly gather around the table with the others. The more they talk, the more excited I feel. We're finally doing it!

I'll be back with you soon, Khazak. I've got a promise to keep.

Chapter 14

Khazak

"**You look like shit.**"

"Funny enough, I feel that way too."

Understandably, I have not been sleeping well, or much at all, after the dragon attack on the shipyard four days ago. When it happened, the only thing on my mind was rescue. While our new friend Jillian took off to find more help, Wari and I ran toward the blaze to try and evacuate everyone we could. It was a grim scene inside, the flames climbing so high I could swear we had opened a mouth to hell.

Even after help arrived, putting out the blaze was no easy task. Rain cannot penetrate the barrier, and creating water inside is no easy task, forcing the few druids and shamans we had to siphon it directly from the nearby bay. I can only imagine what those implications might mean for the rest of the environment here and hope the dome will be gone long before that can become an issue.

The survivors were back to our safehouses and their injuries treated as best we could. In one of the few bright spots, we managed to reunite some of the abandoned children with their families, but others... Well, let me just say that overall, morale has been very low.

It was not all bad though. Jillian was a bright spot, not just for her personality but the information she had from the outside. Once the dust had settled, she was quick to update Lieutenant Gwar on the situation outside of the city and how their own plans for getting back inside had been progressing. Gwar shared our own information with her and then sent her off back outside the city with the intention of coordinating our plans with their compatriots. A lot of hope has been riding on her back for the past few days.

"Not sleeping well?" Liss asks me as we wait for more people to arrive.

"Not sleeping at all." I sigh, hanging my head. "Not for lack of being tired. Even when I can sleep, I have strange dreams to deal with."

"Yeah? What are they about?"

"I was in a forest of some kind." I try and remember more of last night's dream. "I remember black fur and dodging sharp claws. Perhaps I am just worried about Sona back on the mainland."

The two of us, along with Yuta, Adam, Jace, and Wari are in Safehouse 12. We received word early this morning that Jillian had returned, hopefully with updates on the world outside. Lieutenant Gwar has asked people from every safehouse to attend this meeting, intent on putting together a final plan to rid us of the necromancer once and for all. There was an undercurrent of nervous energy running through the group as our thoughts turned to finally being able to defeat him and escape this prison, but it was thoroughly tempered with caution—as though we are afraid to hope. This might be our only chance.

"Okay, I think that is everyone," Gwar announces as a final group enters the safehouse. "Let's get started."

"Between the people in Kiweni and the troops Litkalaa is sending us, we have about 800 people coming in from the north." Jillian references the northern bay on the map. "Then another 200 from the south, and 150 from the west."

"Won't that many boats be easy to spot coming?" one of the guards asks a very good question.

"Normally yes, but tomorrow night a very thick fog is due to roll in over the bay." Jillian hovers her hand over the entire island.

"*Tomorrow?*" Yuta asks, and several others also make shocked noises at the speed with which this is happening.

"You heard right." Gwar nods. "They're already on their way, so we have to be prepared for their arrival."

"Assuming we manage to get the barrier down in time," Jillian continues, "everyone will be trying to reach shore as quickly and quietly as possible. But once it comes down, the necromancer will know *something* is up."

"Which is where we come in," Gwar says to the entire gathered group. "Once he realizes something is wrong, the necromancer will send his army to try and prevent anyone from reaching the shores. So we are going to set up ambushes at strategic points along the way and cut them off before they get there."

"The incoming troops will then join us and help with any cleanup, and then together we'll make our way to the center of the city and the necro's main camp." Jillian points to Progress Park at the center of the island.

"What about the dragons?" a different guard asks another very good question.

"We know the dragons are another of his creations, so it is safe to assume he is controlling them in the same way he is the other undead—with that strange crown of his," Raso explains this next part. "If we can take him out, the rest of his army should follow."

"At the very least, if we can get a hold of it, we should be able to control all of his 'creations,'" Jillian adds. "Including, hopefully, the dragons."

"Hopefully?" another voice questions. "What if that doesn't work?"

"It may not be easy, but dragons *can* be killed," Gwar says with a firm look. "Hopefully it won't come to that, but none of this matters if we can't shut off the barrier. Someone is going to have to infiltrate Testament Island and disable it."

"How do we do that?" Adam asks with a raised hand.

"We just need to disrupt the spell array," Jace cuts in, ready to explain the specifics. "It's set up to absorb magic from the leywell. All you need to do is move some of the crystal geodes out of alignment. The hard part will be getting past the dragon and undead army that have been posted there since day one."

"Lombat, Virit," Gwar says to two specific guards. "You two are the stealthiest we've got. Are you up for the mission?"

"Of course, ma'am," the first man says confidently.

"You can count on us," says the second, and they both salute.

"Since we can't exactly pass messages back and forth with the people on the outside, we have to be mindful of our timing," Gwar explains carefully. "They'll be waiting for the barrier to fall at 22:00. It doesn't need to be exact, but if we move too soon, they may not have everyone in position, and if we're too late we risk them being seen. Either way, we lose the element of surprise."

After that, Gwar begins assigning roles and ambush positions to the other safehouse heads, leaving the responsibility of putting together a team to each of them. Yuta, and therefore the rest of our group, are being sent to the south toward the port we first used to enter the city. As soon as we're finished and everyone has their assignment, we start filing out of the safehouse to prepare.

"Khazak," Jillian calls to me as everyone begins to disperse, "I'm glad you came. I have a message for you. From David."

"What? Really?" My heart skips a beat at the very mention of his name. "He is alright?"

"In his own words: he's okay, and he's on his way back to you." She wears a pleased look on her face. "He was very happy to know you were okay as well."

"I… Thank you." I am speechless if only because I am trying not to cry. "Thank you so much."

"You'll see him soon, I'm sure." She smiles. "Now let's get to work."

We spend the next twenty-four hours preparing. After spreading the word at our safehouse, everyone began to pitch in, even the civilians. Weapons are sharpened, leathers are polished, and the guards even attempt a few last-minute drills.

Adam, Liss, Corrine, and Tsula were relieved when I shared the news of David's survival. On top of the upcoming battle, there is so much nervous excitement between everyone that I doubt any of us slept well. All I can think of is that we will be together again soon.

Our preparations continue in the morning and into the afternoon. The closer the hour draws, the more anxious the safehouse becomes. We have divided all of our capable fighters into two groups. While one will proceed to our assigned ambush location, the other will remain here to defend the safehouse and the civilians inside should the worst happen.

I am on guard duty, this time with Adam, taking a whetstone to my blade. We still have at least two hours before we need to start taking our positions, and I plan on using every second making sure I am ready. I'm just about to take a look at the strings on my bow when I hear the sounds of crashing come from the other side of the secret entrance.

"What was that?" Adam is already up, sword in hand.

"I'm not sure." I take up my own weapon and inch toward the door. "We need to alert the others."

Yuta, Onas, Wari, Jace, Jillian, and more—every capable fighter we have here at the moment—crowds into the entrance as best they can. With everyone in position, I inch toward the door and prepare to throw the switch. I hold the handle on this side to stop it from swinging out, wanting it to open it slowly and hopefully not alert whoever it is of our presence.

Then a skeleton steps into view and hisses at me.

"We've been found!" I announce, kicking open the door and charging forward.

Chaos erupts as I force my way into the main room of the bookstore, where at least a dozen skeletons are poised and waiting to attack. As we attempt to fight them in the already cramped room, even more begin pouring in from outside. We may be severely outnumbered here.

"How did they even find us?" Wari asks angrily while dodging a club to the head.

"Worry about that later!" Yuta orders. "Form up. Don't let any of them pass!"

As the number of skeletons continues to grow and our chances of survival shrink, a bright flash of light comes from the back of the room, so bright it forces me to close my eyes. When they open again, I see that the only things left standing are those of us with heartbeats. Behind us, Corrine and Jace stand side to side with a single arm out stretched, both panting from exhaustion.

"Nice work," Yuta praises the two priests before quickly looking around at the destroyed skeletons. "Now then: how did they find us?"

"Maybe someone was followed?" Onas posits.

"It seemed they were searching the store without any idea of the hidden entrance." Had I not opened the door, perhaps we never would have been found. "As though they knew we were around the area but not precisely where."

"But even then, if they knew where *our* safehouse was…" Adam trails off, letting his words sink in.

"We need to check on Safehouse 12," Yuta decides and begins point at several of us. "Khazak, I need you." She glances around, her gaze landing on each face as she says the name. "Adam, Wari, Onas, Jillian, and Jace—come with me. The rest of you start reinforcing our defenses here in case they come back."

With our orders given, our group of seven hurry out of the building and rush our way to Safehouse 12. No one says it, but I know we are all thinking the same thing: for this to happen when we are only hours away from enacting our plan cannot be good. He may already be on to us.

It is clear that something is wrong as soon as we reach the building that acted as Safehouse 12's cover, the door ripped from its hinges. Inside is no better; the hatch and stairs leading down have been utterly destroyed. With some careful footwork and a little magic, we're able to drop down safely, but the scene inside is even worse, bodies of the Maname Guard strewn about, and most of the furniture destroyed.

"Spirits…" I mutter as I take in the carnage.

"Checking for survivors," Jace quickly announces, raising his hand and casting a spell. "There, there, there, and there."

We split up, each headed in one of the directions he pointed to begin the gruesome task of checking bodies for signs of life. We find three breathing but unconscious guards, whom Jace quickly works to begin patching up. But we are still looking for a fourth.

"Over here!" Adam calls from the corner that used to house the barracks, lifting a toppled bed off of—*Spirits, Lieutenant Gwar!*

"Lieutenant!" Yuta quickly rushes to her side "Are you alright? What happened?"

"He found us," she answers with a wince and groan. "It was the necklaces. He put some sort of tracking spell on them."

"But the safehouse's lead-lined walls should have stopped the tracking spell from working inside." Yuta sounds as angry as she does confounded.

"Someone would still be able to follow the spells trail—right up until it entered the room." I sigh, realizing the flaw in our thinking. "We led them right to us."

"What happened to the others?" Jace asks as he begins the task of healing her with his magic. "There were a lot more people stationed here than I'm seeing on the floor."

"Kidnapped," she says with a hiss of pain. "We tried to defend ourselves, but they had us boxed in. The necromancer himself was with them, leading them and attacking. When he realized we weren't going to go down without a fight, he started to take the hostages. Even children. That got the rest of the guard to stand down and leave with him."

"Everyone?" Jillian asks, though we all already know the answer.

"Everyone that was still alive," Gwar confirms.

"Were they retaliating?" Onas asks next. "Do they know about our plans?"

"I don't know." She tries to move her head and winces. "But they know where the other safehouses are… and they took Lomba and Virit with the rest of the hostages."

"Which means even if they didn't know about the plan, we still can't enact it in time," Adam concludes.

"We cannot allow that to happen," I forcefully declare, determined not to let Corbin, and by extension Redwish, win. "We have to rescue the children and the other hostages and make sure that barrier is down when it needs to be."

"There's only one place they would have taken them," Wari surmises. "Back to the necro's camp in Paramount Park."

"Then that's where you all need to head to stop them," Gwar says as Jace and Yuta help her to stand. "If you hurry, you might be able to catch up."

"I'll stay here," Yuta insists, looking over the survivors. "Make sure everyone makes it back to our safehouse safely and send warnings to the others."

"We will move into our positions at the docks once we're finished," I quickly agree with her plan.

"Khazak, did you find…" Adam looks grimly at some of the dead bodies.

"I did not see Liss," I try to assure him that she is alright.

"Okay. Let's go."

The six of us exit the safehouse and begin running down the street toward the city center. With as big a group as it must have been, I doubt they are attempting to stay hidden, and my guess proves correct when, just a few minutes later, we can see the shambling army of skeletons just up ahead—with some of our people in the middle.

"Our primary concern is freeing the hostages," I instruct the group as we run. "Once they are clear, we go after the rest."

"They won't be expecting us," Adam says on my right. "Let's hit 'em hard and fast."

"Use this." Jace on my left tosses me a glowing crystal. "It's a great opener."

With the reponiam charge in my grip, I lob it overhead and into the crowd of undead. Most of those at the rear of their death march crumble in an instant, though the dazzling bright flash alerts the others to our presence. Time for the battle to begin.

The hostages are grouped together at the center of the horde, relief on their faces at our entrance. As we fight our way toward them, many of the captured guards attempt to help us, some even grabbing a discarded arm or leg bone as an improvised weapon. We work our way through the crowd, targeting any of the boney creatures still holding a civilian.

"Perfect timing," Liss deadpans as she joins the fray.

"You know us, always trying to be punctual," I joke back.

"It's good to see you're alive," Adam tells her next.

"For now," Liss replies, at least partially serious.

We may be greatly outnumbered, but I am feeling energized enough right now to take on the world. On my left, the Bearfoot Brothers are slinging spells into the crowd, sending skulls flying left and right, while on my right, Adam cleaves through them with his sword. Jillian, in the form of a bear, starts to mow them down in droves, and even her small bird companion is whizzing through the undead army, distracting them anyway it can. I start to think we may actually win here.

Almost.

"So predictable," a voice echoes seemingly from every alley around us, just before bolts of necrotic energy are fired at me and each of my companions from within the crowd.

I'm knocked to the ground, and before I can recover, the skeletons we just finished defeating begin to knit themselves back together, an eerie purple glow overtaking their bones as they are reattached. As I pick myself up, two figures walk out of the alleys on opposite sides of the road—Corbin the necromancer and Naruk Redwish.

"I told you they wouldn't hesitate to come running after them," Corbin says to Redwish.

"*You!*" Redwish spits at me with venom, no doubt shocked by our presence. "I should've known you'd have a hand in this sad attempt at a rescue."

"And I should have known *you* would be the one so craven as to kidnap innocent children and hand them over to a death-dealing monster!" I spit back.

"Friend of yours?" Jace asks Adam just behind me.

"No," he answers flatly.

"In my defense, I only took the children as hostages so that the rest of them would cooperate," Corbin says with a false innocence. "I have no real need for them, especially now that I have what I came here for."

"And what was that?" I ask suspiciously.

"Wouldn't you like to know?" He smirks smugly.

"If you already found what you were looking for, why can't you let everyone go?" Liss questions.

"There is still work to be done." He scoffs. "Just not *here.*"

"Where have you taken everyone?!" Onas charges up a spell.

"Again, I don't believe that's something I need to tell you." He rolls his eyes. "And I'd watch where you're pointing that thing."

With a gesture of his hand, every skeleton in the mob turns to face the angry older gnome.

"Now you're getting the idea," Redwish compliments his co-villain. "There's really only one way to deal with these people."

He reaches for the amulet hanging from his neck—one that looks much larger than the smaller ones we retrieved previously—and his fist glows purple. The crowd of undead behind him parts as a skeleton so large it must have belonged to an ogre lumbers toward us. Then I notice what it has in its bony grip.

"Let me go!" a struggling Remo shouts as the young orc is brought forward.

"You bastard," Wari curses.

"Release him," I order through gritted teeth.

"I don't think you all are in any place to make demands of *me*." Redwish fixes us all with a cool look, and once again gripping his necklace, he aims his free hand, now glowing a sickly purple, at Remo's head. "Either lay down your weapons and surrender, or I kill the boy."

Even Corbin seems caught off-guard by the sudden threat, though he quickly recovers. Redwish has us in a bind, one I don't think I can negotiate out of. But just as I am ready to throw my sword to the ground, Remo surprises everyone, and with a surprisingly strong kick, knocking the large skeleton's tibia out of alignment and throwing the whole creature off balance, sending him tumbling onto Redwish. In the confusion, the rascal manages to quickly run over to join us.

"This is why I prefer to work with people lacking a pulse." Corbin rubs his left temple.

"Godsdammit!" Redwish screeches as he clambers off the ground. "Don't think you're getting away!"

As Redwish grasps his purple glowing neck piece, the entirety of the remaining skeleton army advances on us. We form a circle, pushing Remo into the center as we prepare to defend ourselves. But my mind keeps going back to Redwish's new jewelry and what it seems to be capable of.

"Was he always a spellcaster?" Adam asks, unsure.

"No." I shake my head. "It has to be the necklace."

"It let him control the horde, and I bet it can do a whole lot more," Jace notes, meaning I'm not the only one who noticed. "If we could get a hold of it, I might be able to figure out how it works. Maybe even bring the barrier down with it."

"Then our plan may be salvageable," I finish. "Do you have any more reponiam charges?"

"Two." He hands me one. "Make it count."

"Everyone rush Redwish on my signal," I tell the rest of the group. "We need to get that amulet."

I throw the reponiam charge toward Redwish, clearing much of the path between the two of us. As I run toward my target, Adam and another guard run interference, bashing away skeleton after skeleton as they try to stop me. From behind me, spells are flung in the same way, some knocking the skeletons back, others freezing them in place, or even wrapping them in vines.

Determined to reach that smug bastard, I do not let any of it stop me. Redwish's eyes go wide when I finally reach him, and I'm not even sure I could describe the feeling of pure elation and satisfaction that courses through me when my fist hits his face. As he writhes on the ground in pain, I reach down and rip the amulet from his neck, quickly tossing it to Jace.

"Hurry, we might be too late," I implore as I turn to face our remaining enemies.

"Working as fast as I can." Jace's eyes begin to glow as he tries to examine the spellcraft on the necklace, and then winces. "Oh God. Whatever this thing is, he's connected to his entire army at once. It's almost too much."

"Do you think you can—"

"Got it!" he says with relief. "He's literally just been ordering a minion over on Testament Island to move one of the geodes out of alignment, switching it on and off."

"Does that mean you can—?" Wari starts.

"Done," Jace doesn't even wait for him to finish.

A moment later, the red barrier in the sky fades away, the stars of the night sky visible for the first time in over a week. And even though we are still surrounded, a cheer runs through our group. We may actually stand a chance at winning this whole thing. Sadly though, our small victory doesn't last very long. Only a few seconds later and the city begins to glow red again as the barrier returns.

"No you don't!" Jace once again works his magic to remove the barrier, only for it to once again return moments later. He then tries for a third time, only to get the same result.

"*That* was your plan?" Corbin looks ready to laugh. "I'm standing right here!"

"Then I guess that means you're next." Wari takes aim.

"You sure about that?" His crown begins to glow.

Corbin's lack of concern is bolstered by the sounds of heavy leather wings flapping above us. Two dragons now hover above us, black and green, the air from the beating of their wings threatening to knock us off balance as they descend. And of course, all of the enemies we just defeated are already stitching themselves back together.

"You couldn't have brought them out earlier!?" Redwish asks with frustration as he picks himself up from the ground, blood dripping from his nose.

"Try that again and I'll roast the lot of you," Corbin threatens, hand on his necklace.

"Jillian, you need to run." With her shapeshifting, she may be the only one able to actually get away.

"What? I can't leave you all!" she argues.

"You *have* to," I implore. "You're the only one who can. Go, find help, get the barrier down somehow—even if you have to do it yourself. But you have to go, *now*."

"You're just giving up?!" Remo questions angrily, but I don't have time to explain.

"I'll be back, I swear!" she promises before reluctantly shifting into a bird and taking flight.

Corbin and several of his minions fire bolts of energy at her as she and her animal companion flee into the sky, but thankfully none land. She's soon far enough that she's vanished from sight all together. *Spirits, please let her find some way out of this, for all our sakes.*

"No matter—one little druid isn't going to change any-thing. The rest of you will do," Corbin declares. "Now march—unless you and your friends are that eager to die."

With the looming threat literally hanging over us and no other options, we begrudgingly fall in line. Remo looks back at me, once more with betrayal in eyes, as we are force-marched into danger. I don't know what to say to him, all of our hopes now resting on a small bird.

Chapter 15

David

"**This is always the worst part.**"

"Why, you get seasick?"

"No, I mean the waiting."

I lean against the bow of the ship, bathed in the red glow of the dome surrounding Maname. *We meet again, my old nemesis.* We've been anchored out here for less than an hour, but it feels like forever. We're waiting for the barrier to come down, which is supposed to happen any minute now.

It's been almost six months since I was on a boat, and I can't say I missed it. Though, thankfully, this trip was much, much shorter. We were picked up there by the boats carrying troops from Litkalaa and then sailed our way down the coast. There are about forty of us on this ship and between three and four dozen other ships with their own troops positioned all around the island.

Before we left, there was worry over the dragons potentially seeing all of the boats in the water, so it was decided to wait until after the sun had set to enter the bay. All of the nature casters onboard—druids, shamans, and witches—have been working together to maintain a heavy cover of fog over the island. So far, there's been absolutely no change or movement, no sign of anything. So we just keep waiting.

"If you aren't careful, you're gonna wear a groove in the deck with your pacing," Max comments at my left.

"Or start a fire," Aria adds.

"You say that like riding a flaming ship into battle wouldn't look completely badass." I roll my eyes.

Sona lets out an uneasy whine at my side, and I reach down to stroke through her fur. She was a little unsteady on her feet at first but has mostly gotten used to the rocking of the waves. Still, I don't think she's loving it.

Max and the rest of his pack are on board as well, though Peter is waiting below deck, not intending to join the fight but insistent on coming. I'm a little surprised an *actual* prince would want to be on the frontlines like this, but knowing firsthand what he's capable of, he'll be a big help. All the werewolves will.

"Stowaway!" someone on the ship shouts from behind.

Everyone above deck turns to watch as one of the Litkalaan soldiers reaches into a barrel next to the main mast and hoists the person out by the back of their shirt. Someone short, and kind of young looking… *Oh shit!*

"Lemme go!" Cameron Hurskett demands as he struggles in the soldier's grip.

"The hell do you think you're doing, kid?" the soldier berates. "We're about to go into a battle!"

"I know that!" he argues, still struggling. "I'm here to help!"

"Help *how*?" another soldier scoffs. "You can't even free yourself."

"*Cam?*" I rush toward the commotion. "What are you doing here?!"

"You know him?" the first soldier asks me, placing the boy down on the deck.

"Yeah, I'm friends with his parents," I explain before fixing the boy with a stern look, "who are going to *kill him* for this."

"Come on, you know I'm old enough to fight!" He looks to me to plead his case. *Uh-uh.*

"One: no, you're not." I hold up a single finger, and then add a second. "And two: even if you *were, you don't know how.* You've never had any kind of training!"

"I trained myself!" he argues. "Every single night, I swear! Look, I even have a sword!" He pulls a small shortsword from a scabbard on his back.

"Where did you get that?" He didn't seriously think this was gonna work, did he? "Cam, it's not happening. Now you need to get below deck and—"

"It's down!" a voice shouts, just as the red glow behind me vanishes. "The barrier's down!"

"Raise the anchor!" the ship captain orders.

Everyone on board turns to confirm that the dome is gone, the city visible just beyond the fog. I rush back to the bow, eager for things to get moving. I can hear the rest of the ship's crewmen all rushing to their stations ready to—

The hell? The barrier is back, like an angry, red middle finger, taunting me. I start to panic. *Did we get the timing wrong? Did we miscalculate how to do this? Was that our only shot?!* All around me people are starting to wonder the same things, all of us unsure of what to do next.

A collective sigh of relief washes over the boat when it vanishes again a few seconds later. *Okay, phew. Now we just need to—GODDAMMIT IT'S BACK!* Noises of confusion, worry, and even anger start to spread across the deck, and I'm sure the same thing is happening on all of the other boats.

"Something's wrong," Max states on my left.

"What's going on?" Cam asks on my right, having followed me. "Is it supposed to do that?"

"No." I shake my head. "I don't…"

Suddenly, the barrier drops again, and I make a split-second decision. Probably a really, really stupid one in hindsight, but hey, we all know how great I am under pressure. Before I can second guess myself, I jump up onto the ship's bulwark, run down the bowsprit, and dive off the end.

"David!" I hear Max shout from the boat in surprise. "Wait, what are you—NO!"

I land in the cold, dark water with a splash, hopefully beyond the barrier, but in case it comes back again, I start swimming forward as fast as I can. Above me, I hear Sona's loud barks of worry about my sudden departure, then another splash behind me. I turn to greet who I assume is Max—only to find Cameron surfacing instead.

"Cam! What did you do?!" I freak out, looking from the boy to the boat.

Before he can answer, the barrier flickers back into existence, the red wall cutting us both off from the ship. *Fuck. Fuuuuuuuuuuck.*

"I told you I can help," he tries to assure me, though the way he's barely treading water isn't giving me a lot of confidence. "Gods, this water is so cold!"

"I really hope you can swim." I point toward the shore, which is very, *very* far away. "Because that's where we're headed."

"What?!" His eyes go wide, and he sputters as he stops paddling for a second. "But… Then why did you jump?!"

"Because I'm an idiot! You weren't supposed to follow me! You weren't supposed to be here at all!" I shout in frustration, feeling guilty when I see the way he winces at my tone. *I have to calm down but… Fuck!* "Just… come on. We need to start swimming."

I don't share with Cam that I'm not sure he'll be able to make it to shore, or that my armor is already feeling heavy now that it's soaking wet, or that I have no idea what could be living in these waters. The last thing we need is for him to start panicking more than he probably already is. But the longer we swim through the cold water, the more worried I get.

It doesn't take long before my arms start to get tired, and we aren't even halfway there. If I'm this tired, Cam must be exhausted, and I'm not even swimming as fast as I can because I can't leave him behind. I don't know what to say or do except slow my own pace to stay with him. If we're out here much longer, I'm going to have to think of something to help keep him afloat.

Above me, the loud *caw* of a bird becomes an additional distraction. Then several more, and what sounds a second bird joining in. I look to the sky, just barely able to make out their shape against the red dome as they circle us, getting lower and lower. I let out a yelp of surprise when one of them suddenly dives into the water—and in its place, up comes Jillian. *Oh thank god!*

"David!" she says with glee after spitting out some water. "I am *so* happy to see you."

"The feeling is very, *very* mutual!" I look with relief to Cam, who only looks confused.

"What are you doing out here?" She takes in the somewhat-struggling young man. "And who's this?"

"C-Cameron Hurskett, ma'am." Cam tries to salute and ends up slipping under water. "I'm here to help fight!"

"No, he's here because he *stupidly* followed me when I jumped off the boat," I correct him.

"Why'd you do that?" Jillian asks, confused.

"When I saw the barrier wasn't staying down, I decided to jump in before I lost the chance to get inside altogether," I explained. "And then he jumped off right after me."

"What was the plan?" Jillian is understandably still confused. "Were you going to swim all the way to shore?"

"I didn't say it was smart," I admit. "But hey, it worked out anyway! Wait, what are *you* doing here?"

"Well—"

"Do you think we could talk about this," Cameron sputters, using all his strength to stay above water, "somewhere else?"

"Oh crap, of course," Jillian quickly agrees. "We need to get to Testament Island. I'll explain there. Just hang on and try not to freak out—remember, that it's still me."

Neither Cam or I are sure of what she means by that, for different reasons. Cam's eyes go wide as he sees Jillian's body start to grow and change shape, but it's what she turns into that surprises me. *Shark!*

"Shark!" *Cam too.*

"She's a druid," I quickly explain, though I had hoped that was obvious after the bird bit. "Remember, just hang on. She's not going to eat us," I say as much to myself as to him.

We both take a hold of the large fin just behind Jillian's head, trying not to hurt her as she starts to swim us toward Testament Island, her small bird companion following above. The water is still cold, but at least we're not in danger of drowning anymore. The Pukwudgie statue sits tall in the distance, its hair and torch blazing a dark and frankly evil-looking red flame that matches the color the barrier.

Jillian slows down as we approach the smaller island. I can see at least part of the massive dragon sitting at the statue's base as she swims us around. Once we find a quiet alcove among the rocks around the island, she lets us off and transforms back into her normal form, her bird landing on her shoulder.

"I'd offer to dry you off but…" She grimaces.

"You need to conserve your magic." I nod in understanding. I can deal with wet clothes. "So, what's going on?"

"There was a hiccup in the plan," she starts with a sigh.

"Obviously." *I'm gonna need more than that.* I start to take off my weapons, leather bracers, and chestpiece.

"The necromancer located and attacked some of our safehouses maybe an hour before things were due to start," she continues. "We were caught totally by surprise. They killed half the guards and captured the other half along with some civilians, including the people who were set to bring down the barrier."

"Shit." *That's not good.* "The necromancer found out about the plan?"

"I don't know." She shakes her head. "But it seemed like too much of a coincidence."

"What about the flickering?" I pull off my shirt and try to wring out all the water I can. "The way the barrier went on and off a few times."

"We chased after the captured group. He still managed to surprise us, but we were able to get a hold of one of the amulets he's using to split or amplify is magic. One of our own people was able to figure out how to use it to turn the barrier off." *That's when it came down the first time.* "But the necromancer was able to reverse what we did, almost imme-diately. We tried a few more times, and when things went south, well… here we are."

"Fuck." Everything has gone to shit.

"On a positive note, Khazak was really happy to hear you were okay." She offers a sad smile.

"Yeah? How is he now?" I ask, taking off my shoes and wringing out my socks next.

"Captured," she admits, hanging her head. "When it was clear we weren't going to be able to bring the dome down permanently, he told me to get out of there before I was captured too."

"And then you found us," Cam finishes, trying to dry his shirt the same way I did.

"I was hoping maybe *one* of the ships had managed to make it through." She frowns. "But… at least I found you."

"Alright," I say as I pull my slightly less wet shirt back on. "How do we do this?"

"Do you really think you can?" Jillian asks, looking toward the statue, unsure.

"I've gotta try." I shrug and reach for my boots. No socks are better than wet socks unless you want blisters. "So where am I going and what am I looking for?"

"The first thing you need to do is get up there." She points up the rocky shelf, the stone ledge around the island's courtyard several dozen feet above. "Then you have to get to the array room. It's about halfway up the staircase up the statue behind a set of big doors."

"And what do I do when I'm there?" I tie the laces tight, not liking how wet they are but not trusting my bare feet on these sharp rocks.

"You'll see six geodes on pedestals set around a giant glowing crystal in the center of the room," she continues. "The giant crystal pulls magic from the leywell, and runes engraved within the geodes then process that magic, sync together, and create the dome. All you need to do is remove one of the six to break the array, and the barrier will be gone."

"Okay." I nod. "Doesn't sound too hard."

"They're a lot bigger than you'd expect, so be careful. I can come with you to help," she offers, ready to start climbing herself.

"No, I need you to stay here with him." I point to Cam. "I don't trust him not to run off."

"I guess his track record isn't great." She side-eyes her fellow halfling.

"Come on, you can't just leave me here!" he argues.

"I can and I will." What is with this kid? "This isn't a game, Cam. People are going to die tonight. Some already have, trained soldiers! So just … wait here, please. Okay?"

"Fine." He grumpily crosses his arm, and that's the best I'm gonna get.

I leave the rest of my armor behind. As waterlogged as it is, it'll only weigh me down. With a deep breath, I carefully climb up the rocky side of Testament Island. It's not easy, the rocks slick from the sea water, not to mention how cold I am in these wet clothes, but this has to be done.

Once I make it to the top, I slowly peer my head over the ledge to get a feel for what we're dealing with. I spot maybe two dozen skeletons milling around the courtyard at the base of the island, and on the opposite side is what looks like the back half of a dragon. It's laying down, maybe asleep? Do undead dragons need to sleep? I really hope so.

I *cannot* get caught because even if I wasn't outnumbered, I have no idea how to fight a fire-breathing dragon. The necromancer and the rest of his army are going to realize something is up as soon as the barrier is gone, so I need to make sure they can't bring it back yet again. But I can deal with that problem when we get to it.

I start to carefully climb just below the ledge, searching for a safe spot to hop over. I see my chance when a pair of skeletons guarding the bottom of the staircase start to walk away—a patrol? Whatever the reason, I quickly jump over, landing as silently as I can before climbing the stairs.

They wrap around the statue as we go up, a solid stone railing along the outside. Any hopes that the stairs themselves are unguarded are dashed when I make out the sound of bones hitting stone coming down the stairs, and I quickly jump over the railing, hanging by my hands until I hear the danger pass, and I can safely climb back over.

When I reach the statue's waist, I see what must be the entrance to the array room, a pair of heavy-looking metal doors set into the statue's base. I quickly check, breathing a sigh of relief when I find them unlocked. Then I wince as the door lets out a slight *scrape* as I push it open, slipping inside and pulling it closed behind me.

The room I enter is stunning. I mean literally every inch of this room is bright and shiny, particularly the huge glowing crystal sitting at its center. A stone walkway extends ahead, splitting and wrapping around the giant centerpiece like a hexagon. The walls, ceiling, and floor below the walkway are covered in a layer of crystal themselves, everything tinged the same red as the barrier outside.

Six pedestals are placed at each corner of the walkway, each holding an individual geode. Motes of light lift into the air before entering the giant crystal as it draws energy from the leywell. Then, in turn, light wisps between the crystal and the geodes, powering the spell. Can't wait to tell Mikey that I figured most of that out on my own!

All amazing to look at, but they aren't the only things in the room. Four skeletons are also patrolling around the walkway. I quickly leap off and drop onto the crystalized ground below, walking beneath the walkway until I reach the large crystal. There are plenty of outcroppings so it looks like it should be easy enough to climb, but when I grip onto one, I don't like how smooth and sharp it feels under my hand. Still, it'll put me right next to one of the pedestals… so here goes nothing.

I make my way up carefully and quietly, trying to get an idea of where the skeletons are and looking for a decent blind spot to pop up in. Now level with the walkway, one of the pedestals is just barely out of reach. Holding tightly to the large crystal, I lean across the gap, stretching my hand toward the geode. *Just need to…*

A sudden hiss freezes me in place, and I turn my head slowly to see that, yep, I've been spotted. There goes that idea. The skeleton then "roars," alerting its companions, and all four begin to advance.

Alright, new plan. I jump from the crystal to the walkway, pulling myself up over the ledge. I reach for both of the swords strapped to my back and quickly assess the situation. All four are getting closer, but they're waiting for me to make the first move.

I need to do this fast before they have a chance to call for reinforcements. I dash to my right, ready to cleave through the first boney asshole's chest when I notice his raised hand start to glow. I'm barely able to dive out of the way in time as he tries to blast me with magic. Forgot these guys can do that.

So, with that now in mind I recover quickly, jumping to my feet to finish what I started and beheading and destroying the first skeleton. Then I keep running forward and clip through the second before it even has a chance to charge anything up. Continuing my run around the walkway, I circle behind the third skeleton, who manages to turn and fire off his own spell, but it's simple enough to dodge.

That's where my luck ends though because as soon as I drop #3, I'm thrown back, hitting the floor hard as a purple-black bolt of magic hits me directly in the shoulder. I cry out in pain, the magic raking through my skin, muscle, and bone like hot knives. I swear I can feel the flesh of my shoulder *dying*.

The undead aren't the only ones with tricks though. I use that anger and pain to fuel me, and before the skeleton has a chance to even move, I'm on my feet. I ram my good shoulder into its body and send it flying, smashing into the cave wall before crumbling into a pile of broken bones. *There we go!*

With no time to lose, I turn toward the nearest pedestal and grab the geode. Jillian wasn't wrong—it is *way* heavier than it looks, but I'm able to lift it all the same. As soon as I do, the whole room changes, the other geodes going dark as the large crystal at the center changes from red to white, bathing the room in dazzling light.

No time to enjoy it though, the large roar I hear outside signaling to everyone on the island that the barrier must be down. Time to get the hell out of here. I take the geode with me as I rush to the exit, not willing to risk them flipping the thing back on.

As soon as I shove open the doors, I start to rethink my plan. Mostly because of the huge dragon hovering only thirty or forty feet in the air from me. Throwing the heavy crystal ahead of me and over the railing, I have only a split-second to leap out of the way as the monster rears back its head and unleashes an inferno.

I land awkwardly on the stairs, almost losing my footing as I try to rush down them. That's when I remember that the courtyard is filled with more skeletons—all of whom are waiting for me. And with another roar behind me, there's no time to find an alternate exit.

I start to fight my way through, coming up with a quick plan to make my way toward the docks. From there, I can jump back in the water for cover, and then hopefully find Jillian and Cam so we can get out of here. Easier said than done.

There are over two dozen skeletons out here, and from the amount of spells I have to avoid, most of them are spell-casters. Still, now that I know what I'm doing it's easy to take some of them out while dancing between the others. Just as I near the exit, a glowing purple wall rises up in front of me and then extends around and over my body, trapping me. A number of skeletons converge on the cage, their hands and eye sockets glowing.

"I've got you!" I hear Jillian call from above.

She lands with enough force to make the ground quake, forcing all of them off-balance. I almost join them, but

thankfully stay upright as the magical cage fades from existence. Then I help Jillian destroy my attempted captors.

"Thanks for the assist," I tell her as I finish off another.
"Where's Cam?"

"I left him on the shore with my—" She stops, her eyes
going wide as she stares over my shoulder.

I already know what it is, but I still feel my stomach
drop when I turn and see the dragon hovering in the air.
It roars in anger as it plunges toward the courtyard, Jillian
and I barely diving out of the way as it flies past. Turning
quickly, it hangs over the courtyard, small flames flickering
at the corners of its mouth as it prepares its flame-breath
for another attack.

"Hey!" Cam shouts, running up from the docks and
waving his arms, Jillian's bird circling frantically around
his head. "Leave them alone!"

The young halfling starts to throw stones in the dragon's
direction as he yells. All of them fall way short, of course,
but he's still making enough noise to draw the creature's
attention. *Oh gods, this kid is gonna kill me.*

"Get him in the water!" Jillian yells at my side before
shrinking into a bird and flying straight at the dragon.

I take off running, aiming straight for Cam who is too
busy gawking in terror at the dragon to notice. I grab him
when I reach him, tucking his smaller body under my arm
as I continue to run for the docks. Behind me, powerful
gusts of wind accompany the sound of heavy wings being
flapped as Jillian attempts to distract the dragon, and when
I finally feel the wood of the docks under my feet, I leap
into the dark water for the second time today.

We both surface and turn to watch as the dragon fights
an aerial battle with… well, it's a little too dark to really see
Jillian, small as she is, but we know she's there. The dragon
starts to circle in the air, its head flailing around after losing
track of the small nuisance of a bird. It'd be funny, if it

weren't a second later that it turns to look directly toward me and Cam in the water. Barely a second later, something splashes into the water as Jillian joins us, reconstituting into her normal body.

"Swim down!" she orders as the dragon starts to fly toward us. "Now!"

We do as asked, diving under the water as fast and as deep as we can. I even pull Cam down with me when I'm worried it's not enough. It's too dark so see anything under here, at least until I notice a glowing blue light coming from above us.

I turn to look up and see Jillian, holding her breath with her hands above her as she creates a dome of ice in the water above us—right before the dragon strikes us with its flames. She continues to cast as the ice begins to melt, cooling the water and saving us from being boiled alive.

We surface, drawing huge gasps of air and watching the dragon flying overhead. I think it's looking around for us, but it's too dark for it to see us down here. After circling around the island twice more, it flies toward Maname proper.

"I think we're safe," I say after catching my breath. "Ish."

"Great job!" Jillian says to me, genuinely, and I realize as I watch the dragon flying through the night sky that I can see the stars—the dome is gone!

"We did it!" Cam announces, and I hate to admit it but he did contribute some—though I still want to smack him on the back of his head for being so stupid. Hell, I think even Jillian's bird wants to peck at him. No time for that now, though.

"The ships should all be headed in now." Jillian looks out as the thick fog from outside begins rolling in. "As long as those dragons don't see them coming."

"We have to get to the city and do what we can to make sure that doesn't happen," I say next, already wanting to help the others. "Think you can get us there fast?"

"Of course, just hop on!" Jillian says before she dives under and grows another set of fins. "We'll circle around for your gear first."

As we swim our way to the city, its buildings growing large by the second, my thoughts are on Khazak and my friends. I made it this far; I just need them to hold on a little longer. He promised me I could do any stupid plan that I wanted, and I am damn sure gonna collect.

Chapter 16

Khazak

"*I knew I should've stayed on my own.*"

"Come on, kid. It's not like this was our fault."

"This is totally your fault!"

Unlike Onas, I try not to take Remo's words to heart. Though that is a little difficult to do as I sit in this make-shift prison camp, a glowing cage surrounding our group. But Onas is right; it is not as if we expected any of this to happen.

Corbin, the necromancer, led us into Progress Park, leaving us just outside his camp before raising his deadly purple walls. We are entirely surrounded by the undead, and if that were not enough, there are also two of his three dragons here to threaten us into cooperation, including the extremely large one. Even if we made it past the skeletons, the dragons would burn us to a crisp. Our only hope lies with Jillian, and it has been nearly half an hour since she left us.

"So, what's the plan?" Adam asks at my side.

"I … do not have one." I admit sadly.

"Guess we better start praying then," Wari says wryly.

Suddenly, above us, the red barrier surrounding the island vanishes, revealing dark clear skies. *She did it!* All around me, the other captives look up, eyes filled with hope and reflecting the starry night sky. Any minute now, those ships will hit the shore, and with them, rescue.

"What the hell is happening?" Redwish asks Corbin as they both look up in confusion.

"I'm not sure," Corbin says, eyes narrowed in suspicion as he his crown begins to glow.

A dragon roar echoes across the city, originating in the direction of Testament Island. No doubt because of the barrier. I hope Jillian and anyone that may have helped her got away safely.

"Someone made it past my dragon," Corbin tells Redwish with a growl as he climbs onto the larger dragon. "Something's going on. Stay here and make sure no one escapes."

"As if I have anything better to do," Redwish answers with a roll of his eyes.

As we wait there, most of us, at least those aware of what is happening, do our best to rein in our emotions. If we seem too excited or relieved, Redwish might suspect the rest of the plan. But with only one living person to watch over us, we have a much better chance of escaping. And seeing as I happen to know our jailer fairly well, I have a good idea of how to distract him. I elbow Adam and Liss and look toward Redwish, trying to silently communicate for them to follow my lead.

"Once again someone else's lackey, eh?" I mock the red-haired orc.

"Does he always leave you to babysit?" Adam joins in, catching on.

"Shut up." Redwish rolls his eyes at us. "As if you know anything about what I do."

"What is there to know?" I challenge, hoping he will take the bait. "Just like when you worked for Murbank, all you do is take someone else's orders."

"I was working *with* Murbank—not for him." Redwish narrows his eyes as we question his authority. "And just as it was with him, the only reason I am *assisting* Corbin is because we share a mutual employer."

"Oh, so your boss just keeps sending you on these little pissant missions for *other* people instead of letting you work on your own," Liss says sharply. "Sounds like he thinks you're *really* important."

"You couldn't even begin to fathom what we're doing," Redwish continues, offended.

"And that would be…?" I try to lead him to explain his plans.

"Why would I tell you?" To be fair, I did not expect that to work.

"Murbank was an old fool who became too obsessed with his own plans," Redwish continues to bad mouth his… co-workers? "And the longer I am stuck here, the more apparent it has become that Corbin has fallen prey to the same issue."

"So your boss has a habit of hiring idiots," Adam notes, sounding amused.

"He must be pretty used to failure by now," Liss adds snidely, if the implication wasn't clear enough.

"Who's to say that we failed?" Redwish just smirks, unflappable.

"Right, you have been running away for over a month because you *succeeded* in V'rok'sh Tah'lj." I am unimpressed.

"My escape from that backwater hellhole was unplanned, certainly," Redwish starts to explain. "But what—I should have stayed and allowed myself to be arrested?"

"Yes!" I reply emphatically. "Almost forty people died that night! If you had any decency, you would take responsibility for your part in it!"

"Please, save me the speeches about decency and honor." Redwish rolls his eyes. "Besides, the person most responsible for the *slaughter* that occurred that night was your pet, remember?"

"He *defended* himself after you *murdered* him and were planning to do the same with the rest of us." My plan may have backfired as he starts provoke me in return.

"He got better, didn't he?" he mocks. "I don't see why you're so angry at me; after all, I'm the only reason you two are even together."

"Sharing a common enemy is a good way to bring people together." He may be technically right, but I can't let him get under my skin.

"I'm sure," he scoffs, walking over to his dragon. "You sound exactly like the elders in my old village. And the elders in *your* old village."

"You do not have to be an elder to have *integrity*," I spit in anger. "If the rangers were here…"

"Ah yes the rangers, such an upstanding organization," Redwish mocks. "One that was shockingly easy to infiltrate and corrupt to further my own agenda. And let's not forget that Murbank was essentially one of your *heads of state*!"

"*Pok'ak tch'am,*" I curse in Atasi.

"I don't know what he just said, but it sounded rude," Liss adds with a chuckle.

"I shouldn't be surprised," Redwish says dismissively. "You were as embedded in that system as the rest of them."

"I was not embedded in any 'system'!" I defend myself, incensed. "I joined the rangers to help people."

"And how well did that go for the 'almost forty' whose deaths I am supposedly responsible for?" he continues to deride my home. "People like you are so close minded, set in your ways. Afraid of change and unwilling to make the sacrifices required to make that change happen."

"Okay but you were *literally* sacrificing people, dude." Adam seems surprised by his brazenness—I'm not. "And I don't think they got a say in what was happening."

"As I said, I'm not afraid to do what it takes." Redwish climbs onto the back of the dragon. "To create something new, you first have to burn away the old. And I'm going to start with you and your friends here."

A wave of panic goes through our small group of survivors at the threat. Time almost slows to a crawl as I watch Redwish grasp his amulet. The cage keeping us in place vanishes just before the dragon rears its head back, its midsection glowing as it heats up. Dragon fire was not something on my list of ways I might be killed.

Time speeds back up a moment later when a shadowy blur flies in from the left, striking the dragon's head and sending it swinging in the other direction. The blur lands with a thud between us and the dragon, and as it stands up, my heart soars.

"David!" I shout in joy, confusion, and worry all at once.

"Hey, Sir," he replies almost casually, looking over his shoulder with a smile and holding up a single finger. "Gimme a minute."

"Oh good, we were just talking about you." Redwish glares at David from atop the dragon.

"Yeah, sorry. Ran into a few hiccups on the way." David sounds very sure of himself as he draws his swords. "But now that I'm here: I think you and I have some unfinished business."

David leaps into the air—faster and higher than I would have anticipated—to strike at the dragon again. But this time, Redwish is ready and the creature quickly whips its head at David, sending him back to the ground with a *thud*.

I start to rush over, panicked that he's hurt, only to see him stand up as if the blow was nothing.

"That the best you got?" David dusts off his shoulder.

"You'll burn just as well as the rest of them." Redwish sounds angry and a little worried—David has clearly shaken him. The dragon's chest begins to glow again.

"Hope you've got good aim!" David says, just before he strikes the dragon's head again and takes off into the park, pushing through the undead army as if it was nothing.

Redwish growls in frustration and begins to chase after him, but not before turning the army on the rest of us. All at once, the skeletons begin to advance, and all of us are without our weapons. The few of us that can use magic quickly fan out and put the others behind us.

"Get behind me," I tell Remo as I pull him into the center of our circle of defense. It is looking grim, but if we can get a hold of some of the weapons the skeletons are using, we might stand a chance.

"On three," Wari says to his brother, both of their hands outstretched and glowing. "THREE!"

The spells start to fly, and I prepare myself to run forward and retrieve a weapon in the chaos. But before I can, sounds of combat can be heard on the other side of the army with bones flying left and right through the air. When the creature causing the mayhem draws nearer, I think I recognize it only from a description I've read in a book—a great ape or gorilla.

Jillian (or perhaps some other druid) gets right to work dispatching our attackers while leaving plenty of room for the rest of us to grab a weapon and join the fray. Just as the tides are turning, what must be the sound of a dragon breathing fire pulls my attention back to Redwish flying above as he searches through the trees, periodically firing at the ground.

"He's going to set the whole park on fire," Jillian comments on my left, back in her normal form.

"And David along with it," I add gravely.

Before I have time to focus on the creation of an inferno, two loud roars echo from the opposite end of the city—the necromancer's other dragons. Time for the real battle to finally begin. A low rumble of thunder then sounds out above as clouds begin to grow.

"Is that you?" I ask Jillian after looking around and seeing her back in her normal form.

"No, but I can use it." She stretches both hands upward, coaxing the already stormy clouds to release rain onto the fires Redwish has created. "And I wouldn't worry too much about David. This isn't even his first fight with a dragon *tonight*."

"What?" I look between her and the dragon in shock.

"He's the one who brought the barrier down," she informs me proudly.

"Of course he was." *That's my puppy.*

As if he could hear us, a dark blur leaps from one of the trees and slams into the dragon being ridden by Redwish. The creature begins to flail as it flies through the air in an attempt to dislodge David, firing random blasts of flame at its own body. In the short bursts of light that accompany them, I can just barely make out David struggling for purchase on the dragon's back, holding tightly to its tail—and I can hear him arguing with Redwish.

"Would you get off!" Redwish screeches, no doubt disoriented from the maneuvering.

"Aww, come on! I just wanna talk!" David mocks, and though it makes me smile, I am still worried about him up there.

The aerial battle continues for a few more minutes, and while trying to keep my focus on the task at hand—the army of skeletons—I am unable to keep my eyes from constantly wandering upward. Then after a particular violent looking flail, something is thrown from the dragon—David!

"I've got him!" Jillian shouts in reply, rushing forward with her hands extended. "*Lotenkomo!*"

As she finishes her incantation, gusts of wind rush past us, leaves and grass swirling into a powerful cyclone. The winds slow and cushion David's descent, allowing him to land on both feet with relative grace. In the sky, Redwish is already flying off, though whether it's to join Corbin or make his escape I do not know.

"Asshole," David grumbles as he watches our enemy make his escape.

"David." I smile after rushing toward him.

"Khaz." He smiles, a split second before leaping at me and wrapping his arms around my torso. "It's so good to see you."

"It's good to see you too." I return his embrace, letting the rest of the world melt away.

Only for a moment—we *are* in the middle of a battle.

"What happened to you?" I ask David as we rejoin the fray. "I've been worried."

"Me too!" he replies, as he takes on his own enemy. "I did what you asked and got off the island—right before the barrier went up."

"I assumed as much—then what?" I kick through a ribcage.

"Well, I tried to get back in," David continues, sounding sheepish. "It didn't work, and I… It just didn't work."

"What do you mean?" I take out a trio of tiny skeletons.

"I tried to use my sword to get back in and kind of got … blown back and knocked out for a few days." I can hear him grimace. "Lucky I didn't drown."

"*Again?*" It feels like he falls unconscious unexpectedly at least twice a month.

"It's not like I did it on purpose!" he defends himself. "A family of traders found me, fished me out of the water, and brought me with them north to the evacuation camp in Kiweni. That's where I've been until a few days ago when we got on the boats to come here."

"I assume there is more to it than that," I comment, thinking in particular about the abilities he's just shown off.

"Uh-huh, a lot, but we can talk about that when we're finished cleaning up Redwish's mess," he replies as he mows down a few more undead.

"David!" Adam calls out in excitement when he notices who has rejoined us. "We've been so worried about you!"

"Same!" The two share a quick hug before returning to the battle.

He has similar reunions with Liss and the Bearfoot Brothers as we continue to fight through the steadily thinning horde. Without Corbin or Redwish to guide them, it takes us less than ten minutes to clear the area. Surrounded on all sides by piles of no-longer-moving bones, our group finally relaxes.

"Now, where were we…" David says, sheathing his weapons as he looks at me longingly. A moment later and I have him in my arms again.

"Spirits, I missed you so, so much," I speak into his hair.

"I did too. I—"

"That was amazing!" An unknown but young sounding voice declares, and David's body goes stiff.

"Cameron!?" Jillian yells as she walks up to a young halfling. "What are you doing here!?"

"We told you to stay with those guards!" David joins her in admonishing the youth.

"And I keep telling you to stop pawning me off on other people!" Neither looks pleased with that response. "Come on, I helped you back on the island with the statue and the dragon and everything!"

"That's not the point," David says, pinching the bridge of his nose like I would. "You could get seriously hurt out here—or worse."

"So could you!" he argues to the both of them.

"It's not the same," Jillian tries to explain. "We're trained to fight, to know how to avoid getting hurt. And if we *are* hurt, we can handle it because of that training."

"I get it, Cam." David kneels down to get on the boy's level. "It's great that you want to help—really—but you don't know what you're doing. None of us have the time to teach you right now or to watch your back."

"I don't need anyone to watch my back." He clearly doesn't like that answer, but he doesn't say anything, crossing his arms in a pout and turning away.

"I really hope I wasn't like that at his age," David mutters to me in exhaustion.

"Is that a joke? You act like that *now*," I reply in disbelief, enjoying the look of false-hurt he gives me. "Is he a friend of yours?"

"Sort of. He's the oldest son of the family that rescued me," he starts to explain. "He stowed away on the ship and then followed after me when I jumped off the boat and into the bay."

"Why the hell would you jump off a boat?" Though that would explain why his clothes appear to be wet.

"I saw the barrier flickering, and I was worried it wasn't going to stay down," he says with a shrug. "So I jumped into the water to make sure I was on the other side of it."

"You could have drowned!" I admonish, worried. "Did you expect to swim all the way to shore?"

"I hadn't quite thought that far ahead." *Of course he didn't.* "Don't give me that look! It turned out to be the right thing to do in the end, or else I wouldn't be here right now."

"He's right," Jillian comes to his defense. "After I escaped, I lucked out and found these two floating in the bay. I got him there, but it was David who managed to knock out the dome's array at Testament Island."

"And I helped! I distracted the dragon right when he was about to torch the two of you!" Cameron states proudly, which is impressive but also sounds harrowing for a child who can't be more than fifteen. "You wouldn't have gotten away if it wasn't for me."

"Come on, I'm going to *personally* make sure that you get to safety," Jillian promises as she steers him toward some of the other civilians.

"So, before we're interrupted *again*..." David pulls me in for a kiss that I happily return.

"Is this your ... boyfriend?" *Oh spirits, why?*

"Who's this?" David asks after breaking our kiss far too early for either of our liking.

"This is Remo," I introduce him to the young orc.

"Hi, Remo." David offers him a hand, which Remo stares at for a second before taking.

"That was pretty cool, fighting the dragon," he says with a hint of aloofness.

"Thanks," David accepts the clearly downplayed compliment. "Got a little follower of your own, huh?" he asks me.

"Pssh, no way!" Remo shakes his head violently. "This guy found me and some other kids and *made* us come with them. We were doing just fine on our own."

"I beg to differ," I argue, sounding weary. "Regardless, we need to get you out of here."

"Yeah, come on, no more kids on the battlefield." Jillian calls him over, having Remo join Cameron.

"Been busy, huh?" David jokes as we watch the young men be led away.

"Well, I had to do something until you came back to me." I mean it as a joke, but it comes out much more sincere.

The two of us quickly embrace again, and with no further interruptions, it is easy to ignore the rest of the world for a minute or two. Spirits, how I missed this: his touch, his scent. As we hold each other, all of the emotions and worries that have plagued me since spitting up threaten to bubble up to the surface, and now is really not the time. Though, when I hear David sniffling as we pull apart, I am comforted to know I am not the only one.

"It's been so weird not being around you every day," David tells me while wiping his eyes.

"The feeling is very mutual," I agree. "I am not sure it's healthy, but after seeing you every day for so long… the past two weeks have been almost unbearable."

"You're telling me," David says in agreement. "And *you* haven't had your dick locked in a cage the whole time."

I feel a boulder drop into the pit of my stomach. *He's been in the chastity cage this entire time?! How could I forget something like that!*

"Spirits, David, you've been locked up this whole time!? I am so, so sorry. We can go right now to get the—"

"It's fine," David assures me, pulling me back before I can leave. "I survived this long. A few more hours won't kill me."

"Who are you and what have you done with David?" I ask, checking him for a fever.

"Harhar." He bats away my hand. "Now come on, we've gotta—"

A loud roar echoes from the other side of the city. As we both turn to try and determine its location, we can see the glowing embers of a fire.

"Even with the outside help, those dragons are gonna be a problem," Wari notes, coming up on my left.

"Especially the big one," David agrees, and I can see him starting to think. "We're going to have to do something about it."

"What do you mean?" *He can't possibly be thinking of…*

"Remember what you said about me being allowed to do whatever stupid plan I wanted after I got back and rescued you?" he reminds me, wearing a large grin.

"…You're going to fight the dragon."

"I'm gonna fight the dragon." We speak in unison.

Spirits help me, this is going to be a long night.

Chapter 17

David

"Alright, so, how do we stop a dragon?"

"By taking out Corbin, I guess."

His name's Corbin? I don't know why, but I was expecting something more … evil sounding. While most of the guards and civilians have left, either joining the battle or returning to a safehouse, the remaining group—me, Khazak, Adam, Liss, some guy named Jace, and the Bearfoot Bros.—are still just outside Progress Park. We can hear the fighting in the distance and even see some already spilling into the park. We don't have long before we'll need to join.

"Isn't he *riding* the dragon?" Liss points out.

"He is," Khazak says with a nod. "So…"

"So I need to figure out a way to get on that dragon, too," I finish, already trying to think of a solution.

"But *how*?" Khazak continues with a sigh. "Even with your abilities, you can't jump that high or fly."

"No, but if we could get it to fly close enough to one of the taller buildings…" I look up and start to plan.

"How would we do that?" Adam asks next. "I mean, as big as it is, I'm not sure how to draw its attention for very long without being eaten."

"Or if we even can," Liss points out again. "Aren't the dragons being controlled the same way as the rest of his army?"

"I don't think so," Jace responds. "I mean I'm only guessing here, but there's something different about them. They've got skin and presumably the internal organs to go with it, but they still read as undead to my magic."

"They couldn't breathe fire if they weren't 'alive' somehow," Wari confirms. "But we've seen him use that crown of his to control them, and Redwish used an amulet, and he's not a spellcaster."

"I'm not sure it's the same, though," Onas adds. "They seem to act more like animals. Trained animals, but still."

"Isn't that kind of weird?" Adam asks. "Aren't dragons supposed to be *extremely* intelligent?"

"That is what I have always read," Khazak agrees, "but it is not as though I have encountered one before myself to judge. I'm not even sure when the last living dragon sighting was."

"The one I dealt with at Testament Island didn't seem very smart," I report with confidence. "It was actually kind of easy to distract, though it was also much smaller than the black one."

"We'll need something big and powerful enough to actually threaten it," Wari decides. "Probably with some kind of spell…"

"That's it!" Onas suddenly exclaims. "I've got an idea. We need to get to the shop."

"What for?" Wari is as confused as the rest of us, his brother already walking away.

"No time to dawdle." Onas doesn't even look back, already running off in the direction of his shop.

"Is he usually like that?" Jace asks as we all turn to Wari.

"When he gets an idea," Wari says with a sigh. "Alright, let's go. At the very least we can get everyone some enchanted equipment."

With little more than a shrug, the rest of us chase after Onas. We don't run into many of the undead on the way, but we do see some of the incoming reinforcements in the distance. Everyone will be pushing toward the park, trying to contain the damage.

"So David," Liss asks as we follow Onas around a corner, "what've you been up to?"

"Oh you know, the usual," I joke back. "Got fished out of the ocean, fought some werewolves, figured out how my magical superstrength works."

"We saw!" Adam says with some excitement. "Between that and your sword, you're basically unstoppable now."

"Yeah…" I can't even pretend to match his energy.

"David, where *is* your sword?" *Of course* it would be Khazak who finally notices that it's not with me.

"I kinda … lost it." Ugh, I feel like a kid coming clean to their parents about sneaking out at night.

"What?" *At least he looks more confused than disappointed.* "How?"

"Remember how I said I got knocked out again?" I start to explain as we turn another corner. "I tried getting back inside by piercing the red barrier with the sword. I mean, it's supposed to be able to cut through anything, right?"

"Uh-oh." Liss can already tell where this is going. "What happened?"

"I don't really remember much beyond a bright flash of light and then being thrown back into the cold water," I admit, ashamed at my dumb antics. "Everything went black after that."

"The enchantments on the sword might have caused some kind of magical feedback loop with the dome and overloaded," Wari suggests, already thinking. "Or maybe it was something about the metal itself…"

"We can figure that out later!" Onas shouts from ahead, still leading the charge.

"It doesn't matter anyway." I sigh. "It's somewhere at the bottom of the ocean by now."

"Maybe someone will fish it up?" Adam offers hopefully.

"Yeah, maybe," I say with little enthusiasm. "I feel so stupid."

"I'm just glad you are alright," Khazak tells me. "If the explosion was strong enough to knock you unconscious, things could have been much, much worse."

I know he's not just saying that, but I still can't help feeling like I screwed up something big. I mean seriously, I lost a one of kind, indestructible, *ancient* weapon. Who does that? Or who *else* does that?

Thankfully there aren't any more questions for me the rest of the short trip to the store. When we get there, the brothers seem impressed that the front door hasn't been blown off. I'm just as surprised no one tried to loot anything.

"*Nakiwa,*" Wari disables the sharp tone of the alarm as we step inside. "Now what did we need to get from here that's so important?"

"This!" Onas rushes over to the wall of gadgets, gesturing proudly to one in particular.

I noticed it immediately the first time I was here. It's a metal dragon, or at least it's shaped like one. They told me it flies and was originally going to be used for some kind of magical light show, but they couldn't get it to stop overheating and breaking down. I don't think they ever got it working.

"How is that gonna help us?" I ask, skeptical.

"Yeah, that hunk of junk won't be good for much more than…" Wari pauses. "…blowing up."

"*Exactly!*" Onas grins widely. "It should stay airborne long enough for what we need, and is bright and loud enough that it'll definitely get the dragon's attention."

"And if it blows up in the thing's face, all the better." Wari is already onboard.

"Could we actually do that?" Khazak wants confirmation, but to my surprise, he sounds hopeful.

"I don't see why not," Onas agrees as he helps his brother pull the object from the wall. "We just need to figure out where we're trying to lead it to and the path to get it there."

"And hope the dragon actually responds to and tries following it," Wari adds, more realistically. "But I think we've got a good shot."

"Maneuvering the dragon between all the buildings in the city might be dangerous." Seems like Liss is in on the plan as well.

"What about near the park?" I offer, looking outside. "There are rows of tall buildings all around its edge with a ton of airspace in the middle."

"That could work." Wari scratches his chin.

"So the plan is to lure the dragon to fly by the buildings and then what? Jump on it?" Khazak asks, like it's crazy.

"Yeah, basically." I shrug, knowing it is.

"David, that's insane. You could…" He stops and sighs. "I am not going to be able to talk you out of this, am I?"

"Nope." I shake my head. "Though I am still open to other ideas that *don't* involve me jumping off a building and onto a fire-breathing dragon."

"What about using that thing to blow up the necromancer directly?" Liss offers. "Then we stop the whole army in one strike."

"It's possible, but a smaller target is going to be a lot harder to hit," Onas counters. "And since he's a spellcaster, there's always a chance he could shield himself or counter it somehow."

"Which would basically be no different than a spellcaster trying to take him on one-on-one." It sounds like Jace has had this discussion before. "He won't be expecting someone to hop onto his dragon though. I really think that might be our best bet."

"Well, this baby is more than up to the challenge," Onas says, patting the thing's side with a grin.

"But just in case…" Wari is more sensible. "Let's get everyone stocked up."

The brothers quickly get to work racing around the shop, grabbing different gadgets from shelves and behind counters. They've got bracelets and rings that make us stronger and faster, shields that float and automatically move to deflect incoming arrows or spells, and even some boots that let a person jump *really* high. Confident enough that I don't need the boost, I let the others divide the objects among themselves.

"David," Wari gets my attention at the other end of the shop. "Over here."

I follow him behind the counter and into the back room, which is even more crowded than the rest of the store. Boxes and crates are stacked all around, each filled with gods know what. But Wari seems to know exactly where he's going, and after following him through basically a small maze, he stops at a box of weapons.

"Here." He grabs two swords and hands them to me, pommel up. "How do they feel?"

"Light," I reply, surprised by how little they weigh.

"That's 'cause they're made of mythril," Wari answers my unspoken question with a grin.

"*Mythril?*" I'm in disbelief. "You just keep this stuff lying around?"

"You live as long as we do, stuff starts to accumulate over the years." He waves me off. "Consider them a gift."

"Wari, that's too much." Seriously, he could probably buy someone a couple of horses, maybe even a small house with these things! "I can't take these."

"Then let's call it a loan," he insists. "You hang onto them until we get your *other* sword back."

"If that's even possible," I complain.

"Hey, we're about to fight a dragon, so can it with the negative thinking," he admonishes me sharply. "Now I think you're also gonna need this, and these."

He hands me a long metal chain and a pair of gloves. The chain has a hook at one end and is as light as the swords, so it must also be mythril. The gloves otherwise look normal, but I'm sure he's gonna correct me.

"The grappling hook is self-explanatory, but the gloves are enchanted to improve your grip," Wari explains. "I thought you might need some help keeping a hold of the dragon once you're on board."

"Thanks, Wari." I put the gloves on and give them a test, opening my hand only to see that the sword doesn't drop from my open hand—I have to pull it off with my other hand.

"Take a few minutes to get used to those things and the swords," he tells me. "Then we should get a move on."

After going over the plan again, our group is ready. As we make our way back to the park, we see that the forces from shore have finally reached the park, and the fighting has begun in earnest. A field of the living versus the undead, punctuated by the occasional werewolf growl or spark of fire from one of the dragons.

"Looks like he's using the big guy to guard his camp," Adam points out, nodding in the direction of the giant black lizard in the center of the park.

"Then that's where we're going." Onas, still carrying the metal dragon with his brother, steps forward.

"That's a long walk," Wari complains, "through a battlefield."

"The rest of us will escort you there," Khazak decides with ease. "But first, we need to find an appropriate building for David to get to the top of."

"There's an inn a block down that way." Jace points us in the right direction. "It should have easy roof access."

"I know the one you're talking about," Wari agrees. "I'll go with David."

"You don't need to be with Wari?" Liss asks, looking at the metal dragon.

"We've both got a set of control sticks." Wari pulls out two wooden rods with metal designs set into them. "But we're not positive on what their range is."

"So just in case, I'll get it started and send it your way." Onas continues, understanding his brother's thinking. "Then Wari will take over and make sure it lures the dragon close enough for David."

"Everyone understand their assignments?" Khazak asks, waiting for a group affirmative. "Then let's get started."

"You know, you're going along with this a lot better than I expected," I tell Khazak as we prepare to split.

"I am not exactly thrilled, but I am also a man of my word." Khazak's face softens for a moment. "David… Please be careful. As careful as you can given the circumstances."

"I will, I promise." We wrap each other in another hug, one that feels a little more serious than I wanted it to. "Don't worry. I'll come back to you again."

"You better, or else you're never getting that cage off," he jokes, though I can tell he's trying to mask his worry. "I love you."

"I love you too." With a kiss, he's back to business and leads the others through the battlefield.

The trip Wari and I have to make is a lot less perilous but still not entirely safe. Most of the battle is taking place

in the park itself, but there are still plenty of outlying skeletons to fight through. Wari is an old pro though, blasting
away most of them with magic before I can even reach for
my weapon.

"This is the place," Wari says once we reach the inn.

It's seen better days. The front doors are both missing,
and the lobby looks like it's been pretty thoroughly ransacked. We start to hustle up the stairs, and it looks like the
same is probably true for the rooms. I wonder what happened to the people staying here when the dragons first
showed. There's nobody here now.

We reach the door to the roof easily, though Wari has
to use magic unlock it. From up here, we can see over the
whole park, though all of the trees combined with the lack
of sunlight make it a little difficult to tell what's actually
going on. Occasionally the dragon in the air will breathe
fire at something on the ground, forming little pockets of
flame on the dark field.

"So I guess now we wait?" I lean over the roof's ledge as
I keep my eyes trained on the large dragon. "How are we
gonna know when they set it off? Maybe we should have
worked out some kind of signal."

"Trust me, kid.. There'll be a very clear signal when
Onas starts that thing up," Wari says, joining me at the
ledge which reaches just under his chin. "But just in case…"

He reaches into his pocket and pulls out what looks like
a spyglass. It seems too dark to be useful, but he holds it up
to his eyes and spies through it without issue. He twists a few
times on the casing, adjusting it until he's happy.

"Can you even see out of that thing?" I question.
"It's so dark."

"Yes and no," he admits. "Yes I can see but not our
friends yet. Too many trees in the way."

He keeps a lookout while we continue to wait. I feel like
this is dragging on and on, and I'm starting to get worried

that something might have happened. I start pacing back and forth.

"There!" Wari announces with a shout. "I see them. They're nearing the big dragon."

"They all made it okay?" *Thank the gods.*

"See for yourself." He hands me the spyglass. "Look just to the left of the lake."

I'm surprised when I first look through the glass, shocked at how detailed everything is. It's not quite like things would be during the day; things are still dark but outlines are much more defined. And even without Wari's instructions, it would be hard to miss where to look—the giant dragon is guarding its rider fiercely, breathing fire at anything that approaches.

"I see them." In an open-ish field, between the lake and dragon, is our small group—Khazak still in the lead.

"Alright, any minute now." Wari taps me on the thigh, and I return the requested spyglass. "Get ready."

I resume my pacing as he watches, anxious to get started. The more I think about it, the more worried I am about psyching myself out and choking up at the last minute. I am about to jump off of a very tall building onto the back of a fast-moving fire breathing dragon. *Is this crazy? This is crazy. I'm crazy.*

"Here they come!" Wari shouts with excitement.

He tosses me the spyglass and quickly retrieves the wooden rods from his pocket. They are basically identical, both inlaid with metal all along their length. He takes one in each hand and holds them vertically in front of himself, covering the top with his thumbs.

Before I even look through the spyglass, a series of bright sparks shoot up into the air near the dragon. Holding it up to my eye, I follow the sparks to their point of origin—the metal dragon. It flies in fast circles around the dragon's head, trying to grab its attention. And it works. Obviously threatened, the dragon attempts to blast it with its fire a few times, but the little thing is just too quick for it.

And then it starts to fly away—and the dragon takes the bait and gives chase. As they turn toward us, I realize that I'm only going to get one shot at this. The metal dragon, now glowing a bright red as it streaks through the sky, starts to make a wide turn as it prepares to lead the dragon right past our building.

"I've got it!" Wari announces, the two rods suddenly humming with energy. "Get ready!"

I watch as he slowly turns the two rods in unison at the time that the dragons, real and metal, start to curve back toward us. *This is it.* I jog to the corner closest to my target, watching carefully as it gets closer and closer. As the metal machine moves along the row of buildings, the large dragon roars right behind it, the force of its flapping wings shattering countless windows.

I start to run to the other end of the roof, hitting my top speed just as the sparks zoom by, and before I can hesitate, I jump. As the dark-scaled dragon passes beneath me, I throw the mythril chain given to me by Wari. Relief shoots through my body as it wraps around the dragon's tail—and then the rest of me is pulled forward as its speed overtakes my own.

Fuckfuckfuckfuckfuckfuck! I am *hurtling* through the sky as the dragon drags me with it. With barely a chance to get my bearings and knowing I need to work fast, I start pulling myself along the chain. With the magic gloves on my hands, I manage to reach beast's back, releasing and keeping my grappling hook at the ready as I work my way up the dragon's body, who thankfully hasn't noticed that it's picked up a passenger, still focused on the chase.

Just as I draw near the base of its scaly tail, the explosion the brothers warned about has the dragon suddenly changing direction. It roars in pain, flying straight up and nearly making me lose my grip. While the dragon hovers in place, probably confused about why whatever it was just chasing exploded, I throw my grappling hook again and use my body weight to swing around its tail, pulling me close as the chain wraps around.

By the time I finally get a hold of its scales, it's moving again, though thankfully slower than before. The gloves the brothers gave me are doing the trick, but it's still unbelievably nerve wracking to climb along the back of a giant creature, let alone a flying fire-breathing dragon.

"Damned stupid thing," a voice that has to belong to the necromancer says. "I knew I should have bound a smarter demon."

I'm about halfway up the dragon as we hover above the park. The chains that make up he dragon's "collar" are just up ahead, sitting at the base of its neck. In front of that, I can see the saddle, along with the human sitting on it: my target, who just like the dragon, hasn't noticed me yet.

"What is it now? Why aren't you…" he continues to complain. "Shit, did something damage the bloodstone?"

I have no idea what this guy is talking about, but at least it's keeping him distracted. I can move a lot faster with the dragon not speeding across the sky and quickly finish my climb. As I draw closer to the saddle, I reach for one of my swords, then pause.

Am I really just going to kill this guy? Sneaking up on someone and literally stabbing them in the back doesn't feel right. But this guy is responsible for a lot of death and destruction, and if I don't stop him, he'll—

<Help… Me…>

What was that? I flail, looking around in confusion for the unknown voice echoing in my head, and my sword smacks into one of the dragon's scales with a *clang*.

"Who's there?" the necromancer calls out, looking around wildly before his eyes land on me. "Who the hell are you? And how did you get up here?"

Welp, there goes that worry. "Your friendly neighborhood dragon inspector. Is this thing registered?"

I quickly duck the bolt of magic that flies over my head. Guess he didn't like that one.

"I don't know what you were hoping to do here," the necromancer continues, his hands glowing as he prepares another spell. "But you didn't think this through very well, did you?"

"Not really, no," I admit with a shrug before ducking behind a large ridge scale as he fires off more magic. Then I poke my head up. "But I've always been pretty good at winging it. Get it? Because of the wings?"

"Oh, I got it," he replies snidely. Fine, maybe he's just not a big fan of comedy in general.

As the weird crown on his head glows, the dragon stops hovering and starts to move again. I barely have a second to grab hold of something as we start to twist through the sky, trying to throw me off. Whatever magic he's using, it's keeping his feet glued to the saddle pretty steadily.

Thankfully, my gloves are still working. And even with his grippy feet, he's learning that it's a lot harder to aim when we're moving this fast. I dodge spells while trying to get myself closer to him at the same time, but just as I reach the saddle, his luck changes, and he nails me in the arm.

As pain courses through it, I try to roll out of the way, but all that does is help the second bolt knock me off the dragon's neck. With my arm starting to go numb, I barely manage to use the other to throw my grappling hook in time, wedging into the creature's collar before I plumet to the ground. *Don't look down.*

<*Help me… Please…*> There's that voice again.

"Oh no you don't." That's Corbin the necro-dick up above. "Why are you still struggling? You're only making it harder on yourself."

Is he talking to me? Or is it... I get an idea and hesitate for a moment, but you know what? Fuck it. It's not like I haven't done crazier stuff today.

"I don't know if you can hear me," I start, speaking in a low voice, "but if there is anything you can do to help me, I swear I'll return the favor."

<Yes... Then please... Release me...>

I take a look at my numb arm, and it's not a pretty sight, the skin pale white and covered in black, pulsing lesions. *Here goes everything.* I start to pull myself back up onto the dragon's neck, which is a lot harder with only one arm and my feet, but I make it. The necromancer is still standing, confident that he's alone up here again. Time to burst that bubble.

"Just wait till we're back at the quarry, then I—Aahh! You!" He looks surprised to see me.

"Me!" I reply with a grin. "Gonna take a lot more than that to get rid of me, but first things first: have you been hearing that weird, disembodied voice too?"

"I don't know what voice you could be referring to," he lies, casting another spell. "But if you'll excuse me, I have important things to take care of."

He's panicking, and that's good because it means he's getting sloppier. But I still can't get close enough to actually attack him, and even with my abilities "on," holding onto anything up here with only one good hand is tough. How am I supposed to stop him?

"Give up!" Corbin tries to end this with another spell. "You'll never beat me. Surrender now, and I'll go easy on you."

The dragon suddenly shakes its head—throwing Corbin off balance and sending his spell into the night sky.

<Please...> the voice pleads again. *<The collar...>*

Everything clicks—the voice, the muttering about binding demons, the fact that he's controlling a dragon that very clearly does not want to be controlled—it's the collar. A collar that seems to be made of really cheap iron.

"Now who didn't think things through?" I pull one of the mithril swords from my back and plunge the blade into the bundle of chains.

I hear several of the links crack, but for good measure, I give it a few more stabs. No longer secure, it just takes a little kick for the chains to begin to slip off either side of the dragon neck. With the amulet now loose, gravity does its work and pulls the entire thing off, the chains rattling all the way down.

"No!" Corbin cries, still barely hanging on. "What did you do!?"

The dragon starts to rapidly lose height but gains speed as its body begins to glow a familiar sickly purple. Energy shoots from the dragon's head with howl, and I swear I see the image of something with bat wings and horns fly off into the night. I watch as the scales and flesh around me begin to melt away—barely leaving me time to brace for impact with the ground.

We land with a crash, and I am thrown from the dragon's body, hitting the ground hard and bouncing as I roll onto the grass. In pain but still moving, I pick myself up and watch as the dragon body disintegrates.

<*Thank you,*> I hear one final time, and then all I'm looking at is a pile of bones. But where's the necromancer?

My question is answered when the other two dragons suddenly fly in, circling around the large skeleton. The green one dives down while the red one—which I see Redwish is still riding—stays in the air. I run forward, but even with magical speed, I'm too late. The green dragon is already back in the air with its passenger. Dammit!

I start to give chase, but as they rise higher into the air, it's pretty obvious that they're both going to make their escape. But with him gone, it doesn't take long for the rest of the necromancer's spells to come undone, his undead army falling to pieces. All around me, people are cheering, and I'm caught off guard when I'm suddenly hugged from behind by a pair of strong green arms.

"You did it!" Khazak cries happily in my ear. "And you're alive!"

"I didn't do it though," I complain and turn around. "He and Redwish got away."

"You stopped him, David, that's all that matters right now," Khazak reminds me, smiling warmly.

"Alright. I did it," I acquiesce. It's hard to stay sad when I see that smile, and I have really, really missed it.

"*Kro'mat*, David, what happened to your arm?!" He looks at my injury with shock.

"Was that a curse word?" He *never* curses in Atasi, and I only managed to learn a few of them on my own. "What does it mean?"

"Medic!" he calls out, ignoring my very important questions.

Jace rushes over, takes one look at my arm, and says a prayer—which kind of freaks me out until I realized that's him casting a healing spell. As the feeling returns to my limb and the color returns to my arm, cries of victory ring out all around the city. I can finally let myself relax, and even though there's still a lot more work to be done, I know I'm right back where I belong, with the man I belong to.

Chapter 18

Khazak

"That looks much better."

"Feels better too."

I'm with David at the center of Progress Park as our victory becomes evident to everyone around us. The colossal skeleton of the dragon lies before us, the ivory of its bones shining bright in the moonlight. And though he would downplay his part, it was him who was up there, fighting mid-air.

Redwish *and* the necromancer appear to have escaped, but with him and his magic gone, the rest of his army has quite literally fallen to pieces. But what would normally be a very morbid scene isn't threatening to dampen anyone's spirits, cries of victory ringing out in every direction.

"Great job, David," Liss compliments.

"Nah, that was a team effort," he insists. "I couldn't have done it without everyone else's help."

"I have a feeling you would have found a way." I smile and squeeze his shoulder. The one that wasn't injured.

As much as I know that he would love to argue with me, there is still work to be done. As we begin to clear out Corbin's camp, we find two long metal cages filled with twenty or so captives each, which is still far less than are missing. Any other captives have already escaped during the battle, at least those that hadn't already been taken from the city yet.

"Thank you so much!" one of the captives praises as we break the lock on their cramped prisons. "Any longer and he would have flown us out of here like the others."

"Do you know where he took them?" Jace asks as he starts to check everyone for injuries.

"No, he just told us that he had more digging to do." Another captive shakes her head.

"He said he had what he came here for," I start, remembering his words. "What was it he was having you look for?"

"I'm not really sure what it was." A third captive looks around at the group, none of who are able to describe it. "It was this heavy, long, and sort of rounded piece of stone?"

"It was all black, but with gold marks all through it?" the captive tries his best. "It looked like the stuff the dome in the ritual room on Testament Island is made of."

"Astral stone!" Onas suddenly shouts while slapping his brother on the arm.

"Oww, what?!" Wari glares at his brother in annoyance.

"That's what's mixed in with the ruby in the amulets!" Onas replies cheerfully. "That could explain so much! We need to start testing—"

"*Onas.*" Wari holds a hand to his brother's face in an attempt to stop him. "Later. Bigger things to worry about right now."

"So it was just a big rock?" David asks the captives, back on topic.

"It looked like it could have been a part of something bigger?" they offer, though it is obvious they are only guessing.

"Is he trying to find the pieces of something?" David wonders aloud, mind drifting.

"Your guess is as good as ours." From behind us come Lieutenant Gwar, Raso, and Yuta, along with some faces I don't recognize.

"Lieutenant!" Jace salutes once he notices his superior. "The captives were just telling us more about the necromancer's operations."

"At ease, Jace." Gwar looks to be in much better shape than when I last saw her. "Raso, let's get these people to a medical tent, then we can worry about interviewing them."

"Right away, ma'am." Raso, along with several other guards, begin assisting the freed captives.

"Khazak, I shouldn't be surprised that it's your group at the center of this," the older halfling tells me with a smile. "Who do I have to thank for taking down the dragon?"

"That would be David." Liss shoves him forward.

"Really? We haven't met but I've heard plenty about you." Gwar offers her hand to David. "The city owes you a lot."

"It wasn't all me," David corrects her. "I had a lot of help from everyone here."

"David, this is Lieutenant Gwar and Yuta," I introduce him to the remaining people I know. "They are who we have been working with over the past few weeks."

"I've heard a lot about you." Yuta offers her own hand. "Seems like you lived up to the hype."

"Thanks? It's nice to meet you both," David says to the two women. "But really, I can't take all the credit. I think the dragon might have even helped me it."

"What do you mean?" Gwar asks, each of us just as curious.

"I think it spoke to me?" He taps his forehead. "In my head. It … asked me to get rid of the collar around its neck. After I did, this bright light shot out of its body, and it started to dissolve. Then we crashed."

"That's strange," Onas notes, already in thought.

"I think it thanked me right before the end," David continues. "And the necromancer was having problems controlling it, too. He was saying something about the collar being damaged."

"I knew it wasn't a regular resurrection," Jace says, mostly to himself. "Ma'am, I'd like to inspect the dragon's remains and see if I can glean anything useful."

"It's all yours, Jace," Gwar tells the man. "Set up a perimeter. I don't want civilians getting near it until we know more."

"Yes, ma'am!" The man salutes before heading off.

"Did everyone make it to shore okay?" David asks one of the faces I do *not* know.

"Didn't lose a single ship," a tall human answers. "Whatever you were doing here kept him too busy to look for us out there."

"Good." David smiles. "Khazak, this is Syris and Twyla. They're who I was with in Kiweni."

"You must be Khazak." A gnome shakes my hand, followed by Syris. "He was really worried about you."

"And I him." I greet them both. "Thank you for looking after him."

"Has anyone seen Max and the rest of his pack?" David asks before looking around.

"Yeah. They're helping with the cleanup," Twyla answers with a nod. "More than a few buildings collapsed, and they've got the strength to dig through it."

"Shit, I better get over there too." David turns toward some of the destruction.

"You are not going anywhere yet." I pull him back. "You just fought a dragon. You need to rest for a moment."

"But I can help," he tries to plead with me.

"We've got it covered for now," Gwar assures him.

"What are the current plans for recovery?" I ask Gwar as David settles back down.

"We want to do a quick sweep of the island and make sure the necromancer hasn't left us any surprises," she starts to explain, "then we'll start moving the civilians back in from the refugee camps."

"We'll get shelters and food banks set up in the interim for anyone who needs them," Yuta adds, "and we'll work on reuniting any families that were separated."

"We still need to track down the city leaders and find out what happened to them," Gwar says next. "We're already checking the remaining safehouses. Then there's figuring out how the necromancer accomplished what he did." The lieutenant sighs wearily as more work presents itself.

"I mean, it was the dragons, right?" David questions seriously.

"Not that, the barrier he created," Gwar clarifies. "Turning it on and off is simple, but for him to alter it the way he did, he had to have some kind of intimate knowledge about our security."

"We may need to interview the staff on Testament Island," Yuta continues. "Hopefully Jace will be able to tell us something about the necromancer's magic."

"What about the people he kidnapped?" David asks, still not giving up. "Are you going after them?"

"We've already assigned some scouts to track his route, and we're setting up a search team. But I worry about how long it may take us." Yuta grimaces slightly. "We have to rescue them, but we also have to help those here recover."

"You have all been an immense help throughout this ordeal," Gwar praises our gathered group. "But you're also civilians, so please, rest, recover, and let us handle things."

"Thank you, Lieutenant." I turn to David, who no doubt is still thinking of ways to help. "You want to keep working, don't you?"

"There's so much I can do to help, Sir." David holds one hand up and puts the other on his heart. "I swear I'm not tired, and I promise to tell you if I start to feel off."

"Hmm. Alright." How can I say no to that face? "Let us see what we can do."

We can see the Maname Guard are already setting up medical tents as medics begin to canvas the battlefield. The Bearfoot Brothers join other spellcasters in using their magic to remove rubble or repair damage to the park while Adam pairs with Liss and I with David to assist in locating the injured still on the battlefield and get them to a healer. Or in the case of more critical injuries, lead a healer directly to them.

"Here you go," David says as we drop off another patient. "Try to stay off that foot until someone can take a look at it."

"Thanks," the injured guard says with a nod.

"We've cleared the area by the lake," I tell David as we head back out. "I think we should move north from there and then—"

bark *Is that—?*

"Sona!" David cheers as we both turn to see her familiar black form behind us rushing forward.

"What in the world are you doing here?" I crouch down as she practically runs right into me and pet through her fur as she nuzzles up to me.

<Khazak, happy!> She whines and lick over my hand. *<See red, scared. Follow David.>*

"She's been with me, actually." David crouches down to pet her as well. "She followed me after I got fished out of the bay and then was on the boat here. I think she was really worried about you."

"She was telling me." I smile at the thought of my two exiled pups banding together. "It is very good to see you."

<Miss Khazak.> She trots around me in a circle. *<Sona stay.>*

"Of course you can stay," I inform her with a pet. "We are looking for people who are hurt. Can you help us find them?"

She quickly barks a yes and begins to sniff at the ground, eager to get started. Soon the three of us are working even faster than we were before to clear our section of the park. Between Sona's nose and David's strength, we are able to assist in finding and helping several people buried under rubble. Not every scene we come across is a pleasant one, but we save many lives. I am not keeping track of the time, but when I notice the beginnings of the sun dawning on the eastern horizon, the exhaustion finally hits me.

"I think I may need to rest soon," I tell David as we help another injured person to a medical tent.

"Really? I'm fine, I just—" He stumbles, proving my point. "Okay, maybe I could sit down for a little."

I direct us to one of the larger tents where chairs, water, and food have been placed out for those in need. Sona trots off into the park as I retrieve some water for the two of us, leaving me a moment to just sit in a comfortable silence with David. When she returns, she has a large femur between her jaws.

"That's adorable," David mumbles, leaning against me. "And morbid."

"Best not to think where all the bones came from, I think." I certainly have tried not to focus on it too much.

"Mmmm," David sleepily agrees, I think.

"More tired than you thought?" I give him a small kiss on the top of his head.

"Yeah." He nods and stands much more steadily than before. "I could use a nap."

"Sona," I tell the young wolf currently gnawing on her prize, "we are going to rest. Do you want to come with us?"

<No. Stay, explore.> She huffs, no doubt excited about her prospects. *<Find Khazak.>*

"Stay out of trouble, and find our friends if something happens," I instruct her, receiving a bark in response. The collar should keep her safe, but I never know how some people may react. "Is it just me, or does it look like she has put on some weight?"

David snorts a laugh. "Maybe."

Eager for a bed, I guide David toward the Black Rooster. I think we both try not to focus too much on the scenes of destruction we pass along the way, but they are impossible to ignore. Nothing has toppled on this side of the city, but there are still obvious signs of destruction from the fighting that took place nearby.

"Wait, *this* is where you've been staying?" David asks in surprise as we approach the familiar bookstore.

"It has proven to be quite an effective base of operations," I inform him, leading him inside. "Lead walls, a hidden entrance, and plenty of room."

"Was there an attack of some kind?" He looks around at the feigned destruction inside.

"Yes, though this actually isn't all from that," I tell him, heading for the secret door. "We wanted it to seem like the store had already been looted and was empty."

Inside the Rooster, things are busy, many of the civilians already packing their bags to leave. The remaining are all gathered in the central room speaking excitedly to one another while some guards are running back and forth between our various inventories, prepping it to be moved to where the supplies are most needed.

"David?" Tsula, who is seated at the bar with Corrine, perks her head up when she notices us walking in.

"David!" Corrine hurries off her seat, practically throwing herself into a hug.

"Cory!" David returns her hug. "It's so good to see you."

"We've all been so worried about you." Tsula takes her turn.

"Ditto." David smiles and takes in the rest of the room. "I'm glad everyone's alright."

"It's been rough," Corrine tells him wearily, "but we made it!"

"You look exhausted too," Tsula notices. "We've been up all night helping with the injured outside. What about you?"

"I fought a dragon." He doesn't mean it as a brag, but it certainly sounds like one.

"What? Oh my God." Corrine covers her mouth in shock, then begins to cast a spell. "Hold on, let me make sure you're alright."

"I'm fine. Just need to lay down, I think," David assures her, giving himself a sniff. "And maybe a shower."

"Well, they're open," Corrine tells us. "A lot of people have already left to try and return home or at least see what state it's in."

"Then there should be plenty of beds open," I say with a nod of my head before pointing toward the room with the showers. "Showers are through there. I'll meet you in a moment."

"Kay." David sleepily stretches his arm above his head as he pads off to the bathroom.

I make a detour for the room I have been using, pleased to find that it appears largely emptied out. I grab my bag, and with it my shower supplies, though there's another object in particular that is on my mind at the moment. That and a lot of guilt.

I can hear the shower running in one of the stalls when I enter the large bathroom, pulling back the curtain to find a naked David already inside. Before I join him, I hold up the key to his chastity cage. I cannot even begin to describe how horrible I feel for having left him locked in it for so long.

Before I can say or do anything, he pulls me against him under the spray of heated water, and I groan as it washes over my sore muscles. For the first time in a long while, the two of us hold each other and enjoy a peaceful moment without interruption. I run my hands over his body, up and down his back, and through his hair as the two of us just rock each other back and forth.

"I've missed you so much, puppy," I say low in his ear.

"Me too, Sir." He nuzzles into my chest like the pup he is.

"Now, I believe I have owed you this for some time," I tell him as I drop to one knee.

With the key in one hand, I take hold of his caged cock with the other. Not intending to draw this out, I insert the key and open the lock with a muted click. I pull the cage from his shaft, and then slide the locking ring over his balls, setting it to the side before standing again.

"That feels nice," David says with a happy groan as he reaches down to fondle himself. "I missed being able to do that."

"I cannot even begin to apologize," I start, willing to try anyway.

"It's okay, really," he tries to assuage my guilt. "It wasn't like you did it on purpose. It wasn't even the hardest thing I had to deal with, considering everything else going on."

"Still, I don't think we will be using that for punishment again." I take him in my arms again. I decided that last night.

"I don't know if we need to go *that* far." I pull back to make sure I am looking at the right person—who is still fondling himself. "I mean, I'm pretty sure everything is still working down here."

"It almost sounds as though you *enjoyed* wearing it," I point out, wondering what he is getting at.

"I'm just saying it's been an effective punishment in the past, that's all," he tries to explain, but I'm not sure I believe him.

"I will try to keep that in mind," I tell him, looking down to note that he is already getting an erection.

"That's unrelated!" David insists when he sees me noticing it. "I mean, come on. It's the first time I've even been able to get hard in weeks."

"Mhmm," I reply, still doubtful of his reasoning.

"Oh man, Sir, you won't believe it, but I actually met another collared boy," he steers my attention away from what is now pushing against my leg. "But get this: his sir has *never* punished him."

"He must be a very well-behaved boy," I note with amusement as I reach for some nearby soap. "You'll have to tell me more—later."

I lather up my hands before taking a hold of his cock, which continues its rapid expansion in my grasp, rising like a tree in the forest in mere seconds. Not a surprise, given it's been nearly four weeks without any direct contact. With my pup once more in my hands, I slowly stroke my soapy hand up and down his erect prick, listening to him gasp at the pressure.

"Careful, Sir, or I'm going to—"

"Cum whenever you want to, pup," I tell him, pressing my body against his side and continuing to work his shaft.

He makes a questioning noise but does not actually ask anything, happy to let me work. Even under the water I can feel that he is practically drooling precum as he throbs in my hand. It is not even a full minute before he is spilling pearly white liquid over my fist with a weak moan.

"Good puppy," I praise while grabbing more soap to clean us. "I assumed the first would happen quickly."

"First?" he asks, still dazed from the orgasm.

"Tonight, puppy, you get to cum as much as you want," I inform him how I intend to start making this up to him. "It is the least I can do."

"Whatever makes you happy, Sir." He tries to play it cool but his erection pulses.

I run my soapy hands over his body, scrubbing the grime and sweat of battle from his skin. It feels good to have him under my hands again. It feels *right.* I scrape my blunt nails down the slick skin of his back as I hold him against my chest.

As I rake his flesh with my fingertips, I find myself trying to commit every curve, mark, and scar to memory. David whimpers as my hands press against his sore muscles, leaning against my body for more. The more I pet him, the less tense he becomes.

I groan when David attempts to repeat these ministrations on my body, not realizing how strained I was myself. When this is all over, I should look into booking a massage for the two of us. Especially as my poor David just does not have the strength right now, practically dozing off while standing up.

I finish up our washing session, keeping an increasingly sleepier David upright as I dry us both off. He is cooperative as I dress us just enough to be decent getting from here to the rooms where we can actually sleep. No one questions what we are up to, and I don't expect to be disturbed for some time.

I return us to the now empty room, closing the door behind us. I start to strip us both, pushing a nude David towards the bed. He falls onto it face-first, groaning in pleasure at the softness against his skin. After making sure the door is locked, I join him, climbing over his body.

"Just a few minutes," David mumbles as he turns onto his side, squeezing against my chest.

I don't respond, just chuckle and kiss his forehead as he drifts off. I throw one of my arms and legs over his body, just happy to feel him beneath me once more. I continue to hold and pet him as I join David in sleep, drifting off just as he starts to lightly snore.

I wake at least a few hours later, not nearly enough to feel fully rested. It is probably barely into the afternoon outside, and my stomach feels empty. I consider leaving to get us both something to eat, but at the moment, I have a more pressing matter to deal with.

Pressing on my thigh, to be specific—David's cock. I am not surprised that it is already seeking more attention after its long confinement. I still feel so bad for leaving him locked as long as I did. How could it not cross my mind even once while he was gone?

After carefully detangling myself from David, I shuffle down the bed, not wanting to wake him just yet. Face to face with his turgid member, I take it in hand and aim it at my mouth. I smile to myself as his familiar taste rolls over my tongue after so long an absence.

David is normally the one in this position, so it is nice to be able to surprise him for once. I begin to slowly suck on his cock, easily taking it into my throat as I continue my way down. I start to bob on him lightly, my nose bumping into the forest of hair covering his groin. Still asleep, David begins to thrust, seeking more friction. I chuckle to myself, doing my best to match his lack of rhythm.

"Mmm," David moans in his sleep. "Khaz—Sir?"

"Just like before, pup," I tell him, pulling off for a moment and stroking his slick shaft with my fist. "Whenever you're ready."

"I—unh—thank you, Sir." His thrusts start to slow. "I can cum however I want?"

"However you want," I confirm with a nod.

"Okay." He nods, but then tugs on my hair, pulling me forward to crawl up his body and meet his lips. "Then what I really, really want right now is to feel you inside of me. Please."

"Of course, pup," I nod, not bothering to disguise my eagerness. "Wait right here."

I practically launch myself from the bed toward my bag to retrieve the cleansing stone and oil in record time. I still fully intend to make things up to David, but I am certainly not going to turn down an invitation like that. I return to the bed with both objects in hand, pulling David onto his back with me at his side.

I hold the stone to his stomach, letting its magic do the trick, and then pop open the cork on the oil. Dribbling it over my fingers, my hand finds itself in a familiar position, just behind David's balls. I run my fingers around the outside of his entrance, making him shudder before I press inside.

"Fuck, I missed that," he says as the first of my fingers penetrates him. "So much better than that toy."

"What toy?" I question as I continue to explore his rear. "I thought they were all in my bag."

"Uh, long story short, someone else found out about the cage and lent me a toy to … help relieve myself the only way I could," he answers with a grimace. "Sorry, Sir."

"Who?" I answer, even as I continue to press my fingers inside, feeling a little jealous.

"That couple I mentioned?" The way he frames it as a question tells me there is more to this story—but I will worry about that later.

I bend over and lock my lips to his as I explore more of his tunnel. Familiar muscles stretch around me as I slowly drive my fingers in and out. David groans, spreading his legs further as the tight heat of his body warms mine.

His lips feel like home, his body a grassy plane I have explored time and again. He begins to bear down on my hand, thrusting himself onto my fingers for more. Happy to satisfy him, I add another and begin to pump my fingers more firmly. *Spirits, I have missed this!*

Managing to tear myself away from him, I shift to kneel between his spread legs. Uncorking the vial of oil,

I pour more out into my hand before sticking it over my cock. Without another word, I press the head of my prick against his hole, pressing forward until the pressure forces me to pop inside.

David moans low as he is stretched, and I already know that whatever toy he was using paled in comparison to me. I neglect to hold back my own noises, practically snarling as I bottom out. With David wrapped tightly around my entire length, I bend over and seek his mouth for a kiss.

"Fuuuuuuuuck yes," he moans into my mouth as I grind into him.

With me locked inside his hole, the two of us spend the next few minutes kissing accompanied by the occasional lazy thrust. It has been twelve days since I last felt him, tasted him. I take my time, remapping his mouth with my tongue, relearning his flavor.

Unable to wait any longer, I pull my hips back and plunge back in. I do my best to keep things slow at first, pumping into him gently, the ring of his hole pulling against my shaft. But the more I thrust, the harder it is to hold back, and not even ten minutes in, I am pounding away with all of my might.

"Fuck… More…" David babbles beneath me. "Please, I've needed this so bad."

I recapture his mouth as my growling and grunting turns more animalistic. All of my instincts are telling me to go harder, faster, to bury myself as deep as I possibly can inside of him until I unload. Between my noises, David's begging, and the bed creaking, I am very thankful for Cillian soundproofing these rooms.

"Yesyeyeyseyseysesssssssss," David cries in pleasure, his muscles fluttering and pushing out as he has an orgasm.

Those yesses and the feeling around my cock only drive me to fuck harder. I continue to plunder David's rear, and my mind clears of all other thoughts. Just the tight, hot drag of his skin against mine.

I don't know how long we are actually at it for. I manage block out all other noise and thoughts, the entire outside world, and everything melts down to just me and David. He is practically bent in two as I lock our mouths together, kissing him deeply as the fucking continues.

David has another orgasm only a minute later, his limbs still tightly wrapped around my body. After that, it does not take me much longer to cum—David is not the only one of us who has gone almost two weeks without sex. Still, it catches us both off-guard, my pup mumbling a questionable noise as my shaft starts to grow within him as I unload.

I feel a release like never before when I cum. More than just pleasure, all the stress and worry of the last two months are fired away with it. Before I even finish, feelings of warmth and safety overcome me, feelings which I try to wrap David in as I pull us onto our sides.

Still exhausted from the evening's battle, I slowly fall back under the spell of sleep. I pull David to lay over my chest, petting through his hair. With my puppy once more in my arms, I allow myself to relax, and all finally feels right with the world.

Chapter 19

David

*J***feel good. Great even, safe, and surrounded by warmth.** *A cool breeze flows over my back, making me shiver, and I try to burrow farther into the warmth.*

Wait, I shouldn't be feeling a breeze at all. I pull back and open my eyes to a forest around me, the blue sky visible just through the branches overhead. And looking at my side is the source of my warmth: Khazak.

We're both naked, which would normally be a concern, but I can't find the energy to make myself care right now. It helps that I already know what's going on: this is a dream. Luckily, it seems to be a nice one.

Khazak wakes up next, but he seems just as unconcerned as I am as he takes in the scene. Then he looks over to me and just smiles. A pair of red birds—cardinals, Khazak's called them before—fly overhead, singing their song. With no signs of danger, no anxiety or fear, we're both content to just lay back and enjoy whatever this is.

I wake up peacefully, probably for the first time since being separated from everyone. The room is dark and cool, and

I can feel Khazak's warm and solid body at my side. I feel totally refreshed, like I could take on the world.

"Good morning," Khazak tells me, his voice rough and unused. "Or good evening, more likely."

"Morning." I cuddle up to my Sir. "This is nice. I missed *this*."

"I did too." He squeezes me to his body, just as my stomach rumbles. "Well then, I suppose we need to get some food in you."

"Yes, please." I nod my head against his chest. "I'm *starving*."

I stumble as I climb out of bed and attempt to get dressed in the dark before Khazak pulls a glowstone out of his bag for me. Then I put my clothes on like a normal person. We exit into the club's central room to find it a lot emptier than it was before we went to bed. I don't see any guards at all, just Adam and Liss and a few others I don't know.

"You're finally up," Liss announces with a smirk.

"Sorry," I apologize for me *and* Khazak. "Been waiting long?"

"Nah, we all crashed for a while too," Adam reveals. "You're just the last ones up."

"Where are the others?" Khazak asks while looking around the nearly empty room.

"Getting dinner ready, hopefully," Liss says with a pat to her stomach. "The Bearfoots offered to cook."

"Yeah, Wari got this excited look in his eye when Corrine and Tsula mentioned being hungry," Adam explains. "Said they're making some kind of stew."

"That sounds great." I follow Liss's lead and pat my own belly. "Should we—"

"Khazak… *David?*" A familiar voice on my right gets my attention, an elf with a dwarf at his side. "It *is* you!"

"You two!" I draw a blank trying to remember either of their names, but I'm pretty sure they own this place.

"Novus, Cillian!" Khazak greets the two and saves me some future embarrassment. "It is good to see that you are alright."

"You two as well, especially you, David!" Cillian replies. "We've been holding up here with Khazak and your other friends since the fighting broke out."

"Your sir was very worried about you," Novus tells me next.

"Yeah, I tend to make him do that." I nod, not feeling guilty at all.

"It has been a hectic time for us all," Cillian continues. "I'm sure your family and other loved ones are happy to know you're alright."

"*Shit!*" I exclaim and quickly run back to our room. *He's gonna kill me.*

"David?" Khazak calls out after me. "What's wrong?"

"Be right back!" I shout as I rush to my bag.

As I reach my hand into the magical satchel, I think about the leather-bound journal I bought maybe three weeks ago, feeling the solid weight of its cover in my hand. I pull it out and quickly flip it open to find that the first six pages are covered top to bottom in frantic writing—Mike has been freaking out since yesterday when I told him the boats were almost to the city. I grab a pen and some ink from my bag next and start writing.

That's it, I'm teleporting there first thing in the morning! is the most recent message.

Wait! No! I'm okay! I reply back frantically, not sure that he's even awake right now.

DUDE! I have been freaking out for almost a full day! What happened!?

It's like even his handwriting is trying to yell at me.

We took a bunch of boats from Kiweni back to Maname yesterday. I pause, deciding to leave out the part where I jumped off of one of those boats and tried to swim to shore. *I got back in the city, turned off the barrier, fought a dragon, rescued Khazak and the others from a different dragon, and then killed a* third *dragon.* Alright, I might be starting to feel a *little* cocky about my dragon slaying prowess.

WHAT!!!!

I know! It was awesome! And also terrifying!

You're okay though? What about the others?

Everyone you know, including me, is okay. I bet he wants to ask about Tsula specifically, but he won't.

We got news of the city's liberation but not any of the details. Oh gods, that means I'll probably have to hear people talking about you for weeks. Ugh.

Aww come on, I know they're all nerds, but you don't think being my brother will boost your social standing?

You think I want people to know we're related? I missed us talking like this.

Alright, I didn't do all the work. There were a lot of guards and soldiers on all those boats. The city is in rough shape, but the necromancer is gone.

Good. Me, Piper, and bunch of other students were ready to head out, whether the school approved or not.

An army of dorks.

He draws a little hand sticking up its middle finger.

Alright listen, I really need to go get something in my stomach. I haven't eaten since yesterday, and I'm starving.

Bottomless fucking pit. Message me later!

I will!

I close the book and return it along with my pen and ink back to my bag. Better keep this on me, just in case. Throwing the whole thing over my shoulder, I rejoin the others in the central room.

"What was that all about?" Khazak asks as I sidle up to him.

"I've been updating Mike on everything while I was in Kiweni and might've forgot to let him know I was alright after last night's big battle," I tell everyone. "He was kinda freaking out."

"I would've been too." Liss snorts a laugh.

"But he is alright now?" He and my brother aren't the biggest fans of each other, so it's nice that he's still concerned.

"Yep!" I nod happily. "Probably tired though. I don't think he got any sleep last night."

"Neither did we," Adam notes with a shrug.

"Shall we meet the others for dinner, then?" Khazak poses the question to the entire group. "Cillian and Novus, you are more than welcome to join us."

"Thank you, Khazak, but I will have to decline." Cillian places his hand on his submissive's back. "The two of us are eager to get home."

"Sir is eager for some of my cooking." Novus grins, proud of his ability.

"Then we wish the two of you a lovely evening," Khazak says gracefully.

We exit the bookstore together, Cillian and Novus going in one direction and the four of us the other. The city doesn't look like it's in any better shape than it was before I slept. I can see people working into the night to clear rubble, and I pause as we pass.

"I should be helping them," I mutter to myself.

"We will," Khazak assures me, "but first you need to eat."

"Even these guys are gonna take a break," Liss points out next. "Everyone's been working in shifts, guards *and* volunteers."

"And even *you* need to take one those sometimes," Khazak says pointedly.

"No good to anyone if you're exhausted, overworked, and hungry," Adam finishes.

I don't quite agree, but I keep the rest of my worries in my head. Guilting myself (and everyone else) for not doing enough isn't gonna help. And I really am hungry.

Deeper into the city, the sights start to look familiar. But when we finally enter the marketplace, I can barely recognize it. Carts and stands are in shambles, shop windows shattered; it's harder to find a place that WASN'T ransacked.

The Magic Mart section fared no better than the rest. I can see through the broken windows that people are already attempting to clean up inside—too many people to just be the owners, meaning this has to be their family, friends, and neighbors. It actually makes me feel warm, some light in all of the darkness.

It's easy to spot the Bearfoot Bros. because set up just outside their storefront is a giant cauldron, a roaring fire underneath. By its size, I assume they're feeding more than just us. Wari stands on a stool at the cauldron's side, hands gripped tightly to the large spoon he's using to stir whatever's inside while Onas is chopping vegetables laid out on a small table just to his left.

Our other friends are all gathered around, some helping with the food, others just chatting, and Khazak whistles to get their attention. It feels good to have the entire group together again. Even Sona managed to find her way here, curled up near the fire and gnawing on a (much smaller than yesterday's) bone.

While dinner cooks, we start to catch each other up on everything that's happened. They tell me all about what it was like hiding in the Black Rooster, working with the guards, rescuing civilians, and all the things they had to do to survive. It's especially hard to hear about the razing of the shipyard, reminding me of that fiery dream I had. Then it's my turn.

"You just woke up in the back of their wagon?" Corrine asks in surprise when I explain how I first met the Hursketts.

"Completely naked," I add. "My clothes were soaked from getting tossed in the bay."

"You *really* like taking your clothes off, huh?" Liss's joke makes the others laugh.

"You would too if you looked this good naked," I fire back with a wink, making her roll her eyes. "They were a nice family, even if their oldest son was kind of a handful."

"Was that the kid you were yelling at yesterday?" Adam asks.

"Yep." I remember the way I dressed him down and wonder if I'm turning into *my* father. "He's a good kid, just a little too hot-headed. Jumps into everything without thinking."

"That doesn't sound familiar at all," Khazak says wryly. I don't dignify it with a response.

"Kiweni was okay," I continue. "Pretty standard for a town. Inns, shops, a dock for boats. There really wasn't all that much to do. I camped with the Hursketts and spent most of my time in the refugee came, but it seemed like a decent place."

"What about your, ah, gifts?" Tsula has the next question. "The others were saying you've learned how to use them."

"I think so." On the off chance this has all been a fluke, I don't want to get ahead of myself. "I joined up with the guards leading the resistance group, started helping train the new recruits. But if I was going to stand any chance of getting back and saving everyone, I needed to figure out my *own* skills—so I started training with a pack of werewolves."

"What?" Khazak is the one who asks, but I've got everyone's attention.

"Yeah, there was a group of werewolves that happened to dock there at the same time," I continue my explanation. "One of them was a prince, even. Wait, I'm not sure I'm allowed to tell you that. Whatever—he's the nephew of the werewolf we freed in Richardton!"

"A prince?" Corrine looks up from her food.

"Who the hell is going around capturing werewolves?" Wari says offhand as he and his brother begin to ladle soup into bowls.

"No one worth talking about," Khazak quickly answers as he is handed a bowl. "You mean Achak."

"C'mon, you know I'm not good with names." I nudge him with my shoulder as Onas gives me my own. "And also that I was mostly out of my mind during that whole thing."

"That's a pretty big coincidence," Adam notes before downing a spoonful.

"We keep having those," Liss adds, looking at me with suspicion.

"I didn't do anything!" I'd be offended if I weren't drooling over the bowl of stew Wari pushes in my hands. "Fuck, that smells delicious."

"Old family recipe," he tells me with a grin.

"I think it was just good timing." I eat almost half my bowl before I finish my thought. "He was only traveling this way because we rescued his uncle. The coincidence—or just luck—is that he docked in Kiweni when he did."

"How'd you meet him?" Does Corrine have a thing for princes?

"He was trying to bribe an innkeeper for a room." I hear a few groans. "He's a better guy than that makes him sound. He actually offered his country's help before anyone even asked. They sent troops, supplies, even the boats that got us here. Plus, him and the rest of his little pack helped me figure out my abilities. Didn't really have to worry about accidentally hurting a werewolf."

"So I guess it's really *them* we should be thanking?" Liss jokes again, accepting a bowl from Onas.

"Yes, but also fuck you." I stick up my middle finger in her direction. "I'd introduce you if I knew where they were. Lost track of them when I jumped off the boat, but—"

"David!" who else but Max shouts from down the street. *Okay, maybe that does happen too much.*

"Max!" I wave him and the rest of his pack over, happy to see Peter is with them.

"We were wondering what happened to you," Max tells me once he's closer. "We were worried you might still be out in the water, then we heard from some of the other guards that somebody managed to slay the big dragon. I assume that was you?"

"Did you seriously jump off the boat and try to swim to shore?" Aria asks behind him.

"Yes," I answer Max first, then turn to Aria. "And yes." She only snorts in response.

"So all the training paid off!" Max grins wide, his teeth sharp and white.

"It did!" I return his enthusiasm. "But we still wouldn't have pulled it off without your help."

"Who are your friends, David?" Khazak not-so-subtly nudges me to make introductions.

"Uh. Alright, but that's a lotta names, so…" I turn and start to point at people individually as I list them off. "Adam, Liss, Corrine, Tsula, Wari, Onas, and this is my … Khazak. And you already know Sona."

"The infamous Khazak." Max smiles and holds out his hand for my orc, then gestures to his own group. "We've heard a lot about you."

"All good, I hope," Khazak jokes as they shake.

"Prince Makseka Blackclaw, but just Max is fine. This is my consort Peter, and that is Aria, Gala, Ryse, and Thomas, who make up my personal guard."

"Nice to meet all of you," Khazak says as the two groups merge and make individual introductions. "I understand I have you to thank for David's triumphant return."

"He did the hard work himself." *Hell yeah I did.* "We just helped."

"Royal *and* humble." Khazak is impressed. "You are a rare breed."

"Ah, that's right, it's you all that we have to thank for rescuing Uncle Achak," Max reminds the rest of his group. "David mentioned your run-in with the 'prince' of Richardville or wherever it is we're supposed to be going."

"Yes, that was quite the adventure." Khazak sounds weary as he remembers. "Achak is your uncle? He is no slouch on the battlefield."

"Unofficially—he was a close friend of my parents," Max clarifies.

"He's actually *my* uncle, by blood." Peter raises his hand. "Not that he knows that, yet."

"Long story," Max responds to Khazak's look of confusion.

"We have a few of those," I reply with a sigh. "So now that the city is liberated, what are you doing next?"

"Continue on to Richardton to collect him," Max explains. "And then we'll be headed back to Litkalaa, I suppose."

"I wish you and the rest of your group safe travels, then." Khazak gives him a small bow of the head. "Tell Achak we said hello."

"Wanna stay for dinner?" I hook my thumb toward the cauldron of stew. "We've got plenty."

The werewolves are more than happy to join us, as are many other people from the neighborhood. Once I finish my own bowl, I start to help Wari and Onas in handing out the rest, looking around for anyone in need of a good meal right now. At some point, someone starts to play their lute, then someone else joins in with their guitar, and before I know it, everyone's up and dancing.

"So, I was thinking about that sword of yours," Wari says offhand as we watch the others enjoying themselves.

"You mean the one I lost?" I complain, not turning to face him.

"Yeah, that one," he barrels forward, not noticing or caring about my tone. "I'm thinking it might not be lost for all that long."

"What do you mean?" That, of course, gets my attention.

"I'm not promising anything," he starts, already back-tracking, "but that thing had a pretty unique magical signature. It might—*might*—be possible to use that to search for it underwater."

"Well… let me know if that ends up working," I reply, trying not to sound too doubtful. "Thanks."

After dinner, I start to feel restless again. I try to relax and join in on the fun some of the others are having, but every time I look around, I feel guilty. I should be helping right now.

"You want to get back to work, don't you?" Khazak asks, noticing my fidgeting.

"Yeah." I nod, frowning.

"Alright," he acquiesces with only a little reluctance, "but no overdoing it."

"I promise!" I say excitedly.

Khazak joins me right away, and once the others see what we're up to, so do they. Corrine puts her talents to use in one of the healer's tents while the rest of us assist the Maname Guard with their search and rescue operations. After all that sleep, I'm a little annoyed when I can barely make it two hours without feeling winded.

"I think it may be time to stop soon, pup," Khazak tells me after finding me in an alley, leaning against a wall and covered in sweat.

"I know I've still got some more juice in me," I try to assure him, but I know I'm not very convincing.

"You'll have more tomorrow, especially after another meal or two." He holds out his hand for me. "Most of the others have already called it quits. Come on, my puppy."

"Yes, Sir…" I relent with minimal grumbling.

The walk back to the Black Rooster, where I guess we are still staying for now, is a quiet one. The scene is a little better than last night with small improvements to the city and people's moods. As we pass one of the Guard's tents, I notice Jillian outside, though she doesn't look too happy as she speaks to her pet bird cupped in her hands.

"Hold on," I tell Khazak. "Jillian!"

"David, Khazak." Her expression swaps to a smile when she sees me, the bird flitting to her shoulder. "How are you?"

"Doing well, thank you," Khazak answers first. "I do not think I've had the pleasure of actually meeting your animal companion earlier. A starling, correct?"

"That's right! Khazak, David, this is Stella," she gestures to the tiny bird, who only tweets in response. "What brings you two here tonight?"

"We just finished helping clear out more rubble and are headed back to rest for the night now," Khazak explains.

"What ended up happening with Cam?" I ask, not having seen the boy since last night.

"And Remo." Khazak chimes in about his own problem child.

"They're bunking in one of the safehouses right now and getting along great. Practically inseparable since last night," she tells us, sounding just as tired as we are. "We sent a scout with a letter to Cam's parents last night, who are hopefully already on their way back here to get him."

"Great." I relax a little. "He's a handful but a good kid."

"And what of Remo?" Khazak is less positive.

"I'm not sure," Jillian admits. "I mean, he's doing fine, but I'm not sure what is next for him. Maybe an orphanage, but I kind of expect he'd run away the second someone turned their back."

"I unfortunately understand." Khazak sighs, just as we hear some frustrated yells from inside the tent. "Is everything alright in there?"

"Not exactly." She returns to frowning. "The discussion was getting a little heated, so I stepped out for some air."

"Why?" Khazak asks next. "What happened?"

"Well, the good news is that we found the city council members," she tells me, keeping her tone somewhat low. "The bad news is that the necromancer had been blackmailing two of them for months, getting them to share all sorts of information on our city's security and the dome, leading to all of this."

"Fuck." *Is there any place where the leaders aren't corrupt?*

"It also explains what happened to Captain Revik and some of the other higher ups in the guard," she continues. "They were some of the first people he kidnapped."

"So what happens now?" I look toward the busy tent.

"We're holding the two council members in a holding cell for the time being until we can better interrogate them and find out who else they might have been working with," she tells us with a sigh. "And we're still trying to figure out what to do next. There's a lot to work through."

"Do you mind if we...?" I thumb toward the tent entrance, interested in learning more.

"Might as well." She waves us in, leading the way as she reenters the tent.

"—may as well have handed him the blueprints and plans for all the city's buildings too." Lt. Gwar grumbles in the middle of a heated discussion.

"Cowards, all of them," Syris agrees.

"It will be a while before we're able to get the courts up and running again, so Councilman Geeta and Councilwoman Nimal can rot in a cell for now," Yuta comments angrily. "Which leaves us plenty of time to gather more evidence."

"The recovery plan is ready to move forward, I think," Raso says next, trying to bring up the positivity in the room. "We already have three different construction companies willing to work at cost."

"Good, they can start with the temporary shelters we're going to need," Gwar moves on to tackling the next problem. "Refugees are already returning to the city, and a lot of those people's homes have been destroyed. They're going to need a roof over their head."

"What about the kidnapped citizens?" Jillian asks next, stepping up to the table. "We still don't know where they are. The dragons chased off every scout we sent after them, but we have to keep looking."

"I know, Jillian, and we will." Gwar sighs, trying to reason with her. "But right now, we need to focus on helping the citizens we have here. We know the dragon's general direction and heading. Once we're able to, we can organize a search party to seek them out and bring them home, but right now, we don't have the manpower to spare."

"We could do it," I find myself volunteering, the guards all turning to me in surprise.

"David…" Khazak clearly wasn't expecting that, though to be fair neither was I.

"Khazak, David?" Gwar only just seemed to notice us. "You want to … what?"

"We can look for the kidnapped citizens," I double-down, speaking more clearly. "Rescue them and bring them back here."

"I appreciate it, but I'm not really sure we should be asking a civilian—let alone someone who isn't even from Manamequohi—for something like that," Gwar tries to let me down easy. "We have people trained for situations like this."

"Listen, that necromancer was working with the guy we've been chasing for over a month now, and we're only going to keep looking," I try to convince not only her but Khazak. "The connection between them probably goes way deeper than that, and he's our only lead, so we're going after him one way or another. I don't see why we shouldn't try and rescue your people as well."

"David, I am not sure this is something we should be offering." Khazak is still hesitant, but I can feel him leaning toward my side. "Especially without discussing it with the others."

"Even if it weren't for Redwish, we're headed next in that direction anyway, aren't we?" I decide to use his favorite thing in the world: logic. "Atsadi said that another temple like the one outside of Tah'lj is somewhere on the west coast, right? And it's not like we have any other trails to follow…"

"You really want to rescue them, don't you?" I knew he'd understand me.

"It doesn't feel right leaving them out there," I admit, "especially not if Redwish is connected."

"We still need to talk to the others, first." *Yesssss!*

"Alright, listen," Gwar starts, her tone leaving no room for nonsense, "I know you and your group are more than capable, so I'm not going to turn down the help, but, lacking any oversight of your group, I'd like one of ours to join you in the meantime: Jillian."

"Ma'am?" Jillian wasn't expecting that, but she sounds hopeful.

"We're still going to put together a rescue party of our own, but this way we can communicate and share information should you learn something," Gwar continues her explanation. "Does that sound alright with all of you?"

"Absolutely, ma'am." Jillian looks please as she stands on her stool.

"We would be happy to have her," Khazak agrees.

"Awesome!" I quickly realize I'm acting a little too excited and pull back. "Working together, I'm sure we'll bring everyone back safely."

"I'll get someone to put together a report of everything we already know before you head out," Gwar offers. "Jillian, I'll expect regular reports with updates on your progress. Good luck."

"Understood, Lieutenant." Jillian gives her a salute.

"We will make sure to keep you abreast of the situation," Khazak assures her. "And good luck to you as well. Now, we *really* need to get back to the others."

"I can meet you tomorrow morning if you'd like," Jillian tells the two of us.

"That sounds good," I tell her, still feeling pretty tired. "But not *too* early."

"After breakfast," she specifies.

"Have a good night, everyone," Khazak says as we turn to leave.

"Thank you for that, Sir," I tell Khazak once we're alone.

"I had a feeling this would happen anyway, my heroic puppy." He rubs my back as we walk. "First thing in the morning, we need to talk to the others about what we're doing and come up with a plan."

I hum thoughtfully, not really worried at all. I don't think I'll need to do much convincing, as I'm willing to bet everyone else will want to rescue those people as much as I do. It's what we do. But first, I am really, really looking forward to climbing into that bed and sleeping.

Chapter 20

David

"We're in."

"What, just like that?"

I look at Khazak and Jillian on my left before turning back to Adam and the others on the opposite side of the table. We're outside, having just finished a breakfast that was provided at one of the Maname Guard's shelters. It was mostly just some sort of oatmeal and bits of grilled pork.

We had to pack up from the Leather Rooster this morning, Cillian eager to get the place back in working order. We quickly moved to check into an inn, not wanting to have to worry about finding a place to sleep later tonight. Luckily, the same inn we first stayed at when we got here, The Moonbright Inn, had some rooms open.

I've been nervous about talking to everyone since waking up. I was really thinking I'd have to spend some time convincing them this morning, but I was wrong. I haven't even fully finished explaining everything yet!

"Were you expecting us to put up a fight?" Corrine asks curiously.

"No, but…" I look at all of them dumbfounded. "I guess I just didn't expect you to all agree *that* easily."

"We are going in that direction anyway, aren't we?" Tsula references the temple her uncle Atsadi told us about.

"And of course we'd want to help those people," Adam agrees. "Even if weren't already headed that way."

"Thanks everyone." I don't know why, but their words do surprise me.

"Why do you look so surprised?" Adam asks when he sees my face.

"Because the last few months have basically been all about me, and I figured you'd be tired of it by now," I try to explain why I feel weird. "I guess I just feel bad for taking over the group like that."

"I mean sure, we've been focused on your stuff for a bit now, but it's not like the rest of us have anything we need to be doing," Adam points out. "This is the kind of stuff we signed up for, and it sure beats what we were doing before, which was basically nothing."

"You're joining us too, Jillian?" Tsula looks to the halfling with a smile.

"Sure am." The druid nods. "It'll be a pleasure working with everyone."

"Where's Liss anyway?" It feels good to have such great friends.

"I think she's already helping with the cleanup," Corrine tells me. "She was acting kind of weird this morning."

"I noticed it last night too," Adam adds.

"Weird how?" Khazak questions.

"We were talking about leaving soon, and she seemed a little cagey about what we were doing next," Adam explains.

"Weird," I agree. "I'll try and find out what's up when we see her today."

"Let me know if you figure it out," Corrine says as she and the others stand. "I'll be in the medical tent all day."

We make our way toward the city center, where in one corner of the park is a tent that the Maname Guard seems to be using as a "command center." From there they direct volunteers to where they are needed the most while also helping any citizens that come in. Things are basically in the same condition they were yesterday, but the city feels so much more alive and active now. It reminds me of when we first got here, people moving through the streets like schools of fish.

The large tent is already bustling with other volunteers as our group steps inside, none of whom I recognize. Except for one: Cam, sitting in a chair next to Remo, and neither of them looks happy. *Poor kids.* I think about just ignoring them, but can't bring myself to do it.

"Uh-oh." I poke Khazak in the side. "Should we…"

"Probably." Khazak waves the others to go on ahead. "Hello, boys."

"Oh." Cam's head sinks as fast as it shot up once he sees me. "What do *you* want?"

"Aww come on, don't be like that." Probably still upset that I wouldn't let him fight with us.

"Are you waiting for your parents?" Khazak asks at my side.

"Yeah," he says with a sigh and a nod. "They're not going to be here for another two days."

"It's stupid," Remo complains, crossing his arms. "He just got here, and he's already leaving."

"Are you sad to see your new friend go?" Khazak asks Remo, taking a seat at his side.

"No. He's just way cooler then you." Remo scoffs in the older orc's face and turns away.

"I have no doubt." Khazak chuckles, unoffended.

"So, how mad were they?" I ask Cam, following Khazak's example and sitting next to him.

"Very," he answers, dejected. "It was hard to tell from the writing, but I probably won't be allowed to even leave the wagon by myself for a long time."

"Good." Two young faces and Khazak look at me in surprise. "What you did was *incredibly* stupid."

"I was just doing the same things you were!" he argues.

"And as previously stated, *I'm an idiot!*" I gesture to myself for emphasis. "And even then… I know it doesn't sound like much, but I am six years older than you, and those six years came with a lot of experience. And more recently, a weird amount of durability."

"What do you mean?" Yeah okay, that last part probably didn't make any sense.

"You just need to be patient," I find my point. "Wait a few more years, and look into places that you could maybe get some real training to do the things you want to do."

"Yeah, I'm sure Dad will *love* that." He rolls his eyes.

"So talk to him," I tell him. "Tell him you don't want to do the trading thing."

"He won't understand." Cam shakes his head, already defeated.

"Then make him understand." I shrug. "Or like I said, just wait—A couple more years and you can do whatever you want, and he can't stop you."

"Maybe." He looks like he might actually take my words under consideration, and I'm counting that as a win.

"You know, Remo, you don't have to keep being on your own," Khazak tries to reason with his own charge. "There are a lot of people who want to help."

"I don't need anyone's help." He crosses his arms even tighter. "I don't even need friends." Without another word, he stands and takes off running.

"Remo, wait!" Cameron stands and calls after him.

"Do you think we need to—" I start to ask Khazak.

"No, I should go talk to him," Cam surprises us both with his maturity.

"Yeah? Alright then, we'll leave it to you." I hold my hand out, strangely proud for some reason, and he looks at it oddly before taking it. "It was great meeting you, Cam. You're gonna do great things one day, I know it."

"Thanks." He finally shakes it. "...it was nice meeting you too."

"Think Remo will be okay?" I ask as we watch Cam go after his new friend.

"It is hard to help someone who does not wish to be helped. But I think Cameron has it handled for now," Khazak comments as the two of us walk away. "That was pretty good advice you gave. I don't suppose *you* tried to talk to *your* parents, did you?"

"...No," I mutter, not liking where this is going.

"Might have been worth some consideration." I don't respond.

"Liss!" And thankfully I won't need to, as I see our missing friend has joined Adam, Tsula, and Jillian.

"Hey guys." She waves, a little surprised to see us. "What brings you here?"

"We wanted to volunteer, of course," Khazak tells her.

"Right, right." She nods. What did she think we were here for? "Come with me. I can get you guys all assigned out somewhere."

"I imagine it has been very busy around here," Khazak comments as we follow.

"Yeah." Liss nods in agreement. "Pretty much everyone in the city is helping in one way or another."

It's easy to see what she's talking about, as packed as it is. The community here really takes care of their own, no matter where they may have originally come from. Not counting the dragon attack, I bet this is a really great place to live.

"Lieutenant!" Liss calls ahead as we approach a set of tables. "We've got more volunteers."

"Oh good, it's you!" Lieutenant Gwar is pleased when she looks up to see it is us. "Perfect timing. I just finished compiling those reports for you."

"Reports?" Liss looks at us questioningly.

"We're going after the missing people the necromancer kidnapped," I tell her as Khazak accepts a small stack of papers.

"When did we decide that?" Liss looks at the rest of us, confused.

"This morning," I answer. "Well, Khazak and I decided last night, and we talked about it with everyone else after breakfast."

"Right." She nods, but there's a look on her face I can't quite read.

"Alright, look here." Gwar directs our attention to the table and the large map spread across it. "This is Maname, and this line is the path we tracked the dragon taking."

"Why does it switch from solid to dashed here?" Adam points to the spot in question.

"That is where they managed to scare our scouts off," she continues. "The dashed line is our best guess at his heading before they lost sight of him and had to turn back."

"That leaves a lot of open area," Tsula notes with wide eyes. "How do we know where he went?"

"We don't, but assuming he was headed straight to his destination, our best guess is he's located somewhere here." She points to a set of mountains drawn on the map. "In the Kiz'Urngor Mountain range."

"There are a lot of places you could hide there—even with a dragon," Jillian adds next. "We've already sent scouts back out to try and pinpoint their location, and if they do, they'll pass that along to us."

"I had a question about that," I say, holding a single hand up. "How exactly are we going to pass information back and forth if we're on the road?"

"That part's easy," Gwar continues, reaching into her back pocket and retrieving … a tiny book. "Jillian has already been given one of these."

"A notebook of enchanted vellum." Jillian holds up an identical notepad—its twin. "Standard for long distance assignments."

"We're stopping in the Magic Market again before we leave," I tell Khazak, already decided on buying more journals in case we ever get separated again.

"Sounds like an excellent idea to me." He probably doesn't like that thought any more than I do.

"So, as you head in that direction, we will continue to look and update you on any information we learn while Jillian does the same for us," Gwar finishes her explanation.

"Alright, but where are we actually going?" Corrine asks. "We aren't just going to pick a direction and start walking, right?"

"The city of Kiz'Urngor is a good place to start." Jillian points to a city in the middle of the mountain range. "It's the closest and biggest city in the area. The people there might have even seen something."

"It's as good a place to start as any," Adam decides.

"I agree." Khazak nods.

We spend the next few minutes plotting out our travel route. There are a lot of different roads we can take to get west from here, and the path we're going to try and follow is as close to the dragon's heading as we can get. We figure we could ask anyone in the area if they had seen anything.

It'll take us at least two weeks, and that's being on horseback for at least part of the journey. We'll need to stock up on provisions before we leave, and it might be worth looking for some new equipment too. Nothing we haven't done before.

"Do you think our horses are still at the docks in Venzor?" Adam asks Khazak as we wrap up.

"I doubt it," Khazak answers with a sigh. "If they weren't taken by the people fleeing the dragons, then it is likely they were set free to fend for themselves rather than let them starve in the abandoned stables."

"I've got a list of medical supplies we need to restock on," Corrine says, holding a small piece of paper.

"I can help with the food shopping," Tsula offers with a raised hand.

"Alright." Adam smiles and nods his head. "Then we can probably be ready to leave in the next two days. Sound good, everyone?"

"Uh, actually… we should probably talk about that," Liss speaks up, wearing that same strange look from earlier.

"That sounds ominous." I narrow my eyes. "What's up?"

"I… I don't think I'm leaving with you all." *What?*

"What do you mean?" Corrine asks, and I'm glad I'm not the only one shocked.

"I'm staying in the city," Liss confirms.

"Why?" Adam questions her next.

"Horrible tragedies aside, working with the guard here these past few weeks has been great," she starts. "It's not like it was at home. They *actually* help people here, and being a part of that… I feel more accomplished than I have in years."

"So you're just gonna leave us?" I'm almost surprised by the amount of hurt in my voice.

"Yeah." She nods. "I'm staying here."

"Are you certain?" Khazak's turn.

"I think so." She nods again. "I'm going to apply to join the Maname Guard."

"We'd be happy to have you," Lieutenant Gwar informs her. "After everything you've done for us in the last two weeks, you've already proven yourself capable enough that I think we can skip the interview."

"That's… Thank you, lieutenant!" She gives her best salute. "I won't let you down."

"We can get started training you on procedures once things settle down, but for now just keep doing what you've been doing and report to me or Yuta," she tells Liss.

"I can't believe this is really happening." I'm dumbfounded that she's leaving us.

"It's not like you'll never hear from me again," she tries to assure me. "I mean, if anything, it'll be easier to stay in touch because now one of us will be staying in one place."

"I guess," I begrudgingly admit. "…I'm gonna miss you."

"Aww, I'm gonna miss you too!" She punches me in the arm. "I'll miss all of you."

"It won't be the same without you," Corrine tells her.

"I know, just when we were about to outnumber the boys," she jokes, the two sharing a hug.

"It was only for a few weeks, but it was wonderful getting to you know, Elisabeth," Tsula says next.

"Alright, I don't know why we're getting all sentimental. You're not leaving without me yet," Liss says, clearly wanting to move past the mushy feelings. "Let's get to work."

We get our roles for the day assigned out right after that. Most of us are on duty helping to clear rubble and looking for anyone trapped within while Corrine is doing her thing with the healers and Tsula is assisting in a makeshift kitchen, making sure everyone is fed. I'm thankful for the distraction because I'm still thinking about Liss.

Another friend leaving the group. Well alright, I'd hardly call Nate a friend, but it still feels weird. We traveled so far for so long, and now someone else is splitting off to do their own thing. But if it makes her happy… and she does seem happy…

"Liss was separated from the rest of us for the first half of the occupation," Khazak starts, reading my mind.

"She has seemed very … fulfilled while working with the Maname Guard."

"You think she knows what she's doing?" I ask as we wrap up for the afternoon, dusting off my hands on my pants.

"I do." He nods and wipes the sweat from his brow. "She has been looking for a chance to prove herself, and this may be the way to do that."

I know he's right. I should trust my friend to know what she wants. But that doesn't mean *I* have to be happy about it.

When we get back to the inn, we all take turns showering before changing. Atsadi asked us all over for dinner to celebrate our victory and send us off with a big meal. I guess now it also counts as a goodbye party for Liss.

After dinner, we all go up to the roof for some drinks. Even Khazak enjoys himself, leaving but still sticking close to the doorway leading back inside. I'd like to say goodbye to Liss, but Dr. Tuvat manages to corner me before I get a chance.

"—it's like the astral stone melded with the ruby, forming an entirely different kind of material."

"So what does that mean?"

"Well, we aren't sure just yet," Tuvat answers, not expecting Khazak's follow-up question. "But it would explain some of the necromancer's 'enhanced' abilities."

"How is astral stone formed again?" I ask, confused.

"No one is sure exactly because it's not like other minerals," Wari takes over explaining. "It can be found underground and in caves but usually only around leywells."

"It is notoriously hard to work with," Onas goes on. "It can amplify the effects and strength of magic, but in volatile and dangerous ways. It's normally extremely brittle, which is why it's such a big deal that all of the elven monuments have stood solid and unweathered for thousands of years."

"It always leads back to the elves," Atsadi chuckles. "Tuvat, tell David your theory on crossing the Astral Plane."

"Huh?" I hope she uses small words.

"Discovering that astral rock was powering the amulets had me thinking," she starts. "Your abilities—you only received them after you were killed, correct?"

"There is some evidence of others in his family having above average abilities," Khazak speaks for me. "But no, it was not until the death and resurrection that they resembled anything like this."

"Well, dying is famously one of the only ways for a person to pass through the Astral Plane," she continues. "I believe that when you were killed, David, your soul passed through the Astral Plane to another realm, before being sent back with… Well, I'm not sure what, but it triggered your transformation. And given all of the evidence we have thus far, I believe that you were brought to the Olympian realm of Elysium."

"The mural we saw, the prophecy from the temple…" Adam joins our conversation. "David's really been empowered by the Olympian gods?"

"I believe so." Dr. Tuvat sounds very confident for a person who just proposed all of *that*. "Now tell me about these 'above average' abilities that run in your family."

"Uh, well, my brother's been called a magical prodigy, and apparently my little sister is going to follow in his footsteps." I'm starting to feel like I'm being studied. "My dad was a pretty successful knight, my brother even better, and I'm not too bad myself."

"He is also a fairly skilled acrobat," Khazak adds for me.

"Okay, so I was really good at running climbing as a kid—"

"—and an adult—"

"And an adult." I roll my eyes. "Lots of people are. You want me to tell her about all my weird dreams, too?"

"Weird dreams?" Wait, I think she actually does want me to tell her.

"Uh, well, there have been a lot of nightmares since I died," I start, already uncomfortable. "Mostly about dying again."

"Understandable." Where'd she get that pen? "Anything else?"

"I mean, sometimes I'm a bird, which is pretty new."

"What kind of bird?" She starts to scribble. "An eagle, perhaps?"

"Maybe? I don't really know my birds." Not high on the study list. "Um, there are a lot storms. And Khazak is in most of them."

"I've been having dreams of you too," Khazak adds with a chuckle. "Which shouldn't be a surprise. Sometimes pleasant, sometimes not."

"Same. I've seen wolves in them more than once," I continue. "And then a couple times, there were tentacles."

"Yes, I remember those." Khazak grimaces. "Had one of my own."

"You had a similar dream to his?" *She's still writing.*

"Yes, but we spend all our time together, so is that really odd?" I'm glad I'm not the only one who thinks she's a quack. "Just yesterday, I dreamt we were together in a forest, something I've done many times."

"I had a dream like that yesterday too." When I start saying it, I only mean it as a fun little story, but when I finish, a weird feeling sits in my stomach. "Did you… Were there cardinals in your dream?"

"Yes." Khazak nods, getting the same feeling. "And we were … naked."

"Fascinating." Almost forgot she was there. Almost. "Has this happened before?"

"I dunno." Khazak and I look at each other. "I've definitely dreamed about us in the forest together before."

"I have done the same." But what does it mean?

"The people of Olympia view dreams as prophetic and even a way for their gods to communicate with them directly." She stops writing as she speaks to us. "Are you certain you have to leave so soon? This opens up so many possibilities for research!"

"Shira," Atsadi does his best to calm his eccentric friend, "they have important things to do. We already had the boy running tests for twenty minutes before dinner started."

"Very well…" She frowns but tucks her pen and paper into her waist. "Then I would at least request that the two of you begin to track these dreams more closely. I'm sure you can even come up with some interesting experiments of your own."

"We'll do our best," I say as convincingly as I can. It's enough, and with a nod of approval, she scurries off, probably to take more notes.

"I'm jealous, you know," Atsadi says to me, handing me a fresh drink.

"Of what?"

"Traveling. Getting to see the other ruins," he answers. "I can only imagine what you might learn."

"I just hope I learn *something*," I reply. "Not that you all haven't helped me. There's just still so much I don't understand. So much guessing."

"We will figure it out," Khazak assures me, squeezing my shoulder. "One way or another."

"Before you leave, I'll give you what information I have on the other temples," Atsadi continues. "And I hope you'll do this old man a favor in return by writing and telling me what you find."

"It's a deal," I say, making a show of shaking the man's hand.

"You know, if you find anything special like that sword of yours, we're gonna wanna know about it too," Wari tells me after Atsadi and Dr. Tuvat leave us.

"Yeah? Well, we'll see if I can manage to not lose it in the ocean," I half complain, half answer.

"Is he always this much of a downer?" Wari asks Khazak.

"He does tend to be harder on himself than necessary," he answers. "Though there are some times…"

"You try losing an irreplaceable ancient weapon!" I argue on my own behalf, or at least that of my bad mood.

"I did want to thank the two of you for everything these past few weeks," Khazak continues, ignoring my grumbling. "You have been invaluable members of the team."

"Hey, this is our home. We weren't about to let some asshole with dragons take over," Onas says with a confident nod. "We've got a business to run."

"I was curious—how has business been?" Khazak asks next. "The shop did not appear to have changed much in the last decade. Before present circumstances, at least."

"Steady as they normally are," Onas answers. "Things are usually slow enough that I've got plenty of time to work on my own projects, which is how I like it."

"Speaking of, your translator has been working well." Khazak taps the object wrapped around his ear. "It helped me rescue a young Galatian child separated from his mother."

"I used mine too, in Kiweni," I quickly add. "It worked great."

"I knew they would!" Onas turns to his brother. "See? This could be our ticket to really start bringing in the gold!"

"Uh huh." Wari doesn't look impressed. "Just like the satchels were supposed to be."

"You cannot *still* be mad about that!" With how exasperated Onas's response it, I don't think this is the first time they've had this argument. "It wasn't my fault that we had all those copycats and regulations come out right after."

"Yes, it was!" Wari looks at Onas like he's an idiot.

"What are you talking about?" I ask hesitantly, worried I might make the argument worse.

"Right after we made the very first spacious satchel, an *incredible* achievement of magical ingenuity, *this* idiot decides to blab about it to everyone in town," Wari starts, pointing his thumb at Onas. "Not two weeks later and we've already got *three* different competitors making the same thing."

"They were not the same thing because none of them had the same safety enchantments ours did!" Onas continues to defend himself.

"Right, so after a few people were accidentally *killed*, the city passed laws say that they all to have the same safety regulations *and* require that every single one be inspected before they can be sold." Wari narrows his eyes at his brother. "The paperwork alone took days to finish, on top of the inspection fees, and don't get me starting on the marketing."

"Oh my god, not the marketing again." Onas rubs his temples with his forefingers.

"I wanted to call them roomy rucksacks, but nooooo..."

The rest of the evening goes well, or at least as well as it can with Corrine crying after one too many drinks. Can't really blame her though; once the subject of Liss leaving us comes up again, things get a little emotional. Thankfully Liss insists on no speeches, but we're all still saying our individual goodbyes.

"Gonna tell your family where you are now?" Adam asks as the two finish their own conversation, hugging.

"Fuck no!" She looks at him like he grew an extra head. "Why would I ruin everything when I'm just getting started?"

"Never change, Liss." Adam chuckles and steps away. *My turn.*

"So," I start, leaning over the railing next to her, "staying here is really what you want?"

"It is." She nods. "It'll be a good change I think. Getting to stay in one place because I'm *choosing* to."

"Then I guess I forgive you for abandoning us," I complain, unserious.

"Thanks." She rolls her eyes and punches me in the arm. "Keep an eye on everyone for me, okay?"

"I'll do my best." I nod. "It'll be nice not having to argue over who gets the last watch shift anymore."

"And it'll be great not listening to you complaining about sleeping on the ground every morning," she jokes back.

"I'm gonna miss you, Liss," I begrudgingly admit.

"Miss you too, David." She pulls me in for a hug.

After dinner, we say our goodbyes to Atsadi, but once we're outside, Khazak stops me from following the others back to the inn. They don't seem fazed as he waves them off. Which is a little embarrassing since I guess everyone knows who wears the pants in our relationship.

"We will meet up with them later," he tells me, turning me away from them. "You and I have plans tonight."

"We do?" I ask as we walk in a different direction.

"Mhmm." He doesn't say anything more as he leads me down suspiciously familiar roads until we stand in front of a suspiciously familiar building: The Black Rooster.

The interior of the bookstore has already been cleaned and fixed up. The shelves are all put upright, and most of the books have already been reshelved while others are in a pile waiting to be reorganized. I hope there wasn't too much damage.

Khazak leads me past the shelves and toward the backroom where, to my surprise, the secret bookcase is already open. Stepping inside the lobby, I can see that the place seems practically packed. It's at least as busy as I saw it the first time, if not more.

"Surprised?" Khazak asks as I stare at the crowd through the entryway.

"Yeah." I nod, dumbfounded. "I didn't think people would be in the mood for this kinda thing right now."

"In times like these, the thing people crave most is normalcy." He puts a hand on my shoulder and turns me towards the locker room. "And this is their—and our—normal. Now let's finish getting ready."

Khazak pulls me into the locker room where a dwarf and her human friend are both getting redressed, presumably after finishing their fun. They look from Khazak to me and back as they see us come in before whispering to each other and blushing. I wonder if they're new to this scene (not that I'm an old pro). Khazak finds us a nice spot on a bench and picks us out a locker, which are all free tonight with their keys already in the lock for a user to grab.

"I think we could both stand to dress a little more appropriately for the evening." He sets the bag down on the bench and reaches inside. "I think the blue jock tonight… Are you alright?"

"Huh? Yeah, sorry." I shake what must have been a weird look from my face. "I guess I just… Is now really the time for me to be doing something like this, when there's—"

"Everyone deserves time to relax and enjoy themselves, David." He takes me by the shoulders, pulling us together. "Even you. *Especially* you, after the things you've had to undertake lately."

"But what if—"

"David." He puts a finger over my lips. "Let me take care of you tonight. Or has it been so long that you've forgotten which one of us is in charge?"

"No, Sir." I shake my head, taking in the thoughtful look on his face.

"Good boy." He presses our lips together before returning to the bag and retrieving our "outfits" for the night.

I'm in my blue jock as previously stated, and Khazak is wearing one in black. We both have our leather harnesses on, but other than my collar, that's it. And I'm kinda excited about that because it's been a while since I've been able to show off like this. What has Khazak turned me into?

We enter the packed main area of the club with a decent amount of eyes already watching us. The room is full, and there are plenty of people already engaged in their activities. Spanking, fucking, bondage. Everyone is either participating or watching in some form of debauchery.

That includes Novus and Cillian. The elf appears to be reclining in a large chair—almost a throne—with Novus on all fours being used as a footrest. Cillian seems to be enjoying himself, but Novus looks as though he's concentrating on keeping still.

"Khazak, David, I was hoping we'd see you tonight!" the elf greets us and stands. "After what you've done for the city, you deserve a hero's welcome!"

He makes some gestures toward the bartender, who begins to mix something behind the counter. At the same time, Cillian gestures to Novus, who sits up on his knees, a smile on his face and a bulge in his underwear. Seems like the dwarf enjoys being furniture—that's a new one for me.

"Now then, what brings you two here tonight?" he asks as his sub leaves to grab our drinks from the bar.

"I thought we could use a nice night out," Khazak answers for us. "We are likely to be leaving the city in the next day or so."

"Oh, that's too bad!" Cillian seems to be genuinely sad at hearing we will be leaving. I even catch Novus frowning when he returns, handing us both a blue-colored drink in a short glass. "But I suppose heroes like you must be very busy."

"Something like that," Khazak agrees with a chuckle before sipping his drink. "Thank you."

I sip my own, tasting alcohol and something vaguely fruity. A little too sweet, not something I'd usually drink, but not bad.

"On the house for the dragon slayers." He grins, then looks between us hopefully. "I don't suppose I could convince the two of you to 'perform' for us tonight, could I?"

"I think something like that could be arranged." Khazak looks at me. "Would you like that, puppy?"

I look between Khazak, Cillian, and Novus, and the rest of the bar. At everything going on, and how much everyone seems to be enjoying themselves. After downing the rest of my drink, I decide that yeah, I want to do that too.

"Yes, Sir." I nod my agreement, wiping my mouth.

"Wonderful!" Cillian exclaims, clasping his hands together. "What equipment can I provide?"

"Just a flogger for now, I think," Khazak responds, looking at me with an evil glint and then finishing his own drink. "And if I could use one of the crosses…"

"Of course!" The elf turns to his boy. "Novus, please have some space cleared for our guests."

"Yes, master." The dwarf scurries off to do as asked but not before taking our empty glasses.

"Already have something in mind, Sir?" I question my orc as Cillian retrieves his flogger.

"Nothing you cannot handle." He smirks before pulling me in for a kiss. "Remember your safe word?"

"Jailbreak," I confirm.

Khazak takes me by the hand and pushes me toward the "stage" Novus has cleared. It's a raised platform, one of several in the room, but this one has the cross he requested. It's more of an X really, two long black wooden planks crossing over each other in the middle. At the end of each plank is a leather cuff attached by chain.

Novus steps away with a little bow as Khazak leads me on stage. He helps me with a few light stretches (while making sure everyone can see me doing them) before ordering me to stand with my stomach to the cross. Then, one by one' he locks one of the cuffs around my limbs. Every time he tightens one of the straps, I feel just a hint of anxiety—but the good excited kind.

"Here you are," I hear Cillian's voice behind me, probably handing over the flogger.

"Thank you." That's Khazak, placing a hand on my back a moment later. "Are you ready, pup?"

"Yes Sir." I nod as best I can.

He's used a flogger on me before, so I know what to expect, but it was only the one time. I tense up when I feel the first leather straps hit my skin, though it barely stings. I'm more prepared for the next one, but I'm still having a hard time relaxing.

It's not because of where we are or that we're surrounded by people. It's that part of me still feels bad for being here at all again, for having fun when other people are suffering. And I *know* Khazak said—

"Get out of your head, pup," Khazak orders between flogs. "Focus on the sound of my voice and what your body is feeling."

Not wanting to let him down, I try to clear my mind and stop it from wandering too far. I just focus on my body: the stings of each strip of leather as they hit me, the way it seems to heat my skin afterwards, how with each strike I feel less and less pain…

Soon, I'm floating in subspace, my body warmer than a summer day. The flogger is practically only a tickle now, but one I want more of. These straps are basically holding me up as my body sinks onto the cross.

At some point, I realize the flogging has stopped and that my arms are released from their restraints. Khazak is a warm, solid weight behind me, his arm around my chest to hold me up. With his free hand, he brings a water flask to my mouth, encouraging me to drink.

"How are you feeling, puppy?" he asks, wiping my lips with his thumb.

"Good, Sir." I nuzzle into his hand, sucking his thumb into my mouth.

"Rrrrr…" Khazak rumbles a growl, slipping his digit in and out of my lips. "I think it's time for you to get on your knees then."

"Yes Sir," I respond with a smile, pushing off of the cross and slowly sinking to the floor.

Face to face with Khazak's crotch, I nuzzle my face against his bulge. There are people all around me, but it all just fades into the background as I reach for the pouch of his jock and pull it to the side, freeing his turgid erection. I can hear myself moan as I take Khazak into my mouth, and taste his salty skin on my tongue.

"Good boy," he praises, his hand stroking over my hair.

I'm barely halfway down his shaft, and I can already feel my jaw being stretched to its limit. Clearly, I'm out of practice after being away for so long. I even gag a little when I try to take him into my throat. Only one way to fix that!

Khazak's cock is a heavy weight on my tongue as I bob up and down on his shaft. I continue to push him farther into my throat, fighting my gag reflex every step of the way. Khazak's hand only pets through my hair, encouraging me further and making me determined to do this.

When I finally manage to stop gagging, I'm barely an inch from the base of his groin. The scent of his musk is heady and threatens to overwhelm me—but like, in a good way. After allowing me a few moments to deep throat him at my own pace, Khazak's grip on my hair gets tighter, and I know it's time for him to take over. Letting him move my head as he pleases, he thrusts his hips forward as I bob on him, meeting him halfway.

"*Very* good boy," he praises again as he gently fucks my face on stage.

It's only gentle for the first minute or so. After that, things start to get faster and rougher. And it's my job to kneel here and take it. I can hear people all around me, watching and commenting on the proceedings. I can't quite make out exactly what they're saying, as the sounds of Khazak hollowing out my wet throat drown out most of the words.

My jaw is straining, my knees are getting sore, and I'm sure I've already got a puddle of drool on the floor beneath me. But fuck if I don't feel good. Even while being roughly facefucked, I still feel like I'm floating.

Khazak pulls me all the way down his cock, burying my nose in his public hair as he pushes as far into my throat as possible. He repeats this twice more, and I manage not to gag once. Then he pulls me off his cock entirely and motions for me to stand.

He mashes our mouths together in another hungry kiss while motioning to someone off stage with his right arm. When we finally break apart, I see Cillian stepping forward with a grin. He holds out his hand and Khazak takes what is offered—a cleansing stone and a small vial of lube.

"Thank you, Cillian," Khazak says as he looks down at me hungrily, then turns me around and pulls me against his chest. "Are you ready for what's next, pup?"

"Yes, Sir," I answer, looking up into his brown eyes.

Without any more words, Khazak presses the cleansing charm to my belly. While it does its magic, he uses his mouth to rip out the cork on the vial of lube, pouring some generously into his hand before discarding it and the stone to the side. I feel his hand go down my back, first taking himself in hand to coat it and then snaking his fingers toward my hole.

I bite my lip to suppress a moan as he breaches me with the first finger, which is quickly followed by number two. I look out on the watching crowd with bleary eyes, seeing most of them are just as ravenous as Khazak. Who knows what they might do to me if they had the chance? Luckily, Sir is here.

When he pulls his fingers from my hole, I know what's next. Both of us still standing, he crouches down slightly, and I feel his slick cock swipe through my cheeks as it is aimed at my hole. His arm goes tight around my chest as the head pops in, and I hear myself make a squeak of surprise. I'm still a little sore from yesterday, but I like it—it reminds me of what I've been missing.

Khazak pushes his thick cock all the way into my ass until his chest is flat against my back. His legs are spread on the outside of mine to help angle us better as he starts to thrust, pulling back just a few inches before pushing back in. As he falls into a good rhythm, he moves his arm from around my chest to hold on to one of my hips.

Fucking while standing up is harder than it looks. Without something to hold on to or brace against, Khazak's thrusts threaten to throw me off balance. I panic when I start to fall forward until Khazak grabs me by the back of my harness, using it to hold me up. And then he just … keeps me there as he continues to fuck me.

I have to admit, this angle feels even better—so long as he doesn't get tired of holding me in place. With my upper body more horizontal, Khazak doesn't have to crouch down quite as much and can thrust even harder. I feel the difference almost immediately, his thighs slapping against mine.

That's when I notice the people around us are actually cheering. I almost kinda forgot that we were "performing" for anyone, rather than just being watched doing what we normally do. But if they want a show, we'll give 'em one— even if there's not much I can do to assist Khazak aside from taking it.

And believe me, I do my best to take it. But that cock is just so big! I know it's been a while, but even before we were separated, he stretched me to my limit. I feel like an overstuffed turkey.

I also feel the pressure of an anal orgasm starting to build up, which I'm sure is what Khazak wants. He loves letting other people see how masterfully he handles my ass. And they are eating it up.

I can feel my legs start to shake as the pressure reaches its boiling point. They almost give out entirely when I finally cum with a low groan, my eyes rolling to the back of my head as I dribble onto the floor. The only reason I don't hit the ground is Khazak's iron grip on the strap of my harness.

I can hear the audience audibly cheer as I practically go limp while Khazak continues to pound away at my backside. It only takes a short while before the pressure builds again, all of my muscles getting tight, especially in my stomach. Everything tenses up as I have another orgasm, feeling even more boneless in the aftermath.

The crowd gives another cheer, but I notice not long after that Khazak's pace starts to slow down before he stops entirely and pulls out. Helping me to stand, he turns me to face him, watching my eyes with a smile and kissing me. When he breaks our kiss, he turns to the crowd.

"I hope you all enjoyed the show," he declares loudly, "but if you will excuse us, I need a little alone time with my puppy."

There are a few disappointed murmurs, but everyone seems happy, even giving us some applause—and I don't even blush. I hear Cillian giving Khazak a thank you before directing the two of us to one of the club's private rooms. Khazak leads me there on shaky legs, opening the door for me and pushing me onto the bed. When I roll over, I see him climbing on after me.

"I hope you're not too tired yet, puppy," he says, wearing that lecherous smile I have come to know well, "because our night is just getting started."

He's not wrong. Not even just tonight—we have *so* much to do in the coming days. But there's nowhere else I'd rather be, and no one else I'd rather be with than my Khazak.

Book Club Questions

1. What do you think is the significance of the book's title?

2. The story switches back and forth between David and Khazak's POV. How do their internal monologues differ? Do you think they're rubbing off on each other?

3. Have you ever been separated from a loved one unexpectedly for a period of time? How did you handle dealing with it?

4. Have you ever had to train for something intensely, physical, mental, or otherwise?

5. Have you ever been responsible for a romantic partner's pet that was not your own?

6. What about children? Not counting a babysitting job, have you ever been responsible for a child that was not your own or a relative's?

7. How good are you communicating with friends and family long distance? Who moved away from who, and does that change anything?

8. Have you ever, or would you ever, join a group like the rebellion? What circumstances might push you to something like that?

9. Have you ever had someone look up to or admire you when you really didn't want them to?

10. What would you do if your city was attacked by dragons?

About the Author

Author Bio: Dominic N. Ashen is an author of gay/ male-on-male BDSM-themed romantic erotica. In his youth he would spend a great deal of time searching for books with characters who were more like himself—queer— and when those fell short, he decided to start creating some of his own. His stories feature gay, bisexual, and queer men with heavy themes of dominance, submission, and all sorts of kinks. Dominic loves the fantasy, sci-fi, and horror genres and prefers to write longer stories where the sex and kink are weaved right into the plot.

Website: https://www.dominicashen.com/

Patreon: https://www.patreon.com/dominicashen

Bluesky: https://bsky.app/profile/dominicashen.com

Facebook: https://www.facebook.com/dom.n.ashen

Instagram: https://www.instagram.com/dom.n.ashen

Discover more at
4HorsemenPublications.com

10% off using HORSEMEN10

www.ingramcontent.com/pod-product-compliance
Lightning Source LLC
Chambersburg PA
CBHW020231010826
48973CB00006B/1466